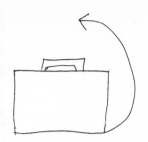  

YOU DON'T HAVE TO BE EVIL TO WORK HERE, BUT IT HELPS

By Tom Holt

Expecting Someone Taller
Who's Afraid of Beowulf?
Flying Dutch
Ye Gods!
Overtime
Here Comes the Sun
Grailblazers
Faust Among Equals
Odds and Gods
Djinn Rummy
My Hero
Paint Your Dragon
Open Sesame
Wish You Were Here
Only Human
Snow White and the Seven Samurai
Valhalla
Nothing But Blue Skies
Falling Sideways
Little People
The Portable Door
In Your Dreams
Earth, Air, Fire and Custard
You Don't Have to be Evil to Work Here, But It Helps
Someone Like Me

Dead Funny: Omnibus 1
Mightier Than the Sword: Omnibus 2
The Divine Comedies: Omnibus 3
For Two Nights Only: Omnibus 4
Tall Stories: Omnibus 5
Saints and Sinners: Omnibus 6
Fishy Wishes: Omnibus 7

The Walled Orchard
Alexander at the World's End
Olympiad
A Song for Nero
Meadowland

I, Margaret

Lucia Triumphant
Lucia in Wartime

TOM HOLT

YOU DON'T HAVE TO BE EVIL TO WORK HERE, BUT IT HELPS

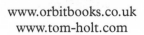

www.orbitbooks.co.uk
www.tom-holt.com

ORBIT

First published in Great Britain in February 2006 by Orbit

A CIP catalogue record for this book
is available from the British Library.

ISBN 1 84149 283 3

Typeset in Plantin by M Rules
Printed and bound in Great Britain
by ClaysLtd, St Ives plc

Orbit
An imprint of
Time Warner Book Group UK
Brettenham House
Lancaster Place
London WC2E 7EN

www.orbitbooks.co.uk

For Kitty, with love

With thanks to the following illustrators: Tim Auvache, Alexandra Barton, Tamsyn Berryman, Cina Bolton, Rachel Bunyan, Francis Charlton, Eddie Clark, Neil Dean, Phillip Fairbairn, Abby Gainforth, Roben Goodfellow, Stephen Gourlay, Graeme Henderson, Wendy Hobson, Caroline Hogg, Sian Jones, Heather Kirk, Shelley Loader, Wil Mohr, Gabriella Nemeth, Bella Pagan, Christina Plowman, Gordon Rivers, Clare Short, Anna Small, Martin Smith, Amy Walker, Lindsay Wallace, James Woodward, Andrea Yates.

feckless-once. No, she reflected; I was young,
getting stuck all the bloody time. 'Listen,' she
's just a tiny bit awkward at the moment, do
ld possibly hang on there till lunch—?'
eaked. 'Look, I'm *stuck*, you've got to—'
nie sighed. 'Tell me where you are, and I'll

the directions on her scratchpad, the corners
h she'd earlier embellished with graceful doo-
sea serpents. 'Please hurry,' Cassie pleaded
be a pain, but—'
s soon as I can,' Connie said, and put the
gger, she thought. It was, of course, only
unger woman should have chosen her as her
and mentor. Even so. She glanced down at
she could always take them home and do
it wasn't as if she had anything else planned.
lection brought her little comfort. She stood
er coat from behind the door, and left the

0 St Mary Axe without (a) official leave (b)
Tanner, assuming you're starting from the
you have to sneak across the landing into the
the rear staircase. This will bring you out in
hat curls round the ground floor like a python,
ll pass Mr Suslowicz's door on your way. But
ause Cas Suslowicz—
Mr Suslowicz, poking his head round his office
oming to look for you.'
lied.
right now, are you?'
e said, in a neutral sort of voice. 'I was just on
ry, as a matter of—'
me a favour, could you?'
he way he said it. You wouldn't expect it to
d vast shoulders, gigantic round red cheeks

CHAPTER ONE

Three weeks, and still nobody had the faintest idea who they were. There were rumours, of course: they were Americans, Germans, Russians, Japanese, an international consortium based in Ulan Bator, the Barclay brothers, Rupert Murdoch; they were white knights, asset strippers, the good guys, the bad guys, maybe even Kawaguchiya Integrated Circuits operating through a network of shells and holding companies designed to bypass US anti-trust legislation. Presumably the partners had some idea who they were, but Mr Wells hadn't been seen around the office in weeks, Mr Suslowicz burst into tears if anybody raised the subject, and nobody was brave and stupid enough to ask Mr Tanner.

'We bloody well ought to be able to figure it out for ourselves,' declared Connie Schwartz-Alberich from Mineral Rights, not for the first time. 'I mean, it's a small industry, the number of players is strictly limited. Only—' She pulled a face. 'Only I've been ringing round – people I know in other firms – and everybody seems just as confused as we are. You'd have thought someone would've heard something by now, but apparently not. It's bloody frustrating.'

Thoughtful silence; a soft grunt of disgust from Peter Melznic as half of his dunked digestive broke off and flopped into his tea.

'I still reckon it's the Germans,' said Benny Shumway, chief cashier. 'Zauberkraftwerk or UMG. They're the only ones big enough in Europe.'

'Unlikely,' muttered the thin-faced new girl from Entertainment and Media, whose name nobody could remember. 'I worked for UMG for eighteen months – it's not their style.'

For some reason, the new girl's statements were always followed by an awkward silence, as though she'd just said something rude or obviously false. *Unfortunate manner* was the generally held explanation, but it didn't quite ring true. Peter Melznic was on record as saying that she gave him the creeps – coming from Peter, that was quite an assertion – but even he was at a loss to explain exactly why.

'I don't think it's anybody in the business,' the new girl went on. 'I think it's someone completely new that none of us has ever heard of. Possibly,' she added after a moment's reflection, 'Romanians. It's just a feeling I have.'

'I don't care who it is,' Connie Schwartz-Alberich lied, 'so long as it's not Harrison's. I couldn't stand the thought of having to take orders from that smug git Tony Harrison. He was a junior clerk here once, believe it or not, years ago.'

Benny Shumway frowned. 'Is that right?'

Connie nodded. 'It was just before I got sent out to the San Francisco office. He started off in mineral rights, same as everybody. He was an obnoxious little prick even then.'

Benny shrugged. 'I don't think it's Harrison's,' he said. 'I happen to know they're in deep trouble right now. In fact, if it wasn't for the bank bailing them out—' He paused, and frowned. 'Anyhow, it's not them. Not,' he added, standing up, 'that it's something we can do anything about. And so far, admit it, they've not been so bad.'

Connie snorted; Peter scowled; the new girl was staring in rapt fascination at a picture on the wall. She did things like that. Benny glanced at his watch and sighed. 'Time I wasn't here,' he said.

Left alone with f
tried to get back to
trate. Benny had b
they'd bought the c
with the rest of the
tionery at valuation;
part of the goodwill
old way to run a ci
the years to the fac
required. Five more
but at her age she
ingly, they had her

Just for curiosity
ture, the one that h
Harbour, in waterc
was something odd
couldn't quite pin

She picked up a
prints. Most people
they were modern
Moon sent back by
the inside view of a
one off the top of th
of her hand on it.

The phone on C
recollections of To
crimson embarras
lifted her hand off
faint cloud of mo
thought, I must be

'Cassie for you.'
'God,' Connie s
The usual click.
'Cassie, dear.'
'I'm stuck.'
'What, *again*?'

I-was-young-an
but I didn't keep
said pleasantly,
you think you c

'No,' Cassie s
'All right,' C
come and get yo

She wrote do
and edges of wh
dles of entwine
urgently. 'Sorry

'Be with you
phone down. B
natural that the
guide, role mod
the pile of print
them this evenin
Somehow, that
up, took down
room.

To get out of
being seen by
second floor bac
computer room
the long corridor
and of course yo
that's all right, b

'Connie,' said
door. 'I was just
'Ah,' Connie
'You're not bu
Yes. 'No,' Con
my way to the lib
'You couldn't
It was, always
look at him; he

and a dense black beard whose pointed tip brushed against the buckle of his trouser belt. Somehow, however, he managed to sound like a very small child who's been separated from his parents at a fairground.

Cassie, stuck, awaiting her with frantic impatience. 'Sure,' she said, 'what can I do for you?'

'It's these dratted specifications,' said Mr Suslowicz; and Connie asked herself if she'd ever heard him use coarse or profane language. Buggered if she knew. 'Some of it I can understand, but a lot of it's horribly technical. It'd take me a week to look it all up, and even then I probably couldn't make head nor tail of it. Do you think you could possibly—?'

'Of course,' Connie said brightly. 'Get Nikki to leave it on my desk and I'll look at it first thing after lunch.'

'Ah.' He could look so sad when he wanted to. 'Actually, it'd be a tremendous help if you could just cast your eye over it terribly quickly now. I've got the client coming in at three, you see.'

Connie thought quickly. Poor stuck Cassie; but stuck, by definition, means not likely to be going anywhere in a hurry. And maybe, just possibly, having to wait an extra forty minutes might encourage her to look where she was going, the next time. 'No problem,' Connie said. (And she thought: just five years to go, and then they can all get stuck permanently, with or without reams of incomprehensible technical jargon, and it won't be any of my concern.) 'How's your back, by the way?'

'Much better,' Mr Suslowicz replied. 'My own silly fault, of course. I just can't get used to the fact that I'm not able to do the kind of stuff I could handle twenty years ago.' He grinned sheepishly – he must have stupendous lip muscles, Connie reflected, in order to lift that bloody great big beard – and held the door for her.

One glance at the wodge of single-spaced typescript reassured Connie that Cas wasn't just being feeble. It was pretty advanced stuff, all about atomic densities and molecular structures, and she was rather proud of the fact that she could understand it.

Explaining it, on the other hand— 'Quite a job you've got on here,' she said. 'New client?'

Cas nodded; she managed not to look at the tip of his beard massaging his crotch. 'Quite a catch, if we can keep him happy,' he said. 'Hence the urgency.'

Connie avoided his gaze. 'Friends of the new management?' she asked, trying and failing to sound casual.

'Yes and no.'

She waited a full half-second, then said, 'Ah' and turned her attention back to the technical drivel. 'Well,' she said, 'it's like this. Imagine the Einsteinian spatio-temporal universe is a globe artichoke—'

Whether or not Cas really understood what she'd endeavoured to explain to him, he let her go an hour later, thanking her profusely and apologising for taking up so much of her time. That was the infuriating thing about Cas Suslowicz, she thought, as she hurtled toward the front office. There ought to be a law, or something in the European Declaration of Human Rights, about bosses not being allowed to be nice. It went against a thousand years of tradition in the field of British industrial relations. Of course, she reminded herself as she pushed through the fire door, Cas Suslowicz is nominally Polish—

'Early lunch?' snapped the girl behind the reception desk. She was slight, slim, blue-eyed, red-haired and to all appearances not a day over twenty-two. She was also Mr Tanner's mother.

'Don't talk to me about lunch,' Connie countersnapped. No chance of even a fleeting sandwich, if she had to go and unstick Cassie and be back in the office by two p.m. The explanation wasn't, however, something that she could share with a boss's mother. 'If Tillotsons call, take a message,' she added, and lunged out into the street.

Poor stuck Cassie – Connie scowled. Impossible, in the circumstances, to take a taxi to Charing Cross and put in a pink expenses chit to get the money back off the firm; which meant that either she'd have to pay for a taxi out of her own money, or take the slow but cheaper Tube. Well, she thought; Cassie's been there a fair old while already, another twenty minutes won't kill her. As a sop to her conscience, Connie increased her pace to a swiftish march (new shoes, heel-tips not yet ground down to comfortable stubs). Halfway down St Mary Axe, however, someone called out her name and she stopped.

'Connie Schwartz-Alberich,' he repeated. 'You haven't got a clue who I am, have you?'

He was short, slim, thin on top, glasses, fifty-whatever; Burton's suit, birthday-present tie. His voice, however, came straight from somewhere else, long ago and very far away. It couldn't be.

'George?'

He grinned. Voices and grins don't decay the way other externals do. 'Hellfire, Connie,' he said, 'you haven't changed a bit.'

'Balls,' she replied demurely. 'You have, though.'

'True.' He frowned. 'I was going to say, fancy meeting you here, but—' His frown deepened. 'Don't say you're still stuck at JWW.'

'Yes.'

'My God.' He shrugged. 'Why?'

'Too old to get a decent job, of course. How about you? Still at M&F?'

He laughed. 'Not likely,' he said. 'I went freelance – what, fifteen years ago. Got my own consultancy now.'

'Doing all right?'

'I guess so.' His grin made it obvious that he was being modest. For over a second and a half, Connie hated him to death. 'Better than the old days, anyhow. Look, is it your lunch hour, or can you skive off whatever you're doing?'

Poor Cassie, stuck; on the other hand, George Katzbalger, apparently returned from the dead. 'Oh, go on,' she said. 'Let's go and have a pizza.'

He looked puzzled. 'A what?'

'Pi—' She remembered one of the salient facts about George. 'You choose,' she said.

'Pleasure. There's this really rather good little Uzbek place just round the corner. Know it?'

'Uzbek?'

'Big bowls of rice with little bits of stuff in it.'

'Yes, all right. But I can't be too long, I've got to go and rescue someone before one-fifteen at the latest.'

George shrugged. 'No problem,' he said. 'So,' he went on, as he fell into step beside her, 'how long's it been, since New York?'

Connie did the maths. 'Twenty years, I suppose,' she said.

'Can't be. My God.' He sighed. 'And you're still with JWW. Is it true, by the way, what I've been hearing?'

'That depends on what it is,' she said quietly.

'About the takeover.'

'Ah.' She smiled. 'So what have you been hearing, exactly?'

Yet another salient fact about George: he always knew less than he thought he did about everything. So, over the rice with little bits of stuff in, Connie learned that J. W. Wells & Co, the oldest established firm in its field, had been having a rough time of it lately – four of the seven partners dead or in permanent exile, public confidence shattered, client base uncertain, the corporate hyenas prowling – and had finally succumbed to an aggressive hostile takeover by an undisclosed buyer. Unfortunately, she knew all that already, and George hadn't heard anything else apart from the kind of vague rumour she'd been swapping with the others over coffee an hour or so earlier. Annoyed, she let George pay for lunch and scuttled off to do whatever it was she'd been on her way to do when she'd bumped into him—

Ah, yes. Unstick Cassie. Connie sighed. One damn thing after another.

In Mortlake, where the shadows lie, the small family business of Hollingshead and Farren have been making small, intricate brass widgets for the plumbing, heating and hydraulic industries practically since the dawn of widget-making in the United Kingdom. Put an H&F widget in the hands of a skilled engineer who truly loves his craft and he'll recognise it at once; most likely he'll comment lovingly on its beautiful lines and exquisite quality of manufacture before pointing out that you can get something nearly as good and made in China for a fifth of the price. Even so, the old firm is still there, pouring, fettling and machining its small brass miracles; and although the Farrens have long since died out or gone away, the Hollingsheads remain: father, two uncles, six cousins and one son, Colin.

'And when you've done that,' Dad had said at breakfast, 'you can nip down to Crinkell's and pick up those end-mills.'

'Fine,' Colin had replied. 'Can I take the car?'

'No, I'm using it. Walk'll do you good. And you can drop in Boots while you're passing and get me some of those heartburn pills.'

Not for the first time, Colin reflected as he trudged down the High Street, collar folded up against the rain, that it really wasn't fair that he didn't have a car of his own any more. True, the business wasn't doing as well as it should have been, and times were hard, and if he absolutely needed a car for something he could always borrow the Daimler, if Dad wasn't using it. Even so. He'd been fond of his perky little Datsun, and they'd got next to nothing for it when it was sold.

Preoccupied with these reflections, Colin was almost through the door of Boots before he noticed it was Boots no longer. Instead, it had at some point turned into a John Menzies. He went in anyway and bought a refill for his pen (a Christmas present from Uncle Phil; it hurt the tip of his middle finger, but you don't want to give offence). That, and a detour to Tesco (who did a practically identical heartburn tablet in a slightly different-coloured box) explained his late arrival at the meeting, which he'd forgotten all about.

It turned out to be the sort of meeting that he'd cheerfully have missed altogether. There was a grim man from the bank, and an equally forbidding-looking woman from the accountants; also some sort of lawyer and a young woman whose name and function Colin didn't quite catch, but what the hell; from context he assumed her to be another species of commercial vulture, wheeling by invitation over the moribund carcass at seventy-five pounds per hour plus VAT.

'The bottom line is,' the man from the bank was saying, 'unless you can find a way to compete with low-cost imports—'

Colin tuned out. The same man, or someone very like him, had said the same thing at the same time last year, and the year before that, and just because something's unpleasant and true it doesn't necessarily mean that it makes for gripping listening. He glanced across the table at the unspecified young woman. Her name, he remembered from the round of cursory introductions, was Cassandra something, and she was rather nice-looking; not that that signified, since it's hard to take a romantic interest in a scavenger who's about to strip the residual flesh off your atrophied remains. Assuming she was a vulture, of course, but it was probably a safe bet. Unless she was a fabulously wealthy widget collector who wanted a hundred thousand 67/Bs by next Thursday, chances were she wasn't there to make things better.

Odd about Boots, he thought. Maybe they're feeling the pinch too. Colin wasn't inclined to take the withering and perishing of H&F personally, since he hadn't been working for the company very long (he'd wanted to go to university and learn to be a vet, but Dad wouldn't hear of it), but he felt sorry for the rest of them – Dad, Uncle Chris, Uncle Phil, the cousins. If Boots was also finishing off its hearty breakfast while the hangman tested the drop mechanism in the prison yard below, at the very least it implied that the hard times were general, and accordingly it wasn't really anybody's fault.

'Anyway,' said the accountant, 'that's more or less the position. Unless you can increase turnover by at least twenty-five per cent over the next three months, or else cut costs by forty-two per cent—'

How old can you be, Colin wondered, and still train to be a vet? All he actually knew about the profession was what he'd gleaned from repeats of *All Creatures Great & Small*, and the hero in that had been, what, about his age (but you can't tell with actors, of course, they've got make-up and all sorts). The careers bloke at school had said he needed all sorts of A levels and stuff, and he'd left as soon as he was legally able to do so, and had come here to start at the bottom and work his way up in the customary fashion. As it was, he'd started at the bottom and more or less stayed there, partly through lack of the killer instinct needed to get on in modern commerce, partly because there wasn't anywhere up for him to go until either Dad, Uncle Chris, Uncle Phil or one of the cousins decided to call it a day. A bit of a waste of time, he couldn't help reflecting, these past few years. His fault? Well, most things proverbially were, but in this case, not everything. If Dad had been a little bit more broad-minded, his life could have been quite different at this point. He could have been standing up to his knees in mud with his arm up a cow's backside, if only he'd been given a decent chance.

'I think that's more or less covered everything,' Dad was saying (and Colin couldn't help thinking of a man in a black suit drawing a cloth over the corpse's face). 'Thank you all for your time, and obviously we'll be in touch as soon as we've reached our decision.'

The vultures spread their wings; all except the nice-looking Cassandra female, who followed Dad into his office. No summons for Colin to follow, so he wandered slowly back to his own miniature lair, crept in behind the desk (he was slim going on scrawny, but he still had to breathe in), stacked his feet on top of the Albion Plastic Extrusions file, and allowed himself to slither into a reverie of petulant thought.

It was all very well cramming his mental screen with images of Christopher Timothy saving the elderly farmer's beloved sheep-dog, but assuming he wasn't ever going to be a vet after all, what was he going to do with his life once Hollingshead and Farren went under? The accountant, he remembered, had been ferociously upbeat about certain aspects of the disaster. The freehold of the factory and warehouse, he'd pointed out, would pay off the debts and redundancies and leave a nice fat lump sum over to provide for Dad and the uncles in the autumn of their lives. That, however, was more or less it as far as comfort and joy were concerned. The machinery had a modest value as scrap iron, maybe enough to pay the accountant's hourly rate for telling them it was otherwise worthless. The patents were about to expire anyway, the office equipment was a joke, and the best thing to do with the Daimler was to leave it parked temptingly in the street and hope a joyrider with an antiquarian bent might take it away and crash it into something solid. The men would be paid off, of course, and that would be that. Apart from one loose end, behind whose desk he was currently sitting. Nobody had ventured any suggestions as to what might be done with him. Like it mattered.

Colin frowned. As a general rule, he didn't do self-pity. Looked at from another perspective, he was tolerably young, more or less healthy and not a complete idiot, and after a child-hood and early adulthood spent chained to the widgetsmith's bench he was free to do whatever the hell he liked. Not so much a disaster, therefore, as an opportunity in fuck-up's clothing.

Opportunity; he considered the concept objectively. To date, opportunities had mostly been things offered to Colin via e-mail by benevolent Nigerian lawyers. Otherwise, he had always fol-lowed a path ordained for him by those who knew better – and a pretty narrow track it had been, running straight through a small and circumscribed world consisting mostly of rather boring work and running errands for senior family members. There had always been an undeniable logic to all of it, of course. Why should he want to move out to a place of his own when the family home was only a minute's walk from the factory gate? What did he need a car for? What conceivable purpose would be served by him spending a year backpacking round the Andes, given that the entire Latin American widget market was sewn up by the big US manufacturers? Furthermore, whence had he got the curious idea that he had time to go running around after girls when there were inventories to be made and quality to be con-trolled? Over the years, widget-making had been held up to him as a combination of Holy Grail, family curse and closed monastic order. Without it, the world would be a big, strange, interesting place, even if his role in it was as yet poorly defined.

Besides (he shifted his feet, nudging Albion Plastic Extrusions off the desk onto the floor) it was by no means certain that the old firm was even dead yet. This time last year, they'd been squinting down the twin barrels of an empty order book and a catastrophic tax demand; then, just as the doctor's finger had been quivering over the life-support machine's off switch, some lunatic in Newport Pagnell had bespoken a quarter of a million J/778c-30s, payment fifty per cent in advance. In due course he'd paid for and taken delivery of his widgets, and nobody had seen or heard of him again. If there was one such loopy philanthropist in the world, why not another? Maybe even now he was stuffing a cheque into an envelope, a crazed look on his face and a lampshade balanced on top of his head in place of a hat.

Enough about that, then; Colin let the unruly Highland terrier of his mind off the lead and let it chase pigeons through the bushes of more enticing improbabilities. The nice-looking female at the meeting, for instance. When the other suits had buggered off to shake their heads and pad their bills, she'd stayed behind to talk to the old man. What was she, then? Some business-school whizz-kid or efficiency guru, come to set them all to rights? Hadn't looked the type, although Colin freely conceded that he hadn't a clue what the type was supposed to look like. Not a customer, or we wouldn't have been giving her a guided tour of the dirty laundry. For the same reasons, not a creditor. So: apart from clients, people we owe money to and charcoal-grey-clad leeches, who the hell else do we know? Nobody.

Not that he'd have spared her one per cent of a passing thought if she hadn't been nice-looking. A realist in matters of self-appraisal, Colin was well aware that he was both shallow (he preferred 'uncomplicated') and unregenerate when it came to nice-looking – not that he got much chance to be either in and around the widget trade, where people tended to be male, middle-aged, harrassed-looking and generally sad. Even five years ago, things had been rather more lively. Now, however, his friends from school were mostly paired off and domesticated, and his social life had accordingly dwindled down to this: surreptitiously ogling nice-looking lady scavengers over the raised lid of his briefcase. He frowned. Maybe H&F going down the bog wouldn't be such a bad thing after all, if it meant that he'd be turned loose in rather more varied society. O brave new world, he said to himself, that hath living, unmutilated females under forty-five in it.

(Slowly but surely, he thought, I'm turning into a real mess. Note to self: do something about that, before it's too late.)

At some point Colin looked up at the clock on the opposite wall and saw that it was gone six. He sat up. Brooding morosely on his own time was something he tried to avoid. True, he had nowhere much to go apart from home. But even he, indentured servant of a family business, had some rudimentary grasp of the great Work/Fun dichotomy that informs the whole of modern Western civilisation. If it was after hours, it was time he buggered off. He went home.

An old-fashioned, rather shiny brown trilby hat on the hook in the hall; for once, Dad was home before him. Colin hung up his coat next to the hat and drifted into the front room.

Mum was there, reading a magazine. She didn't look up as he came into the room, but the cat lifted her head and gave him her trade-mark scowl of disappointed contempt. The TV was on as usual, with the sound turned down. You could tell it was autumn by the small drift of yellow leaves nestling round the foot of the massive tree that grew in the exact centre of the room.

'When's dinner?' he asked.

'Don't know,' Mum replied, eyes glued to print. 'What d'you want?'

'What is there?'

She thought for a moment. 'Fish fingers,' she said. 'Or chicken kievs. You could open a tin for Gretchen while you're out there.'

'Mphm.' Colin nodded, and set course for the kitchen. For

Gretchen the cat he opened a can of chicken fillets in gravy. He made himself cheese on toast. The ad hoc catering implied that Dad was having something on a tray in his study; figures to pore over, books to fiddle, whatever. Just as well; Colin didn't feel like an evening of painfully synthesised conversation in front of the muted telly.

Then to bed. He'd got the latest John Grisham from the library a day or so back, but for once the poet's magic was failing to enthral him. He read the same paragraph three times, stuck a Switch receipt in it for a bookmark and laid it by. He wasn't sleepy but he turned out the light anyway and closed his eyes. Lying in the dark, he fancied he could hear voices – not a Joan of Arc moment necessarily, because Dad's study was in the loft conversion directly overhead, and one of the voices could well be the old man's rumbling growl. The other one sounded feminine, but he couldn't make out any more than that. The nice-looking female, he thought, and then his stream of consciousness flowed out into the delta of drowsiness. He fell asleep, and so presumably what followed was a dream.

There was this girl, for a start. Annoyingly, Colin couldn't see her face – either it was turned away from him or masked from view by the stupid great big hat she was wearing for some reason – but apparently he knew who she was; in fact, as far as he could make out, he was in love with her and (yes, definitely a dream, although somehow it felt more like a memory) she was in love with him. They were strolling beside a river, up and down which young men in straw hats were propelling ditzy-looking boats by means of long, wet sticks. He wished that his dream-viewpoint allowed him to get a good look at the clothes he was wearing, because he had a feeling they were strange and old-fashioned, like the clobber the girl had on. Curious; he had to flounder about in the very back of his subconscious mind before he realised that it was straight out of *Mary Poppins*, a film he'd slept through once many years ago. If the mental pictures he was creating for himself had been refluxed through the hiatus hernia of memory, it was an intriguing comment on his jackdaw mind.

Minutiae of female costume had never interested him in the least; but he was prepared to bet good money that the outfit the girl was wearing was historically accurate down to the last frill and button (although when the historical period thus faithfully recreated was, he had no idea). Not, of course, that it really mattered. The unusual and arresting feature of this dream, surely, was the girl who actually liked him back, in spite of having known him for more than ten minutes.

It got better. He couldn't see her face, of course, so maybe she looked like a springer spaniel under all that hat, but she had a lovely voice and a wonderful sense of humour – she hadn't said anything funny yet, but apparently that was part of the backstory – and it was obvious that just being in her company was the most wonderful thing ever. Here was a girl you could talk to all day and never realise how the time was passing, a girl who saw the world in a wonderfully refreshing different way, a girl he was enchanted by and absolutely at home with at the same time— Fine, it was just a dream, and even at its best real life isn't ever like that (and if it was, ten minutes of it'd be enough to make you want to throw up). Nevertheless, it wasn't at all like his usual kind of dream. For one thing, he wasn't trying to play the cello with no clothes on in front of an audience of his relations, enemies and former headmasters. For another, he never had dreams about girls.

One of the ditzy-looking boats pulled in to the bank, and its passengers climbed out. Ah, he thought, that's more like it. Goblins. Normal service has been resumed, we apologise for any inconvenience.

But the goblins simply strolled past, chatting pleasantly among themselves, pausing very briefly to tip their hats politely to him in a charmingly old-fashioned, courteous kind of way. He reciprocated; the goblins went on their way, chatting about the century that Fry had just made at the Oval.

Century. That was cricket, wasn't it? Colin despised cricket, much as a cat relates badly to water. Arguably that made sense, within the dream's own frame of reference. He didn't like goblins much, either (not that he'd ever encountered one, because of course there's no such thing) so it kind of followed that they'd like a game that gave him a pain in the bum. Dream logic. So that was all right.

Let's sit down on the bench, the girl was saying, and feed the ducks. There was a bench. There were ducks. In his hand he discovered a brown paper bag full of little bits of stale bread.

Bloody odd dream, since he didn't like ducks much either. Colin opened the bag and offered it to her, she took a handful of stale bits and hurled them daintily onto the surface of the water. The ducks closed in, like cruisers cornering the *Bismarck*. So far, apparently, so idyllic.

But then she turned her face toward him (didn't he know her from somewhere? No, but her face was completely familiar all the same) and looked him in the eye. That made her uncomfortable; she looked away, folded her hands in her lap. I've been thinking a lot lately, she said, about us.

(Two ducks were racing for the nearest chunk of floating bread. One of them, mottled brown, beat the other, sort of blue-greeny grey, by a short head.)

Oh yes? he said. Stupid thing to say.

Yes, she said, and – hesitation. Her voice wobbled a bit as she said, And I don't think it's going to work. You and me, I mean. I just don't think we're right for each other.

(Not to worry. Only a dream. Cheese on toast before going to bed.)

You can't mean that, he heard himself say.

I'm sorry, she replied (in a dream, the people speak but you hear the words inside your head). I suppose I've known it for some time now, but I pretended it wasn't true. I thought I could make it work, but I can't. I'm just not the person you think I am.

(And if all this was cribbed straight out of *Mary Poppins* along with the sets and costumes, it must've been one of the bits that he'd slept through, because it didn't ring any bells at all.) That's simply not true, he was saying – hurt, incredulous, angry – we get on so well together, I've never felt like this with anybody else and I know you feel the same really, you must just be—

No. (A passing goblin turns to stare, then looks away hurriedly in embarrassment.) No, we've got to stop lying to ourselves, it only makes it worse. We've got to face it, we can't go on like this any more. It's just wishful thinking. If I could make myself love you, I would; but I can't, and that's all there is to it.

On balance, Colin decided, he preferred the cello-playing dream, even the version with the goblins and the pack of red-eyed howling wolves. At any rate, this would be a good moment for him to wake up, bolt upright, bathed in sweat, tangle of bed-clothes in a white-knuckle grip. Please?

I don't know what to say, he replied, perfectly truthfully. This is such a bolt from the blue. I thought— Damn it, we're supposed to be getting married in a fortnight's time. (A dream with plot twists; sophisticated or what?) We've made all the arrangements. What am I going to tell my parents?

I said I'm sorry, she was saying. I know, it's my fault, I should've said something before now. I should've known it'd upset you dreadfully. Maybe that's why I kept putting it off, because I really don't want to hurt you. But you can see, can't you—?

No. Colin opened his eyes. He was sitting bolt upright, all sweaty, hands gripping the duvet cover; it took him several seconds to make sure that he wasn't still sitting on a bench beside a river, feeding disgusting ducks. Once he was sure that he was safely back in reality, he switched on the light and hopped out of bed. No sound of voices coming through the ceiling. He checked the time; a quarter to midnight.

He padded up the stairs, past the upper section of tree trunk that filled the stairwell, and paused for a moment outside Dad's study door, looking for the crack of light that meant the old man was still in there. Then he knocked and went in.

'Dad,' he said, 'you know all about cricket and stuff. Was there a cricket player called Fry?'

Dad frowned. 'C. B. Fry,' he replied. 'Very famous Edwardian batsman. What about him?'

'Nothing,' Colin replied. ''Night.'

He got as far as the landing, turned round and knocked again.
'Dad.'

'Well?'

'Is there any, you know, insanity in our family? People not right in the head and stuff.'

Dad raised his eyebrows. 'Before you, you mean?'

'Yes.'

'No.'

'Ah,' Colin said, 'that's good. Well, see you in the morning.'

Back out onto the landing, one step down the stairs; hesitate, back up again. Knock.

'Now what?'

'Dad.'

'Well?'

Pause. 'Why've we got a bloody great big tree growing up through the middle of our house, and why can't you see the top of it from outside?'

Dad scowled at him. 'Go back to bed,' he said. 'You need to be up early in the morning.'

CHAPTER TWO

'Assessments,' Peter Melznic wailed. 'Bloody assessments. We never had anything like that before.'

Connie Schwartz-Alberich shrugged. 'Lucky, weren't we? Makes you realise how soft we've had it up to now. Never felt like it at the time, of course.'

The pale-faced girl sniffed. 'When I was at UMG—'

'For two pins,' Peter continued, 'I'd go straight up to Tanner's office and tell him where he can stick his job. I've been in this business seven years, and I've never had to put up with this kind of shit before. And what about this other bloody stupid idea, "ongoing vocational training"? Like I need some snot-nosed academic telling me how to do what I do.'

Connie, who'd been in the trade for five times seven years and seen a dozen Peter Melznics come and go like the flowers in spring, decided not to comment on that. 'It's modern management theory,' she sighed, 'the stuff they teach you at business school and so on. It's just a fashion, some more bloody stupid hoops to jump through, that's all. Did I ever tell you about when I was at the San Francisco office and some pinhead decided we needed a company song?'

'What I'd like to know,' Benny Shumway interrupted, 'is who's going to be doing these assessments.'

'Good point,' Connie said. 'Anybody heard anything about that?'

Nobody had, apparently. But the thin-faced girl mentioned that she'd heard somewhere that Messrs Tanner and Suslowicz, and even Mr Wells himself, were going to have to submit to the same procedure. Connie looked sharply sideways at her, but nobody said anything.

'Can you remember how it went?' Bennie broke the silence.

'How what went?'

'The company song.'

'Oh, that.' Connie grinned. 'Never came to anything. I believe the pinhead sent a memo to Humph Wells, who pointed out that we'd had a company song since 1877, but you needed to be an operatic baritone to get through it without choking to death. It sort of fizzled out after that. But we had a whole month of doing physical jerks on the roof every morning, until the pinhead turned his ankle over. Which sort of proves my point,' she went on. 'They come up with these stupid ideas, you go along with them for a bit till they self-destruct, and then you can get back to doing things properly, like you've always done them. No harm done, everyone's happy, and we remain defiantly unspoilt by progress.'

Benny finished his coffee. 'Where's young Cassie, by the way?' he asked. 'Not stuck again, is she?'

'No.' Connie smiled indulgently. 'In a meeting with clients. Some potty little job south of the river, but I think she's milking it for something to put on her time sheet.'

Peter scowled. 'That's another thing I'm really not happy about,' he said, 'these bloody time sheets. I don't like being treated like I'm some wet-behind-the-ears trainee straight out of college. If the job gets done and the client's happy and we get paid, what the hell does it matter how many six-minute units you took writing a letter?'

'We all had to do time sheets at UMG,' the pale-faced girl said. 'Of course, it was a complete shambles at the Munich office, given the sort of work that we were doing, but it kept the management happy.'

A brief who-let-her-in-here? moment, then Benny thanked Connie for the coffee and left, triggering a general evacuation. It was nearly time for Benny to go to the Bank, but (as usual) he wasn't in any hurry to carry out that particular chore. Instead, he went quietly down to the basement and fed the goats.

He'd raised an interesting point over coffee, he thought as he weighed out the barley, oats and concentrates, though he said so himself. If they were going to have assessments, someone would have to do the assessing, and if the pale-faced girl (what was she called? He was usually good with names, but hers slipped through his mind like car keys through a frayed pocket) was right about the partners having them too, presumably it'd be the new owners, or their trusted representatives, asking the questions. Unless they had in mind some set-up with one-way glass and microphones, it'd mean coming face to face with them at last; and if he was given that opportunity, he had a trick or two of his own up his sleeve, which might help him find answers to the questions that had been bugging him for the last three months.

Benny emptied the feed bucket into the trough, gave Esmeralda her apple, and paused, frowning. There was always the direct approach, he reflected. He could always go to Jack Wells or Dennis Tanner and ask him, straight out. After everything he'd done for JWW over the years, they owed him that. The thing was, did he really want to know the answer?

To the Bank; a wretched business, as ever, and when he got back to his office and closed the door behind him he dropped into his chair and sat still and quiet for a while, until he'd recovered his usual equanimity. Maybe I'm getting too old for this, he thought; maybe it's time I thought about packing it in. Retirement: all the things he'd claimed to have been daydreaming about all these years. A nice little bungalow somewhere on the South Coast; a small open-cast mine of his own, just to keep his hand in; time for hobbies and gardening and stuff. He shuddered. Thoughts like that helped put going to the Bank in context.

His door opened, and one of the more appealing aspects of working at JWW these days appeared in the doorway. He found himself smiling. 'Hiya, Cassie,' he said.

'Are you busy?'

'Not really. Just been and done the banking. I was just about to get a cup of coffee. Can I make you one while I'm there?'

Cassie shook her head with extreme vigour. 'Thanks,' she said, 'but no, thanks. Never touch the stuff.'

'Coffee?'

She nodded. 'Brings me out in blotches. And it's not the caffeine, because I can drink enough tea to kill a whale and be none the worse for it. Funny, but there it is.'

'All right,' Benny said, with a shrug. 'No coffee, tea instead. Won't be a tick.'

He opened a drawer of his desk, took out two empty mugs and gave them a ferocious look, as though they'd betrayed him unforgivably. Immediately they filled with brown liquid and began to steam, and he handed one to her. 'Now then,' he said, 'what can I do for you?'

(Five failed marriages; seven disastrous long-term relationships; and that was only counting the times he'd actually managed to get the girl in the end, albeit temporarily. By now he ought to be completely immune to nice-looking faces, even ones with red hair and freckles. But that was like saying you don't get colds or the flu any more when you're dead.)

'It's these stupid reconciliation figures,' Cassie said, dropping into the chair opposite and dumping a sheaf of papers on the desk. 'I can't make them come out, but I know the numbers are right, because I checked them all three times against the file, so it must just be some stupid slip-up in the arithmetic or something.'

Benny grinned. 'Give them here,' he said. 'I'll go through them this afternoon – I've got time before I cash up.'

'Thanks.'

'You'll owe me, mind. And I always collect on favours owed.'

Cassie scowled at him, mock-ferocious. 'I don't do ironing,' she said. 'Not for anybody.'

'It shows. Now me, I'm an absolute bloody virtuoso. Give me a flat surface and a late-model Rowenta, and basically the sky's the limit.'

She smiled, but her mind was somewhere else. Over the years, Benny had got used to it; nice-looking young women drifting into his office at quiet times of day to think past him. Not a bad thing; they cheered the place up, more so than flowers or a nice watercolour, and they generally only turned nasty if you married them.

'So,' he said, 'these assessment things. I take it you're a hundred and ten per cent in favour.'

She looked up at him. 'What? Oh yes, absolutely. I can't think of anything I'd like more than some goldfish-faced git asking me where I think I'll be in five years' time. Still, it does mean there's a chance we'll actually get to find out who our new masters are at last.'

'I was thinking that just now,' Benny replied, 'while I was feeding the goats. Of course, they might cheat: bring in people from outside, management consultants or whatever.'

'Bastards,' Cassie said absently.

'Management,' Benny paraphrased. 'At least, so far, they haven't come interfering in the actual work. You got anything new on at the moment?'

A slight reaction to that, but too vague to assess properly. 'One new job, came in last week,' she replied. 'Just boring stuff.'

'Boring or really boring?'

'Fairly boring.' She sighed, but her heart wasn't in it. 'When I was at Mortimers, they let me do proper cases, really big stuff for the multinationals.'

Benny nodded gravely. 'You never did tell me why you left.'

'You're right.' A warning grin. 'I never did.'

'They fired you.'

'They did not.' Cassie stood up. 'Well,' she went on, 'better go and do some work, I suppose. Can you let me know when you've sorted those stupid reconciliations?'

Nice girl, Benny thought, as the door closed behind her.

Bright, too; wasted here, of course. Not as smart as she thinks she is, mind, or she wouldn't keep getting stuck and needing Connie to go and fish her out. He pulled a sad face. Twenty years ago, he could really have made a complete and utter idiot of himself over a girl like that. Happy days.

The door opened, and a small face appeared round it; a curious face, in its way, which had made more than one observer think of an early attempt at head-shrinking by an apprentice Javanese headhunter. It belonged to Dennis Tanner, ex-partner and head of the mining and mineral rights department.

'Got a minute?' he said.

Benny nodded. 'What can I do for you?'

Mr Tanner frowned. 'I need the Ibbotson file,' he said, 'and the expenses ledger for June '73. Oh, and the client-account paying-in book, as well.'

Benny clicked his tongue sympathetically. 'The auditors have arrived, then.'

'Too bloody right.' Mr Tanner sighed. 'Nine o'clock, on the doorstep. Miserable sods, by the look of them, typical Moss Berwick. They've taken over Humph Wells's old office and they're demanding files right, left and centre.' He shook his head sadly. 'I said we should never have changed from Andersen's.'

Benny pulled open a filing-cabinet drawer and took out a folder. 'Auditors are auditors,' he said. 'I often wonder what makes someone decide that's what he wants to be when he grows up. A sadistic streak and a total lack of a sense of humour, probably.'

'It's the way they look at you,' Mr Tanner said, 'like you've got your flies undone and snot dribbling out of your nose. And we pay them to do it, too.'

Once Mr Tanner had gone away, Benny glanced quickly at the botched reconciliations sheets that Cassie had left with him, observing in a detached, scholarly manner that it appeared to be an inexorable rule of nature that the prettiest girls always had the most indecipherable handwriting. He dumped them in his in-tray, made a mental note to deal with them later so he could call her and tell her they were done five minutes before coffee-time tomorrow. ('Hell of a job, took me all afternoon, but I got there in the end.') Then he opened a file and ran his finger down a list headed 'Things To Do' until he came to an uncrossed-out entry that read *United Global Finance*. He clicked his tongue. There are some jobs you keep putting off until the thought of them is enough to depress you to death; when you eventually pull your finger out and get on with them, they turn out to be the prover-bial piece of cake. He stood up, crossed the room to a tall, padlocked corner cabinet, unlocked it and took out a long cloth bag, closed with a drawstring, and a small aerosol spray can. Inside the bag was a sword: broad, curved, single-edged, deeply fullered, in a battered black leather scabbard. He drew it, tested the edge with his forefinger (ouch), sprayed a dab of oil on the blade and worked it in with the palm of his hand. He paused for a moment to glance at the familiar inscription cut into the ornate steel hilt: a serial number, and *Property of J. W. Wells & Co*, in runes.

Benny dropped the sword back in its bag, tightened the draw-string, tucked in under his arm and, on his way out of the office, flicked his desk phone to *fax/answer* mode. At the door he paused, went back and retrieved his umbrella.

Colin was stuffing brochures into envelopes in the back office when his father sent for him.

'Got a job for you,' Dad said, stubbing out one cigar and lighting another. 'Take the Tube up to the City – 70 St Mary Axe, I've written it all down for you – and pick up some paper-work. Bring it straight back, it's urgent. Got that?'

Colin nodded. London, he thought, that'll be nice. If I play my cards right and spin it out a bit, I could stop for a burger on my way back. 'Sure,' he said, brightly but not too eagerly, because his father knew him well enough to be suspicious of anything resembling enthusiasm. Colin was painfully aware that he tended to overact when trying to hide an ulterior motive behind a façade of cheerful compliance. Zeal and ham pie, so to speak. 'Anything else you want done while I'm up there?'

Dad grinned. 'Not likely,' he said. 'I want you back here in plenty of time to finish off those brochures.'

Curses. Never mind. At least it was out of the office for an hour or so. Even reading a book on the train was a small but valuable treat, compared with what he'd be doing otherwise.

70 St Mary Axe turned out to be more or less what Colin had been expecting – a bit upmarket, maybe, for the likes of H&F, but that could be explained away easily enough as a hold-over from the days of the company's prosperity, when it could afford to use posh lawyers and accountants. Which of the two J. W. Wells & Co was he didn't know, but it was a reasonable bet it was something of the sort; chartered actuaries, maybe (he had no idea what chartered actuaries did for a living), or just possibly stockbrokers or merchant bankers. Vultures, in any case. But, since they'd afforded him an unexpected outing and possibly a chance of a quarter-pounder with cheese, regular fries, large vanilla shake, he was prepared to give them the benefit of the doubt until such time as they did something nasty to him.

On the way in he nearly barged into a short, broad, bearded man with enormously thick-lensed glasses and a funny-looking cloth bag stuck under his arm. He stepped aside (the man looked so much like Mr Magoo that Colin couldn't rely on him to avoid a collision) and let him pass before going in.

A distinctly old-fashioned revolving door hustled him into a rather daunting, oak-panelled front office. He paused to take in his surroundings.

'Did it get you?' said a musical voice from behind the broad, elegant reception desk.

'Excuse me?'

'The door.' The voice belonged to a startlingly attractive blonde. Good heavens, Colin thought mildly. 'It nips your ankles if you don't watch out.'

'No, I'm fine,' he replied self-consciously. 'Um, I'm Colin Hollingshead, I'm here to see—' He couldn't remember, so he dug the bit of paper Dad had given him out of his top pocket. 'I'm here to see Ms Clay.'

'Oh.' For some reason, the startlingly attractive blonde didn't seem entirely pleased. 'All right, I'll let her know you're here. You'd better sit down.'

There was a lot of space in the front office, entirely uncluttered by chairs. 'Right,' Colin said.

'Through there.' The startlingly attractive blonde (she wasn't quite so appealing with her eyebrows ruckled together like that) nodded at a doorway in the far distance. 'She won't be long.'

The carpet was deep and springy, like bog moss. He felt as though he was leaving a trail of footprints in it.

The waiting room was small and curiously depressing. The chair Colin selected turned out to be wobbly – one false move and it'd probably disintegrate under him – and the best the magazine stack on the table could offer was the *Sunday Times* colour supplement for 16 April 1987. He spent the first five minutes of his wait flicking through it, and the remaining four staring aimlessly at the light fittings on the ceiling. It was still better than cramming brochures into envelopes, but the margin was tightening by the second.

'Hello.' He looked up and recognised her. 'Sorry to have kept you waiting,' she went on, 'I was on the phone. I'm Cassie Clay.'

'Like the boxer,' Colin replied before he could stop himself.

Cassie's rather wan smile gave him a rough idea of how many times she'd heard that one before. 'Absolutely,' she said. 'Now, I've got all the draft papers here, but there're a couple of points I'd just like to run over with you, because they're slightly different from what I discussed with your father after the meeting.'

'Actually.' Colin looked away. 'There wouldn't be very much point, really. I'm just the messenger, you see. I don't know what all this is about.'

'Ah.' She frowned. 'In that case, if you could just let him know there are a few changes, and I'll send him a letter to explain them.'

At that moment, if asked to put a cash value on himself, Colin would've suggested a figure somewhere between £1.50 and a pound. Odd; because although he had practically a complete set of character defects, an inferiority complex was one of the few gaps in his collection. There was something about this girl, however, that made him wish he wasn't so obviously unfit for human consumption. 'Right,' he said, 'I'll do that.' She put a green folder down on the table. He waited for a second, then picked it up. That, as far as he could judge, was that.

'You were at the meeting,' Cassie said; and then she frowned, as if she hadn't meant to say it.

'That's right,' Colin replied. 'I got there late, as usual. Forgot about it, actually.'

'Oh. Well, you didn't miss an awful lot.'

Surreal, Colin thought. 'It'd probably have all been over my head anyway,' he heard himself say. 'I'm pretty much the lowest form of life at H&F.'

'Everyone's got to start somewhere,' she replied.

'That's right,' he said. He felt an unaccountable urge to tell her that in fact he was a managing director in disguise, just pretending to be an underachieving gofer, but he managed to repress it. 'That's what Dad always says. So,' he went on, 'have you been doing this job long?'

'Six months,' she replied. 'Before that I was with Mortimers, in Fleet Street.'

'Oh, right.' Trying to sound suitably impressed; failing. Who the hell were Mortimers? he wondered idly. 'Is it better here, or—?'

Cassie shrugged. 'It's different,' she said. 'Here it's more – traditional.' She sounded as though she was choosing her adjectives carefully; completely wasted on him, of course. 'You've been clients of ours for yonks, haven't you?'

'I think so,' Colin replied, as he realised that his left foot had gone to sleep. All he needed, really. 'Well, thanks for seeing me.'

'No problem.'

'I'll be going, then,' he said, not even trying to move. 'I expect you're very busy,' he added.

'Oh, about normal.' She frowned. 'Are you all right?'

He sighed. 'Pins and needles,' he said. 'In my foot.'

'Oh.'

'I'll be all right,' he said, and shifted his weight. He managed not to scream.

'You'd better sit down for a bit.'

'Yes. Well, no, actually, I can't move.'

Cassie didn't laugh. 'Try rubbing it.'

He looked up sharply at her, not really knowing why. 'It's getting better, actually,' he said. 'There, I can put my weight on it. Sorry about that.'

'Oh, that's all right—' She stopped suddenly, and stared at him. Maybe three seconds; which can be a long time, under the right circumstances. 'It can really hurt, can't it?'

'What?'

'Pins and needles.'

'It's all gone now,' Colin said, exaggerating. 'Right, well, I'll tell Dad to expect a letter from you. Thanks again.'

'All part of the service.'

Cassie opened the door for him. Through it he could see the lovely receptionist, looking daggers at them both. Feeling murderously self-conscious, he crossed the front office, trying very hard not to limp.

As soon as he was out in the street, the pain disappeared completely. He stopped and looked back at the door, then crossed the road. There was a pub quite close by. He lunged toward it like a sprinter clinching a world record.

Two-thirds of a pint later, Colin felt sufficiently composed to rally his thoughts. Something had happened in there, something on a par with Newton's apple or Archimedes' bath; because of it, the world was about to change. Buggered if he knew what, though.

He finished his beer and got another. There was one obvious possibility, but he was fairly sure that he could cross it off the list of possibilities straight away. He'd fallen in love before – how many times? Six? Narrow the search parameters; he'd fallen in love at first sight before, twice. Match not found; the symptoms had been different. Now, technically this wasn't first sight, since he'd seen Cassie before, at the meeting. It still didn't compute. It was more like something else—

Déjà vu? He wasn't a hundred per cent sure what that meant, but what he understood by the term was an uncanny feeling that you're replaying something that's happened to you before. That was closer to it, but not the whole story, not by a long way. Pause to review progress to date. Refine search—

It had been the moment when he'd confessed to the pins and needles, and she'd said something (but he couldn't actually remember what it was; something about the pins and needles, a suggestion). That was the flashback moment. He was certain of it. That was it – she'd said try rubbing it, and he'd been on the point of saying, you told me that the last time and it didn't work.

Of course, there hadn't been a last time. They'd met before, once, briefly, at that stupid meeting, but at that time his feet had been pinless and needle-free. More to the point; hadn't Cassie looked at him, just after he'd apologised for being embarrassing? He'd seen that look in her eyes before, somewhere, somewhen, and at the time it had puzzled him rotten, because he couldn't understand what had been bothering her. Now, though, he did. That look on her face was what he'd have seen if, at that exact moment, he'd been looking into a mirror.

Colin had drunk half his second pint without noticing. He put the glass down and scowled at it. This was starting to get weird, and weirdness was something that he preferred to shy away from, the way a wise dog avoids an electric fence, the second time. But I do know her from somewhere, he conceded unwillingly.

Screw this, he thought. He left the rest of his beer and went outside. A bus was just pulling up; on the front, in the list of destinations, was Fleet Street.

Well, he thought.

Twenty minutes of trudging, and he found it; a little less than seventy yards up the street from the Cheshire Cheese. A simple brass plate that read:

MORTIMER & Co

Mortimers in Fleet Street, she'd said. He shrugged and went in.

Just inside was a reception desk. Behind it was a girl; a singularly attractive blonde. She smiled at him, and said hello.

Colin closed his eyes and counted to five. Originally he'd intended counting to ten, but patience wasn't one of his principal virtues.

'You again,' he said.

She looked at him. 'Excuse me?'

'It's you, isn't it? I saw you just now, at the other place.'

The smile was still there, but it was doing that thing that happened to the J537/Z3 reed valve when incorrectly installed. What was it called? Work-hardening. 'What other place?'

'Where I just came from. St Mary Axe. You were behind the front desk.'

Slight, brittle pause. 'Well, no, actually. I've been here all day.'

'No, it was you,' Colin insisted. 'I know it was. Or, hang on. Have you got a twin sister?'

'Me? No.' She'd moved her left hand off the desk and was fumbling for something under the ledge; the sort of place you'd wire in a panic button.

'Oh. My mistake. Sorry.'

'That's all right. Look, who is it you wanted to see?'

'See?' For a moment it was as though she was speaking a foreign language. 'Oh, *see*. No, nobody. No, I just, um, sort of dropped in. Well, I was passing, and I wondered what it is you do here. Just curiosity, really.'

The blonde girl was definitely looking past him; chances were that the door through which Security would be likely to enter was directly behind his left shoulder. 'How do you mean, exactly?' she was saying.

Colin applauded her training, or her common sense. Keep the nutsos talking and they're less likely to attack. Defending her employer's premises against the invading hordes of fruitcakes and weirdos is all in a day's work for your highly trained and motivated elite-force receptionist. The thin blonde line, and all that.

'Doesn't matter,' he said, taking a few steps back. 'Very sorry to have bothered you. Bloody hell, is that the time?' He turned and fled from the building.

No more pratting around; it wasn't safe, here in the big city. Only when he was safely on the District Line heading for home did he feel secure enough to open his mind to what he'd just seen.

Definitely the same woman, Colin could swear to that, because he never forgot a pretty face. On the other hand, it was highly improbable, verging on outright impossibility. Even if the receptionist at 70 St Mary Axe was moonlighting or job-sharing in Fleet Street, she'd have had to take a taxi and gone like a rocket to get from one office to the other in the time his bus had taken to cross that relatively small distance; and if that was what had happened, why on earth should she deny it? Far more likely that he'd imagined it. It'd be consistent, anyhow, since he'd quite obviously imagined having met the Cassandra Clay female before, and received the benefit of her advice on what to do when pins and needles strike. For some reason (explained Colin's inner Spock) he was going through a phase of thinking that he'd recognised people when he hadn't. There could be any number of explanations for that, ranging from failing eyesight to incipient looniness, without the need to postulate a world haunted by forgotten meetings and duplicate blondes. Served him right, anyhow, for playing truant from the office.

As he walked from the station to the H&F works, he noticed that the John Menzies that had moved in where Boots used to be was now a Virgin Megastore, while the Monsoon three doors down from it had at some point turned into a Halfords. Evolution in action, he supposed.

Dad was on the phone when he reached the office; he scowled and gestured for the green file, and Colin gave it to him. The scowl deepened, and Colin backed out of the room. Back to stuffing brochures into envelopes, then. What fun.

Cassandra Clay, he thought as he worked (fold, fold again, lift flap, stuff, lick flap, press, take another from the pile). While his conscious mind had been on other things, the backroom boys in his subconscious hadn't been idle; they'd produced their report and were ready to discuss their findings. Not, they were pretty sure, love. The symptoms just weren't there, for a start. They'd been through the files (Jackie Ibbotson, May to August 1994; Pauline Fletcher, January 1997 to April 1998; Melanie Mackintosh, September 2000 to June 2002 and 16 to 21 February 2003) and assessed the data. There were a few superficial similarities – daydreaming, wandering about bumping into things, feelings of embarrassment, self-deprecation and general despair – but the really significant features were conspicuous by their absence. True, he was having difficulties evicting her from his mind; she kept popping back, like a computer virus, and scrambling his train of thought, and he'd already played over the dialogue from their brief conversation three times, analysing it for anything that might be considered even remotely encouraging – but it didn't feel like the other times. Really.

The door flew open. Not a SWAT team or Customs & Excise; just Dad not knocking, as usual. And, as usual, Colin was a fifth of a second too late getting his feet off the desk.

'Right,' Dad said, dropping into the other chair and frowning at him. 'So what did she say?'

It only took Colin a second and a half to find the place. 'Not a lot, really,' he replied. 'She gave me the file, I brought it home with me. That's about it.'

Dad's frown thickened. 'Yes, but she went through it with you line by line, so you could report back to me.'

Colin shook his head. 'She's going to write you a letter.'

'A letter?'

'Yes.'

A sigh; such a small sound to come out of such a large body, but it got the message across with perfect efficiency. 'Fine,' Dad said. 'She's going to write me a letter.'

Colin's turn to frown, though it was a pretty feeble effort in comparison. 'Well,' he said, 'there's not much point me going through it with her when I haven't got a clue what it's all about. Wouldn't have meant anything to me.'

'Only because you can't be arsed to take an interest in the business.'

Well, yes, there was that. 'I thought it'd be a waste of money,' Colin offered meekly.

'Right. So instead, they're going to charge me a hundred quid for writing a letter.'

'Sorry,' Colin said. He always apologised. With all the breath he'd wasted on apologies over the past quarter-century he could've inflated a skyful of Zeppelins. 'So,' he said, 'what's it all about?'

Dad looked at him. 'Don't worry about it,' he said. 'You get on with doing the brochures. There'll be a memo in a day or so.'

Colin smiled weakly, and Dad erupted out of the room. One of these days, Colin promised himself, I'll leave home. I'll rent a nice little cottage on the lip of Vesuvius, for the peace and quiet. In the meantime, I'll go on stuffing things in envelopes and honing my esprit de l'escalier. Actually, it'd serve the old bastard right if the company did go bust; which means it won't, of course, because there's no justice.

By a strange coincidence, Colin shoved the last brochure into the last envelope at exactly twenty-nine minutes past five. The felicity of timing made him smile, and he stood up to leave. Home; dinner (overcooked pasta in slimy green sauce; some irresponsible clown had given Mum the latest Delia Smith for her birthday), the telly, bed. I'd get a life, only I wouldn't know what to do with it.

The phone on his desk rang. He frowned. It didn't usually do that. He picked it up.

'Someone from J. W. Wells for you,' said Carol from the front office. She sounded as bewildered as Colin felt. 'Fine,' he said. 'Put them through.'

'Mr Hollingshead?'

That voice. 'Um, yes,' Colin replied.

'Cassie Clay, J. W. Wells. We met earlier.'

'That's right,' Colin said. 'You gave me the documents.' Yes. She knows that, you imbecile.

'Yes.' Pause. 'Just making sure everything was in order.'

She's lying, he realised. That's not why she's phoning me. 'You're going to write us a letter,' he said.

'Yes, it'll be in tonight's post.'

'That's great, thanks.'

'No problem.'

Pause. Now, Colin thought, if it was me phoning her, the motivation would be obvious. I'd be phoning her on the flimsiest of pretexts just so that I could talk to her again, because I'm a pathetic loser. But she's phoning me.

'So,' Cassie went on, 'with any luck, you should get the letter tomorrow.'

'Yes.'

'And if there's anything in it that you want to talk over, please don't hesitate to call.'

'Thanks, I'll do that. Or at least, my dad will. I'll pass on the message.'

'Oh. Right, that's excellent, thanks. You've been most helpful.'

'Not at all.'

At the back of Colin's mind, a small voice conceded the possibility that it might have been wrong. He ignored it. It wasn't me who picked up the phone and dialled a number, he pointed out.

'So,' she said, 'how's the pins and needles?'

'What? Oh, fine. Completely better.'

Actually, that was a lie, too; they'd come back, but not in his foot. Sharp, tiny pinpricks were driving into his brain, worse than any hangover he'd ever inflicted on himself; it was a bit like bee-stings or really savage nettles, and it was something to do with something he'd just said, and if he put the phone down it'd get better right away. On the other hand—

'Sorry,' he said quickly, 'call for me on the other line. Thanks again, bye.'

Click; purr; clunk as the receiver went down on its cradle. The pain (miniature fireworks going off half an inch in from his temples) stopped as abruptly as it had started, so completely that he found it difficult, a second later, to remember how they'd felt.

Bloody odd.

Colin picked the phone up again and looked at it. Seemed harmless enough – he put it to his ear, but nothing happened. Just the phone, something so mundane and ordinary that you'd never spare it a second's thought, but a moment ago he could've sworn it was hurting him, *eating his brain*, like something from an old B movie. (Query: what sort of monstrous life-form would cross the galaxy at x times the speed of light just to eat Colin Hollingshead's brain? An alien on a diet?) There must be something wrong with it, he decided, maybe it was sending out an incredibly high-pitched squeal that he could feel but not hear. Better get the engineer in, or scrap it and get another one. Not that it mattered, because it never rang. Until today.

Perplexity; and on his own time, too. But the oddness of it all was nagging at him like an abscess under a favourite tooth. He dialled a number, and waited.

'Tony?'

'Hello, mate. Haven't heard from you in a long time. What can I do for you?'

'It's all right,' Colin said. 'I'm just ringing to see if my phone hurts my head.'

That hadn't come out quite right; but he and Tony had been at school together, known each other for years and years, all through adolescence. It wasn't the weirdest thing one of them had said to the other, not by a long way. 'Does it?' Tony enquired with interest.

'Doesn't seem to. Keep talking.'

'All right. What about?'

'I don't know, do I? How's things?'

'Oh, fine. Nothing much happening. I broke up with Nikki, of course.'

'I'm sorry to hear that, Tony. Who the bloody hell is Nikki?'

'My girlfriend.'

'I thought that was Sarah.'

'Sarah? Bugger me, that's going back a bit. How long is it since you last called me, anyway?'

'Can't remember.'

'Nor me. Is it hurting yet?'

'Don't think so. But I was talking to someone just now, and I suddenly got this really bad headache, and I was wondering, was it just the phone, or what?'

'I see. So, do you want me to carry on talking? I could tell you about my new MP3 player, it's got—'

'No, thanks, I think that'll do. How's your mum, by the way?'

'Oh, fine. How's your lot?'

'Same as usual. Right, sorry to have bothered you.'

Not the phone, then. Colin was also inclined to discount the alien theory, at least for the time being. How about a fault on the other end of the line; something wrong with *her* phone? The obvious way of testing that hypothesis would be to call Cassie back, but he shied away from that. Probably best to let the whole thing go, pretend it hadn't happened. He was really good at doing that, turning a blind mind's eye to things he couldn't or didn't want to try to understand. It was, he reckoned, a skill that came with living in a house with a bloody great big tree growing right up through it.

About that tree— No, this wasn't the time or the place. He'd lived with it for twenty-five years, and had long since learned the knack of not seeing it. He'd asked about it exactly twice; once the other night, and once when he was seven, the first time he'd had a little friend back for tea. The little friend had said, 'Why have you got a tree growing up through the middle of your house?' and Colin had realised that he didn't know the answer.

Looking back, he realised he'd assumed it was perfectly normal, that everybody had trees growing up through their houses, but the little friend's reaction gave the lie to that assumption, so he'd asked Dad, who hadn't replied. Furthermore, he'd not replied with such a ferocious scowl that Colin had resolved never to raise the subject ever again; and for eighteen years he'd kept to his resolution, even when he noticed – he was eight or nine at the time – that although the stupid thing's trunk went all the way up into the loft (he'd been up there one time with Dad, to hold the torch for him while he saw to a jammed ballcock) there was nothing to be seen of it from outside the house. Which was odd, even to a kid who'd still believed in Father Christmas when his classmates had already discovered tobacco, strong drink and the opposite sex. Trees don't just stop, unless someone goes out of his way to trim bits off them, and he couldn't remember ever having seen Dad coming down out of the roof with secateurs or a pruning saw, let alone bits of amputated tree.

Still. It couldn't be important, could it? He'd lived with it this long and nothing had come of it. There was probably a perfectly rational explanation that he alone was too stupid to see, and he'd only embarrass himself by admitting his ignorance.

Colin went home. Dinner, telly, bed. When he was asleep (he snored) his father, quiet as a little mouse, crept up to the top landing, opened the loft-flap, pulled down the folding aluminium ladder and climbed up it. Over his shoulder was an empty sack.

CHAPTER THREE

'**M**s Schwartz-Alberich,' the stranger said, with a patronising grin. 'Come in, take a seat. Thanks for your time.'

Connie folded herself neatly into the small, straight chair on the other side of the desk, and put down the buff-coloured file she'd brought in with her.

'Your time, actually,' she said cheerfully. 'Anyhow, what can I do for you?'

The stranger's grin didn't increase or diminish, but its curvature shifted slightly. Good, Connie thought, I've annoyed him. She was a great believer in Potter's Law (the first muscle stiffened is the first point won). 'First,' he said, in that salad-dressing voice of his, 'I'd like to make it absolutely clear that there's nothing at all sinister about this. We're not looking to make any compulsory redundancies or anything like that –' he lifted his head, and the morning light glanced off the steel rims of his glasses '– at this stage. This is purely a routine exercise to help us to get to know you, and vice versa. Are you okay with that?'

Ah, Connie thought, threats. Threats I can handle. 'Absolutely,' she said. 'What a very good idea. Fire away.'

'Now then.' The stranger looked at her, blinked like a lizard. 'You've been with the firm for let's see—' Glance down at dossier open on desk. Connie could, of course, read upside-down words almost as easily as right-way-up ones, a skill she'd learned long ago when she first began attending meetings with colleagues, clients and other enemies. 'Gracious,' the stranger said, 'thirty-two years.'

'Thirty-four,' Connie replied. 'Look, it says on your bit of paper, nineteen seventy-one. Two thousand and five take away one thousand, nine hundred and seventy-one is thirty-four.' She smiled pleasantly.

'Thirty-four years.' The stranger moved his sleeve to cover the dossier. 'Quite a long time, then.'

Connie shrugged. 'Actually, I'm a relative newcomer, compared with John or Dennis or Cas.' Dropping the first names of the ex-partners was a tactic that she'd been planning to save till later, but since the hostility level was escalating rather more sharply than she'd anticipated she thought that she might as well deploy it straight away. It only takes one trick, as her whist-playing aunt used to say. 'And Benny Shumway's been here, what, forty-seven years, and Peter—'

'Quite.' The stranger frowned. 'I see that you've spent most of your time at the San Francisco office.'

'Seventeen years,' Connie replied promptly. 'And I was sorely pissed off when young Dennis ordered me home, trust me. Still, I can't blame him, what with all hell breaking loose.'

'Ah.' The stranger looked at her again. 'You liked it out there.'

'Well, I was more or less running the office, wasn't I?' Connie said. 'Sure, Kurt Lundqvist was nominally in charge most of that time, being a partner and all, but of course *he* wasn't doing any work, or anything else much.'

'You liked being your own boss?'

'I wouldn't put it quite like that,' Connie replied. 'More a case of being able to get on with my work without people interfering. Much more efficient.'

The stranger nodded. His dossier obviously told him how successful and profitable the San Francisco office had been during her tenure there, because he changed the subject. 'So, has it been hard adjusting to being back here again?'

'Nah.' She shrugged. 'I've known all of this crowd for yonks – apart from young Cassie, of course – and the work's exactly the same, over there or back here. But the coffee and doughnuts were better.'

Meanwhile, she was guessing at his age. Difficult to tell with someone so reptilian, but almost certainly the unfashionable side of forty. Not that it mattered, but she liked to ground her assessment of people in basic data, and as she got older herself she found age increasingly significant. 'Fine,' the reptile said. 'Now I'd like to talk a bit about how you feel about your place in the team.'

'Which team?'

He frowned. 'Well, JWW, of course. I don't—'

'Sorry,' Connie said brightly, 'thought you were talking about the pub quiz. We have a showdown with Mortimers twice a year; deadly serious stuff, as you'd expect. We lost last year, so obviously next time it'll be to the death. Sorry, I interrupted you.'

So he didn't know who Mortimers were; she could tell from his expression. Interesting.

'We like to think of JWW as a team,' the reptile said, broadening his smile until Connie was sure that his teeth were about to fall out. 'All of us pulling together, working for common goals on a level playing field. We believe—'

'Sports imagery,' Connie interrupted. 'I get you. Jolly good. Go on.'

He subsided for a moment or so, just a little. 'Ms Schwartz-Alberich,' he said, 'where do you see yourself in, say, five years time?'

'Oh that's an easy one,' Connie said cheerfully. 'Let's see, quarter past eleven, so at this precise moment, five years from now, I'll be wheeling my little wire trolley round Tesco's, filling it up with cat food. I haven't got a cat,' she added, 'but I've always promised myself I'll get one when I retire. Mysterious old hags living alone in remote country cottages always have cats, it's traditional.'

The reptile blinked. 'Ah. So you're planning to retire at—'

'Sixty,' Connie said promptly. 'Till then, I guess I'm just clinging on limpet-fashion for my pension.' She smiled. 'And there you have it.'

'I see.' The stranger breathed out slowly through his nose. 'Well, I appreciate your frankness. Of course, we like to see a fresh, achievement-oriented attitude in our team players, which—'

'Well, of course you do,' Connie chirruped. 'And if you care to look at your bit of paper there, top left-hand corner, more or less where your watch is, you'll see exactly how much I achieved for the firm in the last fiscal year. Fourteen per cent up on the previous year, and that was when Dennis was doing most of it himself. I like to keep busy,' she added. 'It helps pass the time.'

'Impressive,' the stranger said sourly. 'Nevertheless, one thing we do insist on in our team is commitment, a hundred and ten per cent—'

'Absolutely,' Connie interrupted. 'I've always said, there's nothing so boring as sitting behind a desk picking your nose all day. Trouble with me is, I work so fast – wonderful powers of concentration, it's a knack I was born with, I guess – I get through it all so quickly that it's hard to make it stretch out to five-thirty sometimes. We're all a bit like that here, really.'

'Moving on,' the stranger said, 'what would you say is your greatest weakness?'

Connie thought for a moment. 'Kryptonite,' she said. 'Other than that, I can handle most things.' She paused. 'That's the green kryptonite,' she went on. 'The red stuff used to bother me a bit but these days I can just sort of shrug it off, mostly.'

Long silence. 'Thank you,' the reptile said, 'this has been extremely useful, and I hope—'

'Oh, is that it?' Connie pulled a sad face. 'Pity. It's ever so much more fun than what you actually pay me for. Can we have another go soon, please? Oh, hang on,' she added, 'you're supposed to ask me if there's anything I want to ask you. It says so, look, on your bit of—'

'Another time, perhaps,' the reptile said. 'I've got an appoint-ment at half-past.'

'But it's only twenty-five—'

'Thank you so much for your time.'

Connie stood up. 'Not a bit of it. Ah well, back to the coal-face. Nice meeting you, Mr—'

Mister didn't say anything; not, at least, until her hand was on the door handle. Then he called out, 'Oh, I nearly forgot.'

'Yes?'

'Here,' he said. He was holding out a little plastic bag, sealed with sticky tape. 'For you.'

'Oh.' Connie hesitated, then went back and took it from him. About the size and feel of a large apple turnover. 'What's this for?'

'Appropriate occasions,' the reptile answered, and in his small round eyes there was a tiny flicker of satisfaction snatched from the jaws of frustration. 'Goodbye.'

Back in her office, Connie ripped the bag open and retrieved from it a baseball cap, one-size-fits-all. It was fluorescent green, and on the front was a bright orange logo made up of the letters JWW, hideously twisted together, as though they'd been melted in a fire. Under the logo was printed, also in orange: *The A Team*

Connie stared at it for a full five seconds before shoving it in the bottom drawer of her desk, which she then locked. Hm, she thought, that's right. Like the old saying goes: never under-estimate a bastard.

'Well,' Cassie demanded, 'how did it go?'

Connie handed her a mug of tea and sat down. 'Actually,' she said, 'it was fun.'

'Fun.'

'Fun.' Connie nodded. 'Thinking about it, I could've been just a teeny bit stroppier if I'd really tried, but I'd have had to set fire to his tie or squirt shaving foam up his nose, something like that.'

'You were stroppy.'

'Very stroppy.' Connie ladled two spoonfuls of sugar into her coffee and stirred it with a pencil.

'It was basically, "If you want to fire me, here's two dozen perfectly good excuses, and if you don't, piss off playing silly games and let me get on with some work." I remain unfired. You've got to be firm with these people, or else they'll make your life a misery.'

'I see,' Cassie said neutrally.

'On the other hand,' Connie conceded, 'he did give me a baseball cap.'

Cassie blinked. 'A what?'

'Here, see for yourself.' Connie removed it from the drawer, using thumb and forefinger-tip only, and laid it on the desktop like a cat delivering a nicely matured dead mouse. 'In particular I'd like to draw your attention to the colour.'

Cassie frowned. 'It's revolting.'

Connie nodded. 'There are some pretty sick minds in this world,' she said. 'It's also about twenty years behind the times, isn't it? I thought all this crap went out with paintball weekends and motivational t'ai chi on the roof every morning.'

'I believe it sort of goes in cycles,' Cassie said absently; it was taking her longer than she'd have anticipated to get over the fluorescent greenness of the thing.

'Ah, well.' Connie improvised a pair of forceps out of two biros and put the cap away where it couldn't do any more harm. 'So on balance,' she went on, 'I'd have to put it down as a draw. Not that I'm bothered, really. It's like what they say about being a successful knife-fighter.'

'Really?' Cassie looked at her. 'What *do* they say about being a successful knife-fighter?'

Connie smiled. 'You can only do it if you don't really care if you lose. Like me; if they fire me, so what? I miss out on a bit of pension, but that's okay, I hardly ever spent anything all the years I was in America – company apartment, obscene bonuses – so if they chuck me out tomorrow, all it means is that I get to be a little old lady in a country cottage a few years ahead of schedule.

Compared to Third World debt or the ozone layer, it's no big deal. You, on the other hand—'

Cassie shook her head. 'I've only been here five minutes compared with the rest of you.'

'True. No, I think the worst thing would be the feeling that somehow they'd won – you know, come in here and beaten us at something.' Connie shrugged. 'The hell with it. Got anything interesting on today?'

'Hardly,' Cassie replied, but as she said it she looked away. The movement caught Connie's attention like a bramble snagging tights. 'I've got a presentation to work up for the manganese people, and I suppose I'd better do a bit more on the Hollingshead and Farren thing.' She paused, then went on: 'Connie, did you ever do one of those?'

Connie's brow furrowed a little. 'Sale and purchase? Yes, actually, years ago. Before I joined JWW, even. Not since, though. Not exactly my favourite line of work, to be honest with you.'

'Ah,' Cassie said. 'Well, I can relate to that.'

'Acting for both sides—'

'Yes.'

'But there you go,' Connie said briskly. 'It's legal and it's profitable, so what the hell. No pun intended,' she added quickly. 'And if you overlook the sort-of-creepy-and-yuck side of it, then really it's just pretty basic contract-drafting. Not exactly rocket science.' She twitched her nose. 'Actually, I did some rocket science once. Didn't like it much, though. Lots of maths and Americans, and very short lunchtimes.'

'Right,' Cassie said. Miles away. She knew that look. She also knew, to nine decimal places, when not to interfere. 'I'd better be getting on,' Cassie continued, swallowing a gulp of her lukewarm tea. She stood up. 'I take it you didn't manage to find out anything. About Them, I mean.'

'One thing,' Connie said quietly. 'He didn't seem to know who Mortimers are.'

That reached her. 'You're kidding.'

, several times, but she couldn't remember off-
life in Mergers and Acquisitions?'

ed. 'Boring,' she replied. 'I don't know, I just can't
my mind on my work right now.'

morphed into the equally characteristic Shumway
wled. 'Don't start,' she said.

arting, promise. And besides, a man can dream.'
an't.'

Benny held up his hands. 'So it isn't that, then.
u aren't fretting over these stupid assessments, are

he lied. 'Had yours yet?'

his head. 'But Connie dropped in just before I left
.' He raised his eyebrows and sighed. 'Mind you, she
he fearless kind. Fearless as two short planks, as my
Robertson's used to say. And she always gets away

iled. 'I think it helps that she's too good at her job to

that,' Benny conceded. 'But there's more to it, I
y, she's wasted in Mineral Rights. Should've gone in
ntrol years ago.' The grin broke out again. 'She'd
pretty cute in chain mail.'
er you said that.'

ven think about it,' Benny replied quickly. 'I have
the deepest respect for Connie, bordering on abject

to tell her you said *that*,' Cassie replied, with a smile.
on, what've you found out about Them? You're
g how nothing happens in this business without you
out it first.'

Benny said ruefully. 'For once, however, colour me
ot for want of asking around; but the weird thing is,
ms to know anything. Which leads me to the conclu-

They aren't in the business at all,' Cassie interrupted.

'Which implies,' Connie said, 'that whoever they are, they aren't in the biz. In which case, what the hell are they doing buying up JWW?'

'I don't know what to make of that,' Cassie replied.

'You know what?' Connie grinned. 'Neither the hell do I.'

In her office, Cassie sat down, drew the green folder across the desk towards her, and opened it. She took out a stapled-together wodge of A4, about five-eighths of an inch thick.

This agreement—

But her eyes glanced off the words like gravel chipping off tank armour. What in God's name had possessed her to phone him like that?

This agreement made the   day of   2005 between (1)   Hollingshead of 17 Mere View Drive Mortlake Surrey (here-inafter 'the vendor') and—

Cassie frowned, rummaged in the file for a page of handwritten notes and filled in the client's missing first names. Which reminded her. What on earth could possibly have induced her to do such a stupid, ditzy—

(hereinafter 'the vendor') and (2) the Prince, governors, directors, supreme council and diabolical parliament of the Powers of Darkness (a statutory corporation; hereinafter 'the purchasers') witnesses as follows:

(1).

Although, she had to admit, it wasn't the first time she'd done something like that. And that was the disturbing thing about it. The last time she'd done it, she'd been seventeen and madly in love with— She shuddered slightly. Not a pleasant memory, if you valued your self-esteem.

(1). By a letter of agreement dated the 19th March 2005, the vendor agreed to sell his soul (hereinafter 'the soul') to the purchasers in consideration of the sum of money, services and other matters detailed in the first schedule hereto (hereinafter 'the purchase price')

She frowned and went back a line. In pencil she inserted the word *facilities* between *services* and *other matters*.

And there was another thing. All right, she'd done a strange, uncharacteristic and bloody stupid thing. The question remained: why? Deliberately, as she corrected a typo in the fifth clause of the contract (if the stupid girl didn't know how to spell 'brimstone', why didn't she use the spellcheck?), she called up onto her mind's screen an image of Colin Hollingshead. Yes, Cassie thought, well. Nothing special; absolutely nothing special. She played back as much as she could remember of what he'd said. Nothing special there, either. It was beyond question that she'd fallen for some real waste products in her time, but in each unhappy instance there'd been something that had baited the hook: nice eyes, a Brandoesque swagger, tight buns, a passable imitation of Robin Cook. Colin Hollingshead? Nothing. Nondescript, charmless, thick as a fantasy trilogy, pointy nose, devoid of any vestige of appeal whatsoever. Hand on non-fluttering heart, she wasn't in love with him one teeny-tiny bit. So why the phone call? It was as though someone else had hijacked her hand and ear and made her do it. Weird.

7. *The vendor covenants with the purchasers that he will not—*

(a) in the ordinary course of business commit any mortal sin (as defined by the Mortal Sins Classification and Consolidation Regulations 1975) that would render him liable to eternal damnation irrespective of the terms of this agreement

(b) adhere to any faith sect religion or philosophy whose precepts do not acknowledge the existence of the purchasers

(c) notwithstanding the provisions of the Unfair Contract Terms Act 1968, seek by any act of repentance absolution contrition or charitable good works to frustrate the terms of this contract by incurring divine forgiveness

And yet another bizarre thing. When they'd been talking, after Cassie had given him the folder to take away, and he'd happened to mention that he'd got pins and needles in his foot – déjà vu, or whatever it was called: it was as though she'd heard him say exactly those words before. She could practically hear his voice in her head, except that it wasn't his voice, and

when she tried to listen, it
of it; a feeling that she kne
it wasn't him really, just
respect.

8. *In the event that the D*
term of this contract, or such c
be opened and the dead to be r
purchasers agree and declare t
referred to arbitration in accord
hereof, the arbitrator's decisio
express term of this agreement

Cassie read Clause 8 over
the words like court shoes o
posed to be another sympt
concentrate at work? Stuff it,
can't even proof-read a basic s
attention wandering. She sto
her ears, sat down again. *Con*

She couldn't.

'Bugger,' she said aloud, an
But Connie wasn't in her o
flights of stairs, across two lan
ridor, to see if Benny Shumw
She was just in time to see th
wall of his office opening, an
slamming the door shut and s
bolts. He looked more than u
until he'd sat down, taken seve
blood off his hands with a swath
anything.

'Did they give you a hard tim
Benny shook his head. 'No wo
closed his eyes for a moment. '
goats instead of doves. Sometim
over from Barclays. Anyhow,' he
mark Shumway smile (how many

He'd told h
hand), 'how'
She shrug
seem to kee
The smil
grin. She sc
'I wasn't
'No, you
'All right
What is it? `
you?'
'Maybe,'
He shool
for the Bank
always was
old boss at
with it, too.
Cassie sr
sack.'
'There's
think. Rea
for Pest C
have looke
'I'll tell
'Don't
nothing bu
terror.'
'I'll hav
'So, com
always say
knowing
'I know
clueless.
nobody s
sion—'
'—Tha

'Like Connie was saying. The creep not having heard of Mortimers, and so forth.'

Benny nodded. 'And that just doesn't make sense. For one thing, it's not allowed. Outsiders can't go around buying into the business, there's rules about that sort of thing, understandably. I think there's even a British Standard or something.'

Cassie picked up a paper clip and started to unbend it. 'One of these days,' she said, 'you're going to have to tell me exactly what did happen, when all the old partners left, and—'

'They didn't *leave*,' Benny said, with a deep chuckle. 'Let's see. Theo Van Spee was killed, ditto Ricky Wurmtoter; last we heard of Judy di Castel' Bianco, she was permanently marooned on the Isle of Avalon; and Humph Wells got turned into a photocopier.'

Cassie couldn't help shuddering a little at that. 'Not the big old one in the computer room?' she said. 'The one that always chews up spreadsheets.'

Benny laughed. 'Nah. Humph broke down about three months before you joined, and he was an old model, we couldn't get the parts. He's up in the roof space somewhere, along with the broken chairs and the old VAT receipts.'

'Yetch.'

'Don't worry, he asked for it. Long story, I'll tell you about it some time. No, it's a rough old game we're in, and from time to time bad stuff happens. You know that.'

'Of course. But losing so many partners one after another—'

'You're starting to sound like Lady Bracknell.'

'I've heard people talking about some bloke called Carpenter,' Cassie said. 'Apparently it was all his fault.'

'Up to a point,' Benny replied. 'Paul Carpenter and Sophie Pettingell. Last heard of happily married and fabulously rich somewhere in New Zealand.' He paused. 'You didn't come here because you're fascinated by industrial history. What's the matter?'

'And wasn't there another partner, Kurt something, who came to a bad end?'

'Don't change the subject.'

'All right.' She frowned. 'God knows why I'm telling you, of all people. You'll just do your lewd grin and make unregenerate sexist remarks.'

Benny rubbed his hands together. 'You bet. Go on.'

So Cassie told him; about Colin Hollingshead, and the phone call, and even pins and needles. To her complete surprise, however, Benny didn't leer, grin, snigger or say things. He hardly moved at all, except that while she was explaining about the déjà-vu thing he frowned deeply and put his hand in front of his mouth.

'Is that it?' he said.

'Yes, I think so. You're pretty quiet.'

He nodded. 'A bit weird, if you ask me.'

'Coming from you—' She glanced across at the plywood door, with its seven massive bolts. 'Now I'm really starting to worry.'

'Don't,' he said quickly. 'Honestly, I don't think it's something horrible, anything like that. Actually, it sort of reminds me of something, but buggered if I can remember what.'

'You're a great help.'

'Proverbially,' Benny said graciously, 'but not on this occasion. Not yet, anyhow, but I promise I'll give it some thought.' Suddenly, his face lit up in a huge, no-holds-barred smile that took Cassie completely by surprise. 'We'll figure it out, don't you worry. Meanwhile,' he went on – the smile vanished as suddenly as it had appeared – 'I'd better get on with some work. Fortunately, I can think and do mental long division at the same time.'

Cassie headed back to her office. As she was passing the closed file store, she very nearly collided with the pale-faced girl whose name nobody seemed able to remember. She apologised. The pale-faced girl looked at her intensely for a moment, as if reading small print reflected in Cassie's eyes.

'That's all right,' said the pale girl. 'It wasn't your fault, though you weren't looking where you were going. But I came round the corner too fast, and I should've kept to my side of the corridor. I could easily have trodden on your foot if you hadn't swerved at the last moment.'

'Ah,' Cassie said.

'So really, it's me who owes you an apology.'

'Oh well,' Cassie said. 'That's all right.'

'Thank you,' the pale-faced girl said gravely. 'In return, please accept this gift as a token of my appreciation for your forbearance.'

She held out her hand; the fingers were clamped tight around something, and the knuckles were white.

'Gift?' Cassie repeated.

'Present,' the thin-faced girl explained. 'Go on, please take it. It's all right, it won't bite or anything.'

Cassie looked at the outstretched hand and made no move. 'That's very kind of you,' she said cautiously. 'What is it?'

'Take it and you can see for yourself.'

'Would you mind awfully telling me what it is first?'

The thin-faced girl's eyebrows cuddled together, then parted. 'Oh, it's nothing really. Just a small glass bead.'

'Ah.'

'It does, however,' the thin-faced girl went on, 'have some interesting properties. If you hold it up to the light and look into it, you can see the face of your own true love.'

'Gosh,' Cassie said; and she was about to add that it was a really, really nice thought but even so, if it was all the same to her, she'd pass on it just for now, when the thin-faced girl grabbed her by the wrist and pressed something small, round and hard into the palm of her hand. 'Well, bye for now,' she said. 'And if you want to drop by my office later on and tell me what you saw in there, do please feel free. There's nothing I enjoy more than some really juicy girl-to-girl gossip.'

The thin-faced girl opened the door of the closed file store and went inside. Cassie wasn't sure, but she had an idea that she heard the click of a lock, or the graunch of a bolt. *You don't have to be weird to work here*, she thought, *but—*

On her desk, when she got back to it, was a small stack of those little red-and-white While-You-Were-Out notes. All of them urged her to phone Mr Hollingshead, at Hollingshead and Farren, ASAP. She sat down, realising that she was still holding in her hand the small round thing that the loony girl had given her. She opened her hand, and something dropped onto her desk, bouncing and rolling a bit before finally coming to rest beside her stapler. After all that, it turned out to be nothing more exciting than a perfectly ordinary kid's marble. Then she picked up her phone and called the front desk.

'Which Mr Hollingshead?' she asked.

'You what?' replied Rosie on reception.

'There's more than one of them,' Cassie explained. 'An old one and a young one.' Pause. 'You left a note on my desk saying I've got to call back a Mr Hollingshead, of Holl—'

'Yes, all right. No need to make a three-hour bloody mini-series out of it.'

'Sorry. Look, did he say which one he was?'

'No.'

'All right,' Cassie said, driving away the small yapping Yorkshire terrier of frustration from around her mind's ankles. 'Did he sound old or young?'

'Search me. All you humans sound the same.'

'Look—' Cassie snapped; but Rosie on reception went on: 'He sounded really pissed off and swore a lot, if that's any help.'

'Ah,' Cassie said. 'That'll be Mr Hollingshead senior.'

'There you go, then.'

Cassie put the phone down and picked up the file, which was on her desk where she'd left it. Father Hollingshead, calling to ask about some detail of the draft contract. For some reason, she felt mortally disappointed. But *why*?

She found the number on the information docket stapled to the back cover of the file and dialled it.

'At last,' said Mr Hollingshead. 'I called five times.'

'Six, actually,' Cassie replied amiably. 'How can I help?'

'It's this Clause Three. What the bloody hell is it supposed to mean?'

So she explained Clause Three. This process required no conscious thought whatsoever; she'd explained that clause, or clauses just like it, a hundred times to a hundred different clients. She wasn't even listening to herself. Instead she was thinking, if Benny Shumway thinks it's weird, it must be really out-of-this-world bizarre; and then he tells me not to worry about it. Yes, right. No problem, I'll dismiss it from my mind this instant. Like hell I will.

'And that,' she caught herself saying, 'is all there is to it, really.'

'I see,' grumbled Mr Hollingshead. 'Then why in buggery can't you just say that, instead of wrapping it up in all that legalese bullshit?'

'Why indeed?' Cassie replied. 'Well, actually, it's because a contract like this is a highly technical document, and all the words in it have very specialised meanings, which aren't necessarily the same as in everyday speech, so—'

'And another thing. Schedule Five, paragraph two, five lines up from the bottom.'

'What? Oh yes, the jurisdiction clause. What about it?'

'I can't understand a bloody word of it. What's all this about the Acapulco Convention, for a start?'

So Cassie explained about conflicts of jurisdiction, and how some kinds of dispute that might arise from the contract could be dealt with by an ordinary County Court in Britain, while other kinds would have to be referred to the Supreme Tribunal of Absolute Evil in Pandaemonium 'It's a bit of a pain,' she conceded, 'but I'm afraid there's nothing we can do about that, it's a standard clause, take it or leave it. Besides,' she went on, 'that sort of dispute is pretty unlikely to crop up, it's only really relevant if—'

'Fine,' grunted Mr Hollingshead, 'so what's all this in Schedule Ten, Section 6B? You never mentioned any of this shit at the meeting.'

Ten more minutes of that sort of thing; which was good in a sense, because it meant that Cassie could score another two six-minute units on her time sheet, which in turn meant a proportionate increase in Mr Hollingshead's bill, about which he would unquestionably complain bitterly. Fine. Then a little crackle of inspiration jumped her mental points.

'Look,' she said, 'obviously there's quite a lot in the draft contract that we need to talk about, so wouldn't it make more sense to go over it together face to face rather than on the phone? If you could maybe drop by the office—'

Derisory snort. 'No chance. Far too busy.'

'That's all right,' Cassie said smoothly, 'I'll come and see you. Would ten-fifteen tomorrow morning suit you?'

Pause; silence of a man who should've seen it coming. 'Yes, all right. We can get it all sorted and out of the way, and then maybe we can get on and see some action. Ten-fifteen sharp.'

'As a needle,' Cassie said cheerfully. 'Goodbye.'

She put the phone down and leant back in her chair. So, she thought; so tomorrow I'm going to where he lives, to see his old Dad. Maybe he'll be sitting in on the meeting too, in which case— In which case *what*, though? Still no trace of an answer to that question.

Sigh. She dumped the corrected draft of the contract into her out-tray, with a yellow sticky attached that read *Revised draft by 9.15 a.m. tomorrow, please.* The sooner the contract was signed and out of the way, the sooner she could close the file, bang in a whopping great bill and move on to something else. Wouldn't that be nice.

Something caught her eye; that stupid marble, the present from the thin girl. On a whim Cassie picked it up and held it up to the light, but all she could see was the little red swirly bit in the middle.

That evening, on her return to her small, expensive flat in Chessington, she found six messages on her answering machine. Messages one to five inclusive were from her mother. Message six, on the other hand, was a bit odd. She couldn't make out what it was; either birdsong, or someone whistling very badly, or the warble of an unusually melodious fax machine. She played it through three times out of sheer naked curiosity; then she deleted it and went to bed.

CHAPTER FOUR

'In here,' Dad growled.

With his default now-what-am-I-supposed-to-have-done? grimace on his face, Colin followed Dad into the study and sat down. He noticed that the green file he'd been to London to collect was open on the desk.

'That bird you went to see the other day,' Dad barked, 'is coming in at quarter past ten.'

Colin hadn't been expecting that. 'Oh yes?' he said.

'I've decided that you'd better sit in on the meeting,' Dad went on. He was pacing up and down, tense and majestic as a caged lion. That wasn't like him; usually he lounged in his expensive office chair, into which he fitted the way a pint of beer fits into a mug. 'All right?'

Another odd thing, because Colin's consent wasn't usually asked for; it was one of those commodities where supply vastly exceeded demand. 'Sure,' he said (and he was thinking: her? Coming here? And his right foot was already starting to tingle).

'And before she gets here—' Dad had his back to him. 'Before she gets here, there's a few things you need to know, so sit quiet and don't interrupt. Got that?'

Colin nodded, realised Dad couldn't see him, and squeaked, 'Yes.' Dad sighed, took a long stride forward, like a fencer lunging, and poured himself a medium-large glass of whisky from the bottle that lived on top of the filing cabinet.

Colin knew that bottle. In fact, it was an old family friend, since its remote ancestor had been the source of his first experience of strong liquor ten years ago, practically to the day. He'd since found out that Dad's office bottle was strictly industrial-grade whisky: crude, functional and cost-effective. Nevertheless, it had put him off the stuff for life. Furthermore, he'd never known Dad touch a drop before a quarter to six.

'These people—' Dad stopped, glugged a fair-sized dose of the whisky, and turned round to face him. 'J. W. Wells & Co,' he said. 'Very good firm, probably the best in the business. You know what they do?'

Colin frowned. 'Some sort of lawyers, aren't they?'

Dad grinned, but the expression on his face had nothing whatsoever to do with humour. 'Sort of. Actually, they're—' He hesitated again; then he fished about in the file and took out a sheet of paper; thick, heavy cream paper, with an old-fashioned embossed black letterhead. 'Read that,' he said.

So Colin read –

J. W. Wells & Co

Practical & Effective Magicians, Sorcerers and
Supernatural Consultants
70 St Mary Axe, London EC3

Then he read it again. Unfortunately, he'd been right the first time.

'What,' he said, 'you mean, like, conjurors and kids' birthday parties and stuff?'

'No,' said Dad.

'Oh.' Colin read it a third time. Under the address, he saw:

Partners: J. W. Wells, MAA (Oxon) LLB FIPES DipN; C. N. Suslowicz, FSEE AIBG; Dennis Tanner, BA (Plymouth) BG

'Magic,' Dad said, and there was a weight of sadness in his voice that Colin had never heard before. 'That's what we've been reduced to, son. It's enough to make you bloody weep.'

Colin screwed his eyes up and relaxed them again. 'They're putting in an order for stuff,' he hazarded. 'Those little brass interlocking rings, or whatever it is they hide up their sleeves for holding the spare ace of spades, or—'

'Not,' Dad said (you could hear the fraying of his patience), 'that kind of bloody magic. This is—' He stopped, closed his eyes. 'This is *real* magic. It's what they do. It works.' He breathed out a long sigh. 'It's the only thing that can stop H&F going right down the pan. So we haven't any choice.'

'Magic?' The word burst out of Colin's mouth like water from a cracked pipe. 'Oh come on, Dad, you've got to be—'

'I'm fucking not.' Dad rounded on him so fiercely that Colin took a step backwards. Then he seemed to deflate a little, and went on in a slightly calmer voice: 'It was Ben Phillips from Amalgamated Box that put me on to them. They were in the same fuck-awful mess as us three years back; then someone told them about these people, JWW, and look at them now. Amalgamated Box *plc*, and they've just bought a fifteen per cent stake in Kawaguchiya Integrated Circuits. So I thought, well, we've got fuck all to lose, so why not?'

'Magic?' Colin repeated.

'Keep your bloody voice down!' Dad roared. 'You want the girls in the back office to hear? They'll think we've gone round the bend.' He sat down heavily, as though he'd just run a marathon. 'Yes,' he said, 'magic. Turning stuff into other stuff; casting spells; doing curses, reading the future, disappearing things, the works. Ben says they can even raise the dead and fight dragons.'

'Dragons.' Colin rubbed his eyes. 'Dad, have you paid these jokers any money yet, because I've got a feeling they're—'

'It works,' Dad said firmly. 'I know it does, because I've seen it. That bird who came here—' He leaned forward, unlocked his desk drawer and pulled out a small leather bag about the size of a baby's sock. 'See this?' he said, and opened the top. Colin peered inside. It was stuffed full of gold coins. 'That's a genuine authentic bottomless purse,' he said wretchedly. 'You keep on taking the gold coins out, and they just keep on coming. Turn it upside down over the floor, and before long you're ankle-deep in gold, quite literally. That girl showed me, I nearly shat myself. Unfortunately,' he added with a rather disturbing grin, 'if you don't enter your PIN code the gold turns into little wriggly worms in about ten seconds.'

'Ah. So what's the—'

Dad smiled. 'You don't get the PIN till you've bought the purse. This is just, like, for demonstration purposes.' He emptied out a palmful of softly chinking coins, looked at them wistfully and put them back; all except one, which he allowed to fall on the floor. Then he started to count, slowly. As he reached ten, the coin stopped being solid and became a very tightly wound spiral, which gradually straightened itself out into a straight line and squirmed away under the desk. 'No kidding,' he said. 'They're the genuine bloody article. They're also,' he went on, 'bloody extortionately expensive. No, we aren't keeping the bottomless purse, because we couldn't ever afford it in a billion years. Real pity, that.'

Colin thought for a moment. Then, in a very quiet voice, he asked: 'Dad, has this got anything to do with the damn great big tree growing right up through—?'

'All we can afford,' Dad went on, as though Colin hadn't spoken, 'is to hire them to broker a deal for us, a deal with one of their other clients.' He frowned, then continued: 'You know what our biggest headache is?'

Colin nodded; easy peasy. 'Cheap imports,' he said.

'That's right. And you know why we can't compete with those—' (Here Dad said something highly reprehensible about the Chinese.)

'Labour costs,' Colin replied promptly. 'You told me all this.'

Dad nodded slowly. 'These clients of JWW,' he said slowly, 'are going to solve all that. What we're going to do is, we make all the workforce redundant, effective immediately, and these friends of JWW are going to supply us with replacement workers. No minimum wage, no pension contributions, no sick pay, maternity leave, equal opportunities, investing in people, health and safety, nothing like that. We've got their cast-iron guarantee that their workers'll work an eighteen-hour shift, no tea breaks, no unions, per capita productivity like you wouldn't fucking believe and – this is the really good bit – they don't want paying. And—' the grin on Dad's face extended from ear to ear, like a professionally cut throat '– the joy of it is, it's all absolutely hundred-per-cent legal.'

'Legal?'

'Couldn't be more legal if it tried.' Dad slumped forward and covered his face with his hands. 'And we can afford it,' he went on, sitting up again. 'All we got to pay is JWW's bill – which is going to be bloody enormous, but compared to the sort of money we'll be making from now on, it's a short pee in the ocean. In eighteen months we'll have driven those [inexcusable racial epithet] out of business, and the Yanks and the Poles too, most like. It's absolutely sure-fire. We can't lose.'

'Oh,' said Colin. 'That's—'

'Yes.' Dad sat up sharply. 'It is, isn't it? And that's what that thin cow from JWW's coming here to sort out; and since you're – well, you're part of the business, so you're involved too, so I thought I'd better tell you now, before you get the wrong end of the stick or anything.'

Colin thought for a while. 'It sounds really, really good,' he said cautiously, 'and I know we're in a really bad position right now. But sacking everybody – some of them have been with us for years and years, Dad, it's not—'

Dad lifted his head and gave Colin a scowl that brought back some very bad memories. 'Sure,' he said. 'But if we carry on like we are at the moment, the firm'll go bust, they'll be out on their ear anyhow, so what's the difference? And this way, they'll get their full redundancy, all legal and by the book, so they'll be all right. And besides,' he added, his scowl blossoming, 'to be absolutely bloody honest with you, I don't give a toss. All I care about is this business, which I've worked fucking hard for all my life, and I'm damned if some slanty—'

'All right,' Colin said. 'I take the point.' He hesitated, considering various aspects of the matter. He was, he realised rather to his surprise, a man of principle who felt nothing but disgust at the kind of measures that his father seemed so blasé about; but he was also a coward. 'And if like you say, it's all completely legal—'

'No doubt about it,' Dad said. 'All checked out with the lawyers, they even got counsel's opinion from a top barrister. Five thousand quid for six sides of A4,' he added with a shudder. 'But no matter. Got to do these things properly. And yes, it's completely legitimate and they can't have us for it.' He scowled violently at a blank space on the wall then shrugged. 'It's not like there's any other way out,' he said. 'And I'm buggered if I'm going to stand by and watch the company go down the toilet. It means everything to me, son. You got problems with that, keep 'em to yourself.'

'No, really, that's fine,' Colin said awkwardly. There are few things on earth as embarrassing as a display of raw emotion by a parent. 'I was just wondering. If this scheme or whatever you call it – if it's so foolproof and easy and legal, then why doesn't everybody do it?'

Dad chuckled. It was, for some reason, a rather disturbing sound. 'Because they don't know about it, of course,' he said. 'It's what you might call a well-kept secret.'

'But for crying out loud,' Colin broke in. 'Magic. I thought that was just Harry Potter and stuff.'

'Ah, well.' Dad looked past him, as though he wasn't there. 'There's all sorts of rules, apparently. Like, they aren't allowed to advertise or anything like that; and they're so bloody extortionately expensive, it's kind of self-regulating. I don't know,' he said, with unexpected vehemence, 'maybe half the blue-chip companies in the *FT* use magic, wouldn't surprise me in the least, it'd explain a lot of things. Who gives a damn? All I know is, it works and we've got this chance to use it, and it'll save us from ending up on the shit-heap along with the rest of the manufacturing sector. Look, if you're drowning in the North Atlantic and someone chucks you a lifebelt, you don't turn round and say, no thanks, I'm not using that, it's not made out of eco-friendly recycled plastic.' He frowned. 'Well, you might, because you're an idiot, but a sensible person wouldn't. All right?'

Colin nodded. Only a small part of him was engaged in the debate. The rest of him was analysing the extraordinary fact that *she* was coming *here,* out of all the billions of places in the universe where she could be instead, and that he was going to see her again, in a matter of minutes. Compared to that incredible miracle, stuff like magic seemed practically mundane.

Dad led the way to the small back office they used for meetings. 'Sit down,' he said. 'You've got a pen and something to write on? Fine. I want you to take notes. That's all. If anything occurs to you, any point you think needs clarifying or whatever, keep it to yourself.'

The phone rang. Dad picked it up, listened, grunted, put it back. 'She's here,' he said. 'Remember. Seen and not heard, got it?'

He left the room, closing the door behind him. Colin listened to his father's footsteps (clump, clump, clump, like a heffalump in rigger boots). He thought: I don't really care about the company. The thought of it not being there any more scares me, but really it's just force of habit. And all that bullshit about magic being real; of course I believed it while Dad was talking, because I've been trained to believe him ever since I was a kid. But he lied to me about Father Christmas, so—

Pause. In the light of what he'd just been told, maybe Father Christmas hadn't been a lie after all. Think about it, he urged himself. Which is more likely: a thousand-year-old perfect stranger capable of defying all the fundamental laws of physics coming all the way from the North Pole to climb down our blocked-up chimney and leave me presents, or Dad buying me stuff with his own money? Put like that, maybe Santa wasn't so implausible, after all.

Not that he cared terribly much. If charmed quarks and electric eels exist, then why shouldn't magic? Probably it's all just science that we haven't found out about yet. Besides, it could all be shunted neatly into the big black plastic sack marked Not My Problem, along with global warming and earthquakes in South-East Asia. Far more immediate and personal was the fact that *she* was, by now, probably no more than forty yards away and closing, and he still hadn't figured out why that fact should be so all-consumingly important—

The door opened. Dad (perfect gentleman of the old school/patronising sexist git) was holding it open for her. Colin stood up as she walked across the threshold.

She looked at him.

'This is my son Colin,' Dad was saying, in that too-late-to-do-anything-about-it-now tone of voice that he'd honed to silky-sharp perfection over the years. 'Thought he might as well sit in, if that's all right with you.'

She was still looking at Colin and his right foot was suddenly a pincushion. Agony. I can't move, he realised. I can't even sit down, I'm going to have to stay standing up like this till it gets better.

'Hi' she said.

'Hi,' he echoed.

'Please take a seat,' Dad was saying – not to Colin, as witness the P-word. She folded herself elegantly into the plain, straight-backed chair. She was still looking at him. He knew that look on her face.

'Right,' Dad was saying, 'I want to start off by looking at some of the terms in this— Colin,' he snapped, 'sit down.'

Twenty-five years of training had made Colin physically incapable of disobeying a direct order spoken in that tone of voice. He shifted the agonised foot; the whole leg sort of buckled under him, and he only just managed to control the resulting collapse. He landed heavily in the chair, which creaked painfully but held together.

She was opening a green folder, fishing out wodges of stapled-together paper. Dad was talking; something about whether time was of the essence in Clause Two, subsection four (b). Colin fixed his stare on the blank sheet in front of him; he uncapped his pen and wrote the date in the top left-hand corner. His foot had stopped hurting, but only because it had gone completely numb.

'Well?' Dad said.

'What? Oh, sorry.' Her voice. 'Could you just repeat what you just said?'

'I asked you,' Dad said, 'if this stuff in Clause Seven, subsection five, subclause roman two means that if they do anything that counts as a substantial breach, all we're entitled to is damages rather than being able to cancel the contract. Because if it does—'

'I—' She sounded – Colin realised that she sounded like he felt. 'To be absolutely honest,' she said, 'I'm not entirely sure. It's a bit of a grey area, really. I'll have to check up on it and let you know.'

Colin was suddenly aware that he was meant to be taking notes. *Grey area*, he wrote, then underlined it twice. Dad, meanwhile, wasn't happy.

'That's all very well,' he was saying, 'but you can see, can't you, it's a pretty bloody important point. And what about this here, Clause Twelve, subsection three? "Insofar as is reasonable in all the circumstances of the case." What's that supposed to mean when it's at home?'

'Ah,' she said. Colin remembered sounding just like that, many years ago, when called on to explain why he hadn't handed in his homework. 'That's just a standard clause, it isn't really . . .'

In fact, Colin decided, she's doing this pretty much the way I'd be doing it if I was in her shoes; but that's wrong, because you can tell just by looking at her that she's smart, clever, much more clever than me. It's like she can't concentrate worth a damn, for some reason.

And so on. Slowly, inexorably, Dad was getting annoyed.

Because she wasn't his only begotten son, with whom he was never well pleased, he was struggling to stay civil; but the effort was making him talk louder and faster, and he was scowling a lot. She – she was fighting too, wrestling with her concentration like someone trying to catch whitebait with their bare hands, and Colin could see clearly that this was a disturbingly unfamiliar experience for her. She was used to being in charge of meetings, to knowing the answers and trotting them out pat and sing-song like the Speaking Clock. And she kept looking at Colin whenever he wasn't looking at her. He knew she was doing it, because he could feel the pressure of her eyes on the side of his face as he jotted down scraps of gibberish on his piece of paper. He felt a powerful urge to make an excuse and leave the room, but his foot was as dead as the last sabre-toothed tiger; if he tried to stand up now, he'd fall flat on his face.

'Look,' Dad was saying. 'All due respect, but it strikes me we aren't getting anywhere, and if you expect me to pay you a hundred and fifty quid an hour for sitting there saying that's a good question and you don't actually know the answer—'

'You're right.' She lifted her head and looked at him. It was the sort of look that could punch a hole through a wall. 'It's my fault, I'm sorry. Let's just forget about it for today; no charge, we'll just pretend this meeting never happened. Give me a couple of days, then—' She frowned. 'Maybe you could call in at the office and we can go through it there. All right?'

Colin was expecting something in the nature of an explosion, but instead his father nodded and mumbled 'Fair enough.' She stood up. 'Sorry to have wasted your time,' she said.

A moment or so later, Colin was alone in the room. His foot was much better, and he'd stopped worrying about magic being real. In fact, he'd clean forgotten about it. Completely beside the point. Instead, his mind was full to bursting with the most important piece of information in the history of the universe; namely, that her car was parked round the back, under the lamp-post. He had no idea how he knew that, but he knew it. He jumped up and tore out of the room, heading for the fire escape.

The fire escape led out into the back yard, and he knew from his childhood that if you jumped up on the roof of the old coal bunker you could scramble over the back wall, landing on the pavement about five yards south of the lamp-post. If he ran, he might just get there before she had a chance to unlock her car door and drive away.

Colin hadn't done much running in the twenty-first century, but he found it came back to him. He vaulted onto the coal-bunker roof like a pentathlete, scrambled over the wall and dropped down the other side. No sign of her, but presumably her car was the soft-topped Golf. He caught his breath, and was leaning against the lamp-post when she turned the corner.

Colin wasn't the sharpest scalpel in the tray, but he was capable of learning from bitter experience. The leaning-on-lamp-posts thing wasn't just a homage to George Formby. If his foot packed up on him again, he wanted something robust to bear his weight and stop him from falling over. Foresight, you see; attention to detail, the ability to plan ahead.

Just as well, as it turned out.

'Oh, hello,' she said.

'Hi,' he replied. Nor had his newly discovered tactical acuity been confined to lamp-posts. He'd thought of an excuse for being there. 'I think you left your pen behind,' he said, unclipping his own Parker from his top pocket and pointing it at her, like Bogart covering the bad guys with his gun.

'What? Oh, thanks.' She took it without looking at it. 'Sorry,' she added.

He knew exactly what she was going to say next. She said it.

'You used to have a moustache,' she said.

'Me?'

'Didn't you?'

'No,' Colin said accurately. 'I wanted to grow a beard when I left school, but Dad made me shave it off after a week. Said it made me look like a clown.'

'Did it?'

'Yes. Well, not a clown, because they've got red noses and coats with big buttons. But it wouldn't have suited me at all.'

She looked at him, as if trying to visualise something. 'No, you're right,' she said. 'It'd make you look all round-faced and—' Her eyes widened a little. 'Sorry,' she said.

'No, that's all right.' He forced about forty per cent of a laugh. 'Brutal honesty's what makes the world go round. Well, I'd better be getting back. Bye for now.'

'Bye.' She looked down at the pen she was still holding. 'Actually, this isn't mine.'

He shrugged. 'Oh, keep it, anyway,' he replied, trying to sound like a Medici scattering florins among the rabble. 'I'd better be – well, see you.'

Colin turned and walked away, brisk as a platoon of Grenadier Guards. He heard a car door slam and an engine start, but he kept going until he was sure that she'd driven away. He was, of course, walking in the wrong direction. He stopped and turned round.

Moustache?

Unbidden, through his mind passed a progression of Notable Moustache-Wearers Through The Ages – King Harold, Genghis Khan, Prince Albert, Charlie Chaplin, Hitler, Hercule Poirot, Captain Wainwaring. Not my style, he thought; and I bet it'd tickle, and bits of food would get trapped in it. The thought never crossed my mind. I'd look a right prune.

He walked in through the factory gates, under the wrought-iron H&F in a gilded oval, and turned left, heading for the side door. As he passed the stack of pallets, it struck Colin that if she was from JWW, and they were professional magicians – what did that make her? A witch? He grappled with that concept for a moment, but it slithered through his mind's fingers like a greased fish. Instead, he tried to guess which stations her car radio was tuned to: Radio 4 for the news, Classic FM for motorways and dual carriageways, and probably she had one of those radios that defaults to the local traffic news just as you've got to the interesting bit in *Book of the Week*; and in the glove compartment, quite possibly, was a small stack of home-made compilation CDs, for tailbacks on the M25. Something along those lines. A witch? No, he couldn't really see it.

'Where the hell did you get to?' Dad thundered at him, as he came through the office door. 'I came back and you'd gone.'

'Slipped out for a pee,' he said, without thinking.

'Out in the yard? Bloody hell. I know you've got your faults, but I had hoped we'd got you house-trained.'

'Breath of fresh air.'

'Since when have you needed fresh air?'

'I felt like some,' Colin mumbled helplessly. 'For a change.'

Dad grinned. 'Fine,' he said. 'In that case, you can nip down to the newsagent and get me two packets of my cigars.'

Colin was, of course, supposed to resent being sent on a menial errand. Not this time, however, since he needed time to recover from the profoundly weird conversation he'd just had under the lamp-post with the girl who thought he'd once had a moustache. Also, he needed a drink; not alcohol, since Dad would be sure to smell it on his breath, but a coffee or something.

There's something about your average suburban high street that anaesthetises even the most blatant weirdness. By the time he'd passed Marks and the DIY place, it had occurred to him that there was at least one rational explanation for the whole moustache thing. For instance: it was entirely possible that somewhere in the vastness of London there was someone who looked quite like him, and who had at one time insulted his face with foliage. She'd mistaken him for this taste-impaired speci-men, hence all the confusion. As for the magic stuff; well, Dad did have a rather off-beat sense of humour. Maybe it amused him to make up an obviously ludicrous story and see if he could bully his only-begotten into taking it seriously. There was also, Colin reminded himself, the Santa episode. Putting all issues of filial respect on one side for a moment, he had clear evidence that Dad wasn't above telling porkies when it suited his pur-poses. Following up that line of argument led him into even richer areas of speculation. If he had to sum up his father's character in two epithets, the second one would have to be *devious*. Just because he didn't understand what Dad was up to, it didn't follow that there wasn't some cunning plan underlying it all. It'd be about fiddling the VAT or wriggling through the meshes of some obscure EU directive, and his own role in it would be fairly trivial – deputy assistant sucker, something like that. And as far as the déjà-vu stuff went—

He stopped outside the door of the little café next to Currys. (Except that it wasn't next to Currys any more; the café was still there, all dark blue, stripped pine and tubular chrome steel, like something out of Kafka, but Currys had turned into a very small Monsoon. Definitely hard times all round in the retail sector.) Coffee, he told himself; and, since he'd been through a rather unsettling experience which was bound to have played hell with his blood sugar, a custard Danish.

The déjà-vu stuff. Well, it couldn't be all that rare, or there wouldn't be a word for it. Probably happened every day, and there was nothing to worry about. Really, he was ashamed of himself for ever having given the weird stuff the time of day.

Kitted out with food and drink, Colin looked round for somewhere to sit. The place was unusually full, but there was a seat at one of the tables in the window. He'd have to share, but what the hell. He didn't mind. He'd long suspected that there was a latent streak of bohemianism in his character, and here it was, bursting out like a lava flow.

'Anybody sitting here?' he asked, putting down his cup and plate.

'No that's—'

They recognised each other simultaneously, and by then it was too late. He sat down. She twitched – you couldn't really call it a shudder. 'Hello,' she said.

Typical of his luck that thieves should have chosen that moment to break into his head and steal all the words. 'Hi,' he replied.

'I was going to drive back to the office,' she said, 'but then I thought, I'll take an early lunch.'

'Why not?' he said. 'Excellent idea.'

She wasn't a big eater, then, if lunch consisted of a cup of tea. 'Fancy bumping into you again,' she said.

'Yes,' he said. 'Where are you parked?'

'The multi-storey round the corner.'

'Ah.'

This was clearly hopeless. Sooner or later he was going to have to—

'Can I ask you something?' he heard himself say.

'Sure.'

'Well—' Colin rallied his intellectual resources, what there were of them. However he phrased it, it was going to sound as daft as a containerload of brushes, so why not just open wide and have at it? 'Excuse me,' he said, 'but do you do magic?'

She nodded. 'Yes,' she said.

Oh, he thought.

'Actually, that's a pretty vague term,' she went on. 'Since I've been with JWW, I've been mostly working in the ancillary and administrative sector, rather than the actual practical and effective side of things. I did a year of spatio-temporal engineering in my last job, I guess that's the last actual hands-on magic I did. I wouldn't mind getting back into the field, so to speak, at some point further down the line, but at the moment I think Mergers and Acquisitions offers quite a lot of scope for some pretty exciting challenges—' She paused. Colin guessed that she'd probably heard the last bit of what she'd been saying, and had realised that she was babbling. 'Yes,' she said, 'I do magic. Why?'

'Oh, no reason,' Colin replied, in a quiet, strangled sort of voice. 'So, is it interesting work, most of the time?'

She shrugged. 'It's all right,' she said. 'It's like a lot of things. When you start off, you think it's going to be glamorous and exciting and fun, and after you've been doing it a bit, you find out that all work is basically just work – on balance, better than being dead, but it really cuts into your free time. Is that what it's like in the ball-bearing industry?'

'Precision casting and hydraulic fittings,' Colin corrected her. 'Yes, pretty much. Except I always knew it wasn't going to be glamorous and what you just said. But I was brought up with it from when I was a kid – family business, see – so there wasn't the disappointment.'

'Probably better that way,' she said. 'Changing the subject completely, is there a Boots around here anywhere?'

'Ah.' Colin smiled. 'That's actually a very good question. There always used to be, about six doors down on your left, next to the baker's, but it suddenly disappeared – can only have been a few weeks ago, but now it's a John Menzies.'

'Oh' She frowned. 'Well, not to worry. All I wanted was some nail varnish remover – it's not urgent or anything.'

Pause. Her introduction of the Boots motif had sounded like a well-I-must-be-going line, but she made no effort to move. It was almost as if she was being held there against her will.

Come to think of it, that was how Colin felt. Not a chained-to-a-dungeon-wall feeling or anything like that, it was more a case of waiting politely while someone you don't want to risk offending finishes telling a long and boring story. Something like that, but not quite. It was as though both of them knew that there was something expected of them; you can't go and play till you've finished your nice greens. On the other hand, it also had the feel of that first ghastly, small-talk-ridden interview that always has to be got through in between the first lightning-bolt meeting of eyes and the headlong fumble for bra straps. Except—

'Other than that,' he heard himself say, 'I think the nearest one's in Richmond.'

'What?'

'Boots.'

She stared at him. 'Boots? Oh, right, *Boots*. Sorry. Really, it doesn't matter.'

'There might be one in Kew, I suppose, but—'

'Really,' she said firmly, 'it's not important.'

'There's a Superdrug in—' Colin forced himself to shut up.

There was an almost desperate look in her eyes now; it seemed to say, *I don't know what to do next, help me.* No good looking at him like that. He felt like he was in the school play again, and had forgotten all his lines.

Then – it was as though the unseen puppet-master had said, 'The hell with it' and let them both go. They stood up simultaneously, like sprinters out of the blocks.

'Well,' Colin said, 'nice to see you again.'

'Absolutely,' she said. 'You haven't eaten your pastry thing.'

'What? Oh, not hungry.'

'I'll be seeing your father tomorrow, then. I'm really sorry about the mix-up today.'

'Maybe you're not feeling too good.'

'I – I'm not sure,' she said. 'Bye.'

At the door they parted; the full one hundred and eighty degrees, no hesitating, quick march, no surreptitious backwards glances. Colin hadn't paid much attention to GCSE physics, but he could dimly recall something about opposite poles repelling. It was that sort of thing. Maybe, he thought as he marched briskly down the street, all witches are like that—

My God, he thought. She's a *witch.*

Somehow, when Dad had been trotting out all that utterly weird stuff, he'd – he'd believed it, but with a subconscious reservation that came of the knowledge that Dad was always up to something and therefore wasn't to be trusted; a deeply buried awareness of the points he'd been rehearsing to himself just before he bumped into her, about lies and expediency and Father Christmas. Hearing it from her, on the other hand, was something quite other. If she said that she was a witch and magic really existed, then he believed her.

Bloody hell.

It was at this point that Colin realised he was going the wrong way. Easy mistake to make, since he'd just passed Argos, and surely Argos was next to the Post Office – apparently, not any more. He was practically at the end of the High Street. He turned round.

If magic really *really* existed, and Dad was getting them both mixed up in it, then he desperately needed to know what the hell was going on. He ran.

CHAPTER FIVE

'So,' he asked her, 'where do you see yourself in five years' time?'

Cassie snapped out of her train of thought like a dog surprised with its nose in the shopping. 'Well, here, I hope,' she said. 'I like it here, really.'

She could see him mentally counting – two, three, four. 'I'm delighted to hear it,' he said. 'But what I meant was, do you feel that you're likely to progress exponentially inside the team structure? Do you regard yourself as essentially goal-driven?'

She blinked. 'Actually,' she said, 'I don't know very much about football. I didn't even know we had a company team. Someone told me about the pub quiz, but—'

Seven, eight, nine. 'What we're looking for, essentially,' he said, 'is predators. Team players who'll go out there and take the market place by the scruff of its neck. Which is why, among other things, we're actively evaluating a more performance-related salary mechanism.'

If Cassie had been paying attention, she'd probably have been able to figure out what he was getting at. 'Ah,' she said.

'Predators,' he repeated. 'Proactivity. The days when we could just wait for clients to come in through the front door are over,

Ms Clay. In today's market environment, you've got to go into the long grass and flush them out. Do you think you're prepared to do that?'

'Oh, absolutely,' she replied.

'What we all need to take on board teamwide,' he went on (he had a little pointy nose, like a hamster), 'is that we've all got to take our share of responsibility for ensuring that we get out on the street and fight for every last scrap of business we can get our claws into. Hence the performance-correlated pay structure concept. In today's business arena, Ms Clay, the rule is, you only eat what you kill.'

Cassie frowned. 'I'm a vegetarian.'

He looked at her blankly for a moment, then wrote something on his piece of paper. 'Have you got any hobbies?' he asked.

'No.'

He ticked a box, paused, tapped his glasses down his nose an eighth of an inch so that he could read his own handwriting. 'What key performance indicators do you feel would be most indicative, given your position in the team network?'

She looked at him. 'Sorry,' she said, 'I was miles away. Do you think you could repeat that, please?'

He repeated it. Still drivel. 'Well,' she said, 'I suppose whether I'm getting my work done properly and on time. Is that the sort of thing you mean?'

He folded his arms. He had tiny wrists poking out of billowing white cuffs, as though he was wearing his big brother's hand-me-down shirt. 'What I want you to think about,' he said, 'is benchmarks.'

'Benchmarks.'

'You've got it. Preferably, we want to be working toward a steeply escalating benchmark curve, ideally within a six- to nine-month time-frame. Do you think that's something you could fully commit to?'

'Rather,' she said.

'Excellent. So how would you set about achieving target attainability?'

Cassie looked at him and thought, I wish you'd shut up, you stupid little man. 'Well,' she said, 'the usual way, naturally.'

He closed his eyes, then opened them again. 'Maybe you don't quite understand. I'm talking about how we can work together to make sure you push the envelope in your particular post.'

She had absolutely no idea what he was drivelling on about. 'You mean, letter-boxes?'

'Fine.' He drew a great big black cross in one of his little squares. 'So, how would you characterise your performance over the last nine months?'

'I've only been here six.'

'Whatever.'

'Oh well, you know.' She shrugged. 'Just sort of jogging along quietly, I suppose.'

'Jogging along quietly.'

'It's about all you can do in Mergers and Acquisitions,' she said. 'Like, mostly it's run the standard form contract off the computer, fill in the client's name and address in the blanks, and that's about it, really. I mean, it's not exactly neurosurgery. And of course you've got to explain it all to the client.' She frowned. 'That's usually the tricky bit. Like the job I've got on at the moment. But we'll get there in the end,' she added, trying to sound positive and dynamic.

He leaned back a little. 'Tell me a bit about it,' he said. 'This job you've got on.'

'Oh, that.' Cassie pulled a little face. 'Should be a piece of cake, really. Standard sale and purchase; seller's a very old-established client, and the buyer—' She pursed her lips. 'Well, you know what it's like acting for Them. If there's one thing They aren't short of, it's lawyers. But you know how it is, you muddle through.'

'Sale and purchase,' he repeated. 'Sale and purchase of what?'

It was the step off the escalator, when you try and put your full weight on thin air. 'The usual,' she said. 'You know. A Section Thirty-two transfer, no set term, with consideration in kind and the equity of redemption barred with a McEwan clause.'

'Ah. Right.' He scratched the side of his neck. 'One of them. As you say, a piece of bread.'

'Cake.'

'Cake. Well, I think that's enough for now. Thank you for your time, Ms Clay.'

'Does that mean I can go now?'

'Yes.'

So Cassie went, glancing at her watch as she did so. An hour till going-home time, which she spent staring at the Hollingshead file without taking in a single word. It was as though that loathsome hour between three and four a.m., when you lie awake fretting yourself to death over some trivial worry that evaporates completely in daylight, had lasted all day. It wasn't like her, she told herself. Normally, she went after problems like a ferret after a rat; grabbed them, dragged them out into the light and dealt with them. But the key to that admirable approach was being able to identify what the problem actually was.

At five past five, Mr Tanner came in to ask her for the Delgado file, which the auditors were apparently demanding to see. Cassie considered asking him if he could shed any light on the problem, but she decided not to. For one thing, he had the harassed look of a man who's been fetching and carrying files and ledgers for a pack of grim-faced accountants for several days, which meant that he probably wasn't in the mood. For another, she still wasn't any closer to figuring out what the problem actually was.

At five twenty-five, she got up, put the file in the cabinet, sighed and took it out again, slung it in her briefcase (when she'd first joined the profession, she'd taken a solemn and dreadful oath never to take work home with her; the Furies that enforce such solemn oaths swore at her, but she ignored them). It was important to be out of the office by five-thirty prompt, because that was when the doors were locked and the building's other occupants came out of hiding to play. They were, in fact, relatives of Mr Tanner, the partner in charge of the mining and mineral rights department, and they hadn't actually eaten anybody in years, but there was no point pushing your luck.

On the stairs she met up with Connie Schwartz-Alberich and Benny Shumway, and her inner Miss Marple deduced (on the basis of a tiny bit of body language and a bucketful of intuition) that running into them wasn't just a coincidence. 'Cassie,' Connie called out, before she could get away, 'we're just popping down the road for a drink. Join us?'

Which proved just what a clever old biddy her inner Miss Marple was. Connie Schwartz-Alberich never indulged in after-work drinking bouts; she went straight home like a racing pigeon. What Benny did in the evenings, nobody knew or wanted to know, but it didn't involve bending a congenial elbow with his co-workers. Cassie sighed. Probably they just wanted to hear all about her stupid assessment thing. The weight of the file in her briefcase tipped the balance, so to speak. 'Love to,' she said.

While Benny was at the bar getting the drinks, Connie settled herself in her seat on the other side of the table and folded her hands. It was more than Cassie could resist.

'I know,' she said. 'You're going to ask me where I see myself in five years' time.'

Connie frowned, but the frown quickly warped into a grin. 'Sorry,' she said. 'Were we being obvious?'

'The purpose of this outing was better signposted than Birmingham, yes,' Cassie replied. 'But that's all right.' She felt something loosen up inside her; it was a bit like slipping out of your office shoes on a hot day. 'Actually,' she said, 'yes, I've been acting bloody weird for a few days now, and yes, I'd really like to talk about it.'

'Thought so,' Benny said, an inch or less from her left ear. 'Yours was the orange and bitter lemon, right? Well, of course it is, because Connie and me'd sooner be eaten by rats than drink that stuff. Peanut?'

'Shut up, Benny,' Connie said, before Cassie could accept (she liked peanuts). 'Right, begin at the beginning. It's not that skinny bloke from Moss Berwick, is it, the one with the neck like a turkey? I could've told you straight away he'd be nothing but trouble.'

'Who?' Cassie thought for a moment. 'Oh, him. No, certainly not. Besides, that was more than three months ago—' She scowled. 'It's nothing like that,' she said. 'Or at least, I don't think so.'

'It's that client, presumably,' Benny put in. 'Hollingshead and Farren; the son, wasn't it?'

Connie darted him an exasperated glance. 'You never told me anything about—'

'No,' Benny said, and grinned.

'More to the point,' Connie added, turning her glare on Cassie, '*you* never told me. How am I supposed to spread salacious gossip throughout the industry if people can't be bothered to keep me up to date?'

'It's no big deal,' Cassie protested. 'Look, I don't even know where to start. There's this bloke – Colin Hollingshead.'

'Got that,' Connie said. 'And?'

'And,' Cassie replied. 'And what? I don't know, that's the really stupid thing. I don't fancy him even one tiny bit, I'm quite definitely not in love with him. But—' She thought for a moment, then shrugged. 'I don't love him, but I'm getting all these symptoms—'

'We'd noticed,' Benny said. 'Ouch,' he added. Cassie remembered that Connie was wearing extremely pointy-toed shoes today. She winced a little in sympathy.

'Describe,' Connie said.

'What, the symptoms? All right.' Taking a deep breath, Cassie recited the whole miserable catalogue, starting with listlessness and inability to concentrate, and working right through to the dreaded phone call, which of course Benny already knew about.

'Yup,' Benny said when she'd finished. 'Those are without doubt the second-stage warning signs of a massive, industrial-strength crush. Witness asserts, however, that no such crush is in progress. Which assertion,' he added quickly, before Cassie could say anything, 'the Court is prepared to accept unreservedly. The question is, though: if it's not that, what the hell is it?'

Cassie leaned forward a little. 'Connie?'

'Well—' Connie hesitated and looked away; both uncharacteristic procedures, for her. 'Cassie, dear, would you mind if I ask you some very weird questions?'

'Not at all.'

'Fine.' Connie lifted her head, and there was something worrying about her expression. No gleam in the eye, for one thing. 'Probability wells. Consequence mines.'

'Oh,' Cassie said. 'Them. What about them?'

'Really,' Benny put in, 'it's nothing to be ashamed of. We've all blundered into one in our time.'

Cassie scowled. 'One, yes,' she said. 'Five—'

'It was just bad luck, that's all.'

'Of *each*—'

'Extremely bad luck,' Benny said firmly. 'Honestly, there's times when I don't understand people in this business. Leaving bloody dangerous things like probability wells and consequence mines littered about the place where anybody can just stumble into them—'

'But that's the point,' Connie interrupted quietly. 'We don't. They're highly specialised, strictly controlled—'

'In theory,' Benny scoffed. 'But I could go into any pub between here and Blackfriars, and I bet you I could have my choice of prob wells and still have change out of a grand.'

'Strictly controlled magical weapons,' Connie said firmly. 'Now, naturally, you don't go advertising the fact you've laid one, that'd defeat the object of the exercise. But neither do you lose them, or carelessly leave them lying about in the street. But you,' she went on, looking Cassie in the eye, 'in the six months you've been with JWW, you've contrived to get yourself stuck in *ten* of the revolting things.' She pulled a face. 'And don't tell me

I'm exaggerating, because each time you stick your foot in one, it's me you call, and I'm the one who has to come and unstick you. Not that I'm moaning or anything, I'm just reminding you of the facts. Has it occurred to you that, just possibly, somebody out there doesn't like you very much?'

Cassie nodded slowly. 'It's occurred to me, yes,' she said. 'And really and truly, I can't think of a single person who'd go to all the hassle of trying to catch me in one of those things.'

Connie sighed. 'Me neither,' she said. 'And if there was a feud or a turf war going on with any of the other firms, I'm sure I'd have heard about it by now. And each time I've come along to unstick you—'

'Look, I'm really sorry about that—' Cassie began.

Connie smiled. 'It's all right,' she said, 'really. And I'm sorry you had to wait so long the last time, only Cas Suslowicz—' She frowned. 'What I'm trying to say,' she went on, 'is that it can't be a concidence but, equally, it can't be deliberate. And I'm pretty sure you haven't been setting the things yourself and deliberately walking into them out of a perverted sense of fun; so where does that leave us?'

Cassie shrugged. 'Haven't a clue,' she said.

'Exactly. It's my fault,' Connie went on. 'Really, I should've given it some thought a long time go. I mean to say, *ten*—'

'Yes, all right,' Cassie snapped. 'What you mean is, if only I'd learn to look where I'm going . . .'

'No, that's not what I mean at all. Look, when Ricky Wurmtoter – before your time, dear – when he was just starting in the business, he got hit by seven consecutive Groundhog Day loops on seven consecutive days; and he was in Pest Control, for pity's sake, he was supposed to be an expert. So really, it can happen to anybody.'

'True,' Benny put in. 'Or what about Kurt Lundqvist and the Sheldrake anomaly? Laugh? I nearly—'

'The point is,' Connie went on, ignoring him, 'somebody's been laying booby traps for you – expensive, and difficult to get hold of.' (Benny grunted, but said nothing.) 'But you say, and I believe you, that there's nobody in the trade who's got it in for you enough to go to that much trouble. Right?'

Cassie nodded. 'I honestly can't think of anybody,' she said.

'All right. Likewise,' Connie continued, 'you're showing all the symptoms of a really colossal crush on this bloke that you're adamant you don't fancy in the least. Sounds to me,' she said, 'like all this stuff isn't meant for you, but for somebody else.'

'Ah,' Benny said. 'Mistaken identity.'

'But that doesn't work,' Cassie interrupted. 'Yes, it'd account for the booby traps, I suppose. But not the, um, other thing.'

'Oh, I don't know,' Benny said. 'If someone's playing dirty tricks on you, thinking you're somebody else. I mean, a love potion's about as dirty a trick as you can get.'

'Benny, you're drivelling,' Connie said affectionately. 'If someone had spiked her tea with a love potion, regardless of motive, she'd be in love. The whole point is, she isn't. Got all the symptoms, but not the actual disease. That's the funny part of it.'

'All right,' Benny said, 'suppose it's someone who doesn't know what he's doing. He tried to slip Cassie the love philtre, but he got it wrong – put sugar in it or something – and it's not working properly. Sugar'll do it every time, actually,' he added. 'I owe several lucky escapes to the fact that I have two sugars in my coffee.'

'But then it doesn't work at all,' Connie pointed out. 'Besides,' she went on, 'I really don't think it's that, because that'd still mean there's some moustache-twirling villain out there, and we're pretty sure that's not the case. And also there's the—'

'The what?'

But Connie shook her head. 'Ignore me,' she said, 'red herring. No, there's something a bit funny going on here, but there's more to it than simple malice. And colour me paranoid if you want to, but I think it's a bit suspicious that all this should be going on just now, with the takeover and everything. Bear in mind that Cassie's the most recent recruit to the firm; maybe that's got something to do with it.'

'Actually, you're wrong there. What about—' Cassie paused. 'Sod it, I can't remember her name. You know, the pale-faced girl in Entertainments, came to us from UMG. She joined the month after I did.'

'True,' Benny said. 'What *is* she called, by the way? I can never remember.'

'No,' Connie said thoughtfully, 'neither can I. You know,' she went on, 'this is one of those problems where the more you think about it, the harder it gets. Still,' she said firmly, 'there's bound to be a nice, straightforward explanation. Answer's probably staring us in the face, like relativity or Fermat's last theorem.' She glanced at her watch. 'I think I'll go home now,' she said. 'I need to rinse out some tights and clean the kitchen floor.'

'Oh, fine,' Cassie snapped petulantly. 'You're going to waltz off and leave me worrying myself to death in case there's someone out there trying to screw me over with probability wells and love philtres. Thank you ever so bloody much.'

Connie smiled. 'Cassie dear,' she said, 'there's something about the profession you really ought to know. We've got all these horribly dangerous toys we love to play with, but really and truly they're no big deal. At least; yes, they're horrible and scary and they can do unspeakable things to you—'

'Specially Sheldrake anomalies,' Benny pointed out. 'And continuum twisters, and 5-D snakes and ladders, and dragons' teeth and —'

'But compared,' Connie went on blithely, 'with all the really vicious stuff you're apt to find in everyday life, such as love and marriage and families and personal finance, they're really no bother to anybody. The most a Barrington Fly-trap can do to you is rip your body into atoms and freeze your consciousness for ever at the exact moment of death. If you really want something to lose sleep over, imagine living with a couple of teenage daughters. Which is why,' she added, standing up, 'I never got married. I may be exceptionally brave, but I'm not stupid.'

She left. Benny still had an inch of his drink left. Cassie stayed where she was.

'The thing with Connie is,' Benny said after a medium-length silence, 'she's absolutely brilliant at what she does. If they'd made her a partner like they should've back in the 1970s the firm wouldn't have got into the mess it's in now. But sometimes she has trouble remembering we aren't all as Sherman-tanklike as she is.' He sighed. 'She can walk through walls without even breaking a fingernail. The rest of us have to use the door.'

Cassie smiled. 'I'd sort of worked that out for myself,' she said. 'And you know, I think she's right. I don't think it's a wizards' feud or a magical war or anything like that; or else I'd be on a plane to Nova Scotia right now, and the hell with the lot of you. Actually, I don't think it's really anything – well, anything to do with *work*, if you follow me. It's just, somehow it's got mixed up with the work side of my life, and it's easier to spot in that context, because it makes a more obvious mess. Does that make any kind of sense to you?'

Benny finished his drink. 'Cassie,' he said, 'I've been working for JWW ever since I left the mines of my ancestors. Nothing whatsoever makes any sense to me any more. I find that strangely comforting. Cheerio.'

Cassie went home. Uneventful journey; seven messages on the answering machine when she got in, all of them from her mother. She made herself cheese on toast and tried to get to grips with the Hollingshead file. In the silence of her lonely room, by the pale orange glow of the electric fire, it was all perfectly straightforward: a mundane, everyday little sale-and-purchase, the sort of thing that she could explain with her eyes shut and a kipper in each ear. Which dragged her back, ineluctably, to context. And she didn't want to think about that any more, thanks all the same.

Instead, she reflected for a moment on the complete and utter bog she'd made of her assessment interview. She thought it over; so what? If they wanted to sack her, they could do that any time they liked. As for squandered opportunities to impress and sneak a toe onto the fast track to promotion; she found it perfectly easy not to get the least bit worked up about that. Screw the lot of them, she thought happily.

To drown out the noise of her own thoughts, Cassie switched on the telly. That was a good move on her part, since it reminded her that although her life was in many respects sad and dreary it wasn't such a hopeless mess that she wanted to escape from it for an hour by watching an Australian soap opera. With a faint smile, she picked up the remote, drew a bead on one of the actors on the screen like Kirk aiming his phaser, and thumbed the off-button.

No result. Frowning, she tried again, but the intolerably young, bronzed, angst-riddled Strines were still there. She tried standby and mute, but they weren't working either. Batteries, she growled to herself; she got up, crossed to the table on which the set rested, and jabbed at the off switch with her left index finger.

This time, something did happen. She cracked a nail. The loathsome Aussies didn't seem to care (fair enough; they had troubles enough of their own). So, Cassie thought: batteries flat and switch jammed. Not worth having it fixed; have to get a new one. Expense, ruin, aggravation. She reached round the back and turned the power off at the mains.

Still nothing. The beautiful golden young people on the screen gabbled on. The hell with this, Cassie thought, and she pulled the plug out of the wall.

Oh, she thought.

The young woman was called Holly, apparently, and the young man's name was Ross. As if that wasn't bad enough, they were talking about a pair of mutual friends of theirs, Chelsea and Josh. According to Ross, Josh was having trouble expressing his true feelings, while Chelsea still couldn't make up her mind whether she loved Josh or Zack, although since Zack was now seeing Pixie, who'd broken up with Vince—

At this point, Cassie snatched up a small but chunky brass travelling clock and threw it at the screen. It bounced off.

Vince, meanwhile, was sort of still interested in Christy, which was a bit of a problem since Christy had just been dumped by Lee because he thought she still fancied Zack, whereas in fact she'd just had a brief but torrid fling with Shane, who was on the rebound from Tabby—

The toaster had no more effect than the small brass clock; likewise the cast-iron Le Creuset omelette pan her mother had given her the Christmas before last. Screaming at the set didn't help matters either, which was hardly surprising. Cohere, Cassie ordered herself. Get a grip.

She went back into the kitchen. There, at least, the authentic voice of the Southern Hemisphere was muffled to the extent that she couldn't hear the words. But she was damned if she was going to spend the rest of her life hiding in the kitchen from her own TV set. Think, she told herself. She thought.

Compared to being stuck in a probability well, it wasn't too bad after all. She screwed up two little bits of paper towel into plugs and jammed them into her ears; but they itched, so she had to take them out again.

All right, then. When all else fails, try unconditional surrender. She went back into the living room, sat down on the sofa, and paid attention.

'And another thing,' Ross was saying (they were on the beach now, carrying surfboards under their arms), 'I'm really worried about Cassie.'

'Me, too,' Holly replied. 'Her and Colin. Like, when are those two going to get their act together?'

'It's always the same with them,' Ross said. Behind him, a motor boat skimmed a water-skier across the limpid blue backdrop of the bay. 'Every time they come close to getting it all out there in the open, something goes wrong and they're back to square one. I think they're like so afraid to commit.'

(At this point, Cassie had another go with the omelette pan. The handle snapped off.)

'I mean, it's obvious they're crazy about each other,' Holly whined. 'It's like they're physically incapable of coming to terms with how they feel. Which is so lame,' she added, as the water-skier wheeled round for another pass. 'They orta pull themselves together and just go for it. I mean, how long've they been an item for?'

'Practically for ever,' Ross said. 'That's the really dumb part of it. They just keep going round and round and round in circles.'

So much, Cassie decided, for unconditional surrender. After a frustratingly long search, she found Connie Schwartz-Alberich's home number in the phone-book drawer.

'Connie?'

'Cassie.'

'Help.'

Short pause. 'Cassie, you aren't stuck *again*, are you?'

'Maybe,' Cassie replied. 'I'm not sure. Look, do you think you could possibly come round?'

'At this time of night?'

'Please?'

'And it's really awkward getting to Chessington from here, you've got to—'

'*Please.*'

Sigh. 'All right,' Connie said. 'But it'll take me a while to get there. Look, it's not just a spider in the bath or anything like that, is it? Because—'

Cassie explained what was happening.

'Oh. I'll be right over.'

Cassie put the phone down and glanced at the TV. The Australians had gone, and a woman with an unfortunate dress sense was doing the weather. Cassie thumbed the remote at her, and the screen went blank.

So she rang Connie.

'I think the programme just sort of finished,' Cassie offered by way of explanation, 'and it switched off perfectly happily after that.'

'Did it really.' She could tell that Connie wasn't easy in her mind about something. 'Well, don't touch it again tonight, what-ever you do. Also, I'd put a towel or a pillowcase over it for now. Just because you can't see it doesn't always mean that it can't see you.'

Which was about as reassuring as waking up and finding the head of a racehorse on the pillow next to you. Cassie draped the TV with a duvet cover, a sheet and two dressing gowns, made herself a strong cup of tea, then went to bed.

Several hours lying on her back in the dark convinced Cassie that the Sandman had got a better offer somewhere else, so she switched on the light and reached for her book: *Time's Arrow* by Martin Amis, an old favourite, warmly recommended to her by a fellow insomniac and hitherto infallible. For once, however, it failed; twelve pages and she was still wide awake. With a primeval-sounding grunt she shoved it back on the bedside table and got up. As she pushed open the bedroom door, she noticed something that shouldn't have been there: her two dressing gowns, neatly hung up on the hook.

In the living room the TV was alive again, burbling away to itself like a drunk on a park bench; the duvet cover, she noted, was lying on the sofa, folded with more precision than she ever managed. She frowned. This wasn't just weird and inexplicable, it was bullying, and she wasn't having it. 'Stop it,' she said, in a loud, clear voice. It took no notice.

Fine, Cassie thought. Stifling a yawn (probably the unabridged Amis working its way through her bloodstream) she sat down on the sofa, tucked the duvet cover round her, and looked at the screen. Open University, by the look of it; where else were you likely to find two grown men and a sensible-looking woman sitting round a table discussing thematic resonances in Shakespeare at one in the morning? Serendipitous, nonetheless. If these three didn't fast-track her to Nod Central, nothing would.

Seemed to be working. Her eyelids drooped, her train of thought stopped in a tunnel just outside Birmingham, the edges of the world smudged. It was just comfortably snug under the duvet cover. She relaxed into the languid warmth.

One of the talking-head people was reciting poetry, no doubt to illustrate some point he was making –

Ay me! For aught that I could ever read,
Could ever hear by tale or history,
The course of true love never did run smooth.

Right, she muttered to herself, tell me about it. Been there, endured that, and they'll have to build an annexe to the Hayward Gallery to house my T-shirt collection when I die and bequeath it to the nation. Star-crossed lovers; the talking head was banging on about star-crossed lovers. *Star*-crossed, don't know they're bloody born. If they'd had to deal with what I've had to put up with all these years, over and over and over again; you think *star*-crossed is such a big deal, you should try—

Cassie sat up. The TV had switched itself off. The brass travelling clock (which had picked itself up off the floor and somehow got back onto the mantelpiece) told her it was a quarter to three.

Go on, then, she asked herself. What should I try?

No answer. Insufficient data; please try again.

Damn, she thought. It would've been perfectly simple to dismiss it as having been one of those dreams where you wake up convinced you've got the next *Xanadu* or a sensational new theory that'll revolutionise particle physics as we know it or the best recipe ever for scrambled egg, knowing all the while that it's an illusion, an undigested belch of subconscious waste. I had a dream, and suddenly I remembered all my previous lives in one go—

Not that kind of dream, though, because she hadn't been asleep; she had the folded-up duvet cover as proof. No, not any more, because she'd unfolded it, silly cow; but there were two dressing gowns hanging on the back of her bedroom door that she'd last seen draped over the screen. Even Lord Hutton couldn't turn a blind eye to evidence as compelling as that.

Just to be sure, she got up and checked. They were still there. Next she went to the kitchen. In the bin was her Le Creuset omelette pan (one careless owner, unwanted gift) with the handle snapped off.

The course of true love never did run smooth. Cassie ate a couple of Ritz crackers and a small pink yoghurt. It seemed a great deal of trouble to go to – telekinesis, strong effective magic, quite a lot of difficult technical stuff which she could appreciate, being in the trade herself – just to remind her of that. A bit like buying the last surviving Concorde and retrofitting it with huge smoke canisters just so you could skywrite *A stitch in time saves nine* over the Manchester rush hour. Besides, she wasn't at all sure about true love. Rather, she'd come to the conclusion that it was a bit like God or Santa Claus; something you take on trust when you're young, until you eventually get to figure out why they want you to believe in something so innately improbable. You had to have something like true love, or else there'd be chaos: the fabric of society in tatters, the apocalypse of the film and music industry, a total lack of anything for the retail sector to hype in February. It was, therefore, a necessary myth, something you subscribe to but know deep down is a fallacy and a sham, like parliamentary democracy. Accordingly, it never runs smooth because it doesn't actually run at all. Fact.

Fat chance of getting to sleep with all that churning round inside her head. She looked round for something to do. Well, there was the ironing; but the ironing is always with us, and Cassie held to the view that doing it only encourages it. Or there was the Hollingshead & Farren file, which she'd thrown aside earlier as too easy-peasy for words. Nevertheless, she still had to draft a couple of covering letters, forms for registering the transfer at St Peter's House, routine guff like that. If she did it now, she wouldn't have to do it later, at the office; she could go and chat to Connie, or stare out of the window. What fun.

True love, indeed. Whatever next? The tooth fairy?

Cassie duly fell asleep at 5.25 a.m. in the middle of filling in Form G37. She woke up at 7.35 with a cricked neck, in plenty of time to burn her tongue on her morning coffee, miss her usual train and arrive at the office twenty minutes late – with Mr Tanner's mum on reception.

CHAPTER SIX

Dimly glowing, Colin's watch dial told him that it was a quarter past one in the morning. Without switching on the light, he levered himself out of bed, padded to the door and opened it a sliver. All dark, all quiet. He took a deep breath and started to climb the stairs. He reached out to guide and steady himself, and his fingertips brushed the bark of the tree. He'd know its texture anywhere: familiar without being the slightest bit reassuring, like everything in this house.

He'd realised, long before he got back to the office after his strange, serendipitous meeting with her in the tea-shop place, that asking Dad straight out what was going on would be at best counterproductive, and most likely traumatic. That left him a stark choice: accept passively and wait, or go snooping in the wee small hours. Normally, he'd have gone for the first option like a terrier after a rat. But normality seemed to be distinctly out of fashion these days, so here he was.

Colin had never done anything like this before, of course, so he didn't actually know whether Dad kept his study door locked during the night. Wouldn't put it past the old bugger; but on balance he decided that it'd be worth the risk of frustration. If the door was locked, he'd turn straight round and go back to bed. On balance, he hoped very much that he'd find it locked.

It wasn't. The door handle had a singularly powerful spring – he had to use both hands to turn it. Once inside, he closed the door carefully before flipping the light switch.

The file was there on the desk, its flap open, a big, thick type-written document lying flat with its first few sheets folded back. Apparently, snooping was as easy as the made-for-TV movies made it look. Colin lowered himself into the chair – he'd never sat in Dad's study chair before, and he felt like a royal footman trying out the throne when nobody's looking – and pulled the document towards him. He'd filed away a mental picture of where it had been before he touched it, and the page it was open at.

This agreement –

First time lucky. He started to read.

This agreement made the   day of   2005 between (1)   Hollingshead of 17 Mere View Drive Mortlake Surrey (here-inafter 'the vendor') and (2) the Prince, governors, directors, supreme council and diabolical parliament of the Powers of Darkness (a statu-tory corporation; hereinafter 'the purchasers') witnesses as follows: (1). By a letter of agreement dated the 19th March 2005, the vendor agreed to sell his soul (hereinafter 'the soul') to the purchasers in con-sideration of the sum of money, facilities, services and other matters detailed in the first schedule hereto (hereinafter 'the purchase price')

Fuck, Colin thought, and that was putting it mildly. He looked up and read it again. The Powers of Darkness; well. Not much scope for ambiguity there. Likewise the bit about souls. This couldn't be happening. That's it, he lied hopelessly to himself, I'm sleepwalking, and—

He read on. Maybe he was hoping he'd get to a clause that said, *Fooled you, really it's only a second mortgage on the house but we like to make these things as scary as possible.* If so he was disappointed. As a piece of draughtsmanship it was laudably clear. No melodrama here. It was a plain, functional businesslike instrument for getting a job done, rather like a bullet or a hang-man's noose. A chunk of legal bumf for selling your soul to the Devil.

Oh boy. Much, much scarier than melodrama. Pentangles and goats' blood and circles chalked on the floor he could've handled, because everybody knows that's just Hollywood, and if the special effects look so convincing that you can't begin to imagine how they're done, it doesn't matter. Deep down, you still know they're just Mr Lucas's brilliantly crafted illusions. A piece of paper calling itself *This agreement* and ending up with dotted lines for signing on is in a completely different league.

Yes, but—

Yes, but what? Either it wasn't true, in which case everything would be fine, or it was true, and everything was going to be as bad as it could possibly get. No compromise, no negotiated settlement, odds-playing, damage limitation. Straight heads-or-tails call, no big deal, or the end of the universe.

Bloody *hell*—

No pun intended. Colin rummaged in the file, and found what he'd hoped to find: the covering letter she'd written to explain the fine print. No wonder Dad had wanted to go through the contract in detail, clause by clause and line by line. Just this once, it was possible to justify Dad's habitual pickiness.

He read the letter. Basically, it said the same thing, but without the Latin salad. If the letter and the contract were to be believed, Dad was proposing to deliver his immortal soul to eternal damnation to save the company from going bust.

'That's the spirit,' said a voice behind him.

Colin jumped like a teal rocketing off a pond. There was Dad in the doorway, in that old-fashioned tartan wool dressing gown that Mum had been threatening to chuck out for years. He wasn't shouting. He wasn't even doing the glare that flayed you alive. He just looked unhappy.

'What?' Colin said.

'I said, that's the spirit,' Dad repeated. 'Getting some work done instead of lounging in bed like a pig in shit. And there's me been thinking you're nothing but a waste of space.'

'Dad,' Colin said.

'So.' Dad perched on the edge of the desk, leaned over his shoulder to see how far he'd got. 'What do you make of it, then?'

'It's a joke, right?'

Dad frowned slightly. 'If that's your idea of funny, you want to see someone about it.'

'It's for real, then.'

'Yes, son, it's for real.'

Not the answer he'd been wanting to hear. 'Dad,' he said, 'are you completely off your head? You can't do this. It's—' But they didn't make words big enough to describe what it was, or if they did, they didn't leave them lying around where losers like him could pick them up and play with them. 'You can't,' he said. 'That's all.'

Dad laughed. 'Don't talk daft,' he said. ''Course I can; I checked it out with that thin bird. Perfectly straightforward transaction; and, like I told you, totally hundred-per-cent legal.'

'That's not what I meant,' Colin whispered.

But Dad simply shook his head. 'Don't vex your pretty little head about it,' he said. 'It's the original win-win scenario. As in: if it's all make-believe and bullshit, I'm no worse off. If not – well, you know what sort of a life I've led, the way I've had to treat a few people who've got under my feet. It's not like I was ever likely to wind up in the other place.' He grinned. 'Don't suppose I'd have liked it there, anyway,' he went on, 'sat around on a cloud all day long with a load of wimps and goody-goodies being nice to each other. And I don't imagine it'll be all that bad where I'm going. Compared to running a small manufacturing business under a Labour government, it'll probably be as good as a holiday.' He turned his head and stared into Colin's eyes; Colin tried to look away, but couldn't. 'You weren't worried about me, were you, son? I'm touched.'

'Of course I—' Colin shut up. No point in trying to talk to him. That had always been a mug's game, ever since his first lisped 'Dada', a quarter of a century ago. 'Fine,' he said. 'You go ahead.'

'I mean to,' Dad replied. 'Else I wouldn't have gone to all this trouble. I never start something unless I plan on seeing it through.'

And that was true, God knew. 'So all that stuff,' Colin said, 'about your grand restructuring plan, sacking the workers and taking on trainees—'

Dad laughed. A different timbre this time; genuine amusement. 'You what?'

'Isn't that what you told me you were going to do?'

'Trainees.' Dad pursed his lips. 'I guess you could call them that.'

'I thought—' Colin frowned. 'I thought you'd signed up to one of these schemes where you take on a load of school-leavers for work experience, and the government pays their wages. It's not that, though, is it?'

Dad shook his head. 'Better than that,' he said. 'Much better. You wait and see.'

'So you're not going to tell me, then?'

'Nah. Spoil the surprise. Besides, it's got nothing to do with you. Strictly between me and—' He scowled. 'Me and Him,' he said. 'That's the thing about business,' he went on. 'Sometimes it means you've got to get a bit intimate with people you don't like terribly much. Can't be helped, you do it for the company.' He stood up, suddenly restless. 'I don't suppose I could ever make *you* understand. You always were a bit of a disappointment to me, you know. I don't think you've ever really felt what it means, being responsible for the company. It's like it's a living thing, you know; you can't help it, you've got to look after it, keep it going, protect it from all the bastards who want to kill it. I've fought them, all my life. In the 1980s it was the Yanks, coming over here, buying up good little firms like us, stripping out the good stuff, selling off the rest. Then there were the unions, and the men from the ministry with their gadzillions of bloody forms and regulations, and then it was the Chinese and the East Europeans, dumping their tat over here at way below cost, just to starve us out. I've seen them all off, over the years, and you know what? We're still here, and so help me, we'll still be here in a hundred years. It's all I care about, Colin, and I'm buggered if I'm going to let them win. That'd be so much worse than—' He shrugged. 'I guess eternal damnation is like anything else, in the eye of the beholder. Fire and brimstone's something I can learn to put up with, it can't be so bad. Losing—' He shook his head. 'No, I won't stand for it. Not while there's something I can do.'

Colin looked at him. If it had been anybody else, he might just have found it in himself to make the effort, to go on resisting – tear up the contract, scream, shout, plead, whatever. But Dad was the one person in the world who he knew would never, ever listen to him. Wonderful thing, family.

'What about the others?' he said feebly. 'Uncle Phil and Uncle Chris. What've they got to say about it?'

'Haven't told them. Can't be bothered. They're useless, they'll do as they're told.'

'Like me.'

'Like you. It's been my bad luck,' Dad said, 'to be surrounded all my life by weak, useless people. It's made it so hard for me, you know? In the end, it's always had to be me, me against the whole fucking universe. On the other hand,' he added, with a violent gleam in his eye, 'I've always won, haven't I? Guess that says something about me.'

Guess it does, Colin thought. I guess it means I've lost him; and so what if he's a vicious, bigoted old bully who's screwed up my life for me, he's still my Dad. At the back of his mind, a small voice made a suggestion. What you ought to do, said the small voice, is offer to take his place, sign the contract instead of him. It'd be an absolutely pointless, idiotic thing to do, obviously you'd regret it every second of every day for ever and ever, it'd be completely unjustifiable and just plain *stupid*, but on the other hand he's your father, so maybe you should. Because it's the right thing to do. You know it is.

Colin shut his eyes. There was a moment, maybe a second and a half, when the offer was capable of being made. It passed.

'Fine,' he said. 'Well, thanks for filling me in. I'll go back to bed now.'

'You do that. Sweet dreams.'

So he went. And of course, he had no chance whatsoever of getting to sleep after what he'd heard; nevertheless, he woke up to the shriek of his alarm clock, tumbled out of bed and, just before his feet hit the carpet, he realised what he had to do.

Cassie and Mr Tanner's mother had disliked each other from the very beginning. Mainly, this was because Mr Tanner's mother, who amused herself by looking after the reception desk at 70 St Mary Axe, was a goblin, and there's always been bad blood between goblins and humans. Not that Rosie Tanner was a bigot. She liked humans, or young human males at any rate (hence, among other equally regrettable occurrences, Dennis Tanner), with the result that she took a great deal of trouble over her appearance when she worked on the front desk; and, like a daytime soap star, she never wore the same outfit twice. Today, she'd chosen red hair, green eyes, high cheekbones and a creamy complexion with just a faint sprinkle of freckles.

There was also, of course, something of a clash of personalities. Cassie tried to avoid being judgemental, but nevertheless had reservations about anybody who transformed herself into a different superbimbo every day and chased after anything in trousers like a ferret down a rabbit hole. Rosie Tanner, by contrast, had long maintained that human women had simply lost the knack of having fun and were seriously out of touch with their inner orc.

Accordingly, she leered menacingly at Cassie when Cassie arrived late, and wrote something down on a piece of paper. In fact, the something was nothing more malicious than the answer to seven across, but Rosie dwelt with relish on the thought of That Thin Cow fretting herself all morning in case she'd been reported to the boss for deficient timekeeping. She was still smiling to herself over it when a young man – tall, solid, a bit gormless but who wants an intellectual? – turned up at the front desk asking if Ms Clay could spare him ten minutes.

Carelessly, Rosie Tanner left the smile in place and loaded as she turned to answer his enquiry. To her annoyance, it didn't have the usual effect. Either the young man was smileproof (and she hadn't met one yet) or he had something pretty substantial on his mind.

'I'll ring through and see,' she said. 'What name, please?'

She recognised him and of course the name was familiar, since the Hollingshead clan had been clients for yonks; now that she looked, he reminded her quite a bit of his great-grandfather, except that the relentless march of evolution had dispensed with the cute nose. Pity.

'You're in luck,' she said, putting the phone down. 'She can see you straight away. If you'd care to go through into the waiting room.'

He went. Rosie Tanner sighed, and fished a small mirror out of her desk drawer. What she saw in it gave her no pleasure – to her, one monkey-suit was much like another – but her proper sense of craftsmanlike pride was offended by the lack of reaction she'd had to what she knew was a perfectly well designed and executed flame-haired bombshell. Frowning, she made a few adjustments: the eyes a trifle bigger, a hint more fullness to the bottom lip, a few experiments with nose length and eyelash density. No, she'd got it more or less exactly right the first time. Maybe young Mr Hollingshead simply didn't like girls. In which case, she reflected, Cassie Clay was welcome to him.

Talk of the Devil (must stop using that expression now They're clients of ours); here was Ms Clay in person. Rosie jerked her head toward the waiting room, and went back to her crossword.

'You can't let him do it,' Colin said.

Cassie closed the door and sat down. 'Oh,' she said.

He was standing by the window (extensive views of the back alley and the dustbins; because of the rather unconventional geography of 70 St Mary Axe, the back alley was only there on Tuesdays when there was an R in the month, which made emptying the bins even more hit-and-miss than is usual in Central

London). 'You can't,' he repeated. 'It's so *stupid*. It's only a poxy little company. We'd all be better off stacking shelves in Tesco's anyway.'

Cassie opened her mouth to say something, but hesitated. There were lots of things she could say at this point; client confidentiality, only obeying orders, was he sure he hadn't got entirely the wrong end of the stick. She'd said all those, and several other variants on these themes, to other clients' families on other occasions. It was part of getting the job done. Long ago she'd come to terms with the fact that magic isn't all flower remedies and the ends of rainbows.

Instead, she said, 'I'm sorry.'

'You're *sorry*?' He spun round and looked at her. 'My Dad is going to go to Hell, and you're bloody sorry.'

She shrugged. 'It's not up to me. I'm just the—'

'Look.' Cassie noticed how awkward Colin was in the fairly straightforward business of displaying anger; a greenhorn, a newbie. Probably this was the first time in his life he'd allowed himself to lose his temper with a virtual stranger. 'I don't want to hear about it. It's not going to happen, all right?'

'Sit down,' she said. He sat down.

'Sorry.' He didn't mean that. What he meant was, *I can't risk pissing you off by shouting at you*. 'Listen, can't you see what this means? He's my Dad.'

She looked at him. 'So talk to him,' she said. 'Persuade him.'

'He won't listen to me.'

Cassie thought about that. No, quite probably he wouldn't. She imagined herself having a conversation along those lines with her own father. 'Don't fuss, kitten,' he'd say; his mind made up, her objections dismissed unheard, because of course she was still a little girl who wouldn't eat up her nice casserole. And she'd never had any trouble talking to her parents. It helped that they'd been in the trade, of course, but that only covered superficialities. No, she could see his point.

'Fine,' she said. 'So, what do you want me to do about it?'

'Easy. Tell him the deal's off.'

She sighed. 'I could do that,' she agreed. 'And then your father would ring up my boss and say, what the hell – what on earth's going on? And my boss would apologise and make up some excuse, he'd pass the file on to one of my colleagues, the deal would go through just the same and I'd get the sack. Do you think that'd help?'

'All right.' Colin scowled in thought. 'How about this: you get in touch with—' He hesitated. 'Whatever you call them,' he said. 'You get on to Them and say, my Dad's changed his mind, terribly sorry. They go away. Then you tell Dad that They've cried off. He accepts it, so there's no call for him to go to your boss. Would that be all right?'

Cassie shook her head. 'It doesn't work like that. Technical reasons which I can't go into. I'm very sorry,' she said. 'You could burn down this office, or blow it up with dynamite, and it'd still go through. They're pretty persistent, I'm afraid, once they've got their hooks into someone. Imagine a combination of AOL and the National Trust – it might give you some idea.'

'So there's nothing you can do,' he said.

It was his tone of voice. She'd heard it before, but *when*? It was the voice in which he'd once said, I'm asking you to do this one thing for me, to show that you really— Almost she could hear him saying it, if she closed her eyes and ignored his face.

'I don't—' she said, and stopped. Maybe there was something she could do after all, but it was still tentative and vague in her mind: an approach, not a strategy. 'I don't know,' she said. 'Has he actually signed anything yet?'

Colin thought, visualised the last page of the contract in his mind. Dotted lines, pencil crosses to show where the signature had to go, but nothing in actual ink. 'No,' he said. 'Actually, that's odd. I guess there's still some details he wants to iron out. He's like that, picky.'

Cassie smiled. She knew that already. 'All right,' she said. 'Look, I can't promise anything—'

(And by saying that, of course, she'd just given him a solemn

undertaking.) 'I might be able to think of something, but—'
Again she hesitated, and thought about what she was getting
herself into. She was, after all, a professional. Her work wasn't
her entire life or anything like that, but it was what she'd chosen
to do (Have you thought about what you're going to do when
you leave school, kitten? You're going to go into the trade, aren't
you? Yes, Daddy, of course) and it mattered to her to do it reasonably well, because she wanted to get on. The fact that doing
her job occasionally involved arranging for strangers to go to
Hell was one of those things. Of course, she could pack it all in
and do something else – computers, aromatherapy, a job in a call
centre somewhere – but there'd have to be a damn good reason.
True love, for instance; assuming that such a thing existed. She'd
never had any trouble believing in magic, because she'd grown
up with it, but true love was, well, a bit far-fetched. She looked
at Colin again, and took a deep breath.

'Do I know you from somewhere?' she said.

He was leaning forward, massaging his leg below the knee, the
way you do when you've got pins and needles. 'I don't – I'm not
sure,' he said quietly.

'Oh,' she said.

Colin looked up at her. 'I've been assuming it's that thing,' he
said in a rush. 'Déjà vu. You know, where you're convinced
something's terribly familiar, but it can't possibly be. I heard
something about it on the radio. Apparently it's all just brain
chemistry or something.'

Cassie held her breath for a moment, then let it out slowly.
'That's what I've been telling myself, too,' she said. 'But we
can't both—'

The light bulb blew. It didn't matter terribly much, since
there was plenty of daylight to see by, but the soft plinking noise
made them both jump. 'That's beside the point,' he said firmly.
'Do you really think you can stop this stupid deal happening?
You've got to. You must see that.'

'I don't know.' She was only playing for time, though, keeping
him talking. 'It's like – I don't know. It's like I'm a fox and you're

a chicken, and you're trying to talk me into turning vegetarian.' She scowled. That hadn't come out right. It wasn't even anything like what she'd actually wanted to say.

'Is that how you see yourself?' Colin asked her.

'No, of course not. Look, all I do is draw up paperwork. If my boss knew I was even having this conversation—'

'I'm sorry.' She wished he wouldn't say that. 'But I've got to try.'

'Yes.' Cassie looked away. This – she really wished she knew how she knew it – this wasn't the conversation they were supposed to be having. It was as though they'd both drifted so far away from the script that they were hopelessly lost, and hadn't got a clue how to wind up the scene or escape off the stage. 'Leave it with me, all right?' she said. 'After all, we get paid whatever happens, so I don't suppose it'll be the end of the world.'

Colin looked at her one more time, then nodded and got to his feet. He staggered and grabbed hold of the desk to steady himself. 'Thanks,' he said.

'That's all right. I'll show you out.'

Mr Tanner's mum gave Cassie an extra-special glower as she passed through reception, but it hardly registered with her. Part of her was protesting *I'm going to get into so much trouble for this*, but most of her didn't care about that; it was desperately trying to figure out what it should be caring about.

She sat at her desk the rest of the morning, going through the motions of drafting a building contract for Mr Suslowicz. It was by no means straightforward, and should have engaged her full attention. A major international leisure consortium had engaged JWW to design a castle in the air (Cas Suslowicz was widely recognised as the best flying-freehold architect in the business); it was going to be their flagship shopping-mall-cum-casino, floating serenely above all terrestrial jurisdictions, tantalisingly out of reach of mortal laws and taxes, hanging in the sky like a free-enterprise heaven. Cas was pulling out all the stops, because the client was on a strict schedule, and it was vital that the paperwork should be sorted out as soon as possible. Normally, Cassie would be chuffed to nuts to be involved in such a high-profile job, so much more prestigious and exciting than a routine little sale-and-purchase for the clients we prefer not to think too much about. Instead, she turned the pages of the precedents book, trying to find a form of words that she could adapt for the snagging clause, and her mind was jumping and snapping like a performing seal trying to get at the just-out-of-reach gobbet of fish.

Colin had a thoroughly rotten afternoon. Dad wasn't talking to him; there was no work for him to do but he didn't dare skive off, so he sat in the post room stuffing more of the stupid brochures into their stupid envelopes. At five-thirty he went home. Mum was out at her yoga class. She'd left a meat pie in the oven, but he wasn't hungry. He went up to his room and shut the door.

When this is over, he thought; when all this is over, I'm definitely leaving. I'll move out, get a flat or a bedsit, find a job, don't care what. Once I've cleared out, Dad can do what he bloody well likes. This is the last and only time.

He lay on the bed and stared at the ceiling. Years ago there had been plastic Spitfires and Messerschmitts up there on bits of fishing line, wheeling endlessly above his slumbers like guardian angels, ready to shoot down the bad dreams, the disturbing thoughts. It was well over ten years since they'd gone: outgrown, discarded, squashed in the jaws of the council dustcart. Now, when he needed them most, he missed them. Bad thoughts were zooming down in squadrons. (In his mind he pictured the Ops room, where WAAFs in neat uniforms pushed little wooden blocks with flags sticking in them around on a tabletop map of his life, as the radio burbled about more bandits crossing the Channel.) It occurred to Colin that he was only able to keep going because he had so many different bad thoughts circling over him that he couldn't choose between them. As soon as he made that choice, it'd get very bad for him. Implications would start raining down on him like enemy paratroops – the implications of magic being real, of there being a Hell where you went if you sold your soul, of that crazy déjà-vu thing, of the realisation that he'd probably already screwed his life up beyond any possibility of repair or redemption. Compared with all of that, the prospect of living in a fleapit and spending his days flipping burgers was as enticing as the New World to the crew of the *Mayflower*.

So: I'll do this one thing, and then I'm out of here.

He wriggled round to face the wall, and tried to think of something else. Counting sheep. His all-time greats fantasy World Cup final teams. Rivers in South America beginning with various letters of the alphabet. No joy; and then he found himself suddenly and unexpectedly engrossed by a thought that had never occurred to him before.

So there's this tree, Colin thought, growing up through the middle of our house. It starts off in the lounge, right, and then it goes up through the ceiling into the first-floor landing and up the stairwell to the second floor— He struggled to figure out the layout of the rooms. For one thing, how could the first-floor stairs be directly above the middle of the lounge? And the place where the tree vanished into the loft; surely that was well over to one side, facing the back-garden fence. He reached for a bit of paper and a pencil and tried to draw it out, side views and seen-from-above, like an architect's drawings he'd looked at once. The more he thought about it, the less sense it made (unless he'd got the whole topography skew-whiff, which wasn't beyond the bounds of possibility). In the end, he managed to wrestle the problem down to two possible alternatives. Either the tree didn't fit the house, or the house didn't fit the tree. Neither of them was satisfactory, and neither of them addressed the question that was bugging him; namely, what in God's name was it doing there in the first place?

Foolish, foolish; because the tree had always been there, as long as he could remember. Therefore it followed that it wasn't an emergency, which meant he shouldn't be wasting his time and his exceedingly small reserve of mental energy worrying about it right now. Instead, he should be tearing himself to bits over the reality of Hell, the existence of witches and the fact that his Dad was trying to sell his soul to the Devil in return for a cunning way round the statutory minimum wage regulations.

This is no good, Colin decided. I can't just lie here, I've got to *do* something.

Like what? Get up a petition? Write to my MP?

He sagged, like a becalmed sail. All his hopes rested on the girl; the strange young woman, the *witch*, who gave him pins and needles in his feet and ferocious mental flashbacks to non-existent memories. Only she could stop Dad doing this dreadful thing; and if anybody could cast some light on the whole déjà-vu nightmare, it had to be her. Right; talk to her. But he'd tried that. She was going to see what she could do; fine. But—

His door opened.

'Dad?' Colin sat up. A thin taper of light gleamed through from the landing.

'Oh,' said a voice. 'Sorry, wrong door.'

Colin froze. It was one of those moment when time slows down; more than that, it crumples, the way the front end of a Volvo's supposed to if you drive it into a tree. It wasn't just that he didn't recognise the voice. It was the pitch, the timbre, the piercing tone. Hardly more than a whisper, but so clear as to be practically deafening.

The door closed. For seven seconds – he could hear the ticking of his alarm clock, as loud as panel beating in the silence that followed that voice – he remained paralysed. Then his bones seemed to melt, and he flopped like a discarded shirt back down onto the bed. How long he lay there, he had no idea. He lost count of the ticks. He couldn't think; it was as though someone had scooped out his brains to fill an ice-cream cone.

Oscar (it wasn't its real name, but it pleased its somewhat whimsical nature to use it on field assignments) crossed the landing, found the stairs and climbed to the second-floor landing. There it stopped, and sniffed. Just follow the tree, they'd told it. Should've known better than to trust them to get anything right.

The smell was strongest in front of a white-painted door with a round brass knob. Oscar turned it and went in. A human was sitting in a chair in front of a desk, smoking a cigar.

Insofar as it had any time for humans, Oscar admired courage. It was very much the admiration of the angler for the cunning and determined fish, but it was sincere. Accordingly, the human's reaction to its appearance earned its respect.

Even so: 'Fuck me,' the human said.

Oscar frowned. 'I didn't know that was in the contract,' it said. 'However—'

'No, it's just an expression.' Remarkable. It had taken the human a mere two-point-three-seven seconds to regain a substantial proportion of his composure. A sturdy fellow, this. 'You're late.'

'Apology.' Oscar checked the time against the schedule and acknowledged a failure, then reviewed the protocols. 'You are entitled to punish me with disembowelling should you choose to do so,' it said. 'If you lack the necessary cutting tools, I can provide them.'

'You what?' Clearly, the human was unfamiliar with the protocols. A sorry creature, for all his courage. 'No, screw that. I mean, forget it. You're here now.'

Also given to stating the obvious. 'We should proceed,' Oscar said.

'Yes, right. You've got the paperwork?'

Oscar nodded. Something about the gesture disturbed the human very much. Oscar didn't understand, but understanding wasn't necessary. 'Rosters,' it said. 'Timetables, shift-rotation modules, requisition forms.' A buff A4 envelope, mildly sulphur-scented, appeared on the human's desk. 'You'll find everything in order.'

The human reached out a pink paw – humans have hair on one side of the hand only – and touched the envelope, then let it go again. Distaste. There had been a briefing on distaste a thousand years ago, but Oscar had been on assignment and had missed it. 'I'll check these over in the morning,' the human said.

'As you wish.' Oscar frowned. 'You haven't signed the contract yet.'

'No.' The human looked away. Humans often did that. 'Still going through the small print with JWW. My Dad always said, don't sign something till you know what it means.'

'I can explain it for you if you like. It's quite straightforward.'

'Yes.' Oscar smelt an emotion it didn't immediately recognise. Guilt, partly. Also distrust; loathing and terror, naturally (it would have hurt Oscar's professional pride if they'd been missing). Something else, too. Not that it mattered. Either the human signed, or he didn't. 'He sends you his regards, by the way,' it added.

The human blinked. 'Who?'

'Your father.'

A curious reaction followed. According to the manual, humans appreciated small, thoughtful gestures and exhibited affection towards those who made them. The human's response, consequently, should have been positive. Complicated creatures; extravagantly over-engineered for their function, in Oscar's opinion.

'So,' the human said (this time, he'd recovered in only one-point-eight-five seconds). 'Are you going to be here full time, or are you just the messenger?'

'I've been assigned to your case,' Oscar replied. 'Both here and –' it couldn't help pausing for effect '– afterwards. We believe that continuity is important in ongoing situations,' it explained. 'Better the Devil you know, and so forth.'

Its little joke. Way over the human's head, of course.

'Right,' the human said. 'So we'll be seeing quite a bit of each other, then.'

'Yes indeed.'

'Well.' The human did that swallowing thing. 'Pleased to meet you. My name's—'

'I know your name.' Had that been a trifle abrupt? Such subtleties of modulation. 'You should call me Oscar,' Oscar said.

'Oscar.'

'Yes.'

'All right.' The human appeared to be having trouble concentrating. 'Well, that's all for now, I guess. Unless you've got—'

'When do you anticipate being in a position to sign the contract?'

'Oh, soon.' Bluster. A symptom of being backed into a corner by the forces he had himself unleashed. Bluster's last stand. Another little joke. 'Just a few bits of mumbo-jumbo I want to thrash out. You know what the legal eagles are like.'

'Yes,' Oscar said. 'Intimately.'

'You— Oh, I see.' The human's body trembled slightly. Low ambient temperature, perhaps, or possibly fear. 'Well, don't let me keep you.'

'Apology,' Oscar said. 'I thought I'd made it clear – I'm on permanent assignment to you.' It frowned. 'Another expression?'

'Yes.'

'Understood. You dismiss me for the moment.'

'Yes.'

Oscar nodded. Humans appreciate an exchange of formulaic salutations at leave-taking. 'Ciao for now,' it said, and vanished in a cloud of yellow smoke.

Reduced to its component atoms, hurtling at inconceivable speed through the interstices of time and space, Oscar reviewed its first impressions of the human. Adequate, it decided. Courage, as previously noted. A brittle, almost flamboyant display of fortitude in the face of the most terrifying entity he would ever meet; such fortitude resembles the snail's shell, in that it generally conceals a soft and vulnerable interior. It would be rewarding to peel him in due course. Regrettably, no sense of humour; but that was such a rare attribute among mortals that it was pointless to hold it against him. A pity, nonetheless; shared humour can have a very positive part to play in the relationship with a colleague – which the human would be, in a sense; someone Oscar would be working with (and after that, of course, working on). Also, it realised at the moment of rematerialisation (as the full force of the heat closed in around it, and the shrieking, and the stench of molten metal), he's hiding something. Even from me. Now that was intriguing, a rare gift among these shallow, bland creatures. Maybe this assignment would turn out to be more challenging than it had anticipated. Faced with the monotony of eternity, the wretched homogeneity of mankind, even the slightest difference was exceedingly welcome. Something to get my teeth into, Oscar thought.

Another little joke.

CHAPTER SEVEN

Never work, they say, with children or animals; a doctrine that Benny Shumway had subscribed to for most of his adult life. Feeding the goats was, however, an exception. It was a pleasantly boring midday chore – sign out a sack of feed from the stores, lug it down to the cellar, fill the trough – which gave him a welcome opportunity to unwind and let his mind drift into neutral. He looked on it as an antidote to the daily trip to the Bank, even though the two tasks were, of course, intimately related.

A year or so ago, in order to take advantage of their highly competitive account structures for business customers, JWW had transferred its custom from Barclays to the Bank of the Dead. Accordingly, Benny's daily trip to pay in the cheques, draw the petty cash, arrange for wire transfers and so on involved him in a trip to the Underworld, to which he gained access through a small door in the back wall of his office. In order for the living to contact the dead on their own turf, a blood sacrifice is required, and a detailed cost-efficiency analysis had shown that goats were the most economical option. Once you got used to it, it was no more of a hassle than topping up your mobile, except that you used a Stanley knife instead of a little plastic card.

Nevertheless, Benny couldn't honestly say that he enjoyed his daily outing. The peace and quiet of the goat cellar was a welcome contrast. Leaning against the manger wall and listening to the soft crunch of feeding ruminants, he could think things over at his own pace, a luxury usually denied him in the frantic rush of the working day. It was hard enough staying on top of his duties as cashier; since the demise of that fool Ricky Wurmtoter, however, he'd also been filling in as the firm's pest-control specialist. Since the pests for which JWW generally got called in included dragons, werewolves, manticores, harpies, frost-giants, ogres, djinns, hydras and all known permutations of the Undead, it could at times be a rather demanding portfolio, especially for someone who stood five feet nothing in his socks and whose spectacle lenses were as thick as the bottom of a beer mug.

Esmeralda lifted her head and gazed at him, her jaws grinding in their slow, circular rhythm. She had character, Benny reckoned, and since she was the brood nanny she was safe from the demands of the financial sector. Benny fished in his pocket and took out a small apple. He felt a little like Lord Emsworth, feeding the Empress of Blandings.

Cassie's problem, he thought; something of a collector's item. Ever since she'd told him about it, he'd had it constantly in the back of his mind, hanging like game to mature. Definitely, something was going on there. In many ways, it reminded him of examples he'd read about in textbooks long years ago: identify the catastrophic anomaly of which these are the perceived effects. The particulars didn't fit any of the cases he'd studied, but it had that sort of feel about it, almost as though someone had made it up to illustrate a specific point.

Another good thing about the goat cellar was that it was a cracking place to hide when you didn't want to be found. According to his watch, at that moment he should have been upstairs, in the interview room, having his assessment. The prospect hadn't bothered him particularly (who the hell else could they find who'd do his job for the money?), but he reckoned it was one of those things you needed to be in the mood for, and he wasn't. So let them bawl him out or send him a snotty memo. It'd do them good to be mucked about for a change. Meanwhile, he could roost down here for half an hour or so, and think about—

About what?

From the sound of it (though Cassie wouldn't appreciate him saying so), true love seemed like a logical starting point. She'd described at least half a dozen classic symptoms; true, the bloke as she'd described him sounded like a pathetic wimp, but Benny (who had to stop and think before he could recite the roster of his ex-wives in chronological order) had long since given up trying to figure out what women see in men.

But it wasn't that. He wasn't quite sure how he knew, but he was quite certain. You could tell when a girl was in love with someone – small modulations of voice, temper and body language, imperceptible as a dog-whistle – and he'd picked up on nothing of the sort. Instead, he kept on coming back to the test papers in the back of Eaton's *Theory & Practice of Commercial Sorcery* (27th edition, Manchester, 1906). He could remember the kind of thing as though it were yesterday. A man walking down the street after murdering his grandfather meets an identical copy of himself coming the other way; a practical sorcerer engaged in summoning malevolent spirits in a village on the Equator in June discovers that his watch is running backwards; the distance between A and B is exactly nineteen miles, but measures twenty-one miles in a leap year. Explain, using diagrams if necessary.

Benny smiled. Of course, it wasn't politically correct to say 'sorcerer' any more. He thought of himself yawning his way through night-school classes, the new suit he'd bought for the exam. Back then, it had all been so wonderfully straightforward – working-class boy from small mining village wins scholarship; a brilliant career; a partnership. It had all been about improving yourself in those days. Am I improved, he wondered, or just different?

Concentrate. A girl shows all the symptoms of being in love, but isn't. Put like that, it could easily have been one of those test exercises; so, start by applying the rules you've been taught. First, find the paradox. Second, reduce it to its simplest terms. Third, formulate your equation.

Benny thought about it, leaning over the rail, brow furrowed. Esmeralda licked the side of his hand, then started eating his shirt cuff. He didn't notice.

One of the rules he'd committed to memory (Friday night in the Working Men's Institute; and it was always freezing cold, because they were too tight to turn on the heating until December) was that a small anomaly usually has big causes. Look, therefore, to the wider picture.

Of course, Cassie wasn't really in a position to supply reliable data; but suppose, just for argument's sake, that the bloke (the wimp, the waste of space) was exhibiting the same symptoms. In which case, you'd have two people acting like they're in love, but they aren't. A small candle flickered in Benny's mind, and he rummaged in his inside pocket for a pen and something to write on. A equals B, but doesn't equal C. D equals E, but not F. Therefore let x (why does it always have to be x?) represent the—

He scribbled for a minute or so, until the paying-in slip he'd been using was almost full of tiny, squiggly letters and symbols. Let x – let it be what? Whisper words of wisdom, let it be—

Ah.

The trouble was, back in the Working Men's Institute, you always had to show your working or you got no marks, even if the answer was the right one. He'd always bitterly resented that; it seemed arbitrary and unfair. Take Danny Earnshaw: nearly always got the wrong answer, nearly always got top marks. Benny, on the other hand, got the right answer ninety-nine times out of a hundred, but they'd put him back a year for lack of progress.

Bloody Earnshaw (whatever had become of him? Benny wondered), could do with him here right now; because Benny knew the answer, or something very like it, but he had no idea how he'd got there. Which was a bloody shame, since he couldn't very well go to young Cassie and tell her what was going on, and then say, 'Don't ask, I just *know*.' He sighed, and noticed that he was missing three-quarters of his left shirt cuff.

The answer was, not two people in love, but *four*.

The phone rang. Benny raised an eyebrow, because last time he'd looked there hadn't been a phone down here in the cellar. He listened, located the source of the noise, picked it up.

'There you are.' Rosie Tanner. 'I've been turning the place upside down looking for you.'

Benny sighed. 'Tell them to reschedule it for early next week. Before half-ten, for choice.'

'I haven't got a clue what you're on about,' Rosie replied. She used her own voice when she talked to him; flattering, in a way, but a pity. 'You've got a client waiting in reception. Been there a quarter of an hour, and he's not pleased.'

'Can't be. There wasn't anything in my diary.'

'It's a new job, emergency.'

'They always say that.'

'This time it's true. Apparently, a balrog's just moved into the Burnside nuclear plant, and they want it shifted.' Goblin chuckle. 'You get all the rotten jobs.'

'Yes,' Benny growled, and hung up.

Burnside, he thought; that's in bloody Scotland. Well, someone else'll have to do the banking, that's all. He gave Esmeralda her second apple, pulled his jacket sleeve down over the tatters of his cuff, and headed for the stairs.

Four, he thought. A crowd. Must remember to talk to young Cassie, soon as I get back.

Out onto the landing, through the computer room, down one flight of the back stairs, across the lower landing (once upon a time they'd tried calling it the mezzanine, but the effort of trying to keep straight faces had interfered with work, so they'd abandoned that), down one flight of the middle stairs, on down the corridor, through the fire door and into the front office.

'I'll be out for the rest of the day,' he told Mr Tanner's mum. She gave him a sympathetic look. 'Scotland?' she asked.

'Yes.'

'Have fun.'

A balrog in a nuclear reactor. 'I'll try,' Benny said, and stepped into the revolving door.

It wasn't what I thought it was. It wasn't what I thought it was. Does lying to yourself make you go blind? It wasn't what I thought it was, it can't have been.

Colin opened his eyes. The first thing he saw was the underside of his bed. Ah yes, he said to himself, I remember now. I came down here because I was scared in case the demon came back.

Not a demon. Not what I thought it was.

The room was full of daylight, and he was still wearing the clothes he'd had on yesterday. He wriggled sideways until he could stand up. The face in the mirror looked even dozier than usual. He shaved its chin, but that didn't help a great deal. Time to go downstairs for breakfast.

Dad wasn't there; he'd gone in early, Mum told him, as she confronted him with a huge bowl full of porridge. It was ten years since he'd first explained to her that porridge gave him raging indigestion. He ate it alone and in silence, then went to work.

'Morning,' he called out as he passed the front desk. It was pure habit, a Pavlovian reaction. Each morning for the last eight years, he'd called out his insincere greeting, and Pam on the front desk had echoed it. He knew what Pam looked like, so there was no point wasting a neck-swivel just to see her. He cocked his wrist to push open the connecting door.

'Hi,' said the receptionist. 'You must be Colin Hollingshead.'

He stopped and turned his head. 'Hello,' he said. 'Who—?'

She smiled at him. 'I'm the new receptionist,' she said.

Compare and contrast. He'd made two recent visits to the office of J. W. Wells, in the City. On both occasions, there had been a (why mince words?) stunningly lovely girl behind the front desk. The first time, he'd experienced that numbed, having-just-walked-through-a-plate-glass-door feeling that besets susceptible young men when confronted with extreme beauty. The second time he'd been too preoccupied to care, but he'd still been human enough to notice. The young female sitting where Pam usually sat wasn't in the same league: nice-looking, on balance, though maybe a smidge on the chunky side. On the other hand—

'Right,' he said. 'You're—'

'Pam's on holiday,' she explained. 'I'm filling in for her. Actually, I'm her niece.'

Colin relaxed slightly. 'Pleased to meet you,' he said. 'What's your name?'

She frowned. 'Ah,' she said.

'That's a funny name. Is it short for—?'

'No, that's not what I'm called.' Her frown deepened. 'Oh well, I suppose I'd better tell you and get it over with. I'm called Famine.'

Colin thought for a moment. 'That's Spanish, isn't it?'

She winced slightly. 'No,' she said, 'English. My two sisters are called Pestilence and War, and my kid brother—' She sighed. 'My Dad's quite religious, you see. You can laugh now if you want to.'

Colin frowned. 'I don't think it's funny,' he said. 'It must be really difficult for you.'

She shrugged. 'You get used to it,' she said. 'And it's sort of a family tradition. Like, Dad's first name is Envy, and he's got six brothers and sisters. Bit of a pain, really.'

'Sounds like it,' Colin said. 'Have you got a middle name? You could use that instead.'

She shook her head. 'Not really,' she said. 'For my middle name, they called me after Dad's sister. I'm Famine L. Williams.' She shrugged again. 'Could've been worse,' she said. 'I heard on the radio once about some family in America that called their kids after Santa's reindeer.'

Colin pursed his lips. 'That'd be worse?'

'Or there's the seven dwarves,' she added, 'or the 1966 England World Cup squad. Mostly people call me Fam, for short.'

'I'll do that, then,' Colin said. Then he grinned. 'My Dad's a nutcase too,' he said.

Fam seemed to hesitate for a moment, then she grinned. 'That's what Auntie Pam told me,' she said.

'She's your mum's sister, right?'

'That's right, yes.'

'How did I guess?'

She smiled at him. 'Well, anyway,' she said, and hesitated.

'I'd better get on, I suppose,' he said, though of course he had nothing useful to do, and all day to fill with doing it.

'See you around, then.'

'See you.'

Colin shoved through the connecting door and pottered down to his office, just in case some splendid task or quest was waiting on his desk. No such luck, so he sat down. He remembered.

My Dad in is league with the Devil, and last night I saw— And this morning, I forgot all about it while I was chatting to some girl on reception. Eek. So what does that make me?

Normal? He considered the interpretation and rejected it. No, he was a callous, shallow, thoughtless bastard. How could any decent human being possibly allow himself to be sidetracked by nice-looking girls when his universe was in tatters and his own father was in mortal peril – no, immortal peril, which was far worse.

Nice-looking? Well, yes. Also bright, cheerful, easy to get along with, nice sense of humour—

There is no *thunk* as the arrow strikes home; presumably Cupid uses a silencer, as befits a sniper. Instead, there's a slight jolt. The subconscious mind registers a change that slightly affects everything. It's like playing with the TV remote: you turn the colour down to black and white, then gradually bring it back up again. That moment, when the shades of grey start to blush into the first faint colours, is pretty much what it's like. Oh, you say to yourself, as you acknowledge the fact for the first time. Right. From there on, it gathers pace; but there's a moment, like the short interval of time when you realise you've caught a cold, when the symptoms are still only slight, but the diagnosis is certain. Whether you then proceed to extremes of daydreaming, mooning about, making a fool and a nuisance of yourself, depends on the severity of the case and your own nature. The start, however, is always the same.

Well then, Colin thought.

Next he scowled at a blank spot on the wall, because it couldn't have come at a more inconvenient time if it'd tried. How often had he laughed in infuriated scorn at the movies, when the hero and heroine discover their true feelings for each other in the middle of a gun battle, car chase, earthquake, alien invasion (or, if it's a Bond film, all of the above simultaneously), because surely you'd be far too preoccupied with blind terror and stuff like that. Apparently not. The world was breaking up all around him, bloody great big chunks of sky were crashing down at him like Newton's apple, but that didn't matter. He was still in the firing line for a fly-by shooting. Maybe that was the rule rather than the exception. Maybe true love always comes at the most inconvenient moment, like phone calls from your mother, or jury service. Maybe that's how you're supposed to know that this one's the—

Colin opened his eyes wide and sat up. Miss Right? Apparently his subconscious mind thought so, or it wouldn't be flailing around concepts like true love. Really, though? He'd barely said two words to Fam and already he was holding a lighted match over a gunpowder trail that led directly to mortgages, soft furnishings, kiddie seats in the car, Sunday mornings at the DIY superstore, family holidays, thinking seriously about pensions, school league tables and Christmas round robins filled with graduating offspring and minor geriatric ailments. When you're about to die, your whole past life's supposed to flash before your eyes. When you fall in true love, on the other hand, what you see in the twinkling of an eye is your entire future. It's very much a matter of opinion which is the more depressing.

Even so, Colin thought. So what? He thought of a father-in-law called Envy and a brother-in-law who, if he opted for a career as a professional darts player, would be seen standing at the oche with DEATH WILLIAMS spreadeagled in big white letters across his shoulder blades, and against that balanced the memory of a smile. No big deal. In fact, the utter unspeakableness of their families was something they had in common which would undoubtedly draw them closer together—

He gave up. Resistance is futile; likewise logic, common sense and the instinctive urge to self-preservation. He glanced at his watch; ten minutes since he'd come in through the front-office door. He might as well amble back to reception and see if there were any messages for him.

Usually Colin slouched along the corridor, though sometimes he dawdled and occasionally he traipsed. This time he practically sprinted. His head was full of sleigh-bells and birdsong, which was probably why he almost failed to notice something unusual standing in the middle of the small room just in front of the fire door, where they kept the photocopier, the shredder and three battered old green filing cabinets.

Almost, but not quite. He stopped, looked at it and wilted, like an Action Man inadvertently microwaved.

It was much smaller than the one at home; hardly more than a sapling.

Finally, as a last resort, Connie tried *Levinson & De Pienaar on Temporal Displacement*. She hadn't bothered looking there before, partly because she was sure it was really something quite simple and straightforward, partly because her copy of Levinson was on the top shelf and she'd have to stand on a chair to reach it.

She stepped back down and blew dust off the top of the book. It fell open at the flyleaf. *Constance Schwartz-Alberich. St Barthold's College, Nuneaton.* She frowned. She'd written that in the same year that the Beatles had recorded 'Eleanor Rigby'. Maybe she was getting too old for all this nonsense.

Or maybe not. She sat down and turned to the index. Cassie's problem had chafed at her mind ever since the poor girl had explained it to her in the pub, and the irritation was getting in the way of her work. Better to get it sorted out once and for all, and then she'd be able to concentrate on doing what she was paid for.

Anomalies: 3, 7, 13, 67, 69–72, 86, 92f; 103— There were some aspects of the matter that definitely rang bells, to the point where, if Connie closed her eyes, she could practically see Quasimodo swinging to and fro underneath them. The difficulty was, they had nothing to do with the particulars of the case. They were out of place, like a torpedo in a salad.

Nothing on page thirteen. She flipped back to the end of the book. Twenty years ago, she felt sure, she'd have been able to put her finger on it straight away, no messing. It was just a matter of seeing the bigger picture.

Knock. The door opened, and Cassie came in. With a sigh, Connie put the book down. 'I was just thinking about you,' she said.

'Oh?'

'This bloody thing of yours. It's really starting to bug me.'

'Me too,' Cassie said. 'But that's not why I'm here. I was wondering, could you just cast your eye over this clause here? I think it means what I want it to mean, but I've been staring at it for so long it could mean practically anything.'

Connie grinned. 'Give it here,' she said. She read it quickly and nodded. 'Seems perfectly clear to me,' she said.

'Ah, right. Thanks.'

'Roughly paraphrased, it means, we've got you by the balls, but deep down we're philanthropists, so we've bunged in this huge great loophole so you can scamper away like frightened woodland creatures and there's bugger-all that we'll be able to do about it. Was that what you wanted it to say?'

'Oh.' Cassie sat down. 'It's no good,' she said. 'It's really start-ing to get to me.'

'I know.' Connie picked up a pen, crossed out some words in

the offending paragraph and wrote some bits in over the top. 'Try that,' she said. 'Better?'

'Yes, much. I guess. Oh, I don't know. Is it all right or not?'

'Search me. I can't concentrate either. A bloody menace, that's what you are.'

'Sorry.'

'Unlike you,' Connie went on, 'I'm trying to do something about it. Or I was, before you barged in.' She swivelled the book round so that Cassie could see the title on the spine.

'Temporal displacement,' Cassie said. 'What's that got to do with anything?'

'I don't know,' Connie admitted. 'But I've tried everything sensible I could think of, so I thought I'd waste my time on something that it couldn't possibly be.'

Cassie nodded. 'I can see the logic in that,' she said. 'Any luck?'

'No, but like I said, I'd only just started. Come back in half an hour, when I've failed properly.'

Cassie stood up. 'It's very kind of you to go to all this trouble,' she said. 'Maybe it's only a load of coincidences, or I'm imagining things, or—'

'Shut up,' Connie said. 'Here, what about this? Porzig's ghost: did you do that at college?'

Cassie frowned. 'It does sound vaguely familiar,' she said. 'What's it all about?'

'Well—' Connie said, but the phone rang. She picked it up, listened, grunted, and put it down. 'Here,' she said, pushing the book across the desk, 'you'll have to read it for yourself. Apparently, I've been summoned.'

'Summoned?'

'By Them. God only knows why, but there's only one way to find out. You read that bit there, and I'll explain what I'm on about when I get back.'

So Cassie picked up the book. Connie had marked the place with an empty After Eight wrapper.

. . . is generally misinterpreted as a reference to Leo Porzig, late Fulbright professor of applied metaphysics at Stanford University. In

fact, Porzig was not the first to identify the phenomenon; however, it was his landmark article in Metempsychosis 67 *(1962) that initially drew attention to the research conducted in Paris by Lehmann and Diakonov between 1927 and 1932 . . .*

Cassie frowned. Skip all that.

. . . his epoch-making 1962 article, Porzig characterises the effect thus: An individual A, of sound mind and subject to no perceptible supernatural influence, becomes aware that he is in fact leading the life of another individual, B – he has some or all of B's memories, finds himself in situations alien to his own circumstances but relevant to B's, experiences emotions or holds opinions entirely foreign to his own nature but in keeping with B's. In some cases reported by Lehmann and Diakonov, at the relevant time B had predeceased A, sometimes by a substantial number of years, whereas in other instances A and B were almost exact contemporaries and B was still alive. Under the influence of the syndrome, subjects had espoused causes they detested, quarrelled bitterly with close friends and family, and in some instances married partners they heartily disliked. Lehmann and Diakonov collated the data but were unable to advance any cogent explanation; it was Porzig who proposed the hypothesis that the effect is a symptom of a temporal anomaly, in essence a massive rupture in the time/causality interface, whereby B, having been preordained to commit some act or suffer some experience but having been prevented by the intervention of some unforeseen and anomalous external force or event, B's destiny attaches itself to A and influences his existence in all relevant aspects as though A were indeed B—

Cassie looked up and rubbed her eyelids. It wasn't quite as bad as tax statutes or EU directives, but it wasn't exactly light holiday reading either. She went back and had another crack at it. Second time around wasn't much better than the first; third time, a glimmer of light began to shine through the cracks. She cast her mind back to college, when she'd had to wade through this sort of garbage all the time. Back then, it had always helped if she stuck in a few names, so she did that, and went through it in her mind to see if it made any sense.

All right. Suppose Sean Connery's got a destiny; he's destined to be the first man on Mars. But, the day before the Mars rocket's due to blast off from Canaveral, Sean trips over the cat, falls down the stairs and sprains his ankle. Destiny is foiled; but what's written is written, so instead Destiny darts out into the street and press-gangs the first remotely suitable person it comes across – Jim Carrey, say – into taking Sean's place. Accordingly, Jim abandons his promising career in insurance, signs up with NASA and becomes an astronaut. Destiny is happy, because in the end a human toe leaves a print in the chartreuse dust of an alien world; whether Jim likes it or not is neither here nor there. Fine.

Back to the book—

. . . complications arise when the superimposition of B's destiny on A prevents A from fulfilling his own destiny, which in turn lights on a random third party C, and so on in a rapidly escalating chain reaction. That no such sequence of events has yet been detected or recorded, Porzig argued, is beside the point; given the right circumstances, such a chain reaction could quite possibly develop, with obviously disastrous consequences. Dismissing Porzig as unduly alarmist and seeking to refute his basic conclusions, Hrozny and Crossland (JTS 105, 1972, pp 156–94) argued that such an effect would immediately be neutralised and readjusted by Meilhac's Phenomenon, and accordingly . . .

Cassie shut the book. She couldn't be arsed with Hrozny and Crossland right now. In fact, if they both fell down an open manhole cover, and Meilhac tumbled in after them and broke his stupid neck, it'd serve them all right for complicating her life to the point where she wanted to scream.

Living someone else's life instead of my own, she thought; well. In a sense, she'd been doing that for years (Daddy's voice: *You don't want to be a boring old accountant, kitten, you're going to be a sorcerer just like me*) but that wasn't an effect or a phenomenon, that was her own fault for not digging her heels in and saying no. The recent stuff, though; that was something else. Suppose, then, that somebody she didn't know, hadn't ever met, had been destined since Time began to fall in love with Colin

Hollingshead. A nasty thought, that, although it was always possible that this unknown person had been very naughty in a previous existence. Suppose, though; and suppose somewhere along the line true love had cast a shoe or blown a tyre; and suppose that, in consequence, there was this huge splodge of romance ricocheting around like a stray bullet, and she just happened to be in the way—

Eek, Cassie thought.

Or maybe it happens all the time, which would at least go some way towards explaining some of the bizarre combinations you see wheeling trolleys round Homebase together on bank holidays. Very nasty thought. But it was all going to be all right in the end, because that nice Mr Porzig, or one of his fellow researchers, would undoubtedly have come up with an antidote or cure, something you could get from Boots in your lunch hour and gobble down, and everything's fine again. Cassie grabbed for the book and flicked through to Connie's bookmark.

Drivel, drivel, drivel – ah, here we go. *As regards counteracting an existing anomaly or circumventing one believed likely to occur, at the time of writing there is a general consensus among the leading authorities. Even Falkenstein and Shah, the leading proponents of the revisionist approach, agree that once the syndrome has taken effect, absolutely nothing can be done to set things right.*

Cassie closed the book and dumped it on the desk. Thank you ever so bloody much, she thought. Of course, she didn't believe a word of it. It was all just a bunch of stupid academics making up the most appalling garbage simply so they could justify their research grants. And even if it wasn't, there was bound to be some other perfectly rational explanation for what was happening to her, which was really no big deal in any case, hardly worth sparing a moment's thought for.

She thought about hurling the book on the floor and jumping on it, which wouldn't solve much but might soothe her immediate need for self-expression; but it was Connie's book. It was ridiculous, though. There had to be something she could do instead of dropping a meek curtsy and trooping off to choose a wedding dress. To hell with it; it was bullying, and she wouldn't stand for it –

'You still here?' Connie had come back. Cassie was about to tell her all about Porzig and the stars in their courses and everything when she caught sight of the look on Connie's face. 'Something's up,' she said.

Connie nodded and sat down. 'You could say that,' she said. 'Something bad.'

'Oh, I don't know.' Connie shrugged. 'Define bad. If you mean something really shitty and unfair, then yes, something bad.' She sighed, and leaned back in her chair. 'Guess what,' she said. 'The bastards have given me the sack.'

CHAPTER EIGHT

'They can't do that,' Cassie said.

'Really?' Connie glared at her. 'Oh, I see what you mean. I could take them to the industrial tribunal for wrongful dismissal, or whatever it's called. Well, it'd be fun, I suppose, watching a whole roomful of lawyers getting turned into white mice, but I don't think it'd achieve anything positive. Of course they can do it. They can do anything. Look it up in the dictionary, under M for Magic.' She sighed. 'Well,' she said, 'that's that, I suppose. Nobody's going to give me another job at my age. In six months' time, I'll be one of those sad old creatures you see in supermarkets wheeling round a trolley full of frozen dinners and cat food. I'll be able to do gardening and watch the daytime soaps. Won't that be bloody fun.'

'But that's stupid,' Cassie objected. 'You know more about the business than anybody I've ever met. You earn them pots of money. You—'

'Not a team player, they said,' Connie interrupted grimly. 'They feel I'm too set in my ways to adapt to the challenges of the new post-rationalisation corporate structure. Also, they seem to have got it into their heads that I'm a teeny bit stroppy. What gave them that idea I honestly couldn't say.' She shook her head sadly. 'Two weeks' notice, though of course they'd understand if

I want to leave earlier. Fat chance,' she spat. 'I never did get the hang of knowing when I'm beaten. Lack of practice, I guess.'

'But it doesn't make sense,' Cassie maintained. 'You were going to retire anyway.'

'That's management for you,' Connie said wearily. 'The maximum brutality working hand in hand with the minimum logic to achieve the worst possible outcome – it's the proud old tradition of British industrial relations. No, they could see I wasn't going to wear my baseball cap and be a happy camper, so they've flushed me down the bog, and the hell with thirty years of bloody hard work.' She shrugged. 'It's not like it matters,' she added. 'Like you said, I was going to pack it in anyway. It's letting the little shits beat me that I don't like. It goes against the grain, somehow.'

Cassie couldn't think of anything to say that wouldn't be irritating at best. 'I'm really sorry,' she said. 'I think it's a rotten thing to do. In fact, I've got a good mind to tell them where they can stick their stupid job.'

'You could do that,' Connie replied. 'And we could go into business together making soft toys and home-made jam, since neither of us'd be able to get a proper job. Sweet idea but don't bother on my account. Now, if you don't mind, I want to sit quietly on my own and think despairing thoughts. Push off,' she translated, and Cassie left.

So, Connie thought. She looked around her, considering the boundaries of the life she'd just had taken away from her. From where she sat, she could see the filing cabinet whose drawers had never closed properly, the carpet that rucked up under the door, the empty bubble where the wallpaper had come away from the wall, the standard-issue print of London Bridge that had suddenly turned up one day without any explanation (she'd taken it down and thrown it out once; it was back in place the next morning), the floor-to-ceiling books stuffed with information she wouldn't be needing any more, the visitor's chair that squeaked. It was a cage, and the zookeepers came round from time to time to push work under the door, and when she'd gone they'd probably knock through to extend the computer room. She thought of all the hours she'd bled in this room, irreplaceable units of the slim margin between birth and death. What, after all, is Life but eighty-odd quid you get out of the cashpoint to pay some bill or other, and end up frittering away on impulse buys and special offers that you don't actually want?

Yes, but she knew all that already. The interesting aspect was why they'd chosen to dump on her *now*, as opposed to, say, later. Lying on her desk was that old copy of *Levinson & De Pienaar*; suddenly she remembered why she'd taken it down off the shelf.

Coincidence.

Absolutely. Nevertheless, Connie pulled the book towards her and flicked through until she found the place. She was reading and making notes when there was a knock at the door and Mr Tanner came in.

'Dennis,' she said. 'Haven't seen you in a while.'

Mr Tanner wasn't looking her in the eye, which meant he'd heard about her getting the sack. 'Been run off my feet by the bastard auditors,' he said.

'They're still here, then?'

'Oh yes.' He sighed. 'Busy little bees. They've been through half the files in the building, they've had all the ledgers and the paying-in books and the VAT stuff and the PAYE accounts, and now they want a whole lot more files and the bank statements for the last three years. I'll say this for them,' he added, 'they're thorough.'

'Apart from that, though,' Connie said. 'You've made friends with them, I trust; passed round the family snapshots, talked about United's chances in the League this season, all that sort of thing.'

Mr Tanner laughed. 'Yeah, right,' he said. 'There's three blokes who look like the Nazgul in pinstripes, and a skinny hatchet-faced bird who keeps saying "Well?" at me every time she asks me a question and I don't answer her inside half a second. If death's half as scary, I'll have to think seriously about living for ever. You got the Takemura file handy?'

Connie opened her filing cabinet and handed it over. 'What do they want that for?' she asked. 'It was just a poxy little job, and it was all wrapped up three years ago.'

Mr Tanner shrugged. 'You ask them if you like,' he said. 'And if you do and that bony cow looks at you and turns you to stone, can I have you for a bird-bath stand? You'd look good on our lawn with starlings hopping about on your head.'

When he'd gone, Connie reached for the book and read a little more. Then she reached for the phone.

'Rosie?' she said. 'Do me a favour, get me Hollingshead and Farren. Not the boss,' she added, 'the son. What's-his-name, Colin Hollingshead. Thanks.'

From time to time, you do get trees growing inside industrial premises. The difference is, they're neatly planted in pots, strategically placed so that visiting buyers can discreetly empty their glasses of disgusting white wine into them at sales presentations. What you don't tend to get is trees growing straight up through the carpet, and especially not overnight.

Oh God, Colin thought, and he reached out and wiped his fingertips on the bark. Just as he'd expected: the exact same texture as the one at home. It was a curious thing. For some reason or other, he'd spent an unreasonably large amount of time over the years looking through gardening books and tree books, and he'd never quite managed to pin down the species of the stupid big growing thing that filled the stairwell at home. Just when he was sure it was an oak or a sequoia or a Japanese maple, he'd find another book and realise it was nothing of the kind, though it might just possibly be an ornamental dogwood or an Amazonian bubinga. Whatever it was, though, there were now two of it. How nice.

Staring and prodding at the horrible thing wasn't going to achieve anything. He passed it by and went to his office. As he pushed open the door, he heard the burbling of the phone.

Her voice; the sound of it made him catch his breath. No doubt about it, then. 'There's a Connie Schwartz-Alberich calling for you from J. W. Wells,' she said.

'What?' He'd forgotten all about JWW, and everything they implied. How could you possibly forget about something like that? 'Sorry, I mean, right, yes, put her through. Thanks.'

Connie Schwartz-whatever-she'd-said. Who? Never mind. 'Hello?' said a voice.

'Hello,' he said back. 'Colin Hollingshead,' he remembered.

'Connie Schwartz-Alberich. It's all right, you don't know me from a hole in the ground. But you have met my colleague, Cassandra Clay.'

'Yes,' Colin said, and he meant it.

'Right.' Pause. The voice was brisk, normally the sort of tone he'd be intimidated by; and he was, but not nearly as much as he'd usually have been. 'You got a minute?'

'Sure,' Colin replied. 'Is this about—?'

'No.' Another pause, though slightly shorter this time. 'It's really more a sort of personal matter. Look, it's difficult to explain. I don't suppose there's any chance you could spare me half an hour? This evening, preferably. Sevenish?'

'I suppose so,' Colin said doubtfully. 'Why?'

'If I could explain why over the phone, I wouldn't need to come dragging out all the way to Richmond, or wherever the hell you are. Sorry,' the voice added, 'I'm having one of those days. Actually, I've been having one of those lives, but it's only just starting to catch up with me.'

'I don't know,' Colin said. 'Is it important?' He caught the sound of breath being intaken at the other end of the line. 'It's important,' he added quickly. 'Look, excuse me if this sounds really strange, but might it have something to do with why we've got a tree growing up through the middle of our lounge?'

He had no idea why he'd said that; but, to his great surprise, the voice replied, 'Interesting. A tree.'

'Yes.'

'Anything's possible.' Pause. 'You're sure it's a tree?'

'Absolutely fucking positive.'

'Right.' The voice sounded thoughtful. Not thoughtful as in should-I-tell-someone-where-I'm-going-and-be-sure-to-take-along-my-personal-security-alarm. Thoughtful as in Oh. 'Ash?'

'What?'

'Is it an ash tree?'

'No.'

'Oh. You do know what an ash tree looks like?'

'Yes, and it isn't one. It's not any kind of tree I've ever seen anywhere else. Look—'

'Ah.' The dictionaries are pretty useless on the subject, but there can be an infinity of difference between an 'Ah' and an 'Oh'. 'Right, where shall I meet you? I'll be coming on the train from the City.'

The rest of Colin's working day was almost mockingly orthodox. He stuffed circulars into envelopes. He went down to Crudgington's to pick up five boxes of dovetail cutters for the big CNC mills in the tool room. He filed some letters for Uncle Chris. Life was teasing him, pretending to be normal when it patently wasn't. On the positive side, Fam smiled at him four times, laughed at two jokes, agreed with his views on the latest Trinny and Susannah show and happened to mention in passing that she quite fancied seeing the new Mel Gibson film. All of that was, of course, wonderful. It was only its juxtaposition with all the sub-Koontzian melodrama that made it seem bizarre.

He got rid of the ninety minutes between end-of-work and seven o'clock after the fashion of the sea grinding down a cliff. Most of it he spent in a grim little pub just down from the station, where he spun out a glass of Pepsi and failed to read the *Evening Standard*. At five to seven, he got up and wandered over to the ticket barrier. At ten past seven he'd just resolved to give it ten more minutes and then go home, when a middle-aged woman in a Marks & Spencer coat appeared in front of him like a decloaking Romulan and said, 'You're Colin Hollingshead.'

'Yes.'

'Fine. I need a drink. Lead the way.'

Which he did, with tolerable efficiency. She bought, which both impressed and relieved Colin, since he suddenly realised, as they walked into the pub, that he only had two pounds and seventy-six pence on him. For some reason, he felt inclined to trust her – probably because she was middle-aged and female, or some daft superficial reason of that kind. In his narrow and slight experience, middle-aged women were calm, efficient voices on the other end of phones sorting out botched deliveries, explaining incomprehensible Department of Trade export licence regulations, or telling him in words of one syllable how to install broadband on the office computer. Leaving aside his mother (easily done), he'd never been let down or dumped on by a middle-aged female, though of course there was a first time for everything.

'Now then,' she said, as they sat across a table in the quiet corner, next to the broken fruit machine. 'I've got a theory, and I need you to help me prove it. All right?'

Colin nodded. 'Sure,' he said. 'Is it to do with—'

'I'm coming to that.'

'Are you? I mean, fine, sorry.'

'All right.' She seemed to brace herself, as though she was nervous. The thought of someone being nervous talking to him struck Colin as faintly absurd. 'You've met my colleague, Ms Clay.'

'Yes.'

The woman thought for a moment. 'All the time you were with her, you had this unaccountable feeling that something extremely weird was going on, but you couldn't quite figure out what it was.'

Colin nodded.

'You know what it is we do at JWW.'

'Sort of.' He took a deep breath. 'You're wizards. Sorry, witches, I suppose, in your—'

Connie gave him a weary look. 'Hint,' she said. 'Not the W word. It's got the wrong connotations; you know, old men in long white beards, crones with cats, teenagers larking about in the sky on broomsticks. We prefer the word "magical practitioners", though old-timers like me still say sorcerers. Amounts to the same thing, but it doesn't make me cringe when I hear it.'

'All right,' Colin said. 'Sorcerers. You do magic.' He hesitated for a moment, then added: 'You're arranging for my Dad to sell his soul to the Devil.'

'Hm.' The relative positions of the woman's nose, mouth and eyebrows gave Colin the impression that she didn't hold with that sort of thing, but wasn't quite prepared to admit as much to someone outside the trade. 'I imagine you're not thrilled by that.'

'Not really.'

'Don't blame you. If I were you, I'd talk him out of it.'

'You don't know my Dad.'

'True. But that's beside the point. Listen.' She then told him about temporal displacement theory. She was better at explaining than Messrs Levinson and De Pienaar which was just as well.

'Ring any bells?' she concluded.

It was Colin's turn to think. 'Yes,' he said. 'I mean, yes, that could be me. But hang on. You're saying that I'm being – well, like *possessed*, or something.' He heard himself say that, almost as though he was eavesdropping on someone else, and his hand shook, spilling beer on his knees. 'Someone else has taken me over, and they're making me feel like I'm in love with her.'

Connie pursed her lips. 'Nearly,' she said, 'but not quite. It's not a case of malicious little gremlins squatting inside your head and ordering you about. It's more – I don't know; more impersonal than that. It's got more in common with catching a cold than invasion-of-the-body-snatchers. The thing is,' she went on, 'it's a really huge coincidence that both of you seem to have gone down with the same thing. Trust me, that's really unusual. In fact, I can't think of a single case study where it's happened before.' She drank some of her gin and tonic, then said, 'Why don't you tell me about it in your own words?'

That sounded a bit too much like English homework for Colin's taste, but he did his best. 'And the crazy part of it is,' he concluded, with a rush, 'since all this stuff started I've met someone else who I think I really do like, a lot. And some of the things I'm feeling now are pretty much the same, but a lot of them are different. Like, with this – this other girl I mentioned, it's—' He made an effort and found some words that more or less got the job done. 'It feels much more like *me*, if you see what I mean. The stuff with Cassie doesn't feel like me at all. It's like I suddenly stopped talking normally and started saying everything in blank verse. It feels all wrong, but at the same time it's really, definitely *there*, if you get me. Almost,' he added with a frown, 'it's like it's all happened before, and I'm remembering it. Which can't make any sense, surely.'

Connie looked at him oddly and said, 'I'll be the judge of that. Now then, what's all this about a tree?'

'Two trees, actually.' Colin studied her for a moment, and realised that she was actually taking him seriously. So he told her about it, the whole shebang, starting with his early childhood and putting in all the details he could call to mind. When he'd finished, all she said was, 'And you're sure it's not an ash?'

'Yes.'

'OK. Not an apple, either?'

'I've got books out of the library,' he said. 'Alan Titchmarsh and everything. It's not anything in any of them.'

'That's very strange,' Connie said. 'That's the bummer with mysteries, of course. One particular detail catches your attention and reminds you of something, and so you don't pay proper attention to the rest of it, and you wind up completely screwed. I mean, here's me banging on about species . . . But this tree definitely goes up through your roof and then disappears?'

'Oh yes.'

Connie shook her head. 'I'll have to think about that one,' she said. 'There's something lurking at the back of my mind, but I must've ticked it off somehow, because it's sulking and won't come out to play. Meanwhile, we've got to assume that it's nothing to do with the other stuff. Which is hard to take,' she added irritably, 'because two separate lots of weirdness happening to one civilian – no offence – is pretty bloody unlikely if you ask me. Tell me, do you do the Lottery?'

'Sometimes,' Colin admitted.

'No luck so far, obviously.'

'No.'

'Maybe you should stick with it,' Connie said. 'I mean, it'd solve a lot of problems if you won. Well, of course it would, ignore me. Only, you remind me a bit of the old joke about Cyprus being a place that produces more history than can be consumed locally. You do seem to have an awful lot of luck, far more than your fair share. Pity it's all bad luck, really.' She shook herself like a wet dog and went on, 'The tree thing probably isn't anything to worry about, but the other business is turning my colleague into a nervous wreck, and I don't suppose it's much fun for you, either. And the larks your father's getting up to—' She pulled a face. 'I'll be straight with you, if you promise not to breathe a word of it to anybody at JWW. In our profession, ethics is generally just someone talking with a lisp about southern East Anglia, but most of us do draw a line somewhere, eventually. Trouble is, the firm's just been taken over, and the new management isn't too picky about who it does business with. Seems to me,' she added with a slight edge to her voice, 'that if you help young Cassie to sort out her bit of bother – and that'll be doing you some good too, don't let's forget – then she might be inclined to be grateful, which might lead her to make a complete balls-up of this routine sale-and-purchase. Completely out of character, that'd be, because she's pretty good at her work most of the time, but everybody makes mistakes occasionally.'

Colin nodded. 'I think she'd be happy to do that,' he said, 'only she doesn't know how. I mean, how to make a mess of it so the – the other lot pull out.'

Connie smiled beautifully. 'That's just youthful inexperience,' she said. 'When you've been in this trade as long as I have, you learn a thing or two about how perfectly simple, straightforward, do-it-standing-on-your-head-whistling-"Chatanooga-Choo-Choo" jobs can go horribly wrong in the twinkling of an eye. So; have we got a deal?'

'I guess so,' Colin said, feeling vaguely stunned. 'Sorry if I sound a bit out of it, but I'm new to all this. A few days ago, I thought magic was sawing girls in half and Paul Daniels.'

'Did you really?' Connie shook her head. 'Well, don't beat yourself up too much about that. Let me tell you a secret about our profession. Basically, it's all about giving a tiny minority of the population a hugely unfair advantage over everybody else. If everybody could get at it, there'd be no point, because it'd be the proverbial level playing field; and then you'd get cowboy sorcery outfits in every high street, you'd have watchdogs and ombuds-men and EU directives and disgruntled customers ringing up *You & Yours*, and everything'd grind to a halt. So instead, we confine ourselves to the very, very few people who can afford to pay our extortionate bills. We help them to get even richer still and the rest of the world gets screwed rotten without even knowing it; everything's normal, everybody's happy. It's a noble calling, but it's all I've got. Or it was,' she added, frowning. 'But that's none of your concern. Leave it with me,' she said, finishing her drink, 'and I'll see what I can do.' She grinned. 'Think of me as your fairy godmother,' she said. 'I'll wave my magic wand—'

'Have you got one?' Colin said. 'A real one?'

She looked at him. 'I'll pretend you didn't say that. Anyway, I'll be in touch. Now we've got some idea of what the problem actually is, solving it ought to be relatively simple. Probably a great big anticlimax; it usually is. We just like to dress it up in funky long words so we can pad the bill out a bit. Still, I don't suppose you're the first person in galactic history that this has happened to.'

Colin looked at her. 'A moment ago you said I was. You said—'

Connie made a dismissive gesture. 'I say all sorts of things,' she replied, 'it's a side effect of charging by the hour. The more I think about it, the more I'm inclined to the view that it's prob-ably just a little bit of fluff on the points of the space-time continuum. Really screws things up for you, but a wipe with an oily rag and a squirt of WD-40 and you'll be back on the rails in no time.'

'You think so?'

'In the trade before you were born,' she said, getting up. 'I'll call you as soon as I've got anything concrete, as the developer said to the mafioso. Nice to have met you.'

Colin watched her leave. Very strange; she'd appeared to change her mind in mid-flow, and now it was all a storm in a teacup, no big deal. In which case, why had she come halfway across Greater London in her own time to talk to him about it?

He got himself another drink and had a nice quiet brood, with a panic chaser. Forget his Dad making a pact with the Evil One; forget the tree, and now the other fucking tree. Focus instead on the notion that he might be the victim of – he wasn't quite sure how to categorise it, now that he came to think about it. It was either a crossed line in Destiny's switchboard, or a rare and supernatural variation on an arranged marriage. Either way—

That at least was something that Colin could be definite about. Either way, it sucked and he wanted no part of it. All the time he'd been telling the nice lady about it, and listening to her explanation, his subconscious had been chewing doggedly over the available data on Ms Cassie Clay, and to his surprise he realised he'd somehow stumbled into a little pothole of clarity.

He didn't love her. He didn't even like her very much. She wasn't nice-looking, she didn't make him laugh, he couldn't imagine sitting over empty plates with her in a restaurant, with the staff tapping their feet because it was past closing time but these two young lovebirds were still nattering away, oblivious of time . . . Now Famine— Sod it, he couldn't possibly think of her as that. Fam. If you rewound those criteria and replayed them with Fam instead of Ms blasted Clay, it all played very smoothly indeed. Which was probably, he was prepared to concede, why he was falling in love with her.

Because it was boring and of no conceivable relevance to the widget-founding industry, Colin hadn't taken much notice of the history they'd tried to squash into the space between his ears at school. But he did vaguely remember the American Declaration of Independence; which was when a bunch of ordinary people got pissed off with being shoved around by bullies and put a stop to it. No, they'd said, you can take all that, and you can stuff it. Right, then. Here and now, a declaration of not-taking-any-more-of-that-from-anybody. Not from supernature, which had no right to come splurging into his life without any warning. Not from his own pathetic excuse for a personality, which couldn't even make up its mind who it was in love with until the nice lady had explained it all. Not from all the Hollingsheads dead and gone, with their traditions and expectations and demands; and abso-bloody-lutely not from Dad. Screw what anybody thought of him, shame and guilt and all that. Just as soon as this mess was sorted out, and Ms Clay was out of his life for good, and Dad had come to his senses and told the Bad Person to get lost, there would be a new dawn for Colin Hollingshead. On that glorious day, there'd be an empty bed and loads of free shelf-space back at the family home; there'd be a vacancy for a junior gofer and blame-receptacle at Hollingshead & Farren Ltd; there'd be a tree poking up the stairwell with nobody to worry to death. He'd be off, out of it, gone. A flat of his own, a proper job, and with any luck a nice-looking, cheerful girlfriend he could go to the pictures and annoy clock-watching waiters with. One small drift for a wimp, a massive break-up of tectonic plates for Colinkind. Yes, he decided, as he drained his second pint and wiped froth on his cuff. Why not?

He looked up at the clock; half past eight. Options review. Well, he could go home, get moaned at for missing dinner, sit in front of the telly, go to bed. Alternatively, the world was at his feet, ready to thrill, chill and cloy him with an infinity of new experiences.

Qualify that: a rather circumscribed range of experiences that could be sampled without spending money, since he now had a total of twenty-seven pence. The number of things that you can experience in London in the twenty-first century for 27p is still pretty impressive, but offhand Colin couldn't think of many that he fancied. On the short list he was left with were things like a nice walk, a nice sit on a low wall, a nice lean in a doorway, stuff like that. Still, Washington and Jefferson and Ben Franklin had probably had to make their own amusements, and it hadn't broken their resolve. Of course, he reflected as he left the pub, it'd all be different if I had, say for the sake of argument, Fam here with me. Slot her into the equation, and a nice walk, lean or sit on a low wall would have a lot going for it. Now, if only he had her phone number, maybe he could do something about it.

A quiet doorway, the mobile, directory enquiries. Name, please? E. Williams, Mortlake. Could he possibly be more specific, please, since at the last count there were over a hundred and ten E. Williamses in the designated search area. Envy, he clarified, Envy Williams. N. V. Williams, not E. Williams? There's six N. V. Williamses in the designated search area, can you be more specific? Thanks, Colin said, and forget it.

Not to worry; Fam would be at the office tomorrow and he could ask her in person. It'd constitute a significant step, of course, a diplomatic incident signalling a potential outbreak of amicabilities, but a man who's just evicted family tradition, predestined true love and the Devil from his life isn't put off by stuff like that. If she narrowed her eyes and asked him, 'What do you want it for?' he'd simply smile and say, 'So I can ring you up, stupid,' and that'd be that sorted and out of the way. True, he'd known a Colin Hollingshead once who'd have gone all droopy and wimpish at the thought of such a positive course of action. He could almost see him, far away below as he sailed through the clouds of newly accessible possibilities. Screw him, in any case. He belonged in a strange, unreal world of unexplained trees and days spent stuffing envelopes, and Colin was beginning to find it hard to imagine that he'd ever believed in him.

Someone jostled his arm. He opened his mouth for the instinctive automated apology, and stuck like it, face open like a door.

'Sorry,' said the offending passer-by. 'Oh, it's you. We meet again.'

With his jaw still at half-mast, Colin could only nod his head.

He wanted to look away, but his eyes had jammed and wouldn't move.

'You're young Colin,' the passer-by said. 'Allow me to introduce myself. My name's Oscar.'

'M.'

'We didn't have a chance to talk the other night,' said Oscar. 'Since we'll be seeing quite a bit of each other in the future, we ought to establish the foundations of a working relationship. Get to know each other. Bond. Do you agree?'

Colin had once heard on the radio how much the average human head weighs. He couldn't remember the exact figure quoted, but whatever it had been, it was way off. Right now, as he tried to nod his up and down a second time, it definitely weighed at least a ton.

'Excellent. We should have—' Pause, while the nightmare vision calling itself Oscar appeared to be trying to remember something. 'We should drink a large number of alcoholic beverages, play darts, discuss team sports, motor vehicles and women, buy fried fish and sliced potatoes, and possibly urinate together in a shop doorway. That's the correct procedure, isn't it?'

'Love to,' Colin croaked. 'Only—'

Oscar did something with its face that could possibly be interpreted as a frown. 'You have other commitments at this time. I understand. We should reschedule. I can make eighteen-forty-five hours on Thursday the seventh.'

'Eighteen forty-five?'

'Eighteen forty-five precisely. The Devil is in the detail.'

'Right.' Colin tried to shut his mouth but it wouldn't stay closed. 'I mean, I think that's OK, but I'd need to check. I'll call you.'

'Excellent.' A nod, carried out with Prussian precision. 'You can pass a message on to me through your father. If I haven't heard from you by noon tomorrow, I shall contact you. Is that acceptable?'

'M.'

'This was a fortuitous encounter. Be seeing you, kid. Adieu.'

A few footsteps, and the darkness swallowed it. Colin breathed out and flumped hard against the nearest wall.

So much, then, for Paul Revere, Boston Harbour and Yankee Doodle Dandy. Maybe it wasn't going to be that easy after all. Or maybe he'd been more than usually stupid, imagining that he could simply walk out on such a comprehensive assortment of really bad things—

What the hell *was* that?

Since we'll be seeing quite a bit of each other in the future. If Stephen King could put together a half-sentence anything like as scary as that, the talking-book rights alone would be enough to buy him Illinois. As the trembles and the shudders began, Colin tried to remember what it had actually looked like, but nothing came to mind except two eyes. Perfectly ordinary, they'd been, apart from the feeling they gave of being able to see *everything*.

Colin thought of his father. Then he thought about trying to get clever with the likes of *that*. Pulling the proverbial wool over those eyes suddenly didn't seem such a piece of cake any more. (And presumably, that was just the messenger, the gofer: probably, in the diabolical hierarchy, someone of equivalent standing to himself. Somehow, that made the whole thing a lot worse.)

Anyhow, it had cleared up the small matter of where he was going to go next. Back into the pub for a drink stiff as any icicle. No, belay that; he only had twenty-seven pence. He paused on the threshold, and felt something crinkle in his shirt pocket. A twenty-pound note, which he was almost positive hadn't been there before. For some reason, this stroke of un-expected luck made him shudder. For a moment he was locked in a ferocious mental debate. On the one hand, his mother had warned him about accepting money from strange men, and he was pretty sure Oscar could safely be included in that category. On the other hand, twenty quid employed judiciously on licensed premises could make him feel a lot better, if only for a little while. The demon drink, he thought. Humour.

It helped, a little. It didn't make the horror go away, but it took the razor edge off it. Colin followed it up with a repeat prescription, which had no appreciable effect. He thought about that, and reached the conclusion that after a jolt as sobering as that, he'd probably be able to drink for a week before he slurred so much as a preposition.

'Colin?'

Voices calling him again. No wonder Joan of Arc ended up so stroppy. He raised his head and saw a face he sort of recognised. Not that he cared a damn, since he really wasn't in the mood, but at a guess he'd say it belonged to—

'It's me,' said the face. 'Steve Gillett. You remember? St George's Secondary?'

'Steve,' said Colin.

What the face was saying was, of course, true; up to a point, anyhow. Yes, he'd been at school with the face's owner, whose second name (now he came to think of it) was indeed Gillett. But his first name had been Snotty, and Colin was pretty sure that he'd always disliked him intensely, unless of course he was getting him muddled up with someone else.

'Fancy seeing you again,' said Snotty Gillett, sitting down opposite. 'What's it been, nine years?'

'Eight,' Colin said, and added, with the absolute minimum of enthusiasm, 'So, how've you been keeping?'

'Not so bad, thanks. You?'

'Still breathing.'

Snotty seemed to find that painfully funny. He still snorted like a donkey when he laughed. 'You went into your Dad's company, didn't you?'

'That's right,' Colin replied.

'Still there?'

'Just about.'

If anything, that was even funnier. It was so funny that if the game-show comperes ever got to hear of it, they'd send scouts out on camels to find Colin, bearing gold, frankincense and myrrh. 'So,' Colin said, 'what about you?'

'Oh, I'm with Lemon. Joined them eighteen months ago – now I'm area manager.'

'Lemon.'

'Lemon,' Snotty repeated. 'You know, the mobile-phone network?'

'Oh, right.' Colin grinned feebly, aware that his prestige had just foundered. No point being the funniest man on earth if you were still living in the nineteenth century. 'Area manager,' he repeated. 'Not bad.'

Snotty shrugged, a gesture intended to convey modesty; a failure. 'It's a great product,' he said. 'I just stand back and let it sell itself. Oh, hang on a tick.' He turned round in his seat and waved to someone. 'My girlfriend,' he said. 'She's bringing the drinks. Talking of which, what'll you have?'

'I'm fine, thanks.'

'Same again, then.' Snotty stood up and semaphored towards the bar. Apparently two fingers of the left hand uplifted while the right hand pats the top of the head is the international code for a large Scotch. 'So,' Snotty went on. 'Married?'

Colin shook his head.

'Going steady?'

'No.'

'Right, still playing the field.' Snotty grinned, and Colin ached for an apple to stick in his mouth 'See anything of the old gang?'

Colin was about to shake his head when he caught sight of someone over Snotty's shoulder. She was carrying a tray, on which rested a pint of lager, something colourful with fruit in it and (believe it or not) a double whisky. An echo sounded inside Colin's head; Snotty's voice, saying *my girlfriend*.

'Minnie, this is an old mate of mine from school, Colin Hollingshead. Colin, Minnie Williams.'

The penny dropping; the tinkle as it pitched. Fa*min*. Minnie.

She said hello. The way she said it, the word had volume, colour and tone. What a nice surprise, it said.

The other penny dropping, clunk. 'Of course,' Snotty

exclaimed, 'Hollingshead and *Farren*. That's where you're working, right?'

She nodded, but she wasn't looking at Snotty. She was also smiling.

There ought to be a dictionary of smiles; somewhere you can look them up and find out what they mean. It'd be a genuine service to humanity, but instead there're just *Jane's Fighting Ships* and the *Observer Book of British Birds*, useless stuff like that. In the absence of a definitive reference, the only option is a mixture of experience and intuition. Even so. If that smile didn't mean, *Oh good, maybe this evening won't be such a drag after all*, Colin was prepared to comb the local charity shops for a grey fedora and eat it.

As soon as he'd reached that conclusion, Colin was immediately at a complete loss for words. Luckily, though, Snotty seemed to regard a word driven in edgeways as an affront to his alpha-male status. He talked – about the old days at school, the mobile-phone industry, scandalous examples of bad driving he'd recently witnessed – and seemed not to notice that his audience wasn't listening. In fact, they were as lost to him as the cities of the Incas, and the fool was too busy with the virtues of the latest Nokia even to notice. There was something faintly unreal about it; Minnie was smiling at Colin and he was smiling back, while the sound of poor old Snotty's voice hung in the background like the faint whisper of a distant waterfall.

Abruptly, in mid-sentence, Snotty stood up and said, 'Same again?' They nodded; he went away. Colin took a deep breath, but she spoke first.

'Was he that boring at school?' she said.

'Actually, no,' Colin replied. 'As I recall, he was more on the jerk side of things. Mind you, we had some very boring teachers, which must be where he got the inspiration from.'

She smiled, a bit; and if he wasn't the funniest man in the world any more, it really didn't matter. 'Did he say I'm his girlfriend?'

'Yes.' Pause. 'An exaggeration?'

'Too bloody right.' She frowned. 'But at the moment it's go out with him or stay home with the family.' Shrug. 'I thought of signing up for Conversational Spanish instead, but classes don't start till the spring.'

'Ah. Do you like Spain?'

'Not much.'

'I see. Well, in that case—'

Colin contemplated writing down Fam's phone number on a beermat, but there didn't seem any point. Its digits were burnt into his heart and mind like a brand on a Texan steer. He was as likely to forget it on the way home as Moses would have been to forget the Fifth Commandment on reaching the bottom of Mount Sinai.

In a way, the evening turned out something like that scenario he'd been toying with earlier: *so wrapped up in talking that we lost track of time.* It would've been closer to the model if all the talking hadn't been done by Snotty Gillett, but never mind; near enough for country music, as his Uncle Phil insufferably said. Chucking-out time came by; they went three separate ways. 'See you in the morning,' she said, and if they'd been in Berkeley Square instead of Mortlake he could've paused to listen to the nightingale. Instead, when she'd gone, he lifted his head a little, looked at the sky and said, 'Thanks,' just in case anybody was listening; then he recited a string of eleven numbers, which made all the difference.

Still chanting integers softly to the moon, Colin started to walk home. At the corner of the street, someone stepped out of the shadows in front of him, barred his way and said, 'Finally.' It was what's-her-name, Connie Schwartz-Alberich.

'What are you—?' he started to ask.

'Have you got any idea how long I've been standing here waiting for you?' she said, sounding more than a little like his mother.

'Sorry.'

Connie sighed 'Well,' she said, 'never mind about that now,' and stabbed him in the throat with a pair of nail scissors.

CHAPTER NINE

He was the little Aberdeen terrier in a Monopoly set, and he was scampering round the board. It wasn't the conventional format. Instead of Piccadilly and Edgware Road and Fenchurch Street station, the squares were pictures, which moved. As he skipped over one, he saw a woman in a hospital bed holding a baby; the next one was a toddler wobbling awkwardly across a carpet; two squares further on was a small boy arriving at a school gate; the school buildings were squat and green, and he realised that they looked just like the Monopoly houses that make a square very expensive to land on. He was counting as he ran, two, three, four; somehow he knew that he had six squares still to go. He glanced down, and saw himself standing at a bench next to a big three-phase grinder and polisher. Rang a bell; he was pretty sure he'd just seen his first day at work. Nine, ten – he hopped and, as he was about to land, looked down. Not good. There below him was a deep rectangular hole, into which four men in black were lowering an instantly recognisable box, with a brass name-plate and handles. Oh, he thought; then his paws touched down, and he found that he wasn't in the hole after all, but standing off to one side on an L-shaped sort of patio thing made up of square stone slabs, painted on which he could see the words:

JUST VISITING

So that was all right, presumably. He didn't need to lean forward and peer at the brass plate to know whose coffin it was. Late for my own funeral, he muttered to himself. Very droll.

At any rate, he wasn't an Aberdeen terrier any more. Neither, he realised with a slight start, was he Colin Hollingshead. Nothing handy that he could see his face in, but the hands, arms, feet, stomach he appeared to be wearing weren't his own; the scar on the back of his right hand, for example, where he'd cut himself on a jagged Coke-can edge when he was six, quite visibly wasn't there. The fingers were longer, their nails squarer. Who am I? he wondered. Just out of curiosity, he added.

'Finally,' said Connie Schwartz-Alberich, standing beside him. 'Have you got any idea how long I've been standing here waiting for you?'

He frowned. 'You said that just now.'

'That's right, I did.'

'And then you stabbed me.'

'Yes,' she said. She was wiping a pair of nail scissors on a bit of tissue.

'And—' He cast his mind back. Memory like a tea bag, but he could dimly recall . . . 'And I died,' he said. 'I'm dead.'

She clicked her tongue. 'No, just visiting,' she said. 'Can't you read?'

'Sorry.' Something possessed him to reach out, to see if his hand could pass beyond the paved L-shape into the rest of the square. 'Stop that,' she ordered sharply, and he drew it back again. Not a good idea, apparently.

'Why did you stab me?' he asked.

'Ah.' Connie pulled a face as she dropped the scissors into her bag and closed the clasp with a snap. 'D'you want the full technobabble or the abbreviated layman's version?'

'The second one, please.'

She smiled at him. 'For your own good,' she said.

'Ah.'

'Don't worry about it,' she said, and she made a gesture that would've been very reassuring in a rather less disturbing context. 'Just stay on the concrete slabs and you'll be fine.' She was looking at her watch. 'Bloody Shumway,' she was muttering. 'No idea of time. Not,' she added, 'that time has any meaning here, but it's the principle. Punctuality is the politeness of princes, and all that.'

He frowned. 'Who's Shumway?'

'Oh, a colleague of mine from work. He's supposed to meet us here. I suppose he thought he might as well do the banking first and then come straight on here instead of going back to the office. Two birds with one stone.' She grinned. 'No pun intended.'

'What?' Colin asked; and a short man in very thick-lensed glasses materialised beside him. In his left hand was a big, sharp-edged chunk of flint. There was blood on it.

'Sorry,' he said. 'Been here long?'

'Long enough,' Connie sighed. 'I was starting to think you hadn't got my text.'

'I did the banking on the way.'

'Ah. Thought that must be it. Anyhow, you're here now. Colin Hollingshead, Benny Shumway.'

The short man gave Colin a perfunctory nod and said 'Pleased to meet you.' Colin had an idea that he was probably exaggerating. 'She'll be along any minute,' he added. 'She's the racing car.'

A second or two of that particularly awkward silence you get when you're with a couple of strangers waiting for someone or something; then there was a screech of brakes, and a fine example of a late-1930s Bugatti sports car pulled up a couple of inches short of Colin's feet. It revved its engine, switched off and turned into Cassie Clay.

She wasn't looking her best. For one thing, her hair was soaked with blood, and bright red wasn't her colour. She looked round, saw the open grave, noticed Mr Shumway and turned on him ferociously.

'You hit me,' she said. 'With a rock.'

Mr Shumway grinned sheepishly. 'I was just explaining,' he said. 'Two birds with one – never mind,' he added. 'It's no good if you've got to explain it.'

A thought crossed Cassie's mind; if her expression was anything to go by, not a happy one. 'You killed me,' she said.

'I've just been through all that,' Connie Schwartz-Alberich said wearily. 'Look at the ground, dear.'

Cassie looked down. 'Oh,' she said; and then: 'Connie? What're you doing here? And why are those men over there burying me?'

'Cassie, dear—'

'And what's *happened to* me?' Cassie went on, her voice sharp with panic. 'This isn't my body. What've you—?'

'Funkhausen's Loop,' muttered Benny Shumway.

'Oh.' Whatever Funkhausen's Loop was, she'd heard of it and it calmed her down a bit. 'You might've warned me,' she said.

But Connie shook her head. 'You know better than that,' she said. 'Doesn't work if you're expecting it.' She turned to face Colin. 'I'm forgetting my manners,' she said. 'Funkhausen's Loop is magic,' she went on. 'I won't give you the technical stuff because you won't understand it, but basically it's a procedure whereby you can get outside your life for a few minutes and take a look at it.'

Colin scowled at her. 'Oh please,' he said. 'Now you're talking like Oprah.'

'Who?' Connie shrugged. 'Never mind. The point is, this is a tricky enough procedure at the best of times. Having you along – no disrespect, but you not being, well, one of us, makes it harder still. So, if it's all the same to you, let's get on with it.'

'Fine,' Colin muttered. 'Just tell me I get to come back to life again when all this is over.'

'Well.' Connie gave him a thin smile. 'Fingers crossed. Anyhow, it works like this. The Loop shows you a selection of significant moments from your various lives. In order to get a good look at the particular one you're interested in—'

'Hang on,' Colin interrupted. 'Did you say *lives*?'

'Yes. In order to get the one you want, you have to keep throwing dice and moving round and round the board till you land on the—'

'Lives plural?'

'Yes. Look, if you keep interrupting, I'll lose the thread and then we'll all be in the smelly. Right: round and round the board you go, and when you've found the right square, there you are. That's about it, really; other than that, normal game rules apply. Passing Go is good, Chance cards are usually not your friend, and if you wind up back on this square, do try and keep to the paving stones, otherwise it could be a bit awkward. All right? Who's got the dice? Benny?'

'Just a second,' Cassie interrupted. 'Why exactly are we doing this?'

Connie clicked her tongue. 'To find out what's been playing games with the two of you, of course,' she said. 'And while I think of it, a few words of thanks wouldn't be entirely out of place, don't you think? After all, Benny and I've been to a lot of trouble setting this up.'

'Thanks,' Cassie snapped. 'All right, so what're we supposed to be looking out for?'

'I don't know, do I? They're your lives.'

'But—' Cassie protested as Benny Shumway pressed two dice into her hand, folded her fingers round them and waggled her wrist up and down until she dropped the dice on the ground.

'Jammy,' Connie said, 'double six. Means you get two goes.'

Before Cassie could say another word, she was picked up off her feet, as if by a sudden sharp gust of wind, and carried away down the flickering avenue of pictures. Just when Colin was sure that she'd be blown off the board into the shapeless darkness beyond she stopped dead, windmilled her arms frantically for a moment, and looked down at her feet.

'Can you see—' Connie asked nervously.

'From this distance?' Benny Shumway replied. 'No chance.'

The gust of wind caught Cassie again, and again she stopped

as though she'd collided with a plate glass window and looked down. Then she was lifted off her feet and swept back.

'Go back three squares,' Benny explained. 'Very literal-minded man, Funkhausen.'

Colin opened his mouth to say something, but Benny had squeezed the dice into his hand. He felt his wrist twitch and his fingers open. 'A four and a two,' Connie told him. 'Try and ride with the—'

It was as though an invisible giant had pinched his head between finger and thumb and lifted him off the ground. He landed, managed to stagger back without falling, and looked down.

He saw himself. How he knew that, he had no idea, because he looked quite different. For one thing, he was taller, slim, athletic, with thick curly blond hair; also he was in fancy dress, something sort of medieval involving tight tights and a bright red tunic. Furthermore he was on a horse (never been on a horse in his life) and there was a bird sitting on the side of his right hand. Yuck, he thought, because he wasn't fond of animals and birds made him nervous. He didn't like the way they flapped their wings in your face, and he was afraid of the sharp bits, like beaks and claws. This bird was particularly scary; it was some kind of hawk, and it had small, round, mad-looking yellow eyes with a black dot for a pupil. But Fancy-Dress Him didn't seem to be worried at all; his attention was occupied elsewhere. Colin followed his line of sight and saw a female of some description, also on a horse, though unencumbered by large birds. She was swathed from head to foot in what looked like curtain material with a tall dunce's-cap sort of hat on her head. He could just make out her face in among all the cloth and net curtain. Nice-looking woman, smiling at him. He was saying something to her, but for some reason he was talking in a strange foreign language—

'French,' said Benny Shumway.

'How did you get here?' Colin demanded, looking round. There was nobody there.

'I didn't,' Benny's voice explained. 'Let's just say I'm with you in spirit. Want me to translate?'

'What? Oh, right. Yes.'

He expected to hear Benny doing a not-quite-simultaneous translation, like the people with headphones at the United Nations. Instead, he heard the woman's voice but now she was talking ordinary English, with a sort of Kenneth-Branagh-directs-Shakespeare accent.

'Is she heavy to carry?' she said.

'Not really,' Fancy-Dress Colin replied, and Colin was pretty sure he was lying. 'I'll fly her in a moment, if you like.'

'Yes, please. I've never seen a real gyrfalcon working.'

'You'll have to bear with me a second. She's gripping so tight, I think my arm's gone to sleep.'

– Whereupon the wind caught him again and threw him up into the air. *Five and a three,* whispered Benny's voice in his ear. Colin's feet hit the ground, sending a stab of jarring pain up his shins into his knees.

He looked down. CHANCE, said the marble slabs under his feet. He felt something in his hand that hadn't been there a split second earlier.

It was just a rectangular pink card, with his name printed in the centre. He frowned and turned it over.

Get out of death free.

Colin had his faults, but gift-horse dentistry wasn't one of them. He poked the card into his top pocket, and the wind caught him again. Please, no more animals or birds, he thought; then the slam, the wobble, the glance downwards.

Only goes to show how short-sighted he'd been, not paying attention in history. True, he'd salvaged that scrap about the American War of Independence, but that was more or less it. The folly of his neglect came home to him as he stared at the two people in front of him. He knew who one of them was, the man in the funny coat like a dressing gown, but the girl in the enormous dress was a total stranger. She was very odd; in fact, they both were, because neither of them was much older than him, but they were both wearing white wigs. She was holding a fan, though it wasn't particularly warm. This time they weren't alone. They were in a huge room along with lots of other people in funny clothes and wigs; music was playing, and everybody was moving about. Colin supposed you could call it dancing, though that was a subject he knew even less about than history. She was smiling at him; he seemed to be having to concentrate on where he was putting his feet. She did a sort of low curtsy; he stumbled, barged into her and trod on her toe. He didn't hear what she said to him, because the wind got up and tore him away, but he reckoned he could probably guess the gist of it.

The next time Colin landed, he found himself in some sort of hut. No, he was being unfair, it just about counted as a house, because the walls were solid and faced with plaster; there was one window with no glass in it, and the floor was planks covered with dried reeds. There was a cow in the doorway, looking at him and swishing its tail. He saw himself come in from another room; he was limping, and when he dropped into the chair (there was only one) he lifted his knee and started rubbing his foot through the frayed woollen stocking he had on. Only a short stop, that one; next he landed in the middle of a really old-fashioned-looking pub: very dark (no proper lights, just candles stuck in bottles on the tables) and crowded with people dressed like characters in the Dickens serials they used to put on at the weekends when he was a kid. It took him a while to pick himself out of the crowd. He was sitting next to a girl in a big, wide hat with a rather grubby feather sticking out of it. He said something – too far away to make out the words over the background noise – and the girl stood up. He stood up too; she smacked him across the face, and the sound of palm on cheek was so loud that, for a moment, everybody in the pub turned round to stare. He staggered, grabbed at the table – various cheers and general laughter – put his weight on his back foot which crumpled up under him, and collapsed in a heap on the floor. A big, scruffy-looking dog came across and licked his face. All in all, Colin was glad to be blown away from that one.

There were others, nearly all of them involving him and a girl, and in every single one he seemed to have something wrong with his legs or feet. The last one was that day in St Mary Axe, when he'd come in to pick up the file with the contract and everything. It played out more or less as he remembered it; then once again he was a fly swatted against a windscreen, only this time he did lose his balance and fall over.

'Let me guess,' said Benny's voice over his head. 'Pins and needles?'

'Yes, actually.' Colin leaned forward and massaged his foot. 'How did you—? Oh, right. You've been watching.'

Benny's legs materialised in front of him, and Colin realised he was back on the L-shaped pavement. The funeral was still going on; a vicar was talking, and the mourners – not very many of them, he noticed – were yawning and glancing sideways at their watches.

'Sort of,' Benny said, bending forward and offering him a hand to help himself up by. 'Only got the gist of it, but at least now there's a pattern emerging.'

'Is there?' Colin asked, as Benny hauled him to his feet. The left one sent a fireworks display up the nerves of his legs, and he nearly went down again. Benny caught him before he could topple into his own grave.

'Well, yes,' Benny said. 'Didn't you notice? Every time you're about to get somewhere with Cassie – with the girl, I mean – your leg goes to sleep or your foot gets pins and needles, and then it all goes down the toilet. Either she slugs you and flounces off, or she calls you names, or the other way round. If that's a coincidence, I'm Bill Clinton.'

'Yes, all right,' Colin mumbled. 'But what is all this? Who are all these people I've been looking at?' A small landmine of resentment blew up inside his head, and he yelled, 'Why does nobody ever *explain* anything?'

Benny laughed. 'You don't get it? Oh well.' Suddenly Colin felt the dice back in his hand. He tried to drop them before Benny could shake his hand, but he was too late.

This time the giant unseen hand dropped him on a pink square. Which was how he rationalised it later. At the time he guessed that he must be on Mars, because in every direction as far as the eye could see there was nothing but red dusty plateau under a red sky. It was a bit like the sets in the original *Star Trek*, but without the foam rocks.

No pins and needles this time, which was a relief. To make sure, Colin glanced down at his feet and saw he was standing on a black letter C. There were other letters, but the wind had blown pink dust over them, partly covering them so he couldn't make them out.

'Fine,' he said aloud. 'Is it my go again yet?'

A gust of breeze fluttered a small piece of card past his nose. He grabbed at it reflexively, like a cat, and caught it. It said:

GO BACK TO WHERE YOU BELONG

Charming, he thought; I've only been here two seconds and already I'm getting hate mail from the Martian National Party. He opened his fingers and let the card flutter away; at which point— No rush of wind or invisible fingers squeezing his head like a spot this time. Instead, it was as though he'd been there all along, and everything else – Funkhausen's Loop, the past few weeks, his life in Mortlake, Hollingshead & Farren – was just a dream or a funny five minutes. He was sitting down, which was nice, but he didn't recognise the setting, even though it was so very familiar—

Desk. Colin leaned forward in his posh merchant-prince super-duper office chair and pulled open the top drawer. He'd had a funny feeling he'd know what was inside it, and it turned out he was right. Not that any of the stuff in the drawer was exciting or out of the way: no office bottle, pearl-handled .45, diamond necklace. Instead there was a selection of capless biros, some broken pencils, a mélange of paper clips, rubbers, treasury tags, blocks of staples, AAA batteries, rubber bands and tapes for a pocket dictating machine. He slid the drawer closed and looked at the desktop. Couldn't have been any desk he'd ever had responsibility for, since it was neat, tidy and not inches deep in letters that should've been answered weeks ago. Instead, there were two telephones (one red, one green), a keyboard and VDU (blank) and a clipboard with a questionnaire of some kind clipped to it. He frowned and looked at the first question.

1. What do you feel has been your most significant achievement over the past 6 months?

Um, he thought. He'd have explored the theme further, only the red phone rang.

'He's here,' said a female voice. 'Shall I send him in?'

Colin heard himself say 'Yes,' and the office vanished.

It turned into a tea shop, of all things. He was sitting at a table with a neat white tablecloth, and directly in front of him was a blue and white teacup, a brown teapot, a plate of toasted teacakes and a sugar bowl. On the other side of that lot was a girl. She was looking at him.

'Well?' she said.

'I don't know what to say,' he heard his voice reply; and for once in this bizarre experience, he couldn't have put it better himself.

'Really.' He got the impression he'd just given the wrong answer. 'So that's it, then, is it?'

A small part of Colin felt a pang of utterly sincere sympathy for Dr Sam Beckett. The rest of him said, 'I don't know. I suppose it's up to you, isn't it?'

That made matters worse, apparently. The girl (who wasn't anybody he knew: heart-shaped face, high cheekbones, pale blue eyes, thin mouth, mousy hair) sighed and looked away. 'You always do this,' she said, 'it's just not fair. I don't think I can go through it all again, I'm sorry.'

'It's not me, it's you,' he said. 'I don't know, maybe it really would be all for the best.'

'Fine.' She was about to stand up, but then she stopped. Froze, more like. It was as though someone had pressed the pause button; and there on the tablecloth, between the sugar bowl and the teacake plate, was a very small man, apparently dressed as a garden gnome.

Colin looked again, just to make sure. Yes. Tall floppy red hat, oversize baggy trousers held up by braces, big black boots, even the long white beard. He wasn't, however, holding a fishing rod or a spade. Instead, he had a dear little clipboard, with a sheet of paper clipped to it, and a sweet little ballpoint pen.

'Well?' said the little man.

'You're a gnome,' Colin said.

He hadn't meant to. Even he wasn't in the habit of being quite so—

'Yup,' the little man replied.

'I didn't mean to say that.'

Grin, just visible through groves of white beard. 'Nope. But this is me, remember? To whom all desires are known, and from whom no secrets are hid.' He chuckled. 'That's the Bible or something,' he said. 'You remember it from morning prayers at assembly.' He shook his head, and the cute little red hat tilted a little over one eye. 'You're making a right pig's ear of this, aren't you?'

'Yes,' Colin said. 'But maybe it's for the best. I mean—'

'You're still crazy about her.'

'Of course. But she's so bloody—'

'*Complicated.*' The gnome sighed, and the exhalation set the fine down of his moustache dancing. 'They all are, kiddo. It's the free curse hidden at the bottom of the packet of human existence. Why, nobody knows. Pursuit, date, dinner, chat, bed, the same repeated often enough, you move in or she moves in, and suddenly clang, watch out for the falling portcullis.' He ticked a box on his form. 'I've always found it highly significant that *commit* is also the word they use for sending someone to a mental institution because, like it says on the fridge magnets, you don't have to be mad to be here, but—'

'No,' Colin protested, surprising himself with his own vehemence. 'That's not me at all. I really do—'

'Love her, all grown-up and shipshape, and everything should be fine because she feels the same way about you, so where's the problem? You just don't understand what the matter is.'

'That's right,' Colin said. 'But she seems to—'

'Think you understand perfectly well, and you're just pretending not to because you're an insensitive git. Now, don't you wish you'd paid more attention in telepathy when you were at school?'

Colin sighed. 'No,' he said, 'you're still missing the point. I *do* understand, and I've done everything she wanted, and still—'

'Exactly.' The little man shrugged, and the left shoulder-strap of his braces slipped a little further down his bicep. 'And you've reached the point where you're thinking, is it really worth it? Really? I mean, we started off all right, the sex was brilliant, she likes action-adventure movies and she can cook, and then suddenly it started to fall apart and melt like a Dali watch; and surely there comes a time when you've got to cut your losses and move on.'

'*No.*' Colin looked round quickly to see if people were staring, because he hadn't meant to shout quite so loudly. But the rest of the tea shop was still frame-frozen. 'Look, it's not like that. I'm not like that. Damn it, this really is the genuine article, far as I'm concerned. I believe – more than that, I bloody well know—'

'That you're soulmates,' the little man said, with a slight nod. 'That one-in-a-million thing, your actual true love, where it gets to the point where you can't tell any more where you end and she begins, and what's more you don't care about knowing, you don't want to know. Ah.' He sighed, fished in his button-down pocket, took out a darling little clay pipe, caught sight of the No Smoking notice, frowned and put it away again. 'You know what Plato says, of course.'

'No,' Colin said. 'Fuck Plato. And just shut up a moment while I explain. You keep on—'

'Putting words in your mouth.'

'Yes.'

'I know.'

'Then stop doing it.' Colin waited, but the little man didn't say anything. 'Thank you. Oh, screw it, now I've—'

'Forgotten what you were going to say.'

'No. Listen.' Colin took a deep breath. 'It was all going perfectly,' he said. 'We met, right. At first we took it a bit slow, not wanting to rush in for fear we'd spoil it, but before long everything just sort of fell into place, and there we were. It was so perfect. It was glorious. It was *fun*.' Colin scowled; dimly, right at the back of his mind among the old shoes, boxed-up Christmas decorations and broken trouser presses, he could remember how glorious it had been. 'It made sense,' he said, 'and we never had those stupid rows or those tense sulks or any of that stuff. It was like we could see all the problems coming a mile off, when everybody else couldn't see them and walked straight into them; but we'd just look at each other and say "Let's not do that," and we didn't, and that was fine. It was—'

'Perfect.'

'I won't warn you again,' Colin growled. 'But yes, it was perfect. Until a month ago. And then, quite suddenly—'

He stopped. The little man looked at him, and nodded. 'It's all right,' Colin muttered, 'you can say it.'

'No need.' The little man smirked at him. 'I know.'

'It's like—' Colin thought for a moment. 'It's like the fairy story about the boy who flew too near the sun, and the wax holding his wings together melted, and down he came.'

The little man nodded. 'Great story, that,' he said. 'Seminal.'

'And now look at us,' Colin went on, and he looked across the table at the girl, frozen solid in the act of beginning to stand up. 'It's all falling apart, and I simply don't know *why*.'

The little man clicked his tongue. 'It's like you said just now,' he replied. 'Why does nobody ever explain anything?'

'That's right.' Colin looked the little man in his funny little eye. 'Well?'

'Your problem,' the little man said, and he was ticking boxes on his clipboard, 'is that you don't ask yourself the right questions. If you don't do that—' He shrugged. 'I mean,' he went on, 'technology and magic and stuff can only take you so far. Take Funkhausen's Loop, for example. You can lead a horse to water, right? But you can't make it –' He was fading; Colin could see the congealed butter on the surface of the teacake right through his sweet little tummy '– think. But you've got the answer, so all you need to do is work back from—'

He vanished, and the girl stood up. 'Fine,' she said. 'I'll go, then.'

Colin looked up at her. 'Did you just see a gnome?' he asked.
'A what?'
'A gnome. Like in gardens. On the table, right there.'
'What the hell are you talking about?'
'Sorry.' He frowned, wondering what on earth had possessed him to start babbling about gnomes. 'Look, please sit down and we can talk about this.'

'No, sorry.' She started to walk away. She'd gone three yards, four, five; he knew, as though he'd looked it up in a book of tables and specifications, that if he let her get ten yards away before he stood up and went after her, it'd be too late and that'd be that. He had five yards left; she had a head start. He jumped up, and found that his left leg had gone to sleep.

Colin got a whole yard before keeling over, grabbing at the table for support, yanking off the tablecloth and subsiding in a minor landslide of crockery and table-linen. The noise was deafening, but she didn't hear it; she'd gone out through the door into the street.

On the pavement outside the tea shop, she met a little man. He was about ten inches high, and he was wearing a tall red floppy hat and other eccentric garments. Behind him, a car stopped dead, as though someone had just pressed the pause button.

'Well?' he said.
Cassie shrugged. 'Search me,' she replied. 'Was that him?'
The gnome nodded. 'That was him. The first him.'
'Really.' She frowned. 'You surprise me.'
'Not your type.'
'Frankly, no.'
The gnome grinned. 'And he thinks *he*'s superficial. Never

mind. Take it from me, that was him. Actually, you should see yourself. That'd sort of put it in perspective.'

A small mirror materialised in Cassie's hand. She looked in it, taking particular note of the mousy hair and the thin mouth. 'I take your point,' she said. 'But anyway, I think I see now. We were in love—'

'You were.' The gnome grinned; she scowled. 'Absolutely besotted. Embarrassed the hell out of your friends.'

'And then something went—'

'Wrong, but neither of you had a clue what it could possibly be. You'd never—'

'Had any of those problems,' Cassie remembered. 'We didn't do issues, we used to say.'

'A really nauseating phrase, let me point out,' the gnome said. 'So when everything started to come unstuck—'

'You know,' Cassie said, 'it was just like Icarus, in Greek mythology, when he flew too close to the— Sorry,' she added irritably, 'am I boring you?'

The gnome muffled his yawn with his sleeve. 'Sorry,' he said. 'Go on.'

'I just couldn't understand,' she said. 'Suddenly there was this terrible problem; a fatal exception has taken place and this program will be closed down. And I simply—'

'Couldn't make head nor tail of it. Couldn't see why he was being like that. There was no reason.'

'It just happened.' Cassie frowned. 'Things don't just happen, though, do they?'

The gnome winked at her. 'I should cocoa,' he said.

'So there has to be—'

'Quite.' The gnome was growing transparent; she could read the frozen car's number plate through his funny little head. 'I'll send you my bill.'

'All right.' Cassie nodded. 'Thanks, Mr Funkhausen.'

'My pleasure, Ms Clay,' the gnome replied, and vanished.

CHAPTER TEN

Colin woke up and fumbled for the alarm clock.

Another morning. The usual status check; he had a bit of a headache – reasonable enough, since he remembered having indulged in strong drink the previous evening – and one hell of a sore throat. A cold on its way. What fun.

Another day at the office, and then he remembered. She'd be on reception. She wasn't Snotty Gillett's girlfriend after all. She'd said 'See you in the morning' when they'd all left the pub last night. Joy unbounded.

And then he remembered. He'd gone to the pub to meet the strange woman from JWW. When he left it, he'd bumped into that – that whatever, the thing that had barged into his room that night, and hadn't there been something about the two of them having a lads' night out, just him and *it*, getting to know each other better? And then he'd had that extraordinary dream, where the strange woman had stabbed him and he'd—

Yes, he remembered, but just before she said 'See you in the morning,' she'd given him her phone number. Joy still unbounded, and screw all the weird stuff.

Her phone number, which he'd forgotten. Horror.

'Morning,' she practically sang at him as he stumbled through the door. 'Oh, and your Dad's been looking for you.'

'Ah,' Colin said.

'Meeting, in the boardroom,' she said. 'He seemed a bit put out that he couldn't find you earlier.'

A bit put out. Right. 'Anyone in there with him?'

A slight frown on that delightful face. 'There was a blonde woman called to see him, nine sharp.' She said the word *blonde* with a certain inflection, like the clerk of the court reading out charges – blonde with intent to cause grievous emotional harm – and he was wondering about that when she added: 'She asked if you were in so she could have a word with you first, but I told her you weren't in yet.'

'Oh, right.' Just a trace of hesitation, as though scouring his mind for a long-buried memory. 'Was she from J. W. Wells? Clay, I think her name is.'

'Mphm.'

'Oh, *her*,' Colin said, and maybe he went a bit overboard on the heavy sigh 'Dreadful woman,' he added. 'Boring. Still—' He shrugged. 'Better get on and get it over with, I suppose.' Pause. Full eye contact. Deep breath. 'Are you doing anything for lunch?'

'No.'

'Only, I was going to head into town, there's a new sort of Italian place I noticed a couple of days ago—'

'Yes, love to,' she said, cutting him off in mid-dither. And she smiled. 'Go on,' she added, 'you'll be late.'

Up the stairs two at a time; offbeat combination of the spring in the step that comes from a date duly secured and terror at the thought of being late for the meeting. Colin stopped outside the boardroom door and listened, but he could only hear Dad's booming drone. He knocked and went in.

'At bloody last,' his father said. But Colin was too preoccupied to notice or care what sort of mood the old sod was in. Nor was he particularly interested in Cassie, sitting next to the old man, writing something on a big pad of A4 paper. Instead, his attention was monopolised by—

'I gather you've met Oscar,' Dad said, nodding in its direction. 'And Miss Clay, from J. W. Wells.'

Only then did he notice that Cassie was trying to establish non-verbal communication with him; she was opening her eyes wide, twitching her head sideways, mouthing something at him, but he couldn't begin to take any of it in. He sat down, as far away from Oscar as he could get.

'Anyway.' Dad turned away from him and looked down at the papers in front of him. Colin recognised the contract. 'I think we can say that's all pretty well sorted; so, if Miss Clay wouldn't mind being the witness, we can all crack on and get this thing signed.'

Colin opened his mouth, but nothing came out. What with one thing and another, he'd let the whole ghastly soul-selling business slip his mind. After all, hadn't Cassie said she thought she'd be able to derail the procedure before it got to this point? He'd taken that as permission to let it slither down his list of priorities and things to lie awake at night shuddering about; and now here it was, happening, in spite of everything. It wasn't fair; it was an ambush, a sneak attack when his back was turned, and it had caught him completely unprepared. Even so, he opened his mouth to start yelling. Then he saw the pen in his father's hand.

Oh, he thought.

There's always a sort of kids-party-game feel to the signing of a legal document, as it gets passed round like the parcel, and everybody has to have a go. When it was his turn, Colin couldn't resist sneaking a look to see what Oscar's signature looked like, but there wasn't one. Instead there was a circular emblem embossed into the paper, slightly discoloured by scorch marks. He slid the paper back across the table, and Cassie signed both copies for the third time. Dad took one of them and slid it into the folder open in front of him. Oscar took the other copy, and Colin looked away to avoid seeing what it did with it. Then there was a scraping of chairs on the polished wood floor. Oscar nodded to him as it passed, which made him feel sick. Dad said

'Thanks for coming' to Cassie in a mildly distracted tone of voice; he was going to show Oscar something in the factory, apparently. Cassie, on the other hand, was taking an inordinate length of time packing her papers and pens and whatever into her briefcase.

'I need to talk to you,' she hissed, as soon as Dad and the thing were safely out of the room.

'What?'

'We need to talk,' she said. 'About last night.'

'What?' Colin shook his head, as though trying to get rid of the turmoil inside his head by sheer centrifugal force. 'You promised me,' he burst out. 'You promised you'd find a way of stopping it.'

That wasn't what she wanted to talk about. 'I did no such thing,' she snapped defensively. 'I said I'd see if there was anything I could do. But then I found out they'd been talking direct to each other, cutting me out, so—' She shrugged. 'I'm sorry.'

'You're sorry,' Colin repeated savagely. 'My Dad has just sold his soul to – to *that thing*, and you're sorry.'

'Yes.' Cassie's forehead tightened into a warning frown. 'I'm sorry, all right? Now, can we talk about—?'

'No.' He stopped. 'What do you mean, last night? What's any of that got to do with you?'

Her eyes widened, as though he'd just deliberately poured a cup of tea down the front of her blouse. 'What's that supposed to mean?'

'I mean—' Stop; think. 'Well, some stuff happened to me last night, sure, but I don't remember you coming into it. All right, I did have a drink with a really strange woman from your office, Connie something; and then I ran into, um, a couple of old friends in the pub. And then I went home. And yes, I had a bloody funny dream, about being stabbed and dying and being reborn as a—'

'Yes?'

'You were in it,' he said slowly. 'You were in my dreams.'

'Halle-bloody-lujah,' Cassie said sharply. 'Yes, that's right.

Only it wasn't a dream. I know, because I was there too. I was the racing car, and you were the little dog.'

'My God.' For a moment, a sound outside the door snagged Colin's attention; he was afraid it might be his Dad coming back, with or without Oscar. But the door didn't open, so he went on:

'What d'you mean, *real*? It couldn't have actually happened, for crying out loud. I was a dog. I saw my own funeral. That's not—'

'It's called Funkhausen's Loop,' she interrupted briskly. 'It's a magical technique for investigating conditions like avatar slip and Ustinov's Syndrome.'

Colin groaned aloud. 'Could you maybe make a special effort and speak English for a change? Ustinov's Syndrome?'

'Sorry.' Cassie frowned slightly. 'I forgot. Basically, it's about things to do with time; but not like a time machine or anything. It's breakdowns and anomalies in your own temporal network. In this case,' she added, with just a trace of an apologetic simper, 'reincarnation. Funkhausen's Loop means that you can sneak a look at your previous existences, to see if there's feedback or bleedthrough or anything like that.'

'You're doing it again,' Colin protested angrily. 'Bleed-through?'

She closed her eyes and opened them again. He guessed it was her version of counting to ten. 'Where stuff from a previous life seeps through into this one and messes things up. Which is what's happening to us, apparently.'

It was, Colin decided, one hell of a bad time to have a thick head, not to mention savage indigestion and pins and needles in his left leg. 'Is it?' he said.

'Yes. Look, don't you remember? We were people in the Middle Ages, on horseback; you were holding a hawk. And then we were sort of in Jane Austen's time, and—'

Now he came to think of it, yes. 'And peasants,' he interrupted. 'There was a cow inside the house,' he added, 'which is simply gross.'

'That's right.' Cassie sounded relieved. 'Those were flashbacks from previous incarnations. We knew each other in past lives. In fact, we were—' She hesitated. 'But it never worked out,' she went on. 'Something always screwed us up, but we never knew what it was. Things would be going along just fine, and then suddenly we'd find we couldn't carry on any more and we split up.' She was looking at him. 'You know what that makes us?' She had to brace herself to say the next bit. 'Time-crossed lovers.'

Oink, Colin thought. 'You what?'

'Think about it, for pity's sake,' she snapped. 'You *do* know basic reincarnation theory, don't you?'

'No.'

Cassie made a small noise; a cross between the roar of a Spanish bull and tearing linen. 'Sorry,' she added, 'but this is so frustrating. Look, there's no time for the whole deal now, so I'm oversimplifying like crazy. You die, okay?'

Colin frowned. 'What, now?'

'No.' Eyes shut and opened again. 'You die, and your spirit or soul or whatever you want to call it leaves your body and gets put into a new one.'

'Is that what happens, then?' Colin said, in a tiny voice.

'Yes.'

'Oh.'

'And then,' Cassie went on, 'that body dies and you move to the next one, and so on. That's unless you've been really horribly bad, in which case the new host rejects you, and—'

'That's where Oscar comes in.'

'Grossly oversimplifying, yes. Sort of. Anyway, so it goes on, and that's basic reincarnation for you. But just occasionally, you get unfinished business; that's usually where you had something really important going on in your life and for some reason it hasn't been sorted out when you die. In which case, it carries over into the next one.' She paused, searching for the right simile. 'It's like when you're a kid and you won't eat up your greens, so they're served up at you for every meal until you *do* eat them. Right?'

Colin shrugged.

'Anyhow,' Cassie continued, 'that must be what's happening to us. According to Funkhausen, anyhow. You see, we've got all these lives where the two of us come together, and then for no apparent reason it all screws up, so the cold greens get carried forward to breakfast, if you see what I mean. And until we finally get our act together—'

'Hold on,' Colin protested. 'Are you suggesting that we should—? And all because some people in the Middle Ages got their wires crossed? That's sick.'

He could sense that Cassie's patience was running out faster than the North Sea oil reserves, but he didn't particularly care. 'I'm not suggesting anything,' she said, 'I'm just explaining. You wanted me to.'

'All right, fine.' He shook his head. 'But now we know what's going on, we can just ignore it, surely. I mean—' He paused, as huge surges of embarrassment swept through him like flood water. 'I mean,' he said, 'now we know we don't, like, fancy each other, and it's just this sort of hangover from a bunch of dead people. Surely if we just stay out of each other's way from now on, it'll solve itself.'

Cassie bit her lip. 'I don't know,' she said. 'Depends on whether us meeting each other like this was just coincidence and bad luck, or whether the forces acting on us dragged us together in this life same as they seem to have been doing for generations. If it's the second one, I don't think it's going to be as easy as just making an effort to avoid each other.'

That sounded ominous. 'You mean there's someone doing this to us?'

'No, not the way you make it sound. It's more impersonal than that. More like magnetism or gravity. If it really is the second one, our lives will pan out so that we keep running into each other and getting involved, whether we like it or not.'

'If it's the second one.'

'Yes.'

'But you don't know.'

Cassie sighed. 'It's not really my field of expertise,' she said. 'Actually, it's a pretty obscure branch of the profession, partly because it's difficult and vague, mostly because there's not enough money in it to make it worthwhile doing the research. In fact, I can only think of one specialist in this sort of stuff, and that's Professor Van Spee of Leiden.'

'So can you ask him?'

'He's dead.' She shook her head. 'He did publish several articles about it in one of the journals, I could look them up and see if there's anything helpful. Otherwise—' She pulled a sad face. 'I don't think any of the people working at our place would know very much about it.'

'Oh.' Colin felt for a moment as though he was swimming through lumpy gravy; he didn't really understand, or believe, but neither could he simply dismiss what she'd been saying as drivel and put it out of his mind. He'd seen too much: trees, Oscar, his own grave, that sort of thing. Then a small but vital point occurred to him, and its advent was like a flood of harsh white light: that, in the context of all the other shit that was circling over his head like a flock of vultures, it really wasn't that big a deal. If the weird symptoms they apparently shared were bugging the hell out of Ms Clay, naturally he felt for her but not to the extent that he was prepared to do anything about it. As for himself, he had other worries. 'Oh well,' he said. 'I guess we'll just have to wait and see. Meanwhile,' he added, and his voice took on an edge that surprised him, 'perhaps you'd like to tell me how we're going to get my Dad out of this bloody horrible mess that your stupid firm's got him into. Or had you forgotten about that?'

Cassie looked at him. 'I'm sorry,' she said. 'But I don't see there's anything I can do about it. I mean, he knew what he was doing.'

'How can you say that?' Colin exploded. 'He's just sold his *soul*—'

'Yes, all right.' Just a bit shrill there, he noticed. 'But I explained it to him. We're obliged to do that, under the Code of Practice.'

That one hit Colin squarely between the eyes. 'There's a Code of Practice?'

'Oh yes.' Cassie nodded vigorously. 'Like in financial services and stuff. It's even got its own British Standard, and a Kitemark. That's where JWW comes in, mostly. It's our job to explain the terms and conditions to the consumer. And then we certify that we've done it, and that complies with the Code of Practice. So you can see, surely, that there's not a lot I could have done. I'm sorry,' she added, and Colin got the impression that maybe she was, a little bit. That, however, was cold comfort.

'Well, sod that,' he said. 'All right, so he's made the contract. How do you go about cancelling it?'

'You can't,' she said. 'I mean, not without the purchaser's agreement. And really, I don't see them going along with it. I mean, why should they?'

Colin took a deep breath 'What if,' he said, 'I let them have me instead?'

That surprised her all right. 'What?'

'What if I took his place?' Colin paused to listen to what he'd just said. He couldn't remember having taken the decision to say it; it came out because it had to, because he had no choice. His father, after all. 'Look at it from their point of view,' he went on. 'I mean, Dad – well, he's no angel, right? In fact, he's been a right bastard ever since I can remember. I don't think he's ever actually killed anybody or stuff like that; but he said it himself, if there really is an afterlife and a Very Bad Place where you go if you've been a scumbag, then it's a pretty safe bet that that's where he's been heading all along. In which case,' he went on, 'from their point of view it's a very bad deal. What I mean is, they're buying something they'd have got for free in thirty years or so. But if they cancel the deal and take me instead—' He shrugged his shoulders hopelessly. 'Not that I'm a saint or anything, but the sort of life I've led, I never even had the opportunities to do anything evil or bad. I must be a much better bargain, surely.'

Cassie was looking at him. 'Are you serious?' she said. 'Come on, use your brain. By your own admission, no offence, but sooner or later, one way or the other, your father's going to end up— So really,' she went on, 'if we're going to be absolutely brutal about it, he'll be no worse off. But if you get them to take you instead – I mean, it'd be *pointless*. And you saw – well, Oscar. Do you really want to spend all eternity with the likes of—?'

'No, of course not,' Colin shouted. 'But he's my *Dad*, for crying out loud. It's like saying, why bother to save someone from drowning, because we're all going to die eventually anyway?'

She frowned. 'Well, no, actually, because for a start—'

'Quiet.' He hadn't meant to snap at Cassie but he was getting to the point where it really didn't matter. 'I don't actually want your opinion, thanks all the same, just some professional advice. You can invoice me if you want.'

'Go on.'

'All I want to know is,' he said, in a flat voice, 'can you go back and put it to them, see if they'd be interested? And if so, make the necessary arrangements, paperwork and stuff. That's all. Will you do that?'

It was quite a long time, relatively speaking, before Cassie answered. 'Yes,' she said.

'Thank you.'

'Provided—' She was looking at him again. 'Provided you'll help me with this other thing. The reincarnation stuff.'

'What? Oh, that.' Colin made a slightly contemptuous gesture. 'If you insist.'

'Right, then.' She snapped the lid of her briefcase shut. 'I'll see what I can do. No promises, of course, but I will do my best. That's all I can offer.'

'That's fine.' He could feel himself wilting, like a microwaved violet. 'I'd really appreciate it.'

'I think you're stupid,' she added, 'and probably mad, but it's not up to me to pass judgement. Unprofessional.'

'Fine.'

'All right, then.' She moved toward the door. 'I'll be in touch.'

'Good. I'll, um, look forward to hearing from you.'

'Okay. I'll see myself out, I know the way.'

When she'd gone, he sat down in a chair, feeling filleted and rather sick. He wondered if he'd made the offer because he didn't really believe in any of it, so naturally it didn't matter. That'd be good, if it was true, but it wasn't. Instead, he realised, he'd just performed an act of mindless, pointless, gormless heroism, a bit like running back into a burning house to save a cockroach. An image of Oscar formed in his mind, and he squirmed. A truly noble and altruistic act; but there'd be no medal, no headlines in the local rag about have-a-go-hero Colin Hollingshead. Instead (and this really did make him wince) there they'd be, the three of them, in perpetuity; himself, Dad and Oscar. Together for ever, like it says on kids' T-shirts.

Talk about bloody stupid.

The door opened, and it was at least two seconds before he realised who'd come in.

'I thought we were having lunch,' she said.

Christ, he thought, I'd forgotten. Then he realised that it wasn't quite as important as it had been, an hour or so earlier.

'Sorry,' he said. 'Actually, I was wondering, do you think we could possibly give it a miss for today? Only I've got a bit of a headache, and—'

She was looking at him. That made two young women looking at him on the same day. 'It's all right,' she said, in a voice that suggested that it bloody well wasn't. 'You don't need to make up any excuses.'

'Sorry? I don't—'

'I heard you,' she said, tight-lipped with anger. 'I was just passing the door earlier, and I heard you talking to her. That bitch,' she amplified, for the avoidance of any doubt.

'What? Oh, you mean Ms—'

'She said, *we need to talk about last night.* I heard her. You must think I'm really, really stupid.'

Oh for crying out loud, Colin thought. 'Look, it wasn't anything like—'

'And then I went back downstairs to have a bloody good cry,' she went on, 'and then I thought, maybe I got the wrong end of the stick, I'll go back up and see if they're still there, so I came back up and I heard you. *You were in my dreams*, you said. You bastard,' she added. 'So don't you give me any bullshit about a headache, because—'

'It wasn't like that,' Colin said, and even while he was saying it he could feel the fuel gauge of his emotional reserve dipping into the red. An hour or so can make all the difference. Not so very long ago, nothing could have mattered more than putting things right with the only girl in the world for him. Now, though, he was too worn out to care. Nevertheless: 'She's just someone I have to work with,' he said. 'That stuff you heard, it's completely out of context. I couldn't give a stuff about her, all right?'

'Liar.'

And he thought: yes, I do love this stupid woman, very much indeed. On the other hand, life's too short. Very much too short. 'Suit yourself,' he said wearily. 'If you don't believe me, that's your choice. Great pity, but there it is.'

There was some small consolation in seeing on someone else's face the sort of shocked bewilderment he'd been feeling ever since he'd joined the meeting. 'Right,' she said, and slammed the door behind her.

Colin sat down again and tried not to laugh. Comical; what had the Clay female been saying about time-crossed lovers? Nothing like the prospect of eternal damnation to take the sting out of a tiff with a girl. In fact, looked at from that perspective, it was a universal panacea for all possible ills. So he was a born loser with no love life and lousy career prospects, but he was going to hell for ever, so who cared? Might as well toddle back to his kennel and stick a few more of those revolting brochures into envelopes, because it really didn't matter. Once you kick the habit of hope, there's all sorts of tiresome chores you don't have to bother with any more; it's as good as a doctor's note, or a letter from your Mum saying you're to be let off PE. It was enough to make a man next best thing to cheerful.

*

'So, Mr Shumway,' said the face behind the desk. 'What do you see yourself doing in five years' time?'

Benny looked at him through his bulletproof-glass-thick spectacles. 'Exactly five years from now?' he asked.

'Yes.'

'Right,' Benny replied, 'just bear with me a second.' He put a hand to the side pocket of his jacket and produced something the size and shape of an orange, wrapped in a spotlessly clean handkerchief. 'Thought you might ask me that, so I borrowed this from a pal of mine. At the Bank,' he added, whisking away the hanky to reveal a clear glass globe. As he did so, something flat and shiny tumbled out of the folds and fell on the desk, but Benny appeared not to have noticed. 'So,' he went on, glancing at his watch, 'it's two-fifteen on Wednesday the—'

The glass ball started to glow; then its interior went milky. Benny nodded in satisfaction and put it down in the middle of the desk. 'Reception can be a bit tricky sometimes this side of the Divide,' he said, 'but this is the Zone 2 model, they reckon it works in the land of the living as well. Now, let's see.' The milkiness was beginning to disperse. 'Look, there's me,' Benny said brightly, pointing to a small figure in the centre of the globe. 'And—' He paused, and a grin slowly spread across his face. 'And just look what I'm doing,' he said. 'And in the middle of the afternoon, too.' He bent his head over the globe and squinted; the face on the other side of the desk was looking away with a rather stunned expression. 'Can't say I know her,' Benny went on. 'At least, not yet. Definitely something to look forward to, wouldn't you say?'

'Yes, fine,' the face said, in a high, strained voice. 'Could you please cover that thing up or put it away?'

'Sure,' Benny said, swathing the globe in his hanky and pocketing it. 'Right, next question.'

The face had that look on it that suggests its owner has just seen something nasty he's read about in books but never actually witnessed before. Benny made a mental note of that.

'How do you think,' the face went on, after a three-second silence, 'you could best improve your contribution to the success of the team?'

Benny stroked his beard. 'Hm,' he said, 'tricky one. Let's see, now. My job description says I'm the cashier, and of course I do all that, including,' he added, with a slight tightening of the voice, 'the banking. And since young Ricky came to his bad end I've been looking after the pest-control side of things, so that's two people's jobs I'm doing; no big deal, mind you, it's just killing dragons and battling the Undead and so forth, you don't need to be a rocket scientist. How could I best improve my contribution, though?' He frowned thoughtfully. 'I guess the best thing would be for you lot to make me a partner. You see, if I was running the show, instead of just—'

'I see.' The face made a note on his sheet of paper. 'So, how long have you been with the firm?'

'Now you're asking,' Benny said, scratching his head. 'It'd have to be '56 or '57 – not sure which, I think the Crimean War was still on – when Jack Wells first asked me if I'd fancy coming and working for him. I was with Cunningham's at the time, if memory serves, or was it Barker and Earl? I get them mixed up. Anyhow, it was just after I'd married my third, no, I tell a lie, my fourth wife.'

The face glanced down at his notes. 'That would be,' he said, 'Contessa Judith de Castel' Bianco.'

'That's her,' Benny said, smiling. 'Of course, at the time she was still in the chorus at the Gaiety – I didn't find out she was actually the Queen of the Fey until some time later. Bit of a shock, but I still think we could've made a go of it, if she hadn't been so dead set on wiping out the human race.'

'Ah,' said the face. 'Now, then.' He looked at his piece of paper and seemed to draw strength from it. 'If we look at your personnel file for a moment, I see that you were suspended on full pay in June 1963. Could you tell me something about that?'

Benny let his head loll back, and laughed. 'That was a right old game,' he said. 'Of course, old Kurt Lundqvist was still with us back then, before his accident, and he got this call from a very old and valued client of ours, one of those big private hospitals in the States; Florida, I think it was. Anyhow, they'd got a vampire in the plasma store, drinking them out of house and home. Kurt could see it'd be a two-man job, so he asked me if I fancied going along, I said yes, because it was years and years since I'd last been to Florida—'

Twenty minutes later, he said, 'And that's all there was to it, really. Of course, once Humph Wells and Dennis Tanner realised what had happened, and I'd actually saved two hundred and fifty thousand lives *and* landed the firm the Union Tool & Die account, they reinstated me like a shot and gave me a nice juicy bonus to make up for it all. I still kid young Dennis about it from time to time, when he needs taking down a peg or two.'

The face, who'd been trying to interrupt for the past quarter of an hour, made a great show of ticking something on his sheet of paper, put the cap back on his pen and dropped it into his top pocket. 'Well,' he said, 'I think that more or less covers everything, unless there're any points you'd like to raise—'

'As a matter of fact,' Benny said, 'there are. Actually, I made out a short list.' From his other pocket he took a medium-sized spiral-bound notebook and riffled through the pages, all of which were crammed with neat but minuscule handwriting. 'We can quickly skim through them now if you like,' he went on, 'or I could leave my notes with you and we could reschedule. Up to you entirely.'

'If you could possibly leave it with me—'

'No trouble.' Benny handed over the notebook and smiled. As he drew his hand back, he palmed and retrieved the small, shiny flat thing that had fallen out of his hanky earlier. The face was too busy staring in horror at the notebook to pay him any attention. 'Right,' Benny went on, looking at his watch. 'If it's all the same to you, I'd better be getting down to the Bank. I know time has no meaning down there, but they still get a bit funny if I'm late.'

On leaving the interview room, Benny didn't head for his office and the connecting door that led to the Land of the Dead and the Bank; instead, he dashed up the stairs and along a corridor to Connie Schwartz-Alberich's office. He had at least twenty minutes in hand before he had to do the banking, but he'd gambled on Them (whoever They were) not knowing that.

Connie looked up as he came in. 'Well?' she said.

Benny chuckled and sat down. 'Give you three guesses,' he replied.

'Benny, I'm not in the mood—'

'Give you three guesses.'

'Oh, all right.' She sighed. 'A porcupine.'

Benny frowned. 'No.'

'Two porcupines.'

'*Proper* guesses.'

'Just tell me what you saw in the bloody mirror.'

Benny shrugged, and grinned. 'Nothing,' he said.

Connie lifted her head and stared at him. 'What did you just say?'

(The little shiny thing was, of course, a small shard of genuine imp-reflecting mirror: a rare and expensive device of Chinese origin which shows the person reflected in it as they really are. The mirror polish on JWW's boardroom table wasn't just there to look nice; over the years, the partners had found it extremely handy during meetings with clients and fellow professionals for finding out exactly who – or what – they were dealing with.)

'Absolutely nothing,' Benny repeated. 'He might as well not have been there.'

'Oh.' Connie sat back in her chair and blinked a couple of times. 'You sure that's the right bit of glass?' she asked. 'I mean, if it's just an ordinary mirror—'

'No way.' Benny frowned. 'I do know the difference, Con.' He took the shiny fragment from his pocket and put it on the desk where she could see it. 'So no, we're not just dealing with a boring old witch or vampire. The imp-reflector shows you the true shape of what it reflects. So, logically, if I couldn't see anything at all—'

'Bugger me,' Connie said softly.

'So,' Benny went on, 'I've been thinking, and I reckon that when I go to the Bank this afternoon, I'll ask Mr Dao to do me a favour. That ought to settle it once and for all.'

Connie's eyebrows tightened. 'What kind of favour?'

'Let it be a surprise,' Benny replied, and grinned. 'Anyhow, the bottom line is, if I were you I wouldn't start clearing out your desk or looking for another job quite yet. All right?'

Before Connie could say anything, there was a knock at her door. It proved to be the thin-faced girl, the one whose name nobody could ever remember.

'Oh,' the girl said, looking at Connie and then at Benny. 'I'm sorry, I didn't know you were busy. I'll come back another time.'

Benny stood up. 'That's all right,' he said, 'I was just pushing off. I'll drop in later, Con, after I get back. Good idea of yours about the crystal ball, by the way,' he added. 'Freaked him out somewhat, no idea why. See you.'

Once Benny had gone, the thin-faced girl sat down in the chair he'd just vacated. 'I wanted to ask your advice,' she said. 'If it's no bother, I mean.'

Connie shrugged. 'Fire away,' she said.

'Thanks.' The thin-faced girl frowned. 'I came to you because I know you're very experienced and you've worked in all sorts of different specialisations—'

'Don't worry about all that,' Connie interrupted. 'What can I do for you?'

'Well,' the thin-faced girl said and then seemed to stall, like a dodgy old car at traffic lights. 'It's a bit difficult, actually. Personal, if you see what I—'

'Understood,' Connie said, 'that's fine. Mum's the word.'

'Sorry?'

'I said mum's the word.'

The thin-faced girl raised an eyebrow. 'The word for what?'

'Don't worry about it. I mean, it's just an expression. What's the problem?'

'It's not actually for me, you understand, it's for a friend.'

'Got you,' Connie said impatiently. 'So?'

The thin-faced girl paused, visibly collecting her thoughts. 'Well,' she said, 'my friend – let's just say, she's not terribly good at, um, personal relationships.'

Connie's heart sank like an over-insured freighter, but she nodded briskly and said, 'I see. Go on.'

'She has trouble, um, relating to people,' the thin-faced girl said, 'especially in, let's say, a romantic context.'

'All right. And?'

'She was wondering—' The thin-faced girl hesitated. 'Do you happen to know if JWW makes such a thing as a love philtre?'

Here we go, Connie thought. It was the inevitable newbie question, and answering it was very boring when you'd already answered it five hundred times. 'Yes,' she said, and as she said it, a little annoying Microsoft paper clip appeared in the margin of her mind. 'Yes, it's the best in the business, though we say so ourselves. But,' she went on, as the virtual paper clip dropped down into a memo, 'surely they had love philtres at – where was it you said you worked before you came here?'

'UMG,' the thin-faced girl said. 'And before that I was at Mortimers.'

'Well,' Connie said, 'I know for a fact that Mortimers make one. Our main competitor in that sector.'

'Yes,' the thin-faced girl said, 'but it's not—' She frowned, until her face was practically one-dimensional. 'It doesn't last for ever,' she said.

'What?' Connie thought for a moment. 'Oh, I get you. Yes, there's an antidote to the Mortimers philtre. Actually, it's one of their selling points, that you can reverse the effects if you change your mind or something. Just as we make a big deal out of the fact that there's no antidote to ours.'

The girl was looking at Connie with little sharp laser eyes. 'Really?'

'Well, there's death,' Connie said, a bit rattled. 'Till death do us part, and all that. Otherwise no. Drink the JWW philtre and it's for ever. I used to know all the gory biochemical details; something about a resequenced agapotropic enzyme—'

'For ever,' the thin-faced girl said. 'I see. Thanks, you've been very helpful.'

She got up to leave. Red-alert klaxons started blaring in Connie's mind. 'Just a second,' she said. 'This friend of yours—'

'Yes?'

'Look, take it from me, they really aren't worth it. Men, I mean. You spend half your life trying to nab one, and the other half asking yourself how you could've been so bloody stupid. You know, fish and bicycles.' She tailed off; the thin-faced girl was staring at her.

'Well,' the thin-faced girl said, 'she's not a friend, exactly. Thanks. Bye.'

She closed the door behind her. Connie hesitated for a longish moment – about a fifth of a second – before jumping out of her chair, running to the door and yanking it open. But the corridor was empty; fifty yards in either direction.

CHAPTER ELEVEN

Cassie Clay picked up the phone, put it to her ear, reached out for the keypad and hesitated. A promise was a promise. Furthermore – well, furthermore, she was a professional, but she did still have a few conscience-coloured stains in the lining of her soul that wouldn't come out, not even with the boil-wash. And (more to the point) *he*'d asked her to, and even though she now had some idea of what was going on and why she was suffering these stupid symptoms, that didn't stop them having at least some effect. He'd asked; and that was why she was doing it.

Even so. Even bloody so.

She dialled in the number. It's extra-extra-ex-directory, and a hideous fate awaits anybody who discloses it without due authorisation, but here's a hint: it's three digits long, and if you called the Fire Brigade while standing on your head—

Three rings, then the click; then the voice. This was the bit that Cassie hated.

'*Thank you for calling the Powers of Darkness. Your call may be recorded for security and training purposes. For general moral or ethical enquiries, press 1 on your keypad. To make a reservation, press 2. For details of our special discount packages for lawyers, politicians and Microsoft executives, press 3. For the deep blue sea, press 4. To speak to a sales adviser, please hold.*'

She held. They played country and western at her, thereby nailing once and for all the old lie that the Devil has all the best tunes. She waited.

They wouldn't be interested, of course; they'd laugh in her face. But just suppose they didn't, just suppose they were prepared to agree. Was she really prepared to make it possible for them to get their claws on an innocent man in place of a scumbag? If she really did still have vestigal traces of a sense of right and wrong—

'Your call is being stored in a queue. Please hold. Your call will be answered shortly, unless, of course, you are already a resident, in which case—' Cassie held the receiver away from her ear so as not to be deafened by the peals of cackling laughter. The implications of that gave a whole new penumbra of meaning to the phrase 'the torments of the damned'.

The phone sang 'King of the Road', 'Ghost Riders in the Sky' and 'Stand By Your Man'. Cassie shuddered, made a resolution to be very, very good from now on, and endured.

'Enquiries, how can I help you?'

Rumour had it that they, like so many large concerns, had relocated their call centre; being who they were, however, they'd relocated it to Newcastle. 'Hello,' Cassie said. 'My name's Cassandra Clay, I'm calling from J. W. Wells & Co in London, England. I was wondering if I could speak to your reference S/blb/purchases/45115.'

'Please hold.'

To help pass the time, she mused on the strengths and limitations of Funkhausen's Loop. It wasn't easy, resolving the subtle nuances of temporal metaphysics with 'Jolene' thundering through her head like a waterfall, but she considered the final scene of the drama, in the tea shop. The point, surely, was that only in that episode did the pins and needles *make sense*—

'Putting you through.'

Cassie snapped out of her reverie and took a deep breath. 'Hello?'

'Ms Clay?' It wasn't the voice she was used to talking to. In itself, that was no bad thing, since the regular voice wasn't a nice thing to have in your ear; this one, by contrast, was female, quite ordinary, rather bored. 'How can I help you?'

She cleared her throat. 'It's about purchase number 45115,' she said. 'I was wondering—'

'Just a moment, I'll get the file.'

'Sure. Please don't turn on the—'

Either she was too late or it was deliberate; this time it was Roy Orbison. It seemed to take for ever for whoever it was to find the file.

'Right,' the female voice said, eventually. 'Purchase number 45115, that'd be Mr Hollingshead. Yes, I can confirm, that was all signed up earlier today. In fact,' the voice added with a faint trace of bewilderment, 'you witnessed the signatures.'

'That's right, yes.'

'I see. Anyway, it's all done and dusted and we look forward to receiving your bill in due course.'

'Ah.' Cassie's mouth was curiously dry. 'I was wondering,' she said. 'You see, there's been a, well, sort of a last-minute change of plan.'

'Oh yes?'

Deep breath. 'That's right. My client, I mean, Mr Hollingshead – well, to cut a long story short, the wrong person signed. What I mean is, the soul you've contracted to buy is the wrong one.'

'Oh dear.'

'Well, quite; so I was thinking, if we can just quietly put that contract to one side, get another one drawn up with the right name on it – I'll see to all the signing formalities and so forth, free of charge, naturally. And then you can give me back the old contract, the one with the wrong name, and that'll be that. Like you said, done and dusted.'

Silence. For some reason, Cassie found it rather awkward to breathe.

'Well,' said the voice, 'it's not actually up to me, I'm just the assistant personal assistant.'

'Oh.'

'But I can't imagine there'd be any problem,' the voice continued. 'I mean, mistakes happen, don't they?'

Relief flooded into Cassie's mind like the Nile. 'That's right,' she said. 'I mean, yes, they do. Happens to the best of us. I mean, we're only human, after all.'

A long silence followed that remark. Oh, Cassie thought; yup, that was a bit tactless.

'Anyway,' the voice went on, 'I'm sure we can sort it all out.'

'Wonderful.'

'There will, of course, have to be a nominal administration fee.'

Well indeed, Cassie thought. But never mind. 'That'll be fine,' she said. 'What—?'

'May I ask, did you draw up the original contract?'

'That's right, yes.'

'In that case,' the voice went on brightly, 'in order to cancel the agreement and replace it with the amended version, your life and soul will have to be forfeit to the Evil One. Now I can't promise to get the paperwork out to you tonight, but I can definitely make sure it goes out tomorrow—'

'Hang on,' Cassie said. 'My—?'

'Your life and soul,' the voice replied promptly. 'You'll need to sign our standard-form forfeiture agreement, along with the usual disclaimers and stuff, and there'll also be an additional registration fee of five US dollars.'

'*My* life and soul?'

'Correct. Since it was your mistake.'

Cassie didn't shout very often, but she was good at it. 'No bloody way,' she yelled.

'I'm sorry?'

'That's not acceptable,' Cassie said, as firmly as she could. 'There's no way I can agree to that.'

'Oh. You're sure?'

'Yes.'

'Please hold.'

More Roy Orbison, but Cassie hardly noticed. She was too busy shaking.

'Hello? Are you there?'

'What?' Cassie pulled herself together as best she could. 'Yes, I'm here.'

'I've just had a word with the principal personal assistant,' the voice said, 'and as a gesture of goodwill we are prepared to waive the five-dollar fee, if that's any—'

'Sorry,' Cassie said.

'Oh.' Nonplussed voice. 'In that case, I'm afraid I can't see there's a whole lot we can do about it. The current agreement will just have to stand, that's all.'

Well, Cassie said to herself as she replaced the phone, I tried. I really did give it my best shot.

And if it really had been true love, instead of some kind of ditzy trans-temporal fuck-up, maybe I might have—

Nah. Not even for true love.

She got up out of her chair, crossed the room and kicked the filing cabinet, really quite hard.

By no stretch of the imagination could Benny Shumway describe Mr Dao, the suave, sad chief cashier of the Bank of the Dead, as a friend; that went without saying. But, over the years, they'd built up between them a bond of mutual understanding and respect that might possibly be mistaken for friendship, rather as a careless rambler might mistake an adder for a grass snake. Accordingly, Benny asked his favour of Mr Dao, and Mr Dao was pleased to be able to help.

As soon as he was back in his office and the connecting door was safely locked and bolted, Benny lunged for the phone on his desk and called Connie's extension. But there was no reply, suggesting that she wasn't in her room. Sod it, Benny thought, but he wasn't surprised. It was that time in the afternoon when people tended to go walkabout if they didn't have anything desperately urgent to get finished. Connie could therefore be anywhere: in with young Cassie, or dropping in for a chat with

Cas Suslowicz, looking something up on the computer or in the library; generally lurking and making herself difficult to find.

Which was annoying; because what Mr Dao had told Benny corroborated what he'd seen in the imp-reflecting mirror, and the implications of that were both fascinating and obscure. On his own turf, Benny knew his stuff; an account that refused to balance or a manticore nesting in the vaults of the Credit Suisse he could handle easily enough. But this, he readily admitted, wasn't his sort of thing at all, and he made it a rule not to muck about with complicated, dangerous things that he didn't understand.

Immediately, he thought of Judy, his fourth ex-wife, hereditary Queen of the Fey, currently confined in perpetual suspension under the Glass Mountain for trying to obliterate humanity in order to provide Lebensraum for her own vicious, insubstantial people. Judy, of course, knew this sort of stuff backwards and inside out. She'd take one look at it, figure out what was happening and tell him exactly what to do about it. Judy, however, wasn't available. Even by dwarf standards, Benny was as brave as a hatter, but nothing would ever induce him to go snooping round the Glass Mountain.

But—

He picked up a sheaf of petty-cash reconciliations and put them neatly away in the appropriate box file. But, he reflected, there might be another way. After all, he only wanted to talk to her, ask her a question or two, pick her brains. It might—

Nah.

The phone rang: Dennis Tanner, still being tormented by the auditors. Apparently they now wanted the travel-expenses book, the receipted invoices for the 1987 office Christmas party, twenty disposable Bic biros and a laptop Macintosh. Benny said he'd see to it, and put the phone down, before stapling some pink requisition-chit carbons to some yellow designated-deposit slips and filing them in the cabinet. There was a whole world of difference, after all, between brave as a hatter and brave as two short planks. He had more than his fair share of the reckless courage displayed by his ancestors in their relentless wars against the goblins, but he knew better than to pull the electric fire into the bath with him to find out if it worked underwater. The back corridor on the second floor was somewhere he wasn't prepared to go, not for anybody. Not even for Connie Schwartz-Alberich.

He thought about that as he arranged the telegraphic-transfer dockets in date order. Not even for Connie; but if for anybody, then yes, probably for her. The difference being, Connie wasn't a wife or a girlfriend, or a potential wife or conquest. Connie was a *friend*.

There had been a time when Benny would have slaughtered dragons to fetch home golden fleeces for Judy (or Trudy, or Tracy, Sadie, Dominique, Jenny, Monika or Samantha); he'd have stormed heaven for them, and cut a slice out of the moon to make a comb for their hair. That wasn't particularly demanding, that was just doing stuff, and Benny had always been a man of action. It had taken him many years and a lot of scars to figure out that doing stuff is only a very small part of the deal, and it's the remainder that's both difficult and scary. Nowadays he lived alone, mostly because he'd realised that none of them, not even Dominique or Annie or Jill the traffic warden (what is it, people kept asking him, about dwarves and women in uniform?) had motivated him sufficiently to make a serious effort at coming to terms with the not-doing-stuff side of sentient relationships; things like sitting still and listening. With all of them, it had proved too great an effort, for which even red hair and freckled shoulders were an inadequate inducement. With Connie Schwartz-Alberich, on the other hand, inexplicably enough, it was a pleasure.

Yes, Benny thought, as he tapped the keypad of his calculator, while the fingertips of his left hand caressed a column of figures, but even so. If it meant visiting the back corridor on the second floor, then, regrettably, Connie was on her own—

Which makes two of us, he thought. Which is no good. No dwarf, after all, is an island. Besides (he grinned suddenly, like a savage animal baring its teeth) it'd be fun to see Judy again. He missed her; he missed them all, of course, in the way you still occasionally get an itch in a long-since-amputated limb. And anyway, what was the worst that could happen, if he went there and things turned pear-shaped on him? At the very most, he'd be torn apart into his component atoms and suspended for ever, agonisingly conscious, in a dimensionless void outside time and space. A mere trifle, a nanodeal.

The back corridor on the second floor was where the consultants had their offices. It's quite common in many professions for retiring partners to be kept on as consultants, coming in one or two mornings a week to potter round and do a few bits of business, keeping their hands in, looking after a few old and valued clients. It's a good system, providing continuity, keeping in touch with the old-timers' wealth of skill and experience, and giving them something to do with their time. J. W. Wells & Co had always appreciated this; their motto was *Once a partner, always a partner* and, as far as they were concerned, retirement, disability, senility and indeed death were trivial obstacles, easily overcome with a little ingenuity and a simple, everyday receptacle, such as a bottle, jar or old-fashioned oil lamp.

Down one flight of stairs, therefore, turn left at the landing and down the back corridor. Seventh door along, a little brass plate on the door: *The Contessa Judith de Castel' Bianco (ret'd)*. There was no point in knocking, but Benny did so anyway. Judy always was fussy about being taken by surprise.

He opened the door. A small room, no chairs, just a plain cheap desk on which rested a plain pottery oil lamp, the sort whose design has remained basically unchanged since Ancient Egypt. Benny paused on the threshold and frowned. It had never been satisfactorily established which part of a deceased partner remained behind when the rest went to its eternal reward; it was a matter of academic interest only, so long as the work got done and the bills were sent out on time. All that was known for certain was that the residue trapped in the container was sentient, replete with all the ex-partner's memories and character traits, and held there painfully and against its will.

'Hi, Jude,' Benny said.

He took a step forward, then stopped. There was no denying that Judy could be scary sometimes – most of the time, in fact – but he was still convinced that deep down, at some level neither of them had ever been able to explain coherently, he'd always been the special one for her. Even the last time, when he'd turned against her and betrayed her to her unspeakable fate, there'd been a spark of the old magic left. He advanced another step, reached out with the tip of his forefinger, and gently tickled the side of the lamp. Memories of touch are always immediate and vivid, no matter how long it's been. He closed his eyes for a moment.

'Judy?' he said.

The lamp moved very slightly. For a split second, Benny froze; he couldn't remember what he was meant to do, or what was going to happen next. The only thought in his mind was, I'm going to see her again.

He snapped out of it a quarter of a second before it was too late, but dwarves are blessed with superb reflexes. He jumped backwards with both feet as a jet of pink steam blossomed out of the lamp's spout and hung in the air, like mist backlit by a street lamp.

'Hiya, kid,' he said softly. 'How's things?'

The steam billowed, heaved and convulsed, like an animal caught in a net; curdled and thickened, filled out a head and shoulders, a face, as yet without eyes or mouth The hiss was like snakes, and there was a sour smell of sweat.

'Benny,' said a voice, very far away. 'That you?'

'Judy,' Benny replied.

'Get me out of here, Benny. *Please*.'

'Sorry, Jude.' The eyes were being moulded; the thin line of the pressed-together eyelids formed, deepened and split. Lashes sprouted as the eyes opened and looked at him.

'What do you mean, "sorry", you jerk?' Pause, filled with desperation and disappointment. 'You're here to rescue me, right?'

'Wrong.' As he said the word, Benny considered it. Come to think of it, now that he was here, why not? Life would be so much more fun with Judy around again.

(And then he remembered. It was entirely possible for a consultant to leave his office, go back into the outside world and take on a whole new lease of life, just so long as someone took his place. That was all.)

'Oh.' She'd got her colour back, not that she'd ever had very much of it. But that had never mattered very much. By her very nature as one of the Fey, Judy existed almost entirely in the eye of the beholder. As far as Benny was concerned, she'd always been, quite simply, perfect; but ask him to describe her or draw a picture of her and he wouldn't have known where to start. 'I see, fine,' she said bitterly. 'So, to what do I owe the pleasure?'

Benny pulled a sad face. 'Work,' he said. 'I need your help with something.'

She shimmered a little, like smoke stirred by a breeze, then settled until she was practically solid; sitting in her office chair, her hands on the arms, her head slightly on one side. 'Ah well,' she said. 'You realise that you're the first mortal I've seen in six months?'

He could feel her eyes tugging at his face. 'That long? Too bad. What's it like where you are, anyhow?'

'Horrible,' Judy said. 'You?'

Benny shrugged. 'Could be better,' he said. 'You know about the takeover, of course?'

For maybe half a second she went out of focus. 'What d'you mean, takeover?'

'Nobody told you?' He was shocked. 'Jack and Dennis and Cas sold the business,' he said. 'I'm amazed you didn't know. I'd have thought—'

'Sold the business?' She blurred again, as though someone had splashed water over a movie camera lens. 'What the hell did they want to go and do that for?'

Benny shrugged. 'Well, you know what a complete fuck-up everything was, what with Theo and Ricky getting killed, particularly since it was so soon after Humph and—'

'And me.'

'That's right. I mean, losing four partners out of seven in

under a year. Basically, it was sell up or shut down. In fact, that's what I wanted to talk to you about, in a way.'

'The *bastards*,' Judy hissed. 'Screw it, Benny, how dare they? I'm still a partner in this goddamned firm – what about my share? They can't do that, it's—'

It's done,' Benny said gently. 'And just in time, too. As it is, we had to close all the overseas offices – Paris, Hollywood, Frisco, Lisbon, Stockholm, Guadeloupe. Half our Entertainments & Media clients defected to UMG—'

'That stinking bitch Betty Capoferro,' Judy snarled. 'Half? Which half?'

'You don't want to know,' Benny replied. 'It'd only upset you.'

'Which sector, movies or politics?'

'Both,' Benny said wretchedly, feeling her pain. 'We lost Ashford Clent and Maeve Richards . . .'

'Fuck.'

'And Doug Tree and Dermot Fraud, all to UMG; Charlie Wilkinson's gone to Sorcercorp. We only hung on to Alan Titchswamp by cutting our commission to three per cent. It's been pretty rough, I'm telling you.'

For a while, Judy was just a swirl of pink cloud, glittering with incandescent sparkles of furious anger. 'I turn my back for five fucking minutes,' she wailed, 'and everything I worked for goes straight down the toilet. Who are these clowns, anyhow?'

'Ah.' Benny frowned. 'That's the question. See, we don't know. They haven't seen fit to tell us. Jack and Dennis and Cas must know, presumably, but they aren't telling.'

'How do you mean, you don't know? You must've seen them.'

'Seen them, sure. None the wiser. I thought I knew everybody in the business, but they're complete strangers to me. Which makes me think they're outsiders or something.'

'That's not allowed.'

'There's ways round it, you know that. But I've been doing some investigating of my own. Oh, by the way, they just fired Connie Schwartz-Alberich.'

'They did *what*?'

'Exactly.' Benny nodded. 'That's why I'm here, basically. We need to find out who they are before we can stop them. But listen up for a moment—'

'You came here to see me,' she said quietly, 'to help Connie Schwartz-Alberich. I see.'

'Listen,' Benny repeated, his voice both soothing and urgent, 'and I'll tell you what I've got so far.'

And he told her, about what he'd seen in the fragment of mirror, and what Mr Dao had found out for him from the Bank's records. When he finished talking, she was quiet for what felt like a very long time; and when she did speak, she said, 'Benny, you've got to get me out of here. Yes, I know,' she snapped before he could interrupt, 'but this is *important*. This is for the good of the firm. I can deal with these jerks, but not if I'm stuck in here. And you—' Pause. 'Well, no offence, but—'

'Nice try,' Benny said firmly. 'Listen, Jude, if it was—' He took a deep breath. 'If it was anybody else but you, maybe I'd do it, at that. But I can't let you out of there, you know that. You'd be back to your old ways—'

'Benny.'

'No. Please don't ask me again, OK?' He took a step back, then looked over his shoulder. 'Judy,' he said.

'What?'

'The door, Judy.'

(Because, at some point, somehow, the door had vanished, just as if the wall had healed up. A room with four walls and no door is a very bad place to be.)

'What? Oh, go on, then.' The door reappeared. Benny opened it, took off his left shoe and used it to wedge the door slightly ajar. 'It's not that I don't trust you, Jude—'

'Liar.'

'All right. But you know I can't —'

'Fine.' She sighed, like the wind blowing through the last dead leaves of autumn. 'So, let's get this straight. They don't show up in the imp-reflecting mirror, right?'

'Correct.'

'And you asked your pal at the Bank, and he told you that no reservations have been made in their names.'

'That's right. He checked the register for the next hundred and fifty years.'

'Then it's obvious, surely.'

Judy explained it to him, point by point and step by step. 'It's so simple,' she added afterwards, 'I'm amazed you didn't figure it out for yourself. It's the only possible explanation.'

'But it doesn't make any sense,' Benny objected. 'I mean, if you're right, why? Why the hell would anyone bother going to all that trouble?'

'There's a reason,' Judy replied, 'but you haven't figured it out yet, that's all. Now, if only you'd let me come back, just temporarily, for a week or so—'

Benny felt something pressing gently on his left instep. It was, he realised, his shoe; the one he'd wedged the door open with.

'Judy,' he said, 'please put the door back.'

'What? Oh, shucks.' She grinned; the sort of grin a face wears when all the skin and flesh has rotted away, and only bone is left. 'Silly me.'

'The fucking *door*, Judy.'

'It's only because I want us to be together again,' she cooed. 'Together for ever, right?'

'Not like this, no.'

'Then screw you.' Behind him, the door flew open; he heard it bang against the wall. 'Get out of here and solve your own goddamned problems. You know what? I think you never did give a damn about me, Benny. Otherwise you wouldn't leave me here all alone, in this—'

'So long, Judy,' Benny said. 'Thanks, you've been a great help.'

He backed away toward the door. He'd almost made it when a bolt of blue lightning flashed at him from the spout of the lamp. It missed, but not by much; he felt it burn his cheek – cold, not fire. He looked up at Judy, who blew him a kiss before she was sucked back into the lamp.

★

Benny took his time returning to his office. His legs were weak and a bit shaky, and he found it difficult to concentrate on anything, even on where he was going. Partly he was still recovering from the implications of what Judy had told him – yes, she was right, it was all perfectly simple when you looked at it logically, but the simple and obviously correct solution just didn't fit. He was also somewhat preoccupied with other issues that had nothing to do with Connie, the takeover or the identity of the new management—

Mostly, it was something that Judy had said. He knew why, of course. It was nothing more than a blind thrust at his centre of guilt, a pretty obvious and feeble attempt at manipulation. It didn't mean anything, and he would be entirely justified in deleting it from his mind—

You came here to see me, to help Connie Schwartz-Alberich. I see.

Strange, though. Benny was under no illusions about Judy's motivations, or about how close he'd come to taking her place under the Glass Mountain. Attributing any sort of humanoid feeling to Judy was a bit like trying to psychoanalyse a bomb. Jealousy, therefore—

It wasn't Judy's feelings he should be concerned about, of course.

He was just outside the boardroom door. He stopped, and listened. There were no voices coming from inside, so the room was empty. He shrugged, opened the door and went in.

The JWW boardroom was meant to be imposing and intimidating; it had never had that effect on Benny. If anything, he found it vaguely restful, perhaps because it reminded him of home. If it hadn't been for the windows, it could almost have been a room in the house where he'd grown up. That house was long gone, of course: looted, trashed, undermined and filled in by goblins over a century ago in one of the last raids before the peace settlement of 1899. No great loss; by dwarf standards it was a slum, an end-of-gallery two-up-ninety-seven-down. He'd left home when he'd been a mere boy of eighty, hadn't been back since, never regretted it. Nevertheless; the boardroom's dark panelling and massive furnishings always helped him settle his mind. He thought well here. He sat down at the great mirror-polished table, leaned back in his chair and applied his mind.

So simple. The imp-reflecting mirror had shown nothing, and there were no reservations in the new management team's names in the Land of the Dead. Therefore, they didn't exist. Whatever it was he'd spent half an hour with that morning, it wasn't a living being; it wasn't *real*.

There could be all sorts of reasons for that. It could simply be a tax thing, or an elaborate mechanism for circumventing corporate law. The technology wasn't all that complex, though it was pretty long-winded; someone had been to a certain amount of trouble and expense to create the illusions of the annoying little man and his colleagues. Pause; who could do that sort of stuff? A piece of cake for the Fey, all of whom were natural effective magicians. They could create illusions and glamours and phantoms and incubi just by thinking. But ever since Judy's overthrow the Fey were safely locked up in their own shallow, tormented dimension, unable to interact or interfere with anything on the other side of the line. Among humans, pretty well any accomplished effective magician could have done the engineering, and Benny could've filled two sides of A4 with the names of likely suspects without having to pause for thought. The question, though, was *why*.

It only mattered, Benny told himself, because whoever was behind it all had seen fit to sack Connie Schwartz-Alberich, and of course that wasn't on. Furthermore, why would anybody want to? She earned the firm more money per fiscal quarter than Cas Suslowicz or Peter Melznic, she was efficient, reliable, highly respected in the trade, an asset and a credit to the firm. If they were getting rid of her, therefore, there had to be a very good reason, or a very bad one.

Who was it who said '*Never attribute to malice anything that can be explained by incompetence*'? Benny couldn't recall offhand. But, unreal or not, the new management were still Management, and the M-word is, after all, just Latin for couldn't-find-their-arse-with-both-hands. Management tends to do stuff like that, as part of its contribution to keeping the world imperfect and chaotic. Even so; even so.

In which case, he was forced back on the conclusion he'd already jumped to, the moment Connie had told him the news. They were getting rid of her because she'd found out something that they didn't want anybody to know, or she was inadvertently doing something that got in the way of their secret agenda.

Benny groaned aloud. He didn't like conspiracy theories; for one thing, they imply that there's an efficient and competent providence shaping the course of events, even if it's a malign one, and Benny preferred to believe (reasonably enough, in his opinion) that nobody, good guys or bad guys, is capable of being that organised. Far more likely that stuff, good or bad, simply happens, how and when it wants to, and the most anybody can do is be shrewd enough to take advantage, surfing on the crest of the tidal wave.

Even so.

But Connie wasn't like that; she didn't snoop, spy, insert her nose, unless she was compelled to do so by a very good reason. The only things outside the work in her in-tray with which she'd concerned herself recently had been the identity of the new management (and Benny knew she'd been no further forward than him or anybody else at the time of her dismissal) and this stupid business with young Cassie and the guy from Hollingshead's.

Unless—

The vague outlines of an idea were starting to form in Benny's mind; no more than shapes, structures, an aerial photograph of an idea taken from so high up that you could barely recognise it for what it was. Something to do with the— He frowned, then scowled. Something to do—

Quickly, decisively, he looked down. There in the polished table top he saw his reflection; and, since he was no more nor less than he claimed to be, the imp-reflecting surface showed him exactly the same image as he'd have seen in any ordinary mirror. But he concentrated, screwing up his eyes behind the massively thick lenses of his glasses. He was zooming in on the pupils of the reflection's eyes, trying to see if there was anything odd about them.

He saw what he was looking for, and turned his head away.

All dwarves have brown eyes; it's DNA or something equally technical. Benny was no exception; indeed, he owed two of his marriages to the apparent soulfulness of his eyes, though that had been a blessing so mixed as to be practically scrambled. The eyes of the reflection, however, were grey.

'Judy,' he said, quiet but clear.

A sharp twinge, the sort you get from eating ice cream or biting on a bit of silver foil. He looked down again. The brown eyes were back; unfortunately, the idea, or the schematic for the idea, was completely gone.

Ah well, Benny thought, can't blame her for trying. And Judy might have her faults, but nobody could deny she was as sharp as a tack.

At any rate, if she'd solved the problem, then it meant that the problem was soluble. It was a pity he was going to have to figure it out on his own, slowly and laboriously, instead of taking advantage of Judy's superior insight and intellectual voltage. A pity; but the price was too high. Well – any rate, she'd set him on the right path.

Benny glanced at his watch. His chat with his ex had taken longer than he'd anticipated, and he had work to do; he should be getting back, finishing up the daily chores. If there was time, he'd drop by Connie's office and fill her in on what he'd found out. After all, she was much better at intuitive leaping than he was. Maybe she'd solve it in a flash, like Judy had done.

He yawned as he pushed open his office door. These days, mortal peril took it out of him more than it used to; maybe he should start thinking about retiring, while he still—

He stopped dead on the threshold, and stared.

The unthinkable was, reasonably enough, something that Benny didn't think about much. In the early hours of the morning, when most suicides happen and worriers lie awake staring at the ceiling, Benny slept: solid, dreamless dwarf sleep, untroubled by anything. So he'd never scared himself half to death with wondering how he'd react if ever he wandered into his office and found the connecting door to the Land of the Dead unlocked, unbolted and wide open. Which, in context, was a pity. Short-sighted, even.

CHAPTER TWELVE

'So,' said the face of ultimate evil, helping itself to crisps, 'what shall we talk about?'

Colin looked furtively round. It amazed him that nobody seemed to have noticed anything. Here he was, perched on a bar stool next to the quintessence of all nightmares in a crowded suburban pub, and not so much as a head had turned or an eyebrow flickered.

True, Oscar had dressed appropriately for the occasion. It was wearing a fawn suede sort-of-bomber-jacket thing that more or less shrieked M&S casual, with sand-coloured chinos, a white button-down shirt and trainers. Trinny and Susannah would've expressed guarded approval; a bit overstated, perhaps, a smidgeon Nineties in a sort of self-referential way. That, however, was beside the point. Ultimate evil in nice schmutter is still ultimate evil; so why was nobody backing away, or running screaming out into the street?

'Ah,' Oscar said, 'allow me.' A hand extended and laid a shiny coin on the flannel bar-towel. Colin looked at it in mute horror.

'What's that for?' he said.

'A penny,' Oscar replied, 'for your thoughts. It's traditional, isn't it?'

'No, it's just a—' The coin wasn't just shiny, it was red-hot; a wisp of smoke was curling up from the charred towel. As the mopped-up beer evaporated, the penny cooled to a dull charcoal grey.

'Just a what?'

'Expression,' Colin said hoarsely. 'Just an expression.'

'I understand. Humorous?'

'What? I mean, no. Not very. Just something you say.'

'Ah. Just the words, then, but no physical coin.'

'Mphm.'

It cleared its throat. 'A penny for your thoughts,' it said.

'Oh.' Colin tried for a nonchalant shrug, but it came out as a squirm. 'Nothing much. Wool-gathering.'

'Wool—?'

'Another one. Expression.'

'My goodness,' Oscar said. 'You seem to use a great many expressions, if I may say so.' It paused, and sniffed. 'In any event,' it went on, 'I believe I can hazard a guess as to what you were preoccupied with. You were wondering why none of the other mortals in this building have reacted with horror, disgust or distress at my appearance.'

'Mm,' Colin mumbled. 'That sort of thing, anyway.'

'I can explain, should you wish me to do so.'

'Can you? I mean, that's great. Yes, please.'

'It's quite simple,' Oscar said. 'I am shielded by a strong piece of effective magic, known as a glamour, which prevents anybody not party to our contract from seeing me as I truly am. Our fellow customers, therefore, see only an entirely nondescript young man in expensive casual clothes. Of course, if there was such a thing as an imp-reflecting mirror on the premises, my disguise would be wholly ineffectual. Since, however, that is an unlikely contingency, the danger is trivial and can be dismissed. There remains, of course, the possibility that I might be seen and recognised by a sensitive – that is to say, a mortal with strong latent magic power. The odds against that, however, are slightly less than five hundred thousand to one. Having considered the risk and viewed it in the context of the benefit to our relationship of a bonding exercise such as the one we are embarked upon, I resolved to adopt what you might describe as a Devil-may-care attitude. Humour,' Oscar added, 'in the form of wordplay. You need not refrain from laughter on my account.'

Colin stared at it in bewilderment for a moment, then managed to come up with a gurgle, the sort of noise you'd expect from a drowning kitten.

'You have entirely consumed your beverage,' Oscar said. 'Are you in need of a further supply?'

Colin nodded. 'Yes,' he said, with feeling.

'I see. I believe it is your turn to buy.'

'Right,' Colin said. 'Same again?'

'Certainly. I have never sampled alcohol before. Its effects are curious. Although it is a depressant, by sedating the part of the brain that controls natural inhibitions it inspires a sense of well-being verging on recklessness. When you return with further beverages, we should play pool.'

At the bar, Colin seriously considered running away. From the pub to the station – six hundred yards. A train would take him, via Clapham Junction, to Gatwick – bugger, no passport. He could go to Waterloo instead; someone had told him it was possible to dodge passport control on the Eurostar, though he doubted it. Or Dover, somewhere like that; perhaps he could stow away in the back of a lorry—

'I have changed my mind.' Colin's head spun round; Oscar was standing next to him. 'Instead of beer I think I would like to try a measure of fermented spirits. What is the colourless liquid in the bottle with the red label?'

So much for unobtrusive escape. 'Bacardi,' Colin said mournfully. 'It's a sort of rum.'

'Rum,' Oscar repeated. 'What is rum?'

'What? Oh.' Colin frowned, trying to remember. Somehow he found it hard to concentrate on anything with the common enemy of man standing eighteen inches away from him. 'Sugar cane, I think. They sort of squash it up and distil it, and then I believe it's put aside to mature in big barrels.'

'Mature?'

'You've got to keep it for several years before it's ready to drink.'

'Ah.' Oscar nodded a couple of times. 'Rum isn't built in a day.' It made a faint rattling noise, like the cough of a sixty-a-day Nazgul. 'It seems that alcohol is also conducive to humour.'

'Absolutely,' Colin replied. 'Oh look, the pool table's free.'

When he'd racked up the coloured balls and positioned the black and the white, Colin asked, 'Have you played this game before?'

'No,' Oscar replied. 'Explain the rules, and the function of the long, tapered sticks.' It picked up a cue and touched the tip as though expecting it to be sharp. 'These implements have an aerodynamically efficient profile,' it said. 'Do we throw them at each other?'

Colin explained the rules, and they played a game. Oscar's first shot after the break was a fiendishly difficult long pot to the top left-hand corner, flawlessly executed. To his surprise, how-ever, Colin won.

'You have prevailed,' Oscar said. 'State your requirements.'

''Scuse me?'

'The nature of the penalty,' Oscar replied, bowing its head. 'At home, when we play games, the loser has to endure a pun-ishment devised by the winner. Decapitation or ritual disembowelling are traditional choices, but the decision is, of course, yours.'

A few heads were beginning to turn, glamour or no glamour. 'Would you mind keeping your voice down?' Colin muttered in mid-cringe. 'Look, we don't do things like that around here, all right? I mean, thanks for the offer, but—'

'Oh.' More than a trace of disappointment in Oscar's voice. 'Then please explain the purpose of playing the game.'

'Well,' Colin said, 'for fun.'

'Ah.' Oscar shrugged, a complex operation. 'In that case, we shall play again. We shall enjoy fun.'

Depends, presumably, on how you define it, Colin thought.

Oscar's version seemed pretty hard to distinguish from outrageous showing off, culminating in a shot off three cushions that potted five balls simultaneously before nudging the black into the top left. As far as Colin was concerned, however, he was beginning to wonder if he wouldn't have been better off with the ritual disembowelling; messier, maybe, but it wouldn't have attracted quite so much attention. He was also starting to wonder whether pouring ardent spirits down a previously tee-total embodiment of pure evil was entirely sensible. Admittedly, his companion seemed to be having a great time; but there's more to life than sheer naked altruism.

'Right,' he therefore said, after Oscar had won his sixth consecutive game. 'Well, it's been great, but I've got to be up early for work in the morning, so maybe—'

'We should now,' Oscar said, 'play darts.'

So they played darts. Then they had a go on the fruit machines (Colin had never seen anyone get eight jackpots on the trot before; when he mentioned this, however, Oscar replied that if he made it nine in a row there'd be the Devil to pay; into which, Colin later admitted to himself, he'd walked like Custer at the Little Big Horn), then more darts, and then it was closing time. Although Colin had been drinking at four times his accustomed rate in order to keep up with Oscar, when the cold outdoors air hit him he felt wretchedly sober, as though he'd been glugging nothing but Perrier for the past four hours.

'Now,' Oscar said, 'we should consume fast food and become nauseous in a shop doorway. Also, we have not yet discussed football, motor vehicles or the sexual proclivities of female celebrities.' It hiccoughed, then made a noise which Colin later figured out must've been a belch. 'It will be a tight schedule, but not impossible.'

'Actually,' Colin said.

Oscar nodded. 'You would prefer to go to your house, where we can drink more alcohol and watch pornographic videos. Or would you rather encompass a violent encounter with a group of strangers?'

'Actually,' Colin said desperately, 'I think it'd be nice if we—'
He racked his brains for a moderately innocuous suggestion. 'We
could walk down as far as Tesco's and back,' he said. 'A bit of
fresh air—'

'That isn't a traditional male bonding activity,' Oscar
objected. 'However, if you insist.' It shrugged very slightly and
set off at a brisk march, picking up a traffic cone in each hand
without breaking stride. 'Once we've done that,' it added hopefully, 'we could steal a motor vehicle and set light to it.'

'We'll see,' Colin muttered.

Maybe it was the fresh air, or simply a difference in metabolic
rates; as soon as they reached the Tesco's car park, Oscar folded
abruptly at the knees, collided with a stray wire trolley, tripped
over the kerb and fell over. For some reason it seemed to find
this highly amusing; at any rate, it made a noise like bandsawn
aluminium, which Colin assumed on the balance of probabilities
to be laughter.

Now was his chance. A quick sprint, he'd be round the corner
and into Drake Street before the epitome of ultimate evil noticed
that he'd gone. Straight home, up the stairs, grab his passport
and a change of underwear, then a taxi (no faffing around with
trains) to Gatwick and the first available flight to somewhere far
away. He tensed his leg muscles for the first step.

'Your girlfriend,' said Oscar.

Which was no reason at all for hesitating. After all, she wasn't;
they'd been out together once, and that hadn't been a proper
date or anything, and he'd stood her up for lunch. That didn't
constitute a formal relationship, not even in Utah. Besides, in his
mind he'd already committed himself to fleeing the country,
changing his name and therefore, by implication, never seeing
her again, and he was perfectly fine with that. So why the hesitation?

'We should talk about her,' Oscar said, still lying face down in
the gutter. 'Man to man. Further wordplay,' it added. 'You may
now tell me all about your feelings for her. It does good,' it
added, as if quoting, 'to talk about it.'

Colin checked his calf muscles: untensed, not going anywhere soon. His moment of resolution had passed. 'Actually, no,' he said; and added (because it does help to talk about it, even to the epitome of ultimate evil), 'there's no point. We had a row after I stood her up for lunch, and she hasn't spoken to me since.'

'I see,' Oscar replied. 'But this doesn't accord with my information.'

Colin blinked. 'You what?'

'According to my data,' Oscar said, and then threw up. Objectively speaking, it was a sight worth paying money to see: blue fire and cascading fountains of sparks and all sorts. 'According to my data,' it repeated, 'you can't have failed to attend a lunch date, since you have never scheduled such an event with the relevant female.'

There was a dribble of orange flame running down Oscar's shirt front, but Colin didn't seem to have noticed. 'Yes, I did,' he said. 'And anyway, how did you—?'

'Incorrect. You have never broached the subject of sharing food with Ms Clay. Had you done so, I would've been informed immediately.'

'Ms—' Colin shook his head, as though bewilderment was dandruff. 'No, you've got it wrong. She's not the one I—'

He paused. None of ultimate evil's beeswax, surely. And if it knew everything about him, so what? He was too insignificant to have any secrets worth hiding. Mostly, he wanted to go home to bed.

'Not the one,' Oscar repeated. 'Perhaps I used the wrong word. By "girlfriend" I meant to convey a female for whom you feel powerful emotions of romantic and sexual—'

'Yes, all right,' Colin snapped. 'Look, would you mind getting up? Because if a policeman sees you like that we'll both be arrested, and that'd just about round off a perfect day.'

'Certainly.' He didn't see Oscar move. One moment it was lying face down in the gutter, the next it was standing beside him looking relaxed and elegantly dressed. It spoiled the effect rather by falling over again almost straight away. 'Allow me to clarify,' it went on, as though nothing had happened. 'You are passion-ately in love with Cassandra Clay, an assistant sorcerer with J. W. Wells & Co—'

'No, I'm not.'

Zpp; Oscar was standing next to him again, this time hanging on to the wire trolley for support. 'Please,' it said reproachfully. 'We have performed male-bonding procedures. We are now—' It paused, waiting for the right word to drop into place. 'We are now buddies,' it said. 'Accordingly, you feel able to confide in me, and there is no need to deny your true feelings. You madly adore Ms Clay, who returns your love with equal fervour.'

'No,' Colin said. 'Sorry, but that's simply not true. The girl I'm interested in is Fam Williams, our new receptionist, only like I told you, I stood her up for lunch and now—'

'Incorrect.' Colin could feel Oscar's displeasure, like an ice cube down the back of the neck. 'I do not understand why you should feel the need to lie to me. Your mate,' it added; and then the wire trolley skidded sideways under its weight, and it went down like a dynamited chimney stack. 'Pain,' it said, as though reading out a stage direction. 'I can only assume that you are deliberately falsifying data with a view to generating humour. Ha ha. Now, will you please confirm that you are in love with Ms Clay?'

Colin frowned. If only he'd been a bit quicker off the mark, he could be on his way to Vanuatu by now. On the other hand, somehow Oscar didn't seem quite so terrifying now that he'd seen it go arse over tip over a wire trolley. 'Fine,' he said. 'If you get up off the floor and let me go home to bed, I'll say anything you like. Deal?'

'Deal.'

'All right, then. I'm in love with the Clay woman.'

'Excellent,' Oscar said. 'That concludes our lads' night out. Would you like me to give you a lift home?'

'In the state you're in? No, tha—'

It hadn't been an offer, except in the Sicilian sense. Oscar reached out, grabbed a handful of Colin's hair and swung him into the air like a carrier bag. '*Shit, fuck you're hurting me,*' Colin was about to say; but by then he was sitting on his bed, alone, with the bedside light on, staring at the *Deep Space Nine* poster his mum had bought for him ten years ago, and which he'd never got around to taking down off the wall.

She was there, of course, next morning. Colin slouched past her, his head cloudy and fragmented with hangover; she looked straight through him, as though he didn't exist.

Dad intercepted him before he could crawl into his office and build himself a cosy nest out of brochures and envelopes. 'Didn't hear you come in last night,' he growled. 'Had a good time, did you?'

'No, not really.'

'Got a thick head, by the look of you.'

Colin mumbled something about a touch of flu.

'Like it matters. Anyhow, buck your ideas up – we've got a lot to get done today. Meet me in ten minutes in the tool room.'

Aaargh, Colin thought; in the tool room lived a whole lot of big, noisy machines. There was the one that went *scree-scree-scree*, the one that *cachunk-zee-chin*'d its way through solid brass bar stock, the *scrungle-scrungle-scrungle* machine and the screamy-grindy thing. They were enough to set your teeth on edge at the best of times, and definitely not recommended for anybody with a head full of tactical flu. He gobbled a couple of aspirin, which had no effect whatsoever, and drank a glass of dusty, chalky tapwater.

There was a welcome surprise waiting for him in the tool room. All the machines were still and silent; in fact, the place seemed to be deserted. Odd; usually there were half a dozen men working there. Colin looked round for some sort of clue, and saw his father approaching.

'All right?' Dad said. 'Feeling better?'

'No.'

'Well, try not to puke up all over the place, it'll create a bad impression.'

Colin thought about that for a moment. 'We're meeting someone here?'

Dad nodded. 'Our new best friend. Ah,' he added, and maybe he winced just a little. 'Here he is.'

Something had just stepped out from behind the scree-scree machine. It hadn't been there a moment ago, because Colin had looked. This morning, it was wearing a very sharp Italian light grey suit.

'Talk of the Devil,' it said. 'Good morning. You have both rested sufficiently.'

'Fine, thanks,' Dad replied automatically. 'Right, Colin,' he went on, 'this is primarily for your benefit, so pay attention. Now, you'll have noticed there's nobody here but us.'

Colin nodded. Stupid thing to do.

'That's because yesterday I sent all the men home. We don't need them any more, thanks to Mister —' Dad froze, but Oscar simply bowed its head slightly. 'Today we start doing things the new way, right?'

'Correct,' Oscar said, and snapped its fingers.

It was a bit like *Star Trek*, only there was no hum and no shimmering lights. They just appeared, as though the cameraman had stopped filming and started again once they were in position. They didn't look at all like Oscar; and Colin reflected wretchedly that, a mere twenty-four hours ago, he'd have expected that to be a good thing.

They stood at attention until Oscar snapped out a word of command; then each of them headed for a different machine. They moved like second-rate computer animations and when they trod in oil stains or patches of wood shavings on the floor they left no marks. They really did have cloven hooves instead of feet, which goes to show that not all stereotypes are wrong.

'They'll be working twenty-four hours a day, seven days a week,' Dad was saying. 'No tea breaks, no unions, no paternity leave, no minimum wage; no wage at all, come to that.' His face darkened for a moment, and Colin saw him deliberately relax it. 'You know,' he went on, 'if this idea catches on, the manufacturing sector in this country might just still have a snowball's.'

Oscar didn't seem to be listening to him, it was concentrating very hard, like a conductor standing in front of his orchestra. One by one, the machines started to turn, spin and reciprocate. Colin braced himself for the noise, but there wasn't any.

'Completely silent,' Dad said. 'Mister, um, Whatsit here did explain it to me, but it's all a bit technical. Bottom line is, they don't even need the electric, so that's another useful saving. And no noise means we don't have the bloody Environmental Health down here every five minutes.'

'The fundamental principle,' Oscar started reciting in a dead flat monotone, 'is that of the elimination of entropy through temporal displacement. Because entropy only has effect in time, if you eliminate the passage of time you effectively negate the first law of thermodynamics, with the result . . .'

'Something like that, anyhow,' Dad said. 'Bloody clever, these people.'

'Give the Devil his due,' Oscar said. 'There are also significant ecological benefits, including reduced fossil-fuel usage, thereby helping to reduce greenhouse gas emissions—'

Somehow, it came as no surprise to Colin that the powers of darkness were ecologically aware. They probably supported the Kyoto accords and everything.

'And of course,' Dad steamrollered on, 'with these lads on the job the place'll pretty well run itself without us needing to lift a finger. Which is why,' he added, turning to Colin, 'I'm promoting you. Director in charge of production, which means that from now on all this lot's your responsibility. There's no extra money or anything like that, but we might start looking around for a car for you; I was thinking a nice clean Fiesta, something like that.'

Inside Colin's head there was that split second of delay, like during a transatlantic phone call. 'Did you say director?' he asked.

'That's right. I mean, there's no rush, sometime in the next six months, I was thinking, it's a case of waiting till the right car comes along, because it's daft running out and buying the first one you see—'

'As in, seat on the board and everything?'

Dad shrugged. 'Theoretically yes, I suppose so,' he said. 'But don't let it go to your head, we don't actually have board meetings and stuff, we just all do as I say. Still, if it gives you any pleasure.'

'Wow,' Colin said quietly. 'Thanks, Dad.'

For some reason, his gratitude seemed to make Dad uneasy, so he packed it in. Even so. A director of the company, a seat on the board. If he was a company director, surely that meant everybody'd stop treating him like a twelve-year-old, and—

Oscar was grinning. It was, of course, difficult to be sure, given its rather unconventional facial geography, but Colin was convinced that it could see what he was thinking, and the grin was because he'd taken the bait, just as he was supposed to. Fair enough, now he came to think of it. Accepting a seat on the board of Hollingshead & Farren in exchange for his conscience was a bit like selling Manhattan to the palefaces for a handful of shiny beads. He hoped that that was why Dad had just frowned, and that this hadn't been his idea.

Not that it was of very great consequence, since Dad was now just one jump ahead of the everlasting barbecue, and there were strange-looking people with cloven hooves all around him, operating machinery. Colin's head had started to hurt, and he wanted to get out of there. After all, now that the contract had actually been signed and the new workforce had reported for duty and started their first shift, he'd failed, there was nothing more he could do. In which case— 'Look at that.' Dad had picked up a newly fettled widget from one of the plastic bins into which the finished product dropped from the delivery chute. 'Lovely piece of work, better than the stuff the Swiss turn out. They're all right, these lads of yours.'

'I am delighted to hear you say so,' Oscar replied quietly. 'It's a point of pride with us that we always keep our side of the bargain.'

That was about as much as Colin could take. Mumbling something about an upset stomach (not a million miles from the truth) he scuttled across the shop floor and through the fire doors into the back yard. Home; the passport, the station, the airport; after that he wasn't quite sure, but it didn't really matter. He thought of those road signs you get on the outskirts of big towns that say 'All Other Destinations'. That was exactly where he wanted to go, and he couldn't wait to get there.

'Feeling better?'

He turned his head. Oscar was standing beside him, directly between him and the side gate.

'No,' Colin said. 'I think I'd better go home.'

'Of course.' Oscar nodded, and Colin noticed that it was holding something in its hand; sort of burgundy colour, a little book. A passport.

'Excuse me,' Colin said. 'Where did you get that from?'

'Does it matter?' Oscar held it out to him. Colin grabbed at it but as soon as his fingertips brushed its cover, it vanished. Colin opened his hand, and found nothing in it except a few wisps of pale grey ash.

'You won't be needing it,' Oscar reassured him. 'Of course, you could go to the station anyway. You'll find it's closed for renovation: a complete refit, very ambitious. If you're thinking about taxis or buses, you should be prepared for a very long wait. You have no car, and walking, or even running—' It shook its head. 'You could always try.'

Colin looked at it for a moment. 'I might just do that.'

'Of course,' Oscar said, and stood aside.

Colin took two steps toward the gate and staggered. Pins and needles in both feet, worse than he'd ever felt before; worse even than that time in the tea shop—

'Quite,' Oscar said. 'In the end, you see, everything eventually turns out to be about true love. If I were you—' It made a sort of wavy gesture with its left hand, and the pins and needles went away again, 'I'd go into town and buy myself a nice, smart new suit, for being a director in. A small act of celebration would seem to be in order, after all.'

'A suit,' Colin said.

'Indeed. I believe you'd look good in a middle-weight dark grey wool with perhaps the faintest suggestion of chalk-tripes. If you wish, I can come with you and help you choose.'

Colin thanked it but said he'd rather go alone, and left. Once he was a couple of hundred yards away from the factory, he thought, Yes, but I can send away for a new passport, and then realised that most likely he couldn't, not if Oscar didn't want him to. Just for fun he looked in at the station. It was surrounded by hoardings and scaffolding, and a big blue sign told him the name of the contractor and the scheduled completion date for Phase One. There was a long, grumpy queue at the bus stop; he felt that he should stop and apologise to them, but he couldn't think how to explain why it was all his fault.

Even so; he went on a bit further, past British Home Stores to the travel agent's. Only it wasn't there any more. In its place was a large, smart-looking Burton's, and the notice in their window said that they were having a special offer on business suits.

Well, fine. To paraphrase the words of the poet, you can lead a free man to water, but you can't make him drink; all you can do is drown him. So he went in – but he didn't get himself a nice new suit. Instead he bought a tie, light blue with little yellow sunflowers on it. It wasn't much; in fact it was pathetic, a single tea bag thrown into Boston Harbour. Unfortunately, it seemed that it was the best he could do.

Colin went back to the factory. On the way, he made a resolution. So he couldn't save his Dad's soul from eternal damnation. So he couldn't do anything about the fact that the workforce had been fired and replaced by non-union demons (hooflegs rather than blacklegs; dear God, he was even starting to think like bloody Oscar now). So he couldn't even run away to the Andaman Islands and start a new life as a beachcomber. There was one thing he could still do to win himself a little smear of happiness on Life's windscreen; or at least he could give it a go, though he didn't rate his chances very much. And it'd be a minor act of rebellion against Oscar, who seemed very keen on fixing him up with Cassie Clay. Yes; he could find Fam, blurt out a grovelling apology and ask her out for a proper date. It was a bit like asking the lifeboat to go back to the sinking *Titanic* so that he could get his sponge bag, but so what? He'd done his best to do the noble, unselfish things and got precisely nowhere. At least finding true love would be doing something, rather than giving up completely.

Fam wasn't behind the front desk, where she should have been. Instead, there was someone he was pretty sure that he didn't know. He reckoned that he'd have remembered her if he'd met her before.

'Who the hell are you?' he asked.

She smiled at him. It was the kind of smile that should have stopped him dead in his tracks and left him stammering and glowing bright red like a traffic light. 'Hello,' she said, 'I'm Rosie. You must be Colin.'

'What're you doing there?' he said. 'Where's Fam? Ms Williams?'

Rosie looked at him for a moment; Colin had the uncomfortable feeling of being gripped in tweezers, as though she was about to smear him on a glass slide and shove him under a microscope. 'She left,' Rosie said.

'She left?'

'Yes.'

'Why?'

Another smile. If ever they got around to inventing the smile-proof vest, a smile like that would present a very substantial challenge. 'I don't know, do I? I'm just a temp.'

'A what?'

'Temp. Temporary receptionist. There was an ad in the local paper, and I answered it.'

Which was a lie, of course. Fam had been there that morning; unless, of course, she'd given in her notice immediately after

Colin had stood her up, and Dad had phoned in the ad as soon
as she'd crossed the threshold on her way out. Dates, copy dead-
lines: he tried to do the mental arithmetic, but he couldn't
concentrate. 'Oh,' he said. 'Look, I need to talk to her about
something. Did she leave a number or anything like that?'

Beautiful Rosie shrugged; her perfectly straight shoulder-
length auburn hair bobbed slightly, like the most beautiful
maggot any fish had ever seen squirming on a hook. Complete
waste of effort. 'I don't know,' she said. 'I suppose Mr
Hollingshead senior might know. Why don't you ask him?'

No point answering that. 'All right,' Colin said, 'give me the
phone book, I'll look in that.'

Rosie got the book for him. Her nails were blood-red, perfectly almond-shaped and implausibly long. He grabbed the
book and started turning the pages.

Shouldn't be difficult, surely. Her Dad's initial, he remembered, was E. He rifled pages till he got to Williams.

He had no bother at all finding E. Williams in the book.
There was a whole page of them, two full columns in tiny type;
and, by some bizarre coincidence, all of them appeared to live in
Mortlake. He sighed, closed the book and slid it back across the
desk at her.

'What's the matter?' Rosie said.

'Nothing.' Colin was about to slouch off when he hesitated.
Something about the way she'd looked at him; or rather, something about the very corner of her eye.

'Do I know you from somewhere?' he asked.

'Me?'

'Yes, you. Where was your last job?'

A very slight frown. A stunningly lovely frown, sure, but a
frown, as opposed to a smile. 'Oh, up in the City. Packed it in
because I couldn't be bothered with the commuting.'

'Specially now that they've closed the station.'

'That's right, yes.'

Colin looked at Rosie again. Quite definitely he'd never seen
her before in his life. On the other hand, he knew exactly where

he'd seen her last. 'Your last job,' he said. 'It wasn't an outfit called J. W. Wells, was it? Seventy St Mary Axe.'

She looked as though he'd just slapped her or something. 'As a matter of fact, yes, it was,' she said. 'Fancy you knowing that.'

'Yes,' Colin said. 'Fancy.'

'Actually,' she went on, 'that's sort of why I took this job. You see, I remembered the name, what with you being clients of JWW and all; so when I saw your ad in the paper, I thought, there's a funny thing. It felt like it was – I don't know, sort of *meant*, if you know what I mean.'

'Yes,' Colin grunted. 'I get the general idea.'

'So, anyway,' Rosie went on. 'Here I am. I think I'll enjoy working here, after JWW. It was always so hectic there – you know, phone always ringing, clients coming in without an appointment, all stressy. This looks like it'll be a nice change of pace.'

'Sure,' Colin said. 'Nothing ever happens here.'

She looked at him. 'Listen,' she said – it was a sort of stern cooing, like a turtle-dove demanding to see the manager. 'I'm sorry about your friend leaving, but there's no point getting all tense with me about it, is there? So let's just start again and see if we can't be pleasant. Right?'

If Colin had been a cat, he'd have had his ears flat to the sides of his skull by now. 'Absolutely,' he said. 'Quite right. Welcome to Hollingshead and Farren, Rosie. Great to have you on board.'

'Thanks.' She smiled once more, but he saw it coming in plenty of time, and it whistled past him like a cannon ball. 'Oh, I clean forgot. Oscar said, soon as you got in, could you nip down to the foundry and have a word?'

'Foundry,' Colin repeated. 'Got you, yes. Cheerio for now, then.'

He didn't go to the foundry. Instead, he ran up the stairs, two steps at a time, to the manky, dusty, cobwebby old cupboard on the second-floor landing where all the junk and wiffin went to hide. There was all sorts in there: dead typewriters, broken office chairs, worn-out brooms, seventy years' worth of back numbers of the *British Plumbing & Sanitaryware Gazette*. Also, he knew for a fact, there were loads of old phone directories; he'd seen them once, when he'd been looking for something. True, they were very ancient; the most recent one, he recalled, was at least eight years old. But it was worth having a look, on the assumption that Fam's family had lived at the same house eight years ago—

E. Williams: bingo! Instead of a whole page of the bastards, all huddled together in Mortlake like Boers in a laager, there were just two of them; and one of them lived in Putney. He stuffed the book under his arm, scuttled across the landing to the room where the laser printer lurked, nestled like a fairy-tale dragon in its tangled brake of cables, shut the door and sat down. There was a phone on the desk. He reached for it, found the place in the phone book and started dialling. There was a knock at the door, but he ignored it.

He waited for the ring-ring. It didn't come. Instead, he got the bagpipe drone that tells you the number's been cut off.

He swore and dumped the phone back on its cradle. More knocking on the door. Screw it, he thought, and yelled, 'Come in.'

It was Rosie, and she was smiling. 'Thought you might like a nice cup of tea,' she said.

'Not really,' Colin replied, but by then she'd put the cup and saucer down on the desk and gone away. He sighed. As it happened, he was quite thirsty, and it was a shame to waste a nice cuppa that he hadn't had to make himself. He liked milk, no sugar, though he was prepared to bet a million pounds she already knew that.

He picked up the cup and froze.

On the rim of the cup, opposite to where he'd been about to put his lips, was a row of little houses; also a tiny dockyard and a miniature wee jetty, extending a centimetre out to tea. The buildings and structures were quaint and oldy-worldy, and there was a minute little signboard, like the ones you get on the railway telling you the name of the station, that said *Boston*. Seven millimetres or so from the end of the jetty floated a very small sailing ship, on whose deck scuttled teeny-tiny specks of activity. Colin didn't have a magnifying glass or anything like that, but he reckoned he knew what they were doing. They were throwing stuff over the side of the ship. Just as he was about to throw the cup at the wall and run for it, the dinky little sail unfurled, and on it he saw titchy little letters that read:

NICE TRY

CHAPTER THIRTEEN

Banks have a thing about snappy, friendly-sounding slogans. They want to be thought of as action banks, listening banks, banks that like to say Yes. The Bank of the Dead was no exception. Originally founded in China over a thousand years ago as a means whereby the living could provide for the souls of their ancestors in the afterlife, the Bank had pioneered the concept of the snappy, friendly slogan along with paper money and the endowment mortgage. Though some of their earlier efforts at catchy advertising punchlines had, on reflection, struck them as unfortunate ('Now you *can* take it with you', regrettably followed up with 'Why *not* pockets in shrouds?'), they'd always been rather proud of one they'd come up with towards the close of the Yuan Dynasty:

The Bank Of The Dead: We Are Your Future

Small wonder, then, that dealing with them on a daily basis for nearly three years had come to prey on Benny's mind. The one thing that came close to setting it at rest was the door that separated his office from their bleak, dimensionless realm. It was only cheap plywood, but it was hexed, bewitched, shielded and enchanted with every kind of spell, incantation, charm and rune known to the trade, along with a battery of locks whose wards existed on different spatio-temporal planes, and a chain forged from meteorite iron in the flames of the last of the Great Dragons. It's an uncertain world, and Benny had never trusted it or any of its components, but if there was one thing in which he had any degree of faith, it was the door.

Which someone had apparently opened.

He stood and stared at it for close to twenty seconds. Understandable: it's not every day that you see something that's completely impossible. The door couldn't be open, because he knew for a stone-cold fact that he'd locked it himself, personally – it wasn't something he was slapdash about – and he had the one and only set of keys. Just to make sure that he hadn't left them in his desk drawer, he felt his right thigh until he found the chain, looped round his manticore-hide trouser-belt, from which his keyring hung in his pocket. He pulled them out and looked at them. All present and correct.

So, Benny thought, if I didn't unlock it and I've got the only keys, and it's magically impossible for anybody on this side to open the door without the keys, it stands to reason—

He shuddered. The disturbing fact was that the defences, though theoretically perfect and absolute, only really worked from this side. It wasn't supposed to be that way. That was the whole point of the door. But Benny was a realist. Everything real, even magic, obeys certain basic physical laws. But the dead aren't real, it's one of their salient features, and accordingly they are bound by no laws or rules of any kind. Door or no door, deep down in his uncomfortable soul Benny knew that the dead only stayed on their side because of a gentleman's agreement between Mr Dao, the bank's chief cashier, and Jack Wells, the firm's erstwhile senior partner. Under the terms of the deal, J. W. Wells & Co had moved all their accounts to the Bank, in return for higher interest rates on fixed-term deposits, highly competitive business-account charges, free monthly statements and a promise on Mr Dao's word of honour not to come through the door and start abducting the living. Any breach of the agreement, it was strictly understood, wouldn't be tolerated, which meant that if the dead did come marauding through the door, snatching up any hapless mortal who crossed their path and dragging them back with them into their infinity of desolation and despair, JWW would be entitled to close all their accounts and take their business elsewhere without incurring penalty charges or loss of interest. That was, of course, a comfort. But.

Benny backed slowly away until he was standing by his desk. Without turning his head or taking his gaze from the door, he leaned back and fumbled till he'd laid hands on a ten-foot pole he kept handy for all sorts of reasons. With this, he prodded at the door until it swung shut; then he pounced forward and started shooting home bolts and turning keys.

That was better, but only up to a point. He'd locked the stable door, but something told him he was way, way beyond stray horses. Something had come through. Whatever it was, there was a fair chance that it was still in the building. And, since he was the firm's pest-control officer, which is only a PC way of saying hero, it was his job to go and look for it. How jolly nice.

The problem was, how do you set about looking for the dead? The Undead, now, that was a piece of cake. Benny had a whole battery of handy, pocket-size gadgets, ranging from the basic cheap-and-cheerful Pedersen's Zombie-Find-'n'-Stake to the cutting-edge, top-of-the-line RDG200 from Van Helsing Direct. A fat lot of good they'd do him. He didn't know what to look for, because he knew perfectly well that what he was looking for didn't exist. It'd be like searching for WMD in Iraq.

Never mind, said a quiet voice inside Benny's head. If it was easy, they wouldn't need you to do it.

Fine. Benny sighed. The most obvious way to find lurking predators from beyond the veil was to wander about the building looking weak and helpless. He was under no illusions about their possible intentions. They weren't here to see the sights or do a spot of early Christmas shopping. If they'd broken through, it could only be because their insatiable, ravening hunger for some tiny scrap of life had driven them to it. The best way to find them would be to offer them bait and lure them into attacking. How he'd deal with them once he'd found them was another problem he didn't have an answer to right now, but with any luck he'd think of something when the time came.

No point sneaking and prancing round the place Starsky-and-Hutch-style, flattening himself against walls and kicking doors open. Instead, he stuck his hands in his pockets, let his shoulders slump, and strolled down the corridor in the general direction of the stationery cupboard.

Just round the corner he met the thin-faced girl from Entertainment & Media, the one whose name he could never remember. Even at JWW, questions like, 'Excuse me, but have you seen any dead people recently?' would be likely to result in lips pursed and eyebrows raised. Instead he asked, 'Did you see anybody come out of my office just now?'

She frowned before answering. 'You mean the young couple in the funny clothes?'

Just occasionally, it's better to search hopelessly than to find. 'That'd be them,' Benny replied. 'You don't happen to remember which way they went?'

More serious consideration; then she said, 'I think they were heading for the back stairs. You only just missed them.'

'Thanks,' Benny muttered, and started to walk away; but the thin-faced girl coughed meaningfully.

'Have you got a minute?' she asked.

'What? Well, no, actually,' Benny said. 'I wanted a quick word with those people, before they leave the building.'

'Only,' the thin-faced girl went on, as though she hadn't heard him, 'I wanted to ask you about something. Not you personally,' she added, and the tip of her usually sallow nose pinkened a little. 'A senior practitioner. Someone with wisdom, knowledge and experience.'

In spite of what the proverbs say, the difference between flattery and Virgin Atlantic is that, occasionally, flattery will get you somewhere. 'Fair enough,' Benny said. 'What?'

'Love philtre,' the thin-faced girl said. 'I have a job on at the moment where the use of love philtre seems the obvious course.'

Benny grinned. 'You haven't been here long, have you?'

The thin-faced girl narrowed her eyes, making herself look remarkably like a chisel. 'Define long.'

'Because if you had,' Benny went on smoothly, 'you'd know that the firm's fortunes were founded on the stuff. JWW's patent oxy-hydrogen love philtre. Never touched the stuff myself,' he added. 'Never needed to. But it works, no doubt about it.'

'Yes,' the thin-faced girl said, 'quite. I, however, have never used it before. Kindly state the recommended dose and the effects.'

'Right.' Benny thought for a moment. 'Five millilitres ought to get the job done – it tastes funny so, if you're administering it by stealth, best mix it with something. Alcohol is fine, but anything with sugar in it can lead to side effects. What happens when you drink it is, you're fine for between two and fifteen minutes, depending on metabolism, and then you pass out, zappo. When you come round, the first person you see is It. Back in the old days, we used to put something in it to make it opposite-sex-specific, but now we're a bit more broad-minded and flexible. Once it's done the job, that's it. Till death do us part, basically. I remember once, back in '76—'

'Thank you,' the thin-faced girl said. 'You have been extremely helpful.'

'No worries,' Benny replied. 'The intended victims – anybody I know?'

She didn't answer that. Instead, she opened her bag and took out a small jar. 'Manticore fat,' she said. 'Applied liberally to the skin, it will render you invulnerable to dragon-fire and the acidic spittle of harpies. A token of appreciation,' she added. 'Goodbye.'

Benny stood for several seconds after she'd clip-clopped away down the corridor, looking at the jar balanced on the palm of his hand. He knew all about manticore fat, of course; in particular, he knew that it didn't actually work as a dragon-slayer's barrier cream, although it was the best thing on the market for bicycle sprockets. What puzzled him was that it was there at all. People didn't usually give him presents just for answering simple work-related questions. He was both touched and suspicious, in roughly equal proportions.

Who the hell was she, anyway?

Then he remembered what he'd been doing, cursed himself for allowing himself to be distracted, stuffed the pot into his jacket pocket and broke into a run.

There was an unfamiliar knock at Cassie's door. She looked up from the lease that she was studying, and frowned.

Couldn't be Connie, or Benny Shumway; they knocked, but distinctively. Dennis Tanner and old Mr Wells didn't knock, presumably on the basis that it was their door and they could open it how and when they damn well pleased. Julie and Christine, the secretaries, had killer-woodpecker knocks, while Peter Melznic and Cas Suslowicz both tended to stand outside the door and say 'Hello?' plaintively, like dogs left outside in the rain.

Cassie pulled herself together; why speculate, when she could know? 'Come in,' she said, and the door opened.

They stood in the doorway, hand in hand. An objective observer might have said that they were sweet, their fingers tenderly entwined, her cheek resting on his shoulder. Ask any doctor, however, and he'll be sure to tell you: sweet things are bad for you.

'Miss Clay?' the young man said.

Cassie opened her mouth, but some joker had hit the mute button. What she'd been meaning to say was, 'I know you; you were in that tea shop, in the Funkhausen's Loop.' She didn't get around to doing that, however. Mostly it was because she could see the corridor outside and the door opposite, even though they were standing in the way.

The weird was commonplace at 70 St Mary Axe. Even there, however, it was reasonable to assume that translucent people were bad news.

'Are we disturbing you?' asked the girl.

Trick question, surely. In which case, give the reply they aren't expecting. 'No,' Cassie croaked. 'Um, what can I do for you?'

The man and the girl looked at each other. There was a sort of transcendent soppiness in their eyes that would've brought yesterday's dinner to the lips of Barbara Cartland. Then the girl said, 'We'd like to come back to life, please. If that's all right.'

Cassie felt as though someone had parked a large skip right on top of her chest. 'Um,' she said again. 'Are you, like, dead?'

They nodded. They were, she noticed, wearing matching sweaters. With little sheep on them.

'Right.' Instinct, years of meeting clients and taking notes, had her reaching for pen and paper.

'Well,' she went on, 'properly speaking, that'd be necromancy, and that's not really my department. Probably you'll need to see my colleague Mr Wells, or Mr Melznic might be able to—'

The girl looked at her companion, worried and disappointed. He gave her hand a reassuring squeeze. Somehow, Cassie just knew that his pet name for the girl was *pumpkin*. 'Actually,' he said, 'we were rather hoping you could help us. You see—'

'You're me,' the girl said. It wasn't interrupting, more like a sort of staggered chorus. Cassie had always hated it when boyfriends had finished her sentences for her; next thing, she always thought, they'd be stealing her soul.

'What did you say?' Cassie asked.

'You're me,' the girl repeated, 'or at least I'm you. I can never remember which way round it ought to be, though I don't suppose it really matters terribly much. It'd probably be easier to say, we're us.'

Like hell, Cassie's instincts were shrieking. I could be many things, but never such a pathetic bloody drip. 'How do you mean, exactly?' she said.

The man broke in. 'We don't mean to be pushy,' he said, 'but do you think we could possibly come in and sit down, rather than having this discussion where anybody could hear us?'

'Fine.' Cassie waved vaguely at the visitors' chairs. Before he sat down, the man made a point of closing the door.

'All right,' Cassie said, and in her own voice she heard the getting-down-to-business tone she'd perfected over the years for talking to punters. She was impressed by her own professionalism. Pen poised over paper, she said, 'Can we start off with your names?'

Once again, they exchanged glances. 'Well, no,' the girl said. 'You see, we lost them.'

'You lost your names?'

The man nodded. 'When we died, yes. It happens sometimes. It's a kind of—' He hesitated, and then the girl squeezed his hand again, and Cassie could see him drawing strength from her like a tanker refuelling, and it was all so romantic and sad that she wanted to scream. 'It's a kind of punishment,' he went on. 'For, well, suicide.'

Cassie heard the pen clatter on her desk, which suggested that she'd dropped it. 'Suicide?'

They both nodded simultaneously. 'You see,' the girl went on, 'when we found out we couldn't be together—'

'Right.' Cassie groped for a pencil in her desk-tidy. 'I see. No names. I suppose addresses are out of the question too, in that case.'

The girl gave her a small, apologetic smile.

'Not to worry,' Cassie said firmly. 'I'll just put down X and, um, Y. And you're both dead.'

'That's right,' the man said.

'I see. And you want us to, well, do something about that for you.'

'Yes, please.'

Cassie took a deep breath In the back of her mind, she was frantically skimming through dusty old memory folders of day-release lectures and vocational-training weekends, from back when she'd been keen and eager. 'Well,' she said, 'if you were wanting to lodge a formal appeal, there's a fairly straightforward procedure. First, you have to serve notice of intention to appeal within six months of date of death.' She fixed her stare on a small patch of wall about three inches above the man's head. 'When would that have been, precisely?'

'That's complicated,' the man replied.

'Is it?'

He nodded. 'Depends which one you mean,' he replied.

'I see. So which of you died first?'

'Not like that.' The girl was twiddling the ends of her hair round her left index finger, presumably out of nerves. 'You see—'

'Yes?'

'The thing is,' the man said, 'it's sort of happened more than once.'

'More than once?' This time, Cassie stared straight at him. 'What, you mean *death*?'

'Yes, that's right,' the girl said. 'Because of reincarnation, you see.'

The soft *ping* that Cassie heard just then was her pencil-lead snapping. 'Reincarnation.'

'Yes.' The man nodded enthusiastically. 'It's because we're star-crossed, you see,' he said. 'What happened was, we were supposed to get together and get married and live happily ever after, but something must've gone wrong, and we didn't.' Cassie saw the girl's fingers tighten around his once more, and looked away. 'So, well, we killed ourselves—'

(The way you do, Cassie thought.)

'—And when we got to the other place,' the girl said, 'we asked to see the manager, and he looked up his files and said yes, there's been a bit of a mix-up but not to worry, we could come back to life and meet each other all over again and everything would be just fine.' She hesitated, and snuffled loudly. The man fished in his translucent pocket and handed her a see-through tissue. She blew her nose, then went on, 'So back we came, and yes, we met up like we'd been told we I would, but then—'

Cassie waited while the girl did more snuffling, and the man patted her tenderly on the shoulder. Hell must be like this, Cassie thought.

'When we got there,' the girl continued, 'we found out—'

She subsided into snuffledom. The man said, 'Basically, Ms Clay, we found out that we didn't love each other any more.'

The girl looked up sharply. 'No, that's not right, pumpkin.' (Ah, Cassie thought.) 'We loved each other to bits and pieces, but somehow we couldn't—'

'There didn't seem to be any reason to it,' the man said. 'I mean, she knew she loved me, and I knew I worshipped the ground she stood on, but somehow we couldn't seem to make a go of it. We started quarrelling, which we'd never ever done before—'

'We couldn't talk to each other,' the girl whimpered damply. 'It was terrible. We'd always been able to talk to each other.'

'We used to talk for hours and hours and hours and hours,' the man said tenderly.

'And then suddenly we couldn't,' the girl said. 'And it was like there was some dreadful force making me blame him when I knew perfectly well it wasn't his fault—'

'Same with me,' the man put in.

'And then one day we had this awful row, and even though we knew we still loved each other a hundred and ninety per cent, that was it. The end. It was all over.'

'I see,' Cassie said, frowning. 'Excuse me if this sounds silly, but were you in a tea shop at the time?'

'That's right, yes,' the girl said, as though Cassie knowing that was the most natural thing ever. 'Anyway, I ran out into the street, and he didn't follow me, and that was that. Of course, without him life just wasn't worth living—'

'Complete waste of time,' the man agreed fervently.

'And so next thing we knew we were back at the other place,' the girl said, shredding tissue with her fingers.

'The manager was there waiting for us to arrive, I'll say that for him,' the man put in. 'No attempt to pretend it wasn't their fault or anything, we've got no complaints on that score. In fact, we can't speak too highly of the quality of service.'

'And he said,' the girl continued, 'that he couldn't understand what had happened, but naturally he'd send us straight back again for another try.'

'He said that?' Cassie mumbled.

'Oh yes.' The man nodded. 'Nice bloke, we really took to him. So back we went, only this time for some reason we ended up something like a hundred years earlier, in Victorian times; which was a bit of a facer, obviously, but we wouldn't have minded. But exactly the same thing happened all over again: rows, not talking, all that.'

'So you committed suicide,' Cassie said. 'Again.'

'More or less,' the man said. 'Well, this time I was a subaltern in the British army, so I got myself posted to the East and died of malaria, but it was practically suicide.'

'I fell into a decline,' the girl said. 'You know, like in books. I didn't know it was actually possible, but it is.'

'I see,' Cassie said, and she noticed how deep the bite marks were in the pencil she was still holding. 'Let me guess. You went back again—'

'And again,' the girl said with a little sigh, 'and again. Always the same, of course.'

'We used to say we should be clocking up Frequent Dier points,' the man said. 'It was our little joke.'

Something else went *ping* at that point, but this time it wasn't a pencil lead, it was something deep and fundamental inside Cassie's brain. 'Right, I get the picture,' she interrupted brusquely. 'But where the hell do *I* fit into all this?'

'We're coming to that,' the man said severely. 'You see, the most recent time, when we got there and the manager came out to see us—'

'He was really apologetic,' the girl said. 'I think he was genuinely upset about it all.'

'He told us,' the man said, 'that there's some regulation or other about the number of times you can be reincarnated before you, well, sort of come to an end; and apparently, we'd had our ration – no fault of our own, he made that perfectly clear – but he'd been to see his boss and really made a fuss about it, and as a gesture of goodwill they were prepared to give us one last chance.' He looked at Cassie, and through his pale blue eyes she could see the coat hook on the back of the door. 'You,' he said.

'Me?'

The girl's head bobbed up and down. 'And a man called Colin Hollingshead. They – well, you and him – you're our last chance. You're us, you see, reincarnated. If you and he don't get together this time, and fall in love and get married and live happily ever after – well that's all our chances used up, and we'll never . . .'

She dissolved into sobs, like ice cream in a microwave. The man was patting and hand-squeezing and there-thereing, and Cassie had to shout quite loud to make herself heard—

'Just a fucking minute,' she said.

They looked up, startled, and stared at her.

'Sorry,' Cassie said. 'I didn't mean to— Look,' she wailed, 'I really don't want to seem unsympathetic, and it's obvious that you've both had a really raw deal and everything, but I've met this Colin Hollingshead, and he's a nice enough bloke in his way, but—' The power of speech ebbed away from her, as though her battery had finally gone flat, and all she could do was wave her hands, gently and vaguely. 'I'm sorry,' she repeated. 'But there it is.'

The man was staring at her. It was as though a monk or a hermit had spent his entire life praying to be granted a beatific vision; and finally, eventually, one evening in the solitude of his lonely cell the vision had appeared before him in glory and blown a raspberry. 'Are you saying,' he said slowly, 'that you're refusing to help us?'

Cassie gritted her teeth. It was like drowning kittens and decapitating Barbie dolls and whisking up fluffy hamsters in a blender, but it had to be done. 'That's right,' she said. 'Sorry,' she added.

'But you can't—' the girl managed to blurt out, before the sobs overtook her again. The man shot Cassie a furious now-look-what-you've-done glare, and put his arms around the girl, muttering, 'It's all right, sweetness, don't cry, she doesn't really mean it.'

'Yes, I do,' Cassie said crisply. 'Listen to me,' she added, raising her voice above the snuffling and the comforting. 'I really am terribly sorry, but you've got to understand, there's nothing l can do. I can't just make up my mind to be in love with someone, it doesn't work like that. You know that as well as I do. Either you're in love with someone or you aren't. And I'm sorry to say, I've met this Colin Hollingshead, and I have to tell you, I don't love him one bit, and I'm pretty damn sure he doesn't love me. End of story, I'm afraid.'

The couple didn't say anything. She snuffled and he glared, but not a word was spoken. It was one of those silences into which light falls and is destroyed, and no matter what the cost you know you've got to fill it with something before it consumes the entire universe. 'Look,' Cassie said desperately, 'if there was any way on earth I could deliberately make myself fall in love with the bloody man, I'd do it, just so she'd stop making that horrible noise, but—'

It was like treading on a mine; because even as she said the words, Cassie realised that yes, there was something she could do. Not just something, but something easy-peasy; something J. W. Wells and Co had been making possible for over two hundred years.

When it was first invented, round about the time they were laying the foundations of the Brighton Pavilion, they called it *J. W. Wells & Co's Patent Oxy-Hydrogen Love-At-First-Sight Philtre* and that was all right, because there weren't any trade-description laws in those days, and nobody bothered too much about the ropy science because nobody really knew what oxygen or hydrogen actually were. Two centuries later, the label just said *JWW Love Philtre*. It was still the same recipe and it worked just as well as it had always done, and there was always at least one fifty-five-gallon plastic drum of the stuff on hand in the closed-file store. All you had to do was drink it, and make him or her drink it too at the same time, then you'd both fall asleep for twenty minutes or so, and when you both woke up (assuming that each of you was the first person the other one saw), bingo. Easy as falling off a log into a bottomless pit. These days, there were even orange, mango and tropical-fruit flavours. Couldn't be more straightforward.

'No,' Cassie said, to herself as much as to the two translucent lovers. 'I'm sorry, but I can't help you. Has it – I mean, have you ever considered the possibility that you two just weren't meant to get together? Like Romeo and Juliet, or Clark and Lois—' She fell silent. Just looking at them, she knew she was drivelling. Maybe it was a trick of the light, a side effect of their revolting translucence, but where their hands clasped it was as though they'd merged together, like a welded seam.

'Oh no,' the girl said firmly. 'You see, the manager told us, in the other place. He looked it up in the register and everything. We were supposed to live happily ever after, seventy years and never a cross word.' They exchanged a look so gooey that Cassie instinctively wiped her hands on her knees. 'So we know for a definite fact it was meant to be. Also,' she went on, 'Mr Dao – that's the manager's name – he said that if things didn't work out and we never did get married and so on, it'd cause a big problem. Hyperphasic anomaly in the spatio-temporal interface, I think he called it; anyway, it sounded pretty bad. All sorts of things'd start coming unravelled, he reckoned. For a start, you see, we were going to have six children—'

'Three of each,' the man put in dreamily.

'And they were all going to go on and do wonderful things with their lives and make the world a better place; and if we don't, well, that's the future gone wrong for a start. Like, suppose one of our kids was going to be a great doctor who cured a dreadful disease and saved millions of lives—'

'But instead,' the man carried on, smooth as a well-trained relay team, 'he's never born, so all those people who should've lived actually die. Mr Dao was really upset about that; he said it'd cause havoc with schedules and staff duty rosters and accommodation arrangements and sittings for meals and things like that. So you see,' he went on, 'it's not just us who's affected, it's millions and millions of other people too.'

Shit, Cassie thought. Millions and millions of people. She really ought to care about that. And besides: what in the world could possibly be more important than true love? It's the message that everybody's bombarded with, from primary school to crematorium. Love is all you need, they tell you. It's so fundamental that it's practically a duty, like recycling or voting in elections. If she drank the philtre, and spiked Colin's tea with the stuff, there was absolutely no question, they'd be in love, for ever; they'd be just as blissfully, repulsively happy as the two specimens nestling up close in front of her. That had to be a good thing, surely. It was accepted throughout the trade: love philtre was a good thing, because it made people happy. No bitter, traumatic break-ups, broken hearts, ruined lives with love philtre, no ghastly mistaken choices. It was like an arranged marriage made in heaven, stone-cold guaranteed or your money back. So really, there was no earthly reason—

Except that she didn't love young Mr Hollingshead, not one little bit.

Cassie took a deep breath.

'Sorry,' she said.

Up and down the back stairs, along the corridors in every direction, in and out of the conference rooms and the stationery cupboards and the laser-printer bay and everywhere; not a trace of them anywhere. It was as though they'd just walked straight out through a wall or something.

Which, Benny reminded himself, they were probably quite capable of doing. He could feel himself running out of steam, as the hopelessness of his task gradually became apparent. Unless he was lucky enough to run into them by sheer accident, he was wasting his time.

He traipsed back to his office, sat down on a stack of green timesheet pads (just arrived from the printers, still in their shrink-wrap; he spared a moment from his despair to hate the new management) and let his head loll forwards onto his chest. He'd done his best but he'd failed. The question was, what now?

The obvious, logical, sensible thing would be to keep quiet, pretend it had never happened, and get on with the work he was supposed to be doing. The alternative was going and finding one of the bosses and telling him what'd happened, so that he could immediately notify the firm's insurers. If he did that he might get yelled at for a bit, but nothing terribly bad would happen; after all, he was the cashier, the one who had to make the soul-corroding, brain-melting trip to the Bank of the Dead every day. They couldn't fire him, because the job had to be done and who else would be crazy enough to do it? If he went and confessed, like he was supposed to, it'd stop being his responsibility, he could pass it onto someone else and they'd be the one facing sleepless nights and nightmare days haunted with stark terror.

Benny sat up. That'd be a very bad reason for doing the right thing. Benny Shumway had his faults, as his ex-wives knew to their cost, but he wasn't a coward, and he faced up to his responsibilities, one of which was the door in his office. If someone – something – had broken through it and was infesting the land of the living, it was his job to deal with it. The other name for pest control was heroism; in the same way, admittedly, as estate agents describe Swindon as 'edge of the Cotswolds', but never mind. Besides, if he went to one of the ex-partners or (even worse) the new management, who did he think they'd assign to the case? The pest-control specialist. Fine.

He stood up, climbed onto his chair, fetched a book down from the top shelf of his bookcase and blew dust off it. *Necromancy for Dummies*; how long since he'd read it? No matter.

He turned to the index. *Dead, unquiet, exorcising*. Good a place to start as any.

There's one thing every practitioner should know about exorcising. Can't be done. There's a whole heap of books (see Further Reading, pp. 427–558) that'll tell you how to go about it, but guess what. They're all making it up. You can't banish the dead, and for why? Because they don't exist.

Benny sighed, and put the book down on his desk. He remembered now. Oh, he thought.

Next, he tried the office procedures manual, twice as thick and half again as heavy as *Necromancy for Dummies*, and it said more or less the same thing but without the comic patter. There's no point in trying to impose your will on something that isn't there, like the non-existent man on the stair in the nursery rhyme. Dead and gone means what it says. Deal with it.

Yes, Benny thought, but.

Logic; access your inner Spock. The books, who ought to know, said that the dead weren't there any more. On the other hand, something had opened the door, and it hadn't been from his side. Furthermore, he had the evidence of the thin-faced girl, what's-her-name, who'd seen them in the corridor. So either the books were wrong (impossible) or he was wrong (also impossible); or else (entirely possible) he was missing the point—

He growled under his breath Something had opened the door, but obviously it couldn't have been dead. But it had come from the other side, and nothing could possibly live out there, by definition.

Unless—

Benny jumped up. His feet were running before they hit the carpet, like the cat in the cartoons.

CHAPTER FOURTEEN

Colin drifted back into reception. He wasn't quite sure why. Maybe it was the same instinct that motivates cats on wet days to go and see if there's a door where it isn't raining. If so, it hadn't worked. Fam wasn't behind the desk; it was just that Rosie person.

She looked at him and grinned. 'Hello,' she said.

If he'd been wise, he'd have paid more attention to the grin. Humans, with their lamentable tendency to anthropomorphise, are an easy mark for any species that opens its mouth and displays its teeth: they're either unaware of or wilfully blind to the fact that, in most of the animal kingdom, the gesture doesn't mean what they think it does. 'Anything I can do for you?' she asked.

Colin shook his head. 'It's all right,' he said. 'I just, um, I'm waiting for an important fax and I was wondering if it'd come in yet, that's all.'

'Ah.' Rosie's grin widened to Little-Red-Riding-Hood's-surrogate-granny proportions. 'If you're not too busy,' she said, 'could you spare a couple of ticks to answer a question for me?'

'Sure.'

'All right. What the hell is it about young human males and receptionists?'

For a second or so, Colin felt as though someone had accidentally set off a boxful of fireworks inside his head. While he was still thus indisposed, she went on, 'Not that I'm complaining, don't get me wrong. After all, it's why I do this job. It was my cousin Veronica who put me on to it. Be a receptionist, Rosie, she said to me, you can pick 'em off like a sniper up a church tower. I thought she was kidding me until I tried it, and I've never looked back.'

'Um,' Colin said.

'There was this lad at the place I used to work,' she went on, 'a bit like you, he was, only taller and wetter. He had this thing for receptionists; leastways, one of 'em. Not me,' she added with a sigh, 'though not for want of trying. But his receptionist turned out to be an illusion created by the Queen of the Fey to lure him to his doom, and I think he went off us a bit after that. Married a bony little cow and moved to New Zealand. Last I heard he was blissfully happy and richer than Bill Gates, but there you go. Anyhow, you didn't come out here to talk to me. You were thinking about that chubby bird of yours.'

'She's not— How did you know?'

Rosie twitched her nose at him. 'Smell, actually. It's a special talent of my lot – we can smell true love. Like smelling beer on someone's breath. It's a hold-over from the old days. My lot used to track their prey by scent, you see. It's pretty dark, where we evolved.'

A burning eagerness to ask who her lot were fought it out with the sure and certain knowledge that he wouldn't like the answer one bit, and the sure and certain knowledge won. 'Right,' he said; then, 'True love?'

'Mphm. If you're interested, it's sort of a cross between garlic and iodine. The smell, I mean. But you wouldn't be able to smell it, like humans can't hear dog whistles.'

'Then you're saying—' He hesitated. 'Are you sure about that?'

'I'd know it a mile off.' She sighed. 'If it was just a passing infatuation it'd be more like sump oil and violets; and good old plain and simple lust – well, it's hard to describe, a bit like creosote mixed with—'

'Fine,' Colin said quickly. He realised that, in spite of Rosie's breathtaking exterior, he found her about as alluring as a dead badger.

She sniffed, clicked her tongue and said, 'Thank you *so* much. You know, there's times when I think I'm losing my touch. Here, what about this?'

Rosie didn't vanish or anything; there was no single instant when she wasn't there. It was just that there was one moment when she was a screamingly gorgeous redhead, and another when she was a heart-stoppingly lovely brunette; neither of whom would Colin willingly have touched with a ten-foot pole.

'Oh well,' she said. 'Worth a try, no hard feelings. Though in your shoes, I don't think I'd be quite so damn picky.'

Fair comment, but so what? 'Anyhow,' Colin said, a bit awkwardly, 'nice to have chatted with you again and everything. I'd better be—'

She grinned again. 'I know. Used to it by now. You run along, and when your terribly important fax comes in, I'll let you know. I'll bring it down to your office if you like.'

'No, please don't bother,' Colin said quickly, and she laughed. 'Bye,' he said, and fled.

Our lot, he thought as he mounted the last stair and slowed down; and what was all that stuff about tracking their prey by scent? One thing was for sure: he was meeting a lot of new and interesting people these days.

True love. Rosie could smell true love, and—

And a fat lot of good that was going to do him if he never saw Fam again; which was likely, since he didn't know where to find her, and he doubted very much whether she'd be coming round looking for him, given the circumstances of their last meeting.

On his desk was a pile of paper. It looked difficult and technical, something to do with shift rotations and hourly productivity ratios, and he ignored it. Leave it there long enough and it'd eventually turn into coal, maybe even diamonds.

Instead, Colin tried to focus on the miserable tangle that his life had recently become.

Not so long ago, he'd decided against running away to Vanuatu on the grounds that, although everything else had turned extremely weird and smelly, there was still a chance that he might be able to make a go of it with Fam – his one true love, as he'd just found out. Indeed; but apparently that wasn't allowed, in which case there really wasn't anything to keep him here, and every reason for him to clear out as soon as possible.

I'm not really a coward, he thought, or a pathetic loser or any of the other things I use as excuses for not trying. I think my problem's always been history and geography. I'm Dad's son, I'm here at Hollingshead and Farren, of course I'll never have a life if I stay here and let it all wash over me. But if I went somewhere else, where nobody knows me—

Someone – something – was standing over him; something that could open his office door without making a noise. 'You're wanted in the machine shop,' Oscar said.

Colin looked up. 'Me?'

'Yes. You're in charge. You have to go there and take command.' An image of James T. Kirk on the bridge of the *Enterprise* flashed into Colin's mind. Me? Take command? Yes, but not of a machine shop. 'Sorry,' he said. 'I can't come right now.'

'That is untrue,' Oscar said, sounding puzzled. 'You have no other duties.'

Colin looked up; looked the thing, the quintessence of human nightmares, in what he assumed was its eye. 'That's the point, actually,' he said. 'I've got no duties at all. I don't owe anybody anything. Except,' he added, 'possibly me. Sorry, just thinking aloud.'

'I do not understand.'

'No,' Colin replied, 'I don't suppose you do, but never mind. Try this.' He took a deep breath; he was about to be rude to the Devil, and he still wasn't really used to being rude to anybody. 'I quit. I'm leaving. Okay?'

'You're leaving.' Oscar twitched. 'Humour,' it said.

'No.'

'No humour?'

'Not humour. Serious.'

'I see.' There was something about the way Oscar said it. Colin had expected anger, but it wasn't that at all. Quite the reverse; it was something a bit like the still, tense excitement of an angler who sees his float bob. 'You wish to abandon Hollingshead and Farren.'

'Yup.'

Oscar quivered slightly, like a spoilt dog watching a sandwich. 'You intend, then, to forfeit the contract.'

'Y—' Colin managed to bite back the rest of the word in time. 'How do you mean?' he said.

There was a kind of too-good-to-be-true sag in Oscar's voice. 'What I said. You wish to leave the firm and in order to do so you must forfeit the contract. Is that your intention?'

'I—' Colin pulled himself together. All his life he'd said 'Yes' or 'No' to questions he didn't understand, rather than admit his ignorance. This time, however, he wasn't going to do that; not if it was a choice between saving face and saving the rest of him. 'I'm not very good at legal jargon,' he said. 'What exactly does "forfeit" mean?'

Oscar sighed. 'Quite simple,' it said. 'If you leave the firm, it constitutes a fundamental breach of contract, as set out in section 6, paragraph 9, subsection (b) (ii).' Colin was impressed in spite of himself; Oscar could pronounce brackets. '"In the event of unilateral breach by one party, the full consideration falls due immediately on demand."'

'You're doing it again,' Colin said. 'Jargon. Try that again in plain English.'

Oscar seemed almost embarrassed. 'I am sorry,' it said. 'I am not proficient at plain English. It is not much used where I come from. We do not find it conducive to—' It hesitated. 'To productivity. Perhaps,' it went on, 'this is not the best environment for a discussion of this sort. I believe it is traditional to conduct vital negotiations while eating food. Let's do lunch.'

'I'd rather not, thanks.'

'Are you sure? I can provide you with a suitably extended spoon. Humour,' it added, hopefully.

'I think we should get this straight right now. What are you trying to tell me? What'll happen if I just walk out and don't come back?'

It was as though Oscar had closed down or gone off-line; it stood still and quiet for a long time, to the point where Colin began to wonder if he'd killed it. 'You want me to tell you that?' it said at last.

'Yes.'

'Very well. Should you act in the manner you have outlined, the contract will have been breached. We will no longer have to provide workers and material support to your business, and you—' Another pause; was Oscar feeling *squeamish* about something? Surely not. 'You will have to fulfil your obligations under the contract immediately. Do you understand me?'

Colin wilted like a flat tyre. So that was that. If he walked out, Dad would have to go to Hell straight away: not pass Go, do not collect two hundred pounds. Simple as that, once you pared away the legal gibberish.

'Are you sure?' he asked.

'Yes.'

'So I'm stuck here, then. Indefinitely.'

Oscar shook its head. 'Not indefinitely,' it said. 'For the term of your father's natural life.'

'Ah.'

'And now,' Oscar said, 'you must go to the machine shop and exercise authority. At once.'

'Oh, for pity's sake,' Colin snapped. 'Can't I just stay here and sulk? I'm sure you don't need me down there. I don't know how to run a factory. Dad does all that.'

'It is required,' Oscar said.

'Balls.' And now he'd *sworn* at the Devil. Just as well his mother couldn't hear him, or she'd be really upset. Tell him he'd come to a bad end, most like. 'Or are you going to tell me you'll whatsit the contract if I don't?'

Oscar hesitated. 'It is required,' it repeated awkwardly.

'Or?'

'Or there may be a downturn in morale and industrial relations, leading to a decline in productivity.'

Colin stood up. 'I'll risk it,' he said. 'I think I'll go out for a breath of fresh air.'

Oscar sniffed. 'There is air in the building,' it pointed out.

Colin walked past it onto the landing, then sprinted down the stairs as fast as he could go. At reception, Rosie called out, 'That Oscar's looking for you,' but he ignored her and bundled out into the street.

Outside, he paused. Just getting out of there made him feel a lot better, but it was hardly a plan of action. He looked up and down the street, open to suggestions. Sod this, he thought, I'll— He'd what? He knew what he wanted to do: he wanted to go to 70 St Mary Axe, see Cassie Clay and demand that she explained the contract, in language that he could understand, so he'd know exactly what kind of hold the bastards had over him. If he knew that, he could at least start working on an escape plan. That was what he'd like to do, but he had an unpleasant feeling it might not be possible. The railway station was closed until further notice, he didn't have a car yet – come on, he told himself, there's got to be a way to do a simple thing like get up to London. Buses? Taxi?

Colin had a bad feeling about those two options. Somehow, he had an idea that if he went and stood at the bus stop, he'd be there a very long time. He remembered the cup of tea. Even so: there *had* to be a way, even if he was right and there was an exceptionally powerful supernatural force bent on making him stay put. So what if they could sabotage public transport? He could— Hire a car. Yes, of course. Then he'd set off in the opposite direction, make for Kingston or Basingstoke, and then double back and outsmart them that way. Maybe it wouldn't work, but he wouldn't mind trying. It'd be (he grinned sadly) something to do.

Hire a car . . . He remembered. There was a hire-car place

down on the Richmond road, only a few hundred yards away. Into his mind flitted an image of Steve McQueen on a motorbike. Of course, in the film Mr McQueen had been trying to get home, and here he was, desperate to break out of it.

The hire-car place was on the left-hand side, just past Halfords—

Apparently not. It *had* been there; he'd seen it only the other day, a large glass-fronted building on a corner. Instead, he found two small buildings, a florist's and a mobile-phone shop, and, on the opposite side of the road, a photos-while-you-wait place which he could've sworn he'd last seen down the other end of the road, three doors up from Laura Ashley.

This, Colin told himself, is silly.

He stood on the corner, wondering what to do next; and while his mind was wandering, a taxi pulled up next to him. Its yellow light was on, and the driver was looking at him.

Oh well, Colin thought. He went over, and the driver said, 'Where to?'

'Can you take to me 70 St Mary Axe?' he asked.

'Hop in.'

There'd be roadworks, of course; or a burst water main, or a tailback, traffic diverted via Orpington, Salford and the Great Barrier Reef. Humour, as Oscar would say. Colin got in nevertheless. It'd be interesting to see just how far he managed to go before they turned him back. He snuggled into the seat, stretched out his legs and closed his eyes. He was wasting his time, but at least it was out of the office and away from Oscar and the demons, for a little while.

'Seventy St Mary Axe,' the driver called out.

Colin's eyes snapped open, and he leaned forward. 'Are you sure?' he asked.

''Course I'm bloody sure. I do this for a living, you know.'

Colin jumped out, handed over money, waved away the change. Just as the driver pulled away, Colin caught sight of the man's eyes; they were strangely red, as though he was a photo of himself taken indoors with a flash.

'Bugger me,' Colin said aloud, as he stared at the old-fashioned brass plate and the revolving door. 'I made it.' He smiled out of pure exuberant joy. 'Eat your heart out, Steve,' he added, and barged into the door, which whirled him round a couple of times like a rogue centrifuge and spat him out in the front office of JWW.

'You,' said a voice.

His eyes opened wide. Couldn't be—

'Fam?'

'Colin.' She was sitting behind the front desk, staring at him. 'What are you doing here?'

'I came to see—' Fuck that, he thought. 'What about you? What're *you*—?'

She looked at him with a mixture of misery and contempt. 'I work here,' she said.

'Here?'

'Yes, here.' Fam looked round to see if anybody was watching, and lowered her voice. 'It was the only job I could find, after your Dad fired me. Really, Colin, I didn't think you'd be so bloody petty.'

Colin opened his mouth and closed it again, like a whale catching krill.

'He told me, you know, straight out, like it was my fault. You dump my son, he said, you can bloody well get another job. My Mum said I should take you to the tribunal, but I told her, I don't want anything to do with any of them ever again.'

'My Dad said that?'

'Yes, he did.' Fam scowled at him so fiercely that he winced. 'So I told him I never wanted the stupid job and he could go to hell.'

'And what did he say to that?'

'He just laughed. Thought it was dead funny. So I went home and looked through the ads in the paper, and this place was the only one that'd even give me an interview. Took me on straight away, which just shows. Some people *aren't* complete bastards.'

Colin put a hand on the desk to stop himself falling over.

Didn't make sense, his brain was screaming at him. First, all the unseen bloody forces are trying to keep me from finding her, and now they're practically throwing her at me, except that she hates me, because my stupid Dad— Hold it right there. His father, who'd fired her. Go to hell, she'd told him.

And why not?

'Listen,' he said, and the urgency in his voice cut her off in mid-protest. 'It's really, really complicated and bizarre and hard to explain, but I promise faithfully that I'll try, okay? But first I've got to see one of the people who work here, Cassie Clay. It shouldn't take—'

'Cassie Clay,' Fam interrupted venomously. 'Her. The one you were slobbering all over in the office that day, back at your place.'

'I wasn't bloody slobbering,' Colin hissed. 'Look, I'm not the tiniest bit interested in the stupid cow, except that I desperately need to ask her something about a really ghastly, horrible mess we're in at work; and just maybe she might be able to tell me how I can get out of it, and if I can I'm going to leave Hollingshead's and probably the country, and—' Just a fraction of a second's hesitation; but he was right up on top of the wave, so why not carry on and see where it took him? 'And if I do that,' he heard himself say, 'I haven't got a clue what I'll do or where I'll go, and you probably think I've gone barking mad but I genuinely mean this: if it turns out I can go, will you please, please come with me?'

There was a moment's dead silence. 'You what?'

'I love you,' Colin said. 'You're my one true love, you're the only reason my life could possibly be worth living, and will you bloody well come with me or not?'

Maybe, if a trapdoor in the ceiling had opened and swamped Fam in runny custard, she might have been marginally more astonished. Too close to call, really. 'I—'

'Well? I hate to hurry you, but I've got to see this dratted Clay woman.'

'I don't know,' she said.

'Damn.' Colin breathed out hard through his nose. 'All right, tell you what. I'll go and see Cassie Clay, and while I'm in there you can be thinking it over. Then, soon as I'm done, you can tell me what you've decided. All right?'

'All right,' Fam said, in a tiny voice. 'I'll buzz her and ask if she can see you.'

Colin shook his head. 'Tell her I'm on my way up. Where's her office, by the way?'

'Um, I'm not actually sure,' she replied. 'It's a rather odd building, you can get lost in it. I'd better ring through to her – don't want to lose this job as well.'

Colin sighed. 'Yes, all right. But don't ask if she can spare me five minutes. Tell her I've got to see her right now. Matter of life and death. Matter of life *after* death, actually, but that's part of the long, complicated explanation, so we'll save it for later, all right?'

Fam rang through. 'She'll be straight down,' she said. 'Sounded almost like she was expecting you.'

Colin shrugged. 'She's strange. In fact, I think they all are. Fam, have they told you what it is they actually do here? Because—'

'Of course they have,' she replied. 'They're tea and coffee importers, it says so on the brass plate outside.' She frowned. 'What's so desperately important and involves tea?' she added.

Colin felt the grin take control of his face before he could stop it. 'I need to dump about a hundred tons of it in a harbour,' he said. He almost added 'Humour' out of sheer force of habit. 'Look, forget I said that. I really will explain, I promise.' The fire door was opening; that'd be Cassie. 'And think about what I said, right?' he hissed, as Cassie walked into reception. 'Promise?'

Fam mouthed *yes* at him, and he looked away.

'In here,' Cassie said. 'My office. We won't be disturbed in here. I've got all the documents and stuff.'

Colin looked round, and took an instant dislike to the place.

For one thing, there was something very odd about it. No matter how hard they try not to, people can't help leaving an impression on rooms they spend time in. Sometimes it's obvious – fluffy cushions, bead curtains, framed photographs of fat children cuddling dogs, cured and stuffed squirrels in a glass case, the smell of forgotten salad rotting in obscurity. Sometimes it's more subliminal: the perfectly tidy desk and immaculately placed furniture of the neurotic, for example. Cassie Clay's office, by contrast, told him nothing at all. It was as though nobody had been in the room for months.

But he wasn't interested in rooms, no matter how weird and physically impossible they might be. All he wanted to do was get the information he needed and leave, pausing only to sweep Fam off her feet and into his arms on the way out, so, if they'd laid on all this ambience for his benefit, they'd been wasting their time.

'In here,' Cassie went on, 'I've got a photocopy of the contract your father signed, along with the correspondence between us and them, notes of my phone conversations, all that kind of thing. Do you want to work through it together, or what?'

Colin shrugged. 'Do what you like,' he said. 'What I want to know is, how does it affect me personally? Because that bloody horrible *thing* that calls itself Oscar told me I couldn't quit or run away, or they'd foreclose at once and my Dad'd go straight to— Well, you know. So, can you look at the paperwork and tell me if that's really true, or whether they're lying about it.'

Cassie nodded. 'Bear with me,' she said, 'I'll have a—' She broke off. First she stared at the contract – she was only on the first page – and then at Colin.

'What is it?' he asked.

'Sorry if this sounds like a dumb question,' she said, 'but what's your father's first name?'

'Colin,' Colin replied. 'Same as me. What about it?'

Cassie breathed a massive sigh of relief 'That's all right, then,' she said. 'Only, when I drew up the contract, his name wasn't in the file anywhere, or in the letter of instruction, so I left a blank for him to fill in. So when I looked at it just now and saw what's been written in there, Colin Derek Hollingshead, I thought for a moment there'd been some sort of terrible—'

'Did you say Derek?'

Cassie looked up. 'That's right. Here, see for yourself.'

'My father's middle name is Henry.'

'What?'

'And I was called Colin Derek after my Mum's cousin in— Give me that,' Colin snapped, grabbing the contract from her. 'You must've . . .'

Dad's handwriting had always been something of a mystery to him. He'd always wondered how come a forceful, dynamic man like his father could have such childish, girly handwriting.

'Oh shit,' he said.

Childish and girly, but crystal clear. And unmistakable.

'I don't understand,' Cassie was bleating. Colin laughed.

'Don't you?' he said. 'I do. I fucking well understand, all right.' He could feel the anger welling up inside him like a balloon. 'You know what he's done? It wasn't his soul he sold to the Devil – it was *mine*.'

Three seconds passed, during which there was no sound at all.

'Oh,' Cassie said.

Which only went to show: she might've known a very great deal about magical law and spiritual conveyancing, but absolutely nothing about tact. Colin, on the other hand, seemed to have stopped entirely, as though God had hit the pause button. It wasn't that the anger had gone away; far from it. Rather, it was now so huge, filling him so completely, that at first he could neither move nor speak; and when the pressure dropped just a little, all he could come out with was a small, flat voice, like the snotty cow in a Japanese car who reminds you that you haven't put your seat belt on.

'He can't do that, can he?' Colin said.

'Well, no,' Cassie replied quickly. 'I mean, if you're not a party to the contract it's not binding on you, obviously. It'd only affect you if you actually signed—' She tailed off, then added, 'You *did* sign, didn't you?'

'Yes. You witnessed my signature.'

'So I did,' Cassie replied. 'Actually, I remember thinking at the time, why's he got to sign, it's nothing to do with him; but I assumed it was just an indemnity or something, just so they could cover themselves—'

'You thought that,' Colin said, very quietly indeed.

'Yes, but I didn't actually read—'

'You didn't actually read what it said. I see.'

At least Cassie didn't say *sorry* at that point; not because she wasn't about to, her common sense having evaporated like whisky on a hot stove, but because at that moment the door opened and Fam came in, holding a tray. On it were two cups and saucers, a sugar bowl, a milk jug and a small plate of digestive biscuits.

'Thought you might like some tea,' she said, putting the tray down on the table, and left.

It was only after she'd gone that Colin realised it had been her; and the irony of it burst through his stunned numbness like an armour-piercing shell. Just when he'd got somewhere; just when there was a chance she'd say yes and come with him to Vanuatu or the Andaman Islands and help him with the beach-combing and the splitting open of coconuts or whatever the future held for them both, just at that moment, this had to happen. It was just so bloody *unkind*—

'Milk and sugar?' Cassie whispered.

'Yes, please,' Colin replied automatically. 'No sugar.'

'Biscuit?'

'Thanks.' A plate appeared on the periphery of his vision; he reached out and took a biscuit, then stared at it blankly for a second or two, trying to remember what the hell he was supposed to do with it. 'So what you're saying is,' he said, 'I signed the contract, so Dad gets his demon workforce and I'm the one who goes to Hell for ever and ever.'

'Basically, yes,' Cassie replied.

'And the moment I try and quit or escape, I drop dead on the spot and—'

'Yes.'

Without really knowing what he was doing or why, Colin stirred his tea a few times and drank a mouthful. The milk must've been off, because it tasted funny – wasn't there an old superstition that the presence of the Evil One curdled milk? It's started already, he thought wildly. How absolutely bloody wonderful.

'And all this could've been avoided,' he went on – Cassie was trying to hide behind her teacup, but he wasn't having that '– if you could've been arsed to do your job and read the sodding small print.'

'Mphm.'

'Great.' Colin put down his cup, realised he was still holding a digestive biscuit, and closed his hand on it, crushing it into dust. 'Well, since I'm going to go to Hell anyhow, I might as well do something evil and bad while I'm at it. Such as strangling you.'

Something in his tone of voice, perhaps; because Cassie reacted as though she thought he meant it. She choked on the biscuit that she'd been eating, jumped up out of her chair, sending the cup and tray flying, and backed towards the door. Colin, now he came to think of it, actually *had* meant it. 'There's a saying,' he said, as he stood up and took a step forward. 'Something about sheep and lambs,' he muttered. 'And hanging.'

'Now look,' Cassie gabbled quickly. 'I'm not promising anything, but maybe if we talked to them really, really nicely—'

Colin lunged at her. He wasn't blessed with particularly good reflexes or anything like that, but the adrenalin was flowing and he had all the motivation that anybody could possibly need. Cassie dodged, of course, but her chair was in the way and she stumbled against it, which slowed her up a bit. In fact, it'd have been a close-run thing if she and Colin hadn't both suddenly stopped dead in their tracks, dropped to the floor like sacks of potatoes, and immediately fallen asleep.

CHAPTER FIFTEEN

Connie Schwartz-Alberich had many virtues, but patience wasn't one of them. Not that the deficiency bothered her in the least. Trees, she reckoned, were designed to be patient; likewise buildings, stalactites and tectonic plates. Human beings, on the other hand, were better suited to bustling about and getting things done, and she was a great believer in playing to one's strengths.

Now, it seemed, she had a choice. She could wait patiently for her notice to expire, and then she could wait patiently at home for the phone to ring with an enticing new job offer, and then she could resolutely, stoically wither away and die. Or she could get up off her bum and do something.

Define 'something'. There were all sorts of things Connie could do, such as burst her way into the new boss's office and restructure his nasal architecture – fun for about five seconds, but not offering any long-term solution. Or she could get on the phone to every contact she had in the trade and plead for an interview, which would help pass the time but was unlikely to do any good. Or—

Instead, she'd got on with her work. She went at it like a combine harvester in a cornfield, mowing it down in swathes until there simply wasn't any more. That was a pity, because it had helped take her mind off the unpleasant choice that was still unresolved. So she decided to go and see Cas Suslowicz. He might have some work she could be getting on with; alternatively, she could torture him with guilt over the fact that she'd been sacked and there was nothing he could do about it. Yes, that'd be fun.

Connie found him, as usual, slumped in his chair, elbows on the desk, surrounded by a mountain range of files, folders, reports, surveys, architects' drawings and other accumulations of information. Cas loathed paperwork; he was a giant (the shortest giant in the world, but still a giant) and what he liked doing was building things – castles in the air, rainbow bridges, palaces on top of beanstalks, highways to Heaven, anything with a bit of a challenge to it. Trotting up gangplanks with a twenty-ton slab of marble on each shoulder was no bother as far as he was concerned. Filling in a planning application, however, gave him a headache. Pencils broke as soon as he picked them up, and building regulations had been known to make him burst into tears.

'Connie,' he said, looking up. 'I haven't seen you in ages.'

Of course he hadn't. Guilt. That was something else he was good at. Maybe it was a giant thing. If your race memory is all about bearing the weight of the world on your shoulders while someone else is bedding in the acroprop, sooner or later you're going to get into the habit of accepting responsibility for anything that isn't nailed down.

'Oh well,' she said. 'You look busy.'

Cas groaned and nodded his huge, shaggy head. 'It's this rotten job,' he sighed. 'Oh, it's no big deal in itself: Union Bank of Sacramento wants a city in the clouds so they can transfer their registered office there and save a bundle in corporation tax, but the red tape's appalling. There's the Federal Aviation Authority, the California state legislature, the Yosemite National Park people, NASA—' He lifted a vast, sausage-fingered hand, and let it fall on his massive knee. 'I'm telling you,' he went on, 'if we'd had all this kind of crap to contend with when we were building Valhalla, Odin and the boys'd still be beating each other up in a Portakabin on the Oslo fjord.'

Connie pursed her lips. 'You know what, Cas,' she said. 'What you need is someone to look after the bullshit for you and let you get on with building things.'

Cas Suslowicz cupped his chin in his palms and roared softly, like a very sad lion. 'Don't torture me, please, Connie, it's not fair. I know perfectly well, you can do all this stuff standing on your head – didn't I always say you could've been really great in civil engineering?'

'Yes,' Connie said, with a mild smirk. 'And you were right, of course.'

'And now,' Cas went on wretchedly, 'those snot-nosed bastards have given you the sack, and you know as well as I do that it's out of my hands and there's bugger-all I can do about it. Really, Connie, if it was up to me—'

'But it isn't,' she said crisply, 'so there we are. Cas, why the hell did you and Dennis and Jack have to go and sell the bloody firm to those people? And while we're on the subject, who exactly are they? Come on,' she added soothingly, as his brow puckered into a ferocious scowl, 'I know you're sworn to secrecy and if you break your oath you'll get staked out on top of the Caucasus and gnawed at by giant vultures, but you can tell *me*.' She paused, then added: 'I'm your friend.'

Cas grunted like a bull elephant. 'Oh no,' he said. 'Don't start, please. If you could only see the penalty clause they made us sign, you wouldn't joke about it. I promise you, vultures'd be a picnic in comparison.' He sighed, and the window-panes rattled. 'The stupid thing is, they aren't even interested in the business. They aren't in it for the goodwill or the client list or anything like that.'

'Ah,' Connie said sweetly. 'I had an idea they were outsiders.'

'Oh, for—' Cas pulled a terrifying face, which made Connie giggle. 'You didn't hear that from me, all right? Look, the plain fact was, we didn't have any choice. After the Carpenter fuck-up, we had everything go tits-up at once. Half the partners dead or banished, having to hide the office behind a force twelve glamour so that everybody'd think we'd packed up and gone away, the goblins trying to jack the rent up six hundred per cent, losing VogMart and Consolidated Bauxite to the Germans – you know what's at stake for the partners, Con, we could've lost our life savings, houses, every damn thing. It was sell up or be completely screwed. And then these people came along, out of nowhere. We had no choice, really.'

Connie shook her head. 'All right,' she said, 'I'll let you off the hook this time. Just tell me one thing, though. When you negotiated the deal with them, did you have any meetings in the boardroom?'

Cas looked at her for about five seconds before he answered. 'No,' he said, 'we didn't. Jack Wells – well, he thought it wouldn't be appropriate. So we went over to their place and did all the talking there.'

'I see,' Connie said. 'Right,' she went on, 'give it here.'

'Give what?'

'All this bumf you're getting in such a stew over, for the Sacramento job. I'm at a bit of a loose end right now – I might as well have a go at it as sit in my office staring at the walls.'

A big fat tear, enough to drown a mouse in, welled up in Cas Suslowicz's right eye and dribbled down his cheek into his beard. 'Thanks, Con,' he said. 'I'm going to miss you, you know that?'

'Too bloody right you are,' she replied. 'And if only you'd tell me who these wankers are, I might be able to—' She smiled and shook her head. 'It's all right,' she said, 'I'll behave.'

Arms full of papers, she went back to her office. As usual, Cas had been making mountains out of molehills, a speciality of his in both the figurative and literal senses. A couple of hours of pencil-chewing, phone calls, lateral thinking and little-white-lying broke the back of it, and she'd save the rest of it for tomorrow; it'd give her something to fill her day with, and it wouldn't do for Cas to get the impression that it had been easy.

Intense concentration always left Connie with a desire for coffee and trivial conversation. She thought about dropping in on Peter Melznic or Benny Shumway, but she decided that what she really needed was a spot of girl talk, which meant either young Cassie or Rosie Tanner down in reception. Then she remembered hearing something about Rosie taking a week off, for some unspecified reason, presumably something to do with the contents of some pair of trousers or other; hence the fact that there'd been an unfamiliar chubby girl in the front office when she last looked. Cassie, then. Hadn't seen her for a day or so. Maybe there'd been some new development in the mysterious true-love thing. I'll miss all this when I've been slung out, Connie told herself; which is a really sad reflection on how my life's turned out, but never mind.

Connie's approach to office-door etiquette was a nicely balanced compromise; she knocked and went straight in without waiting to be asked. 'Cassie,' she said, and then stopped dead.

Cassie was lying on the floor. Brief panic; but dead bodies don't snuggle up like little field-mice in their nests. She was asleep. So was the young man lying next to her – that Hollingshead boy she'd dragged all the way out to Mortlake to see. Connie's eyebrow started to twitch, but no, it wasn't like that. They were separated by a discreet measure of carpet, and they both had all their clothes on.

In which case— Shit, Connie thought, and backed out of the office at warp speed, shutting the door firmly behind her.

Back on the landing, she tried desperately to think of what she should do. She'd been with JWW long enough to have a pretty good idea what would've led to two young people, one male and one female, conking out all al fresco on the office floor; also, now she thought of it, there'd been the crushed remains of teacups. Someone had been playing games with the JWW patent love philtre; hence her alacrity in getting out of there before anybody woke up. The Hollingshead lad was probably no worse than a bad dose of flu, but he was way too young for her; and she was as broad-minded as anybody, but Cassie simply wasn't her type.

Options. Go away and let chemistry take its course. Knock

loudly on the door and wait for an answer before entering. It'd depend a lot, of course, on who had put the philtre in the tea, and why. Ought she to try and warn them both? And how the hell could she do that? One of the main selling points of the JWW philtre was that there was no antidote: once you'd guzzled it and set eyes on someone, that was it, till death did you part. Trying to intervene at this point would be like telling a pinless grenade not to do anything hasty.

If it'd been late on a midwinter afternoon, Connie could've turned the lights off, maybe. Would that be enough, or would a vague glimpse of a shadowy outline be sufficient to get the job done? She didn't know the answer to that one, and besides, it was purely academic. If she'd been brave to the point of crass stupidity, she could've tiptoed in and blindfolded them both; but even if she got away with it, for all she knew she'd be screwing up a plan of campaign that Cassie had been working on for days. And besides, Cassie and the Hollingshead boy couldn't stay blindfolded for ever, and as soon as the blindfold came off, the closest bystander would be It. Not just your bog-standard two-horned dilemma: this bugger had more pointy bits than a porcupine.

Think it through, Connie, think it through. Here is young Cassie and the drippy young man she's caught up in this daft reincarnated-lovers mess with, and they're both asleep in there, most probably under the influence of the JWW philtre. Coincidence? She should cocoa. The likeliest explanation – not, unfortunately, the only possible explanation, but ahead of its rivals in the polls – was that Cassie had found out something else about the love problem. Maybe it was distorting the fabric of space-time or threatening civilisation as we know it or something equally melodramatic, and Cassie had come over all noble-as-two-short-planks and resolved to give true love a chemical helping hand. It was, she reflected, the sort of thing she might well do. She was like that. If she was a starship captain stranded in the past by a temporal anomaly, she'd be the sort who blew up the ship and crew to avoid polluting the timelines, instead of ransacking the library computer for two-hundred-year-old winning lottery numbers.

In which case, Connie decided, the best course of action currently open to her would be to set off the fire alarm.

Seventy St Mary Axe had, of course, to comply with all the relevant health and safety regulations, and so there was a fire alarm of the approved type. In case of fire, it said on its little red box, break glass. But there was slightly more to it than that. The freehold of the building was owned by a colony of goblins, off-relations of Mr Tanner, the head of the mining and mineral rights division, and one of the terms under which the building was let stated that after office hours the freeholders were allowed to have the run of the place. Goblins are naturally boisterous creatures; and although the partners had got the business of magically repairing the colossal amount of damage they did down to a fine art, it would have been simply begging for trouble to have a fire alarm that could be set off by breaking something. Consequently, the small glass rectangle on the front of the fire box was only there to keep the government happy. If you wanted to ring the fire bell, you had first to remove the half-dozen levels of goblin-proof enchantments, a procedure which called for a twenty-minute ritual involving a pentagram, a sacred chalice, 200 grams of freshly cut mistletoe and the sacrifice of a small goat. This didn't matter, since the building was magically fireproofed to the point where the planet would melt away before the JWW office curtains got faintly singed.

There were, needless to say, always little wrinkles and short cuts round everything, if you'd been in the trade long enough to know about them. Back when Connie had first joined the firm, there had been two young clerks in the Media & Entertainments division with an insatiable appetite for merry pranks. To them, the fire alarm was a sort of Holy Grail, a quest whose achievement represented the absolute consummation of all earthly ambitions. After years of trial and error, involving several quite spectacular errors and a four-day trial at the Old Bailey, they found the answer; which was, of course, salamanders. Being spirits of fire whose natural habitat was the cold heart of the flame, they didn't give off any actual heat, and therefore didn't trigger the magical protection; as far as the alarm's sensors were concerned, however, they were close enough for jazz, which meant that a pair of adult females stuffed up the air-conditioning ducts produced an entirely satisfactory result.

Naturally, JWW kept a wide selection of quality salamanders in stock at all times. They lived in a big glass tank in the closed-file store, and Benny Shumway fed them once a week on gunpowder soaked in diesel. Feeling that she was perhaps getting a trifle too old for such things, Connie darted away and came back a few minutes later with a spoon and two small, glowing amphibians tightly gripped in an oven glove.

The spoon was for levering the grille off the air-conditioning duct. She had to stand on a chair to reach, and one of the salamanders nearly managed to wriggle free and drop down the front of her blouse. Once they were safely installed, she slammed back the grille, hopped off the chair and took cover in the ladies' toilet.

The last time she, or anyone else, for that matter – had heard the alarm was when the two fun-loving clerks had finally attained their ambition, and the passage of time had taken the cutting edge off the memory. It was loud; it would've been loud enough to wake the dead, if the connecting door in Benny's office hadn't been soundproofed with two thicknesses of heavy-duty fibre matting. Luckily, after the two clerks' escapade the alarm had been set to switch itself off after twenty seconds, to prevent structural damage to the building.

The things I do for people, Connie thought, as she unbolted the toilet door. She stepped outside and waited, just in case the corridors filled up with angry, deafened people wanting to know what the racket had been in aid of. She needn't have bothered, since everybody in the place knew perfectly well that whatever it might have been that set off the alarm, it couldn't have been a fire.

Even then, she counted to twenty under her breath before

creeping back to the door of Cassie's office. Some people, she knew, were naturally heavy sleepers. It'd be hard to imagine anybody who could sleep through the JWW fire alarm, but given the circumstances she wasn't taking any chances. She knocked, and waited for a reply.

'Um – yes, right, come in.' Cassie's voice; and she sounded like she'd just snapped out of a daze or reverie. Fine, Connie thought, and turned the handle.

A strong stomach is pretty well essential to a magical practitioner. The pest controller, for example, has to do a certain amount of disembowelling and hammering stakes into the Undead. The sorcerer has to cope with transformation spells that haven't quite turned out the way they're supposed to. Even the mild-mannered minerals-diviner has to do working breakfasts with goblins now and again. Over the years, Connie reckoned she'd seen it all. As she opened the door, however, she realised that she'd only seen most of it, and unfortunately Fate had decided to save the yuckiest sight of all for a special occasion.

They were both still on the floor, though at least they were sitting up, and they were gazing into each other's eyes with a mutual look of such intense, concentrated soppiness that Connie wondered why the hell she'd ever objected to the sight of goblins eating scrambled egg on toast. She looked away, but the damage had been done.

'Hi, Connie,' Cassie burbled. 'You've met Colin, haven't you?'

'Yes,' Connie snapped. 'Look, can I have a word with you outside?'

'Um, it's not really very convenient right now.'

'Cassie, I need to talk to you *right now*,' Connie hissed. 'It's very important.'

'Better do as she says, fluffmuffin,' Colin simpered.

'All right.'

'Hurry back.'

'I will, pumpkin-blossom. Will you miss me?'

'You bet. Will *you* miss *me*?'

'Ever so much.'

'For crying out loud,' Connie moaned. 'Cassie, will you please pull yourself together and get over here *now*?'

'All right.' A catch in her voice. 'I love you, poppet.'

'I love you too, honeybundle.'

'Mww mww.'

'Mww mww *mww*.'

'*Cassie!*' Connie shrieked; and, very slowly, Cassie stood up and backed away, not taking her gaze off Colin's nauseatingly radiant face. As soon as she was within arm's reach, Connie grabbed her and hauled her out onto the landing.

'Cassie—' she started to say, but she got no further. Cassie had grabbed hold of her and crushed all the air out of her lungs with a rib-creasing hug.

'Oh Connie, I'm so happy,' Cassie said, talking very fast, 'and I think it's wonderful that you're the first to know because if it hadn't been for you I don't suppose we'd ever have found each other, and it's so wonderful I think I'm going to cry—'

'Cassie,' Connie said, slowly and forcefully, 'shut the fuck up.' Cassie subsided just a bit, though she was still bobbing up and down as though there was a loop of elastic coming out of the top of her head. 'Now listen,' Connie went on. 'I need to ask you something.'

'Well,' Cassie said, 'originally we were thinking June, but that's such an awfully long way away, I suppose it all depends on getting time off from work, and I'd want my cousin Tracy to be my bridesmaid and she lives in Canada, so there's arrangements to be made, and I'd really like to have the reception at—'

'That's not what I wanted to ask.'

'It wasn't? Oh.'

'No,' Connie said grimly. 'What I want to know is, did you put the philtre in the tea yourself?'

'Philtre?' Connie could practically hear the light switch on inside Cassie's head. 'You think someone made us drink the *philtre*?'

'Well, of course, you stupid cow. Think about it. Why else are you acting like this?'

Scowl; also pout, which was something Connie had never seen Cassie do before. 'Because I've just found the only man in the world for me, of course.'

'But you haven't just found him,' Connie explained patiently. 'You've known him for weeks now, and last time we discussed the subject you reckoned the sight of him made you want to throw up.'

'That's not true. I never—'

'Well,' Connie conceded impatiently, 'maybe I'm exaggerating just a bit. But not by much. Don't you remember?'

Cassie frowned. 'No. Yes,' she amended, her eyebrows shooting up. 'Yes, I do remember. Funkhausen's Loop. And then the dead couple came to see me, and I thought about it then, but I decided no way, because the thought of being in love with a complete loser like—' Her eyes widened, like eggs broken into a frying pan. 'Oh shit, Connie,' she said. 'You're right, it's got to be that bloody love philtre. Not that it matters,' she said, her face relapsing into sickening ecstasy. 'In fact, it's the best thing that could possibly ever have happened to me. Oh Connie, I'm so really, really, *really* happy, I just want to run out into the street and shout out, "Listen everybody, I'm in *love*!"'

Connie, whose jaw had dropped like the loading gate of a car ferry, took a step back. 'Dear God,' she said. 'However much of that muck did they put in that tea? They must've used six times the normal dose.'

Cassie's forehead puckered for a second as memory stabbed its way through the eggshell of joy. 'That's bad, isn't it? Exceeding the recommended dosage, I mean.'

'It's bad,' Connie confirmed, with feeling. 'Five millilitres for an average-sized European female; any more than that, and . . .' She tailed off. 'So it wasn't your idea, then.'

To her credit, Cassie was trying to fight it, but she was clearly fighting a losing battle. 'No,' she said. 'It's the most wonderful thing that's ever happened in the history of the galaxy, but it wasn't me. I wonder who it was.'

'I wonder that too,' Connie muttered. 'Anybody who'd give someone an overdose like that is either completely half-witted or else deliberately trying to do damage. Either way, it'd be a good idea to find out who it was.'

At that point the door opened and Colin's head appeared round it. 'Are you going to be very much longer, sweetness?' he asked wistfully. 'Only it's really awful being here without you.'

'I love you, dreambunny.'

'I love you too, honeypot.'

Gently but firmly Connie closed the door on him. 'Cassie,' she said seriously, 'you do realise there's no known antidote? True love till death, and they *mean* it.'

Cassie let go a sigh that'd have taken a three-masted schooner halfway across the Atlantic. 'That's so romantic,' she sighed. 'It's like Romeo and—'

'Hang on.' Connie cut her off in mid-croon. 'What was that you said a moment ago? About a dead couple?'

'Oh, them.' Cassie fought it again; valiant but fatuous, like trying to mop up the Mediterranean with a tea towel. 'Yes, they came to see me. They explained it to me, the whole thing. They're time-crossed lovers, you see. It's all to do with reincarnation and – it's sort of like a ladder in the tights of causality.' She frowned, as if she'd just realised what she'd said. 'Anyway, they'll be so pleased,' she said. 'It's exactly what they wanted, so isn't that perfect?'

There's only so much that flesh and blood can take. 'Fine,' Connie said, 'and I hope you'll be really happy together. What about these dead people? How did they get in here, for a start?'

Cassie shrugged. 'Don't ask me,' she said. 'They didn't say. I didn't ask,' she said, remembering. 'Does it matter particularly?'

Connie cast her mind back to the last time she'd been madly in love. Had it turned her brains to mashed swede? She was sure it hadn't. 'Does it matter?' she repeated. 'Dead people tramping through here like coach parties in the Cotswolds and you ask if it matters. Oh God,' she added, as the implications sank home like arrowheads. 'The door.'

'Door?'

'In Benny's office. Some clown must've left it open.'

Cassie frowned. 'That wouldn't be good, would it?'

Connie shut her eyes for a moment. Time-crossed lovers; one of her colleagues dosed to the eyeballs with love philtre by an unknown hand; the dead on this side of the door, exercising their right to roam. Just another day at the office. 'Stay there,' she said. 'If they come back, keep them talking. If you see Benny—' She might as well have been talking to the wall. 'Stay there,' she said. 'Both of you. Don't let him out of your sight.'

'Oh, I won't,' Cassie said, with a simper that made Connie wince down to her toes. 'You are happy for me, Connie, aren't you?'

'Bloody ecstatic,' Connie replied, and hurried away.

No sign of Benny in his office, but the connecting door was shut, locked, padlocked and bolted in the usual way. As soon as she saw it, Connie felt the adrenalin drain out of her. She stumbled back to her office like a Sleepwalker, flipped into her chair, closed her eyes and sighed. She felt exhausted, wearier than she could ever remember. A small part of her brain was still chewing its way through the overload of information she'd recently acquired, plotting each bizarre fact on mental graph-paper and trying to join the dots to make something that could be mistaken for sense. But it took too much effort. They fired me, didn't they, she told herself. And if I'm fired, it means I don't have to do this any more. I can bugger off to my little cottage in the country and leave them to it, all of them. For me, the war is over.

How about that? How about the fact that They, whoever They might be, had taken steps to get her out of the way just as the extreme weirdness was about to start? Coincidence – Connie believed in coincidences, and one of these days she might actually see a real one, but that hadn't happened yet, she was quite sure. Whatever was happening, someone was doing it on purpose. Love philtre in the tea, for one thing.

Tea. It doesn't grow on trees; well, it does, or at any rate on bushes. But it doesn't arrive in cups on your desk without help from an intermediary. Either you follow it into the long grass and hunt it down yourself, or someone has to bring it. So; find out who brought the tea. But that would involve going back to Cassie's room and asking a question, quite possibly in highly embarrassing circumstances. Have I got the energy to do that? Connie asked herself.

Her phone rang, and she looked at it for a moment. Cas Suslowicz bleating for help with his planning application; Dennis Tanner demanding to know how much money she'd earned the firm in the last ten minutes; the new bosses, informing her that they'd bet her pension fund on a three-legged greyhound. Only one way to find out.

She picked it up.

'Connie? It's me, Cassie.'

'Talk of the Devil.'

'Well, yes, as it happens.' Slight pause. 'There was something I forgot to mention.'

'Yes, in a minute. First, that tea tray. Did you ask for it?'

'What? No, I don't think so. Listen—'

'Interesting. Can you remember who brought it in?'

'No. I mean yes, it was Thingy. The new girl on reception.'

'Oh.' Connie scowled. 'Only I've been trying to figure out who put the philtre in the tea, and it occurred to me—'

'Connie,' Cassie said plaintively, 'shut up a moment and listen. It's Colin.'

It took Connie a moment to remember who Colin was. Oh yes. Him. 'If you've called me just to tell me that his eyes remind you of deep pools at sunset, I'll come down there and break your arm.'

'It's not that,' Cassie said. 'Actually, there's a slight problem. You know the deal we're doing for his company?'

'It's his father's company, I thought.'

'Yes, yes, all right. Well, it's gone a bit squiffy.'

'Squiffy.'

'Yes. You see, Colin's gone and sold his soul to the Devil.'

'What?'

'It was meant to be his father,' Cassie explained, 'but either there's been a monumental cock-up, or Colin's dad did it on purpose. Anyway, it makes things a bit awkward. For us, I mean.'

Connie leaned back in her chair and massaged the bridge of her nose thoughtfully. 'It does, rather, doesn't it?' she said. 'Look, if I come down there, will you two promise to behave? Only I find it hard to concentrate when people are slobbering all over each other in the same room.'

On the way to Cassie's office, Connie tried to rally her thoughts. She liked Cassie, for some reason she couldn't quite fathom, but did she really want to get involved in something as messy and complicated as this threatened to be? It all depended, she decided, on whether she was involved already.

Connie knocked loudly on the door, and counted up to ten after Cassie had called out, 'Come in.' They were sitting on either side of the desk – holding hands, it was true, but with three feet of melamine-covered chipboard between them: there were limits to the offences against her sensibilities that they could perpetrate. Connie sat down, held up her hand for quiet and looked at Cassie. 'All right,' she said. 'Tell me all about it.'

So Cassie told her. Some of it Connie knew already, of course. Other bits, such as the dead couple's revelations and the details of the Hollingshead & Farren deal, were new to her. When Cassie had finished, Connie sat still and quiet for a moment, and then said, 'That's odd.'

Cassie and Colin looked at each other. Correction: they'd been doing nothing else but look at each other since she'd come into the room, but the expressions on their faces changed. For the better, in Connie's opinion. 'What's odd?' Cassie asked.

'Think about it,' Connie replied. 'The dead couple tell you that their – well, for want of a better word, their *souls* have been born again, over and over again, because there's this ghastly screw-up, time-crossed love and so forth, and this is their last chance to get it right. Obligingly, an unknown hand spikes your tea with philtre; hey presto, you two fall in love till death do you part, which is exactly what the dead couple want. All right so far?'

Cassie nodded. Colin had gone back to gazing tenderly, and Connie shifted slightly in her chair so that she wouldn't have to look at him.

'Meanwhile,' Connie went on, 'his father's gone and done this deal, so now – well, we know what's going to happen,' she added awkwardly. 'The point is – and stop me if I've got this wrong, because spiritual conveyancing was never my thing, I did about three weeks of it when I was still with Robinson's, and that must be, what, thirty-seven years ago; the point is, surely, that if a soul goes down to the Very Bad Place, then as far as reincarnation and stuff goes, that's it. Out of the loop for good, and all previous bets are off. Do you see what I'm getting at?'

'No,' Cassie said, scowling at her.

Connie sighed. 'Fine,' she said. 'Look at it this way. Suppose you hadn't drunk the philtre, right? Pre-philtre, I believe I'm right in saying, you and him were not particularly attracted to each other. Just nod,' she added quickly. They nodded. 'In other words,' she went on, 'the last chance was on track to be a wash-out. You two don't get together, so when you die and the true love hasn't happened, there's an imbalance, anomaly, bloody awful fuck-up, call it what you like. I'm no expert, but I believe that'd be rather serious. Auditors and so forth.'

Cassie nodded. 'It'd threaten the whole fabric of spatio—'

'Quite. Spare me the Latin. But if – sorry, I've forgotten your name again; Colin, that's right. If Colin goes to the Very Bad Place, he's taken out of the loop, there's no imbalance and suddenly everything's all right – from their point of view, I mean,' she added quickly, as Colin started to say something. 'Because if his soul is, well, forfeited, I suppose you could call it, then the auditors can balance their books, the fabric of thingummibob won't go all to cock and everybody – nearly everybody – is off the hook. Convenient, wouldn't you say?'

Five seconds of dead silence. Furthermore, they were looking at her, instead of at each other. It's the way I tell 'em, Connie decided.

'What the hell is she talking about?' Colin asked.

Cassie ignored him. 'But now we've fallen in love—'

'Now that's happened,' Connie went on, 'I'm not quite sure how we stand. I mean, you two have fallen in love, fine, that ought to be enough to sort out the time-crossed thing on its own, so it must follow that whoever did the business with the philtre wasn't in on the selling-Colin's-soul thing, because where'd be the point? Unless,' she added doubtfully, 'I'm barking up the wrong tree entirely, and it *is* just a coincidence. No.' She shook her head. 'Colour me paranoid if you want, but it can't be, it's all too neat and tidy. Someone's playing silly buggers, at any rate, but just now I can't for the life of me figure out—'

'Just a minute,' Colin broke in. He'd been sitting with a stuffed expression on his face, as though he'd drunk far too much fizzy drink; suddenly he seemed to snap out of it, and there was even an actual genuine frown starting to form on his face. 'Someone dosed us with a love potion?'

Connie sighed. 'Yes, that's right.'

'So that we'd fall madly in love for ever?'

As though someone had pulled a string somewhere, Cassie's hand reached out for his. He twitched his arm away at the last moment.

'Sorry,' he said. 'Poppet,' he added. 'But that's all wrong. I shouldn't be in love with her at all. I've already found my one true love. That strange woman on the front desk at our place told me.'

Connie heard a sort of stifled sob from where Cassie was sitting, but ignored it. 'Go on,' she said.

'That's right,' Colin went on, as though he'd just woken up out of a really weird dream, and was gradually coming to terms with the fact that he was back in the real world. 'Fam. Fam Williams.' He paused, and his frown blossomed like a rose in June. 'Who's now on the front desk here, and if somebody'd care to explain that to me sometime, I'd be grateful. Anyhow, it's her. My one true love. Not—' He stopped, as though someone had just stuck something in his mouth. 'Who the *hell* did that to us?' he howled. 'Because—'

Colin was interrupted by Cassie sprinting from the room, dripping tears like a watering can as she went. Connie sighed, waited till the door had slammed behind her, and said, 'Actually, I was wondering that. Think about it.'

Colin looked at her. The penny dropped, gathering momentum; when it landed, it had the terminal velocity of an asteroid.

'Fam,' he said. '*She* brought in the tea.'

'Quite,' Connie said. 'But remember, she's just the hired help. We're a pretty old-fashioned bunch here, Mr Hollingshead, very much the old unregenerate upstairs-downstairs mentality. Which means,' she went on, as Colin opened his mouth, 'that secretaries and receptionists and the like don't take the initiative, they just do as they're told. Meaning, your true love wouldn't have gone making tea off her own bat. Somebody with the necessary authority would've told her to do it. Do you see what I'm getting at?'

Colin shook his head. 'She may not have known that,' he protested. 'About the waiting-to-be-told rule. She's only been here five minutes, after all.'

'No, she'd have been told,' Connie insisted. 'Julie or Christine would've given her the standard dos-and-dont's lecture as soon as she'd taken her coat off.' She sighed. 'Dunno why I'm sitting here theorising without data. Let's go down to the front office and ask her, and then we'll know.'

'Fine,' Colin said; then, immediately, 'No.'

'No?'

He nodded. 'It'd be, sort of, awkward. You see,' he went on, 'when I came in here and saw her on the front desk, I asked her to go with me to Vanuatu.'

Connie's eyebrows shot up like teal off a pond. 'Vanuatu?'

'Or somewhere,' Colin said. 'What I mean is, her and me go away from here for ever and start a new life. She said she'd think about it while I was in seeing Cassie about the stupid bloody contract. The contract,' he repeated. 'Oh shit, what'm I going to do about *that*?'

'Later,' Connie said firmly. 'One world-shattering nightmare at a time, please, or I'll just get muddled.' She frowned, collecting her thoughts. 'Right, I can see why you don't want to talk to her right now, so you stay here and I'll do it. Or better still, you can go and find Cassie and tell her you didn't mean it, before she slashes her wrists in the ladies' bog. You thoughtless, insensitive git,' she added. 'How could you possibly have said that with that poor girl sitting right there?'

'But—' Colin protested, then decided not to bother. 'I'll do that,' he said. 'Where's she likely to be?'

'Don't know, but it won't be hard to locate her. Just listen out for the sound of heartbroken weeping.'

Connie left him and trotted down the stairs, glancing at her watch as she went. It was getting late, and the last thing she needed was to get left behind in the building at half-five when the doors were locked and the goblins came out to play. She marched up to the reception desk and called out, 'Hello?'

The new girl, whom she'd barely registered earlier, popped out from the back office. 'You're Fam Williams,' Connie said.

'That's right. Sorry, I've only just started here, so I don't actually—'

'Connie Schwartz-Alberich,' Connie replied briskly. 'Mining and mineral rights. Got a minute?'

'Sure.'

'Splendid.' Connie perched on the edge of the desk. It felt odd, she realised, seeing a normal-looking person on reception at 70 St Mary Axe. She was, of course, perfectly accustomed to seeing a new and invariably perfect face behind the desk every morning; it didn't bother her in the least, since she knew perfectly well that all those red-lipped, cornflower-eyed supermodels were either Rosie Tanner or Rosie's cousin Vee. Someone normal in that context, by contrast, stood out like a Klingon in Debenhams. 'Right,' she went on. 'A bit earlier, you took up a tray of tea and bickies to Cassie Clay's office, right?'

'Yes.'

'Good. Who asked you to do that?'

One of those awkward moments. The girl – Fam, Connie thought, funny name, wonder what it's short for? – was looking at her as though it was a trick question. 'Sorry?' she said.

'Someone rang down, or came and saw you,' Connie said, 'and asked you to take some tea into Cassie's office. I need to know who it was. Okay?'

A frown, then a shrug. Connie could feel her patience running out. 'Well?' she snapped.

'Well,' Fam said, after another pause. 'You know perfectly well. It was you.'

CHAPTER SIXTEEN

Benny Shumway lived in a small house – two down, two even further down – a quarter of a mile under Fulham Broadway. He'd moved there when his fifth marriage self-destructed in a blaze of emotional fireworks; he'd needed somewhere to move out to in a hurry, and it so happened that a distant cousin of his had the place on his hands and was looking for a short-term tenant. Ten years later Benny was still there, having bought the freehold from his cousin. It suited him; he liked traditional dwarf-built houses, laboriously chipped out of the living rock with hand tools, and it was conveniently situated, small enough to be no bother to maintain, and separated from its nearest neighbour by five million tons of solid sandstone. He only went there to eat, sleep and iron shirts, so its bare functionality suited him perfectly. A bachelor pad, a *pied-sous-terre*. Just the ticket.

Except, of course, on dustbin day. There were some dwarves, avant-garde young tearaways with no respect for tradition, who'd installed lifts to take them to and from the surface, but Benny wasn't one of them. His link with the open air was a spiral stone staircase, as tightly coiled as a spring, each step worn glassy smooth and, of course, no lights and no handrail. It deterred unwanted visitors, for one thing; it looked right, it was good exercise and you weren't at the mercy of electricity. But – the fact had to be met squarely and head-on – it was a real bummer hauling the dustbin bags up it once a week.

Benny paused halfway up and caught his breath. He knew perfectly well what the black sack over his shoulder contained: styrofoam pizza trays, cardboard toilet-roll tubes, empty beer cans, a few discarded plastic carriers. Nothing heavy. He sighed, and shifted the sack across to his other shoulder. Maybe just a small lift, exclusively for dustbin days. Nobody would ever know.

Nobody but me, he thought bitterly, and continued to climb.

To take his mind off his aching neck, Benny considered the previous day's events. There had been a lot of them. The door being open, for one. Somebody must've opened it; somebody on this side of the Line. Motive? That set him thinking about the thin-faced girl and what precisely she'd seen earlier in the corridor. Apparently.

At the top of the stairs, he opened the door, heaved the bag out onto the pavement and began the slow descent. The final act of yesterday's comedy of bewilderments, he remembered, had been his frantic, futile, high-speed tour of the building in search of the two dead people that the thin-faced girl had claimed to have seen. He'd wasted most of the afternoon on it, and eventually he'd ended up in the closed-file store, a place he'd never liked much. No dead people in there, and he'd finally come to the conclusion that Thin-face had either been hallucinating or else she'd told him a deliberate porky just to be mischievous. As he'd been about to leave he'd noticed that someone had left the card-index drawer open, and had been rummaging about like a terrier among the letters F and H. That had in turn prompted him to waste another hour doing some research of his own, the results of which had been mildly interesting. In fact, it was probably a clue, possibly even The Answer, but that wasn't really any help if he couldn't understand it.

Back down the stairs, to finish his lukewarm tea, put on his tie and his overcoat; then back up the stairs again to the bus stop.

All the way from Fulham to the City, Benny worried away at the problem, or at least the parts of it he could get at. It was a bit like doing one of those huge, annoying jigsaws, where the top half of the picture is nothing but uniform blue sky. He'd found two identical sky-blue corners, but that (he was forced to concede) was about as far as he'd managed to get. It was infuriating and humiliating, and he devoutly wished that he'd never got involved in the first place. On the other hand, all the evidence seemed to suggest that Connie's job was on the line, so quietly forgetting all about it wasn't an option.

Thanks to roadworks and other examples of divine spite, Benny arrived on the office doorstep at seven minutes past nine. He hated being late, but at least there didn't seem to be anyone on reception to notice. He barged through the front office and sprinted up the stairs to his office.

He'd read once that the wicked multinational capitalist thugs were despoiling the Amazon rainforest at a rate of twenty-five acres a minute. Bad, obviously; but not his immediate concern. He'd wondered, however, what on earth they actually *did* with all those trees; and now, it seemed, he had the answer. They mashed them into wood pulp, rolled them out into paper, printed stupid annoying forms on them and piled them up on his desk the moment his back was turned. Benny sighed, sat down behind his desk and realised that, thanks to the magnitude of the pile, he could no longer see the door he'd just come in through. Wonderful.

On top of the pile was a memo from Dennis Tanner – handwritten rather than typed, which was probably significant, only Benny couldn't be bothered to work out why. The auditors, it seemed, were still on the premises; this time, they'd called for seventeen closed files, a printout of dollar/yen exchange rates for 1972 to 2004 inclusive, the Greater London phone directory, a quart of tequila and a compass. Benny read it through twice, shrugged and put it somewhere where he'd be sure to forget about it.

All dwarves are occasionally plagued by self-doubt, and

Benny was no exception. One thing he never doubted, however, was his own competence as the firm's cashier. Other people might sometimes drown in the paper ocean; he had the knack of skipping light-footed across its meniscus like a crane-fly. For once, however, he found the requisitions, pink paying-in and paying-out chits, yellow designated-deposit chits, blue petty-cash chits, green client-account chits, reconciliation sheets, telegraphic-transfer authorisations and orange expense-claim dockets hard work. He was having trouble with the numbers. Balances didn't. Twice, he even needed to use a calculator. Something, he felt sure, wasn't quite right. It was almost as though the immutable laws of mathematics had been sat on by someone heavy, and bent out of shape. Impossible, of course, because mathematics is simply a reflection of the supreme order of things, which by definition—

Unless—

Benny swore under his breath, and turned in his swivel chair to look at the connecting door: the one that had been open yesterday when it shouldn't have been. That was something else that couldn't happen, but had. Two impossibilities; he thought about that and ran through the column of figures he'd just been adding up. He added them up again, then double-checked with the calculator, which agreed with him: 67,219. But that couldn't be the right answer, because it had to come out the same as the total of the opposite column in the ledger – that's the whole point of the double-entry system, around which the whole universe revolves – and he'd treble-checked *that*, and it refused to be anything other than 67,217.

I'm not wrong, Benny told himself. Therefore, the universe must be.

Indeed.

He leaned back in his chair and rested his chin on the tips of his steepled fingers, like an elegant saint praying in an illuminated manuscript. The universe is on the fritz; there are tiny specks of shit in the air-filter of space-time, and the gaskets of eternity are leaking entropy all over the place. Fair enough; he'd been warned. He'd been given fair notice that a serious case of time-crossed true love had been unresolved for a dangerously long time; in which case, sums not coming out right would pretty soon be the least of his problems. Pretty soon, gravity would start cutting out, light would be losing races with the second-class mail and the only watch you'd be able to rely on for the right time would be a genuine Dali. Unless, of course, someone – a genuine hero, for example – got up off his bum and did something about it.

Sod, Benny thought. There goes my lunch hour.

Someone knocked, and his door opened. Instinctively he tensed, but it was only Connie Schwartz-Alberich. He started to greet her but she cut him off in mid-syllable.

'Benny,' she said. 'Found you at last. Where the hell have you been?'

He knew her well enough to realise that her question hadn't been designed to be answered. 'Now what?' he said.

Connie sat down, and promptly vanished behind the mountain of paperwork. Benny sighed, and brushed the whole lot off the desk onto the floor, where a stray Filing Charm fortuitously snapped it up and sorted it into neat piles. 'It's got worse,' she said.

No need to ask what It was. 'Define worse.'

So Connie told him: about Cassie's visit from the dead time-crossed lovers, the dosing of the tea with JWW philtre, Cassie and Colin murmuring sweet nothings at each other. When she'd finished, Benny frowned at her and said, 'So it was you, then.'

'Me? Me what?'

'Set off the fire alarm. Maybe nobody told you, Con, but dwarves have sensitive hearing; comes from having evolved in dark places, I guess. Honestly, I nearly swallowed my tongue.'

Connie asked him to do something with the fire alarm that was imaginative but impossible outside a zero-gravity environment. 'Don't you get it?' she went on. 'Someone dosed that poor girl and that young clown Hollingshead with the love philtre, which means—'

'Which means,' Benny interrupted, 'that they reckoned that getting those two to fall in love would solve the anomaly and put the fabric of space-time back together again. But it didn't work. In fact, if anything, it's made it worse.'

Connie looked up sharply. 'What makes you say that?'

Benny grinned. 'Ah,' he said. 'Here, take a look at this. Or rather—' He scrabbled at the remaining papers on his desk, then jumped up and nosed through the piles on the floor. 'Here you go,' he said. 'Look at that and tell me what you make of it.'

Connie stared at the piece of paper he'd given her. 'It's just a load of numbers,' she said. 'Benny, you know I'm no good at sums.'

'Liar. All right,' he relented, 'I'll give you a clue. It's a balance sheet. The numbers on the left are supposed to add up to the same as the numbers on the right. But they don't.'

'All right,' Connie said warily. 'So?'

'So what does that tell you?'

Connie frowned. 'Some cheapskate's been outsourcing their bookkeeping to the Andaman Islands?'

'I,' Benny said gravely, 'compiled that balance sheet. Therefore, I know for a stone-cold dead absolute unalterable certainty that the numbers should add up. They don't. Therefore,' he went on before Connie could say anything, 'it inevitably follows that the laws of mathematics aren't working properly.'

The tip of Connie's nose twitched. 'The anomaly,' she said.

'Exactly. And,' Benny went on, 'I think I've got an idea why. That contract you were telling me about.'

'The Hollingshead boy?'

'That's right. When he dies, his soul goes to Hell, right?'

Connie nodded. 'Which is a bit unfair,' she added. 'I mean, yes, he's neither use nor ornament, but—'

'And if your soul goes to Hell, you can't reincarnate.'

'Sure,' Connie agreed. 'But so what? Doesn't have to, if the anomaly can be put right. True love till death is what's needed. After death, they can drag him down to the brimstone pit and set him to lighting Bill Clinton's cigars for all eternity and it won't make a bit of difference.'

'Possibly,' Benny replied, frowning. 'But I've got a theory about that.' His frown deepened. 'Tell you later,' he said. 'First things first. We'd better have a word with young Cassie, don't you think?'

Connie shrugged. 'If you think it's important,' she said. 'It's not like I've got anything better to do, apart from finishing off some piece-of-shit stuff for Cas Suslowicz.'

Benny stood up. 'It's important,' he said. 'They pay me to keep the books straight, and I can't do that if the laws of mathematics are up a tree. Let's go and find Cassie.'

They found her in her office. She was sitting in her chair with a typescript in front of her: the Hollingshead contract, with big teardrop-shaped splodges all over it.

'Oh, for crying out loud,' Connie said. 'No pun intended,' she added, as she noticed the contract. 'Have you been sitting there moping all morning?'

'Yes,' Cassie said. 'And I know,' she added, with a faint trace of her old self, 'it's pathetic and stupid, and also it's not *me*. But—'

'Quite,' Connie said. 'Look, I've brought Benny up to speed, and he seems to think—'

'*Listen*, will you?' Cassie snapped. 'Yesterday, when we were talking, I quarrelled with Colin and went running off, and then it was going-home time so I tried phoning him at home and he wasn't there.'

Benny shrugged. 'So?'

'So I phoned again. All evening, and then first thing this morning. I kept getting his mother,' Cassie added, with a faint shudder, 'and she kept asking who I was, it was really embarrassing. Anyway, the point is, he didn't go home last night and they don't know where he is. And the representative from the Very Bad People's been ringing too, apparently, which is very bad, because if Colin misses so many days at work without a doctor's note or a good excuse they can forfeit the contract. I'm worried about him, Connie. After you left him yesterday, did he say where he was going?'

Connie scowled. 'Sort of,' she said. 'I told him to go and find you.'

Two and a half seconds of dead silence.

'I see,' Cassie said quietly. 'You sent an outsider to go searching the building on his own, just before locking-up time, at which point the goblins are unleashed and let out to play—'

For a further second and a quarter, Connie was uncharacteristically silent. 'I'm sure nothing's happened to him, Cassie,' she said. 'I mean, the goblins can be a bit rough-and-tumble sometimes, but they don't actually eat people—' She hesitated. 'Not recently,' she added. 'It must be, what, seven years since the last—'

'Five,' Benny muttered.

'And anyway,' Connie struggled on, 'if that'd happened, there'd have been bones and stuff, we'd have heard about it by now, you know what gossip's like in this place. Benny,' she added savagely, 'you really are a complete bastard, scaring the poor girl like that.'

'He's dead,' Cassie said mournfully. 'He came looking for me because I'd been horrible to him, and he got lost and they locked the doors and the goblins got him and it's all my fault, and I'll never ever forgive myself and—'

'He can't be dead,' Benny said suddenly. 'Think about it. If the Very Bad People have been ringing his house asking where the hell he's got to, he must still be alive. If he was dead, they'd be the people most likely to know about it, after all.'

Cassie looked at him in mid-sniffle. 'True,' she said. 'Thank God. But—'

'Tell you what,' Benny went on firmly, 'why don't you ring again now – his house and the factory –and see if he's still missing. Bet you he's turned up by now. Probably what happened was, after you'd run off blubbering – don't pull faces at me, Connie, you'll stick like it – Colin felt really rotten about it, went down the pub, drowned his sorrows and spent the night sleeping it off in a skip somewhere. It's what I'd do. Have done many times,' he added, with a faint nostalgic smile. 'Go on. Or better still,' he added, 'Connie can ring instead, she's marginally more coherent than you are right now. Where's the number?'

So Connie rang; and no, Colin hadn't come home, which was most unlike him; and no (Rosie Tanner at the factory said), hadn't seen hide nor hair of him all morning, and that Oscar's really getting steamed up about it, and normally Oscar wasn't her type at all but there was something about him when he was angry that reminded her a bit of Hugh Grant, or maybe Paul Newman—

'Fine,' Benny said, as Connie replaced the receiver. 'So he's not at home, he's not at the factory and he's not dead. So where the hell is he?'

'Sorry?' Colin said

'There is no need for apology,' replied the elderly Chinese gentleman who'd just materialised out of absolutely nothing at all, with that special kind of automated politeness that only comes through long, bitter years of dealing with the public. 'You do not know me. I . . .' He paused, and a trivial asymmetry at the ends of his mouth could just about have been mistaken for a smile. 'I have been aware of you for a while. You,' he added carefully, 'in various versions. In fact, I knew you long before you were born, which is in itself ironic.' He frowned, as if acknowledging a rebuke. 'Excuse me,' he said. 'My name is Dao Shan-Chen. I am the chief cashier and acting deputy assistant manager of the Bank of the Dead.'

'Bank of the—'

'Exactly what it sounds like,' Mr Dao confirmed. 'Like so many of the world's great institutions, a Chinese invention; set up to make it possible for the living to send money across the Line to pay for the maintenance of their deceased ancestors in the afterlife. Of course, we have moved on since then, expanded our operations, to the point—' This time Mr Dao's smile was almost pronounced. 'To the point where we're even bigger than

Tesco. For the time being, anyway. Although, strictly speaking, time has no meaning here.'

'So you're saying,' Colin said, very deliberately, 'that this is sort of the afterlife.'

Mr Dao nodded elegantly.

'But I thought—' Colin's eyes opened wide. 'How did I get here, then? A moment ago I was in a building in the City of London, and—'

'Ah.' Mr Dao beamed, and nodded. 'Seventy St Mary Axe. J. W. Wells & Co.'

'That's right,' Colin said. 'I was looking for – for someone,' he went on quickly, 'and I sort of wandered into one of the offices, and there was another door inside the room, so I opened it, and then I was here.'

He paused. That was a rather bland way of putting it. What had actually happened was that he'd opened the door and immediately tumbled through out of the light into what he could only describe as a total absence of anything at all. No light, no floor, no walls; no air (but he could still breathe), no sound, nothing he could feel with his feet or hands; nothing. And then, just as he'd filled his lungs with lack-of-air for a really big scream, Mr Dao had popped up—

'Quite so,' Mr Dao said. 'And here you are.'

'The afterlife.'

'Yes.'

'So I'm dead.'

At the very least, Colin had anticipated feeling fear; also despair, maybe a little anger. Instead, just a thick skin of bewilderment overlying a total deficiency of emotion. 'But I thought the afterlife was Heaven and Hell,' he said. 'Well, Hell, at any rate – I'm not fussed about Heaven one way or another.'

'Ah.' Mr Dao moved his head in a small gesture of uncertain meaning. 'Many cultures believe in a very bad place and a very good place. In order to meet their requirements, the Bank has various subsidiary franchises in, let us say, the hospitality and entertainments sector. Those who seek Hell will find it here, and just because it has been carefully designed to accord exactly with their expectations doesn't mean it isn't entirely real.'

Colin nodded. 'The very bad place,' he said.

'Quite so.'

'Right. And the very good place?'

Mr Dao sighed. 'You just left it.'

'Oh.' Colin thought about that for a moment. 'So I'm *really* dead?'

Mr Dao chuckled. 'Of course not, Mr Hollingshead. You would know it if you were. Instead, you accidentally strayed though the connecting door installed in the cashier's office at J. W. Wells & Co. You are still completely and perfectly alive.'

'Ah.' Colin felt his face blossom into a relieved grin. 'So it's all right, then. I can just turn round and go back the way I came.'

'Alas,' said Mr Dao, and quite possibly the compassion in his voice was entirely genuine. 'Unfortunately, there are quite strict regulations and protocols about the use of translinear connecting doors. Access is restricted to customers of the Bank, their employees and agents. You are not, I believe, employed by J. W. Wells?'

'No.'

'Unfortunate. You are, of course, a client of theirs, but the connection is rather too tenuous to be construed as a form of agency. Consequently, the door is not available for your use. You will have noticed,' he added sadly, 'that it has disappeared. You will not be able to find it again. This is not,' he added, 'a matter over which I have any control. It will not allow itself to be found.'

'But that's—' Colin realised he was shouting, and lowered his voice. 'I can't stay here,' he said. 'I'm alive, you just said so yourself.'

'Indeed.' Mr Dao nodded. 'And you will remain alive for the rest of your natural span. Which,' he added, 'in the absence of food, water and air, will not be unduly long. It will then be my privilege to escort you to our associated facility, where of course you are expected, under the terms of the contract you signed with the franchisee.'

Instinctively, Colin breathed in; it felt normal.

'A certain amount of air came through with you,' Mr Dao explained. 'Enough for, perhaps, fifteen minutes. If you wish, we could play chess. Or backgammon.'

'Fifteen—'

'Or perhaps you have unresolved issues about your past life which you would like to explore. If so, I will do my best to assist you.'

Suddenly, it was as though someone had flicked a switch and turned the power on. 'No, fuck it,' Colin said angrily, 'that's not *fair*. All I did was go through a door, to look for—' He hesitated, and breathed out through his nose. 'The point is, I didn't do anything wrong, I just opened a door and walked through it. That doesn't carry the death penalty, does it? I mean, not even Dave Blunkett ever went that far.'

Mr Dao shrugged slightly. 'In these matters,' he said, 'context is everything. As far as the opening and use of doors is concerned, for example, it makes a considerable difference. Opening and walking through a door in your own home is generally quite safe. It would be different, however, if you were aboard a helicopter. Or,' he added, 'in the cashier's office at 70 St Mary Axe. Fairness is also a relative concept. We can explore that, if you like, but I should point out that it's a rather complex issue to cover in –' he paused, and muttered calculations under his breath '– twelve minutes and eighteen seconds.'

At various times in his life, Colin had believed he'd felt afraid; for example, once when he'd overtaken on a blind corner and found a lorry coming straight at him, and again when he'd seen Oscar for the first time. Now he realised that what he'd felt on those occasions was just a free sample, a trailer for the real thing. It was as though someone was winding his guts round a stick while crushing his chest with a hydraulic press. 'You mean it,' he said. 'I'm going to die.'

Mr Dao nodded gravely. 'All living things die,' he said, 'in time; and time has no meaning here. When something is too small to be measured, it might as well be treated as though it doesn't exist. In the context of infinity, human life is that small. Had you not come through that door you might have survived, let's say, another seventy years. Seventy years is nothing. It takes that long to grow two millimetres of a stalactite. Even if you were to spend that time travelling at ten times the speed of light, you'd still be a very long way from reaching Andromeda. Consider your loss, Mr Hollingshead: it is trivial, like dropping a penny through a hole in your pocket, hardly worth stooping to pick it up. Besides,' he went on, 'unlike most of your fellow humans who arrive here, you have a future. Not,' he conceded, 'an entirely attractive one, but the majority of our residents would consider it preferable to the alternative, which is nothing at all. Although,' he added, 'there is a basket-weaving class, and intermediate conversational Spanish.'

Colin was backing away, but it was like going the wrong way on an escalator. 'Come on,' he said, 'there must be something—'

'No.' Mr Dao set his mouth firmly. 'Unfortunately,' he added. 'Concessions are available only in the most exceptional circumstances, such as star-crossed true love. And of course, since you have just now resolved the anomaly in which your previous incarnations were involved, that particular concession most certainly does not apply in your case. Accordingly—'

And then Mr Dao hesitated. It was as if a message had come through on headphones, except that he wasn't wearing any. He froze, stood completely motionless for a moment or so, and then smiled.

'Your door,' he said, and immediately a door swung open to Colin's left. Light streamed through it, bright and hot as a phaser beam. 'We apologise for any inconvenience. Have a nice day.'

Colin took a step toward the door, then hesitated. 'But surely—' he said.

'Mr Hollingshead,' Mr Dao said firmly. 'The difference between luck and a Land Rover is that you don't have to push it to make it work. Quite the opposite, in fact. Goodbye. It was a pleasure meeting you, and of course this is merely *auf wiedersehen.*'

'What?' Colin said, then, 'Oh. Right.' Already the door was starting to drift shut. Colin lunged at it, collided with it, and fell through it into blinding, burning light.

When he opened his eyes again, he was lying on the floor of the office he'd wandered into. Next to him was a door. It was padlocked, bolted, chained and barred, and in case there was still any room for doubt, there was a little notice on it saying *No entry*. Fine, Colin said to himself, no problem.

He was alive.

There had been times over the years when he'd wondered whether being alive was everything it'd been cracked up to be. There were a lot of things wrong with life – unpleasant people, domineering parents, boring, pointless jobs, maths homework, ravioli, girls who burst out laughing when he asked them out on dates, stuff in general – and at various low ebbs in his career he'd wondered whether life was a tooth better removed than endlessly drilled into and root-filled. To be, he'd asked himself, or not to be. Now, at least, he had an answer to that old chestnut. To be, every time, no contest, and bugger not-to-be for a game of soldiers.

Colin lifted his head a little and gave the door a long, hard look. He didn't *ever* want to go back there again.

'You,' someone said; and a hand attached itself to his collar and hauled him to his feet.

He squirmed, and the hand let go. He staggered.

'There you are. We've been looking everywhere for you.'

It took him a moment to place the short, bearded, bespectacled man who'd just let go of him: a Monopoly board, and vague memories of tea shops and pins and needles.

'Benny Shumway,' the man said. 'We met in Funkhausen's Loop. This is my office. What are you doing in it?'

Colin backed away, felt something obstruct him, looked over his shoulder and saw a desk. 'I'm sorry,' he said. 'Only, I was looking for—'

'Cassie Clay.'

'Yes. And then I went through that door there.'

'Oh.' The short man frowned thoughtfully. 'You did, did you?'

'Yes.'

'And now you're back again.'

'Yes. I met a Chinese bloke.'

The short man's eyebrows shot up. 'Mr Dao.'

'That's right. You know him?'

'Oh yes. And he let you go?'

Colin winced. 'I don't think he wanted to, not at first,' he said. 'But then he changed his mind.'

'He changed his mind?'

'Yes. In fact, he pretty well chucked me out.'

'Fine.' The short man frowned, as though trying to crush a beetle to death with his eyebrows. 'Sit down. I'd better give Connie a ring, let her know you've turned up at last. You do realise you've been here all night.'

'No, I haven't,' Colin objected. 'I was only in there a few—'

In his mind he heard Mr Dao's voice: '*Time has no meaning here.*' 'Oh,' he said.

The short man grinned. 'Count yourself lucky,' he said. 'You could've been in there for thirty years, and it'd still have felt like five minutes. Or the other way round, of course. So that was all there was to it, then? He changed his mind and let you go?'

Colin nodded. 'Bloody good job, too. Look, was that place really—?'

'Yes. Now sit still and be quiet while I phone Connie.'

The short man picked up the phone and talked to it for a bit, then put it back. 'She's coming over,' he said. 'Wants a word with you. Me too, for that matter. I don't know if you realise, but you're causing a lot of problems for a lot of people.'

'Am I? I'm sorry. I didn't mean to.'

The short man shrugged. 'I guess being you is a bit like being a landmine. You didn't ask to be left lying around for people to walk all over, and when it all starts going wrong you're the first one who gets blown up. You have my sympathy; but that doesn't mean you're not a bloody nuisance. In case you're wondering, I asked Connie to tell young Cassie that you'd been found, but not that you're here. It might complicate matters, and we've got things we need to talk about.' The short man sighed and sat down on the other side of the desk. 'Right,' he said, resting his elbows and steepling his fingers. 'How much do you know already about this mess?'

Telling his complex and unfortunate life story to a complete stranger struck Colin as a dubious course of action; on the other hand, the short man seemed to know more about it than he did, and besides, he'd just come back from the dead. If there was any chance that this strange person with the beard and the glasses could actually explain any of it, he was prepared to take the risk.

'Well,' Colin said. 'You were there, weren't you, when—' He stopped. The Monopoly incident. It occurred to him that, up till now, he'd been assuming it had all been a dream, like the Bobby Ewing arc in *Dallas*. But the short man knew all about it, so obviously it hadn't been.

'Funkhausen's Loop, yes. So you know about the time-crossed lovers thing. What about the contract with the Bad People? You know that it's you that's for the high jump, not your Dad.'

Colin nodded. 'I had sort of gathered,' he said.

'And you know that yesterday, someone spiked your tea with love potion to make you fall in love with young Cassie.'

'That too,' Colin said, with a faint, humourless grin.

The short man sighed. 'Then you're pretty much up to speed,' he said. 'And now you've been through that door there, you've met Jackie Dao and he let you go. You know, that's rather interesting. In fact— Oh, bloody hell, what is it now?'

The phone on the desk was burbling. The short man picked it up, listened, then started up the beetle-squashing routine again. 'No,' he said. 'She's not here, but don't bother ringing round any more, I'll come and deal with him. Yes, fine. Bye.'

He put the phone down and leaned back in his chair. 'You wouldn't happen to know our new receptionist, would you?' he said.

Colin nodded. 'She's my one true love,' he said. 'Or at least,' he added with a scowl, 'she was, until someone put that stuff in my tea.'

'I see.' The short man was staring into space; then he seemed to snap out of it. 'Well,' he said, 'you may be interested to hear, your old man's just turned up at the front office, and he wants to see young Cassie. I don't think that'd be a good idea right now, and I feel like a word with him myself. You want to see him?'

'No.'

'Didn't think you would, somehow. All right, you push off. Go sit in one of the empty offices or something. I'll get Connie to come and find you when the coast is clear. I'm going down to have a chat with your Dad.' Benny stood up, then stopped. 'I had a look in the closed-file index,' he said. 'Turns out that your Dad's company has been a client of ours for a hundred and eighty-odd years. You wouldn't happen to know offhand exactly what it is that we've been doing for you all that time, would you?'

'Not a clue.' Unlike the short man, Colin didn't have the eyebrows for beetle extermination, but he could probably have managed a small earwig. 'The first I heard about this firm was when Dad was negotiating the contract. And he made it sound like he'd only just found out about you.'

'Mphm. Well,' the short man said, 'it may pain you to learn this, but your Dad's a bit of a fibber. I hope it won't scar you for life, me telling you that.'

Colin smiled thinly. 'I think it's rather nice to have a life to be scarred for, actually. Do you think there's any chance that I might be allowed to keep it?'

The short man breathed in deeply. He had the air of someone who's just agreed to take on yet another tiresome chore he could well do without – organising the Christmas party, being secretary of the Esperanto Club, looking after someone's dog while they're abroad for a fortnight. He gave the impression that he didn't exactly welcome that sort of thing, but he was used to it.

'No promises,' he said, 'but I'll see what I can do.'

CHAPTER SEVENTEEN

It should only have taken Benny Shumway three minutes to get from his office to the small interview room, even if it happened to be a Wednesday, when the boardroom was in the habit of rotating through ninety degrees, thereby blocking the corridor and making it necessary to take the long way round, through the laser-printer room and down the back stairs. As it was, Colin's Dad had been waiting for a quarter of an hour when the interview-room door opened and Benny strolled in. He was holding a dog-eared manila envelope with a long number written on it.

'Sorry to keep you hanging about,' he said cheerfully. 'I got held up on the way here – we've got the auditors in and they wanted some old files. Also,' he added with a frown, 'a set of encyclopedias and a dartboard. My name's Benny Shumway, by the way, and you must be Colin Hollingshead.'

'That's me,' Hollingshead senior grunted. 'Where's the Clay woman, then?'

'Oh, she's a bit tied up at the moment,' Benny said, sitting down and tossing the envelope onto the desk, 'so I thought I'd drop by and keep you entertained till she's available. No charge,' he added, 'just a free service we offer to all our old and valued clients.'

Hollingshead senior scowled at him. 'It's all right,' he said. 'I don't mind waiting till she's ready to see me.'

Benny waved a hand. 'It's no bother,' he said. 'It so happens there's a couple of things I wanted to ask you, saves me the cost of a phone call. What's in the bag, by the way?'

On the floor beside Hollingshead senior was a plastic Tesco's bag; he tried to hide it by shifting his leg a little, but obviously it was too late. 'Oh, nothing,' he said.

'Nothing? Looks like a pretty chunky nothing to me.'

'Apples,' Mr Hollingshead muttered. 'Promised my wife I'd pick some up while I was out. All right?'

'Absolutely,' Benny said, with a pleasant smile. 'I love apples, me. I always say you can't beat a good Cox's, though I'm quite partial to these new Braemars you see everywhere. New Zealand or some place, I gather they're from. Is that what you've got?'

'No idea,' grumbled Mr Hollingshead. 'It just said "apples" on the bay at the supermarket.'

Benny shrugged. 'Whatever,' he said. 'Anyhow, to the matter in hand. I take it you want to see young Cassie about the contract.'

Mr Hollingshead's eyes narrowed. 'You know about that.'

'Here at JWW we're very much team players,' Benny said brightly. 'We don't go in for all that old-fashioned this-is-my-file-keep-your-filthy-paws-off nonsense. No, we all muck in, offering new viewpoints and perspectives according to how the Venn diagrams of our areas of expertise intersect each other. So yes, I know a bit about your case.'

'A bit?'

'Enough.'

'Enough for what?'

Benny smiled. 'Enough to realise that someone's made a complete bog of something, somewhere. I mean,' he went on, 'otherwise I'd have to believe that you deliberately sold your only son to the Devil to keep your poxy little factory going. And you wouldn't do that,' Benny added sweetly, 'would you?'

Mr Hollingshead was breathing heavily through his nose,

making a sound like a sawmill in wet weather. 'What's it to you, one way or the other?' he said, shifting in his seat. 'You people are just here to do the paperwork, not stick your noses in.'

'Absolutely,' Benny said. 'After all, your company – Hollingshead and Farren, isn't it? – you're long-established clients of the firm, excellent customers, the last thing we'd ever want to do is piss you off so that you'd take your business elsewhere.' He reached across the desk and picked up the buff envelope he'd brought with him. 'I did my homework, you see: took the liberty of looking out some of the old files on stuff we've done for you in the past. Seems like Hollingshead and Farren have been clients of ours for well over a century; almost as long as both firms have been in business, in fact. Does your son know that, by the way? Not that it matters particularly.'

'Colin's not really interested in company history,' Mr Hollingshead replied. 'Which is a bit of a disappointment to me, of course, but there you go.'

'Ah.' Benny nodded as he opened the envelope. 'So presumably he doesn't know about the first job we did for your company, way back in – let's see, good heavens, 1839. That's, what, a hundred and sixty-two years—'

'Hundred and sixty-seven, actually,' Mr Hollingshead grunted.

'Is it? Yes, you're right. Well done. Usually I'm pretty good at mental arithmetic, but today's just not been my day as far as maths is concerned. Anyhow,' he went on, 'it's been a long and fruitful association, by any standards. You've got a whole shelf to yourselves in the closed-file store, which means I haven't had time to go back through all the work we've done for you, not by a long shot. So I started at the beginning.' He reached into the envelope and pulled out a folded sheaf of yellow paper. 'Here it is,' he said, 'that first bit of business you ever put our way. Fascinating stuff.'

'Is it?'

'Oh yes,' Benny said, with a brisk nod. 'Of course, you'll know all about it.'

'Can't say as I do.'

'Really? Good heavens. Well, in that case, I'll fill you in on the details. After all, I'm sure you're interested in company history, even if your son isn't.'

Mr Hollingshead yawned ostentatiously. 'Is Ms Clay going to be very long? I could come back.'

'She'll be here any minute, I'm sure. Now then.' Benny smiled and unfolded a piece of paper. 'Actually, it's amazing how little Jack Wells's handwriting has changed over the years. Here we are. If you want to know what a file's about, start with the copy of the invoice. Let's see: *To Alexander Farren, Esq., alchemist, Mortlake, Surrey.*' Benny raised his eyebrows. 'That's a funny word to use, isn't it? I guess back then it just meant someone who did scientific research, what you'd call R&D these days.'

'Fascinating,' Mr Hollingshead said. 'Look, can't you ring the bloody woman and ask her how much longer—?'

Benny frowned. 'Come on,' he said, 'we haven't got to the good bit yet. Ah yes, here we go. *To the procurement and supply of one pip from an apple from the Tree of Life: twelve pounds, eighteen shillings and fourpence.* And then there's a stamp, and someone's written *Paid* and the date.' He paused. 'Now, I'm assuming that Alexander Farren was your great-great-great-grandfather's business partner, yes?'

Hollingshead senior nodded. 'What about it?'

Benny smiled. 'An apple from the Tree of Life,' he said. 'Now there's an intriguing concept to play about with. I'm guessing here, but would that be the tree in the Bible, the one that gives you knowledge of good and evil? Or am I getting muddled up?'

'Don't ask me,' Mr Hollingshead grunted. 'I'm an atheist.'

'Really? Don't let your mate Oscar catch you saying that. But I'm pretty sure it's not that one. Barking up the wrong tree, you could say. Humour,' he added, with a singularly grim expression. 'No, I think what Jack Wells was on about was the tree whose fruit made you immortal. For one thing, that'd tie in nicely with the word alchemist, wouldn't you say?'

'This is all bullshit,' Mr Hollingshead said. 'And you're nuts.'

'Maybe.' Benny shrugged. 'But I had a look at the file index before I came up here, and all those closed files, a hundred and sixty years' worth – you know what? All those jobs we did for you, they're all to do with trees. Funny old subject to consult a firm of sorcerers about, I'd have thought you'd have been better off asking Charlie Dimmock, or *Gardeners' Question Time*. For example,' he went on, taking a file card from his top pocket, 'in 1902 your grandad came to see us about pruning lateral shoots, and in 1921, there was an enquiry about how to deal with apple sawfly; and then there was 1927, nasty scare about what looked like honey fungus, but it all turned out all right in the end, so that's OK. Still, it all seems a lot of trouble to go to, unless it's a pretty special tree. Don't you think?'

Mr Hollingshead gave Benny a stare that should've peeled all the skin off his face. 'I've got no idea what you're on about,' he said.

'Really?' Benny looked surprised. 'Because according to the file index, you came to see Humph Wells about bark scab in 1987, and then you were back in '92 asking Cas Suslowicz about a high-tensile titanium trellis, and then again in '96—'

Mr Hollingshead raised his hands and clapped them together slowly three or four times. 'All right,' he said, 'I give in. What a clever little bastard you are, Mr—'

'Shumway,' Benny replied cheerfully. 'So let's see if I've got this straight. Mostly I'm speculating, because like I said, I haven't had a chance to read the files properly, but this is how I think it went. After your great-however-many-times-grandad stole the apple pip from his partner, Mr Farren—'

'It wasn't stealing. He had a good claim in law, but that bastard was determined to cheat us out of what was rightfully ours.'

Benny raised a hand. 'If you say so. After all this time it doesn't really matter, does it? Anyway, once he'd got hold of it, he had to hide it somewhere so Farren wouldn't be able to find it. So he thought he'd be clever and hide it under the floorboards at home. Unfortunately—' Here Benny failed miserably to suppress a smirk. 'Unfortunately, it grew, with the result that your ancestor found himself with a bloody great big tree growing up through the middle of his house. He couldn't transplant it or it'd die – at least, that was what Jack Wells told him in February 1852 – so he had to put up with it; he pruned off all the lower branches to encourage it to grow, and by the time you were born it'd made its way up into the loft anyhow, so there wasn't anything to see apart from just the trunk. Is that right?'

Mr Hollingshead nodded.

'By that point, of course,' Benny went on, 'it was all getting to be a bit of a drag; because you all knew, thanks to Humph Wells's letter of 15 April 1977, that it'd be another twenty-five years at the very least before you could expect to see any fruit; possibly longer, there's no way of knowing with magic or super-natural fruits. And until you could be sure that there was an apple on the way, your great-great-great-grandad's incredibly cunning plan to make a pact with the Devil and then cheat his way out of it would have to stay on the back burner. But you're a patient bloke, so you bided your time and got on with keeping the company going until – let's see, three or four months ago – you were up in the loft pruning the tree when you saw what you'd been waiting for all this time. Apple blossom. Meaning that finally an apple was on its way and you'd be in business.'

Benny paused, looking for a reaction. But Mr Hollingshead just sat there, arms folded across his chest. Benny sighed, and went on: 'Nice plan, though. Clever. You arrange a deal with the Very Bad People; basically, they save the company and make it a tremendous success in return for the soul of your first-born son. Now it goes without saying, you never had any intention of going through with that. After all,' he added quietly, 'all you and your predecessors ever cared about was the family business, and it wouldn't be any good to you if the family died out, on account of young Colin accidentally breaching the contract and getting carried off to Hell before his time. No, the way to make sure the company goes on for ever is to line up this deal with the Bad People, and then see to it that Colin lives for ever and ever. Beautifully simple. Doesn't matter if he forfeits the contract; he can't give up his soul unless he dies, and if he's immortal that can't happen. Therefore the future of Hollingshead and Farren is guaranteed, until the sun goes cold and the planet crumbles into dust, and quite possibly after that if you land a decent contract for bathroom fittings with aliens from Proxima Centauri. Of course,' Benny added gently, 'it wouldn't do to let Colin in on the secret, just in case he might not want to live for ever and ever, making small brass widgets on a barren rock in space while the interstellar wind whistles round his ears. I have an idea that not many people would. But, of course, his feelings don't really come into it, do they?'

Mr Hollingshead looked at Benny for a long time. 'No,' he said.

Benny nodded. 'Thought not,' he said. 'Anyway, that's more or less it, I guess. You've just had an uncomfortable few weeks waiting for the fruit to ripen – you were a bit concerned in case the deal went wrong and the contract got forfeited before the apple was ready to eat. But at last – I'm guessing late yesterday afternoon, judging by how frantic you were that Colin didn't come home last night – the apple was finally ripe, and all you've got to do now is get him to eat it, and there you are: job done, after a hundred and sixty-five years of careful, patient planning.'

Mr Hollingshead shook his head. 'No,' he said, 'I told you. A hundred and sixty-seven.'

'Of course.' Benny dipped his head to acknowledge the error.

'Anyway.' Mr Hollingshead stood up. 'Obviously you're very clever, figuring it out all by yourself, and you can give yourself a great big pat on the back. But you know what? It's none of your damn business.'

Benny smiled. 'True,' he said.

That didn't seem to appease Mr Hollingshead particularly. He took a long stride and stood over Benny, looking down at him. 'How I choose to run my company is up to me. I pay you people to help, not to go around snooping and making difficulties. If you want to take this up with your senior partner, fine. I expect you'll be able to find another job somewhere else.'

Benny shrugged. 'I'm quite happy where I am, thanks. And like you said, it's nothing to do with me.'

'Right.'

'Besides,' Benny went on, 'there's no harm done. I mean, defrauding the Devil – I suppose that counts as a good deed, really. You probably get a bonus mark for it. Who knows, maybe you'll end up going to Heaven after all.'

Mr Hollingshead laughed. 'Like I told you, I'm an atheist. I don't plan on going anywhere, not in the foreseeable future, which is all I'm concerned about.' He grinned, and sat down again. 'So, now that you've solved the mystery what are you going to do about it?'

'Me?' Benny shook his head. 'Nothing. I was just curious, that's all. Intellectual curiosity. Sorry if I offended you at all, I didn't mean to. I only started investigating when I realised something was a bit screwy somewhere; until I knew what was going on, I couldn't tell whether it affected me personally, or the firm, whatever. Now I know I was right about what's been happening, and that it's none of my business, like you said. It's been a pleasure meeting you, and now I'll go away and get on with some work.' He got up. 'I'll go and see what's holding up young Cassie. It's not like her to keep a client waiting.'

Mr Hollingshead yawned. 'You do that,' he said. 'You know what they say, time is money.'

'Quite,' Benny said. He picked up the papers he'd left on the table, took a step towards the door. 'One last thing, though.'

Mr Hollingshead had taken a magazine from his pocket; he opened it and started to read. 'What?'

'The apple.' Benny reached inside his left sleeve and took out a short length of thick steel pipe. 'Once it's ripe, how long does it stay fresh for? You consulted Humph Wells about that back in '85, but I didn't have time to look up what he told you.'

'Forty-eight hours,' Mr Hollingshead grunted, his face buried in the magazine. 'After that, it's no good, doesn't work. Why?'

'Just interested, that's all. Pleasant dreams,' Benny added as he swung the pipe and bashed Mr Hollingshead on the top of his skull.

When all else fails, do the work they're paying you to do. Cassie went to her filing cabinet, took out the Macziejewski file (a routine surreal-estate transaction involving the sale and purchase of a house in a small Scottish village that only exists for one day in every fifty years), sat down and started filling out a form.

The other thing about really boring work is its anaesthetic quality. While she was calculating the apportionment of fifty years' worth of unpaid council tax between the buyer and the seller, her mind was occupied and therefore not open to disturbing stuff like love, whether true, false or chemically-induced. Unfortunately, the calculation was pretty straightforward, even taking into account the twenty-five per cent tax rebate on properties trapped in a spatio-temporal vortex, and as soon as she'd finished it the thoughts came trooping back, like kids home for the holidays, clamouring to be entertained.

Cassie knew perfectly well that what she felt wasn't real; it was just a bad trip, unwanted stuff forced into her mind by whoever was responsible for giving her that bloody philtre. Furthermore, on one level she was just starting to get good and angry about being used as a component in somebody's grand design. It was particularly unfair that whoever it was should have picked on her, since what she still tended to think of as the soppy love stuff simply wasn't her scene at all.

When all the other girls in her class had been obsessed with eyeshadow, lip gloss and the complex tactical exercises involved in attracting or disposing of boyfriends, she'd watched them with sheer bewilderment and wondered if she really belonged to the same species. Boys simply didn't interest her, for one very obvious reason. They couldn't do magic; they didn't even realise it existed. As far as she was concerned, she had nothing in common with them whatsoever. She'd always known who she was and what she was going to do; Daddy had told her when she was six, and from then on it was just a matter of being patient until she'd grown up and learned what she had to know. Twenty years later, here she was; she'd made it, succeeded, passed the exams and won through to the only prize that mattered, a good job with one of the top firms. Indeed; here she was, sitting at her desk doing apportionments and ticking boxes on forms. Victory.

But at least she'd stuck to the path she'd set out to follow; and yes, what she was doing right now was pretty dull and trivial, not much different from being an accountant or a lawyer or any of the things the other girls had gone on to do. But in ten years' time, fifteen at the most, she'd be a junior partner, or at the very least an associate, and then—

A picture of Colin's face drifted into Cassie's mind, like stomach acid welling up through a hiatus hernia. Love: the thing everybody else was so mad keen about, the thing she'd always known she could take or leave alone. It was so unfair; because it was such a stupid thing, it turned your mind to mush and got in the way of work and progress, and what did it get you in the end? Mortgages and laundry and late-night supermarket shopping and school runs and sewing name tags into gym kit, rapidly followed by lost opportunities, disillusionment, failure, decrepitude and the grave. Partly it was life's fault, for being so ridiculously short and inflexible. You fell in love, you settled down, you compromised; suddenly, all sorts of unimportant things were making demands on you, like a pack of small yapping dogs, and before you knew it you were out of time: too old to have time left to progress beyond a certain point in your career; a part-timer, a reliable old workhorse who cheerfully got on with the stuff the young high-fliers couldn't be bothered to do, put upon and paid peanuts because at your age you daren't leave— That was love, Cassie thought bitterly, a nasty trick played on fifty per cent of the population in order to ensure the continuation of the species. She'd gone out of her way to avoid it, she'd managed it, and now some bastard had rammed it down her throat just to solve someone else's screw-up.

It wasn't fair, yelled the child inside her who'd spent her free time reading Daddy's books while her friends went bowling or rode their ponies. It wasn't fair, and as soon as she caught up with whoever had done it to her . . .

Someone was knocking on the door. Judging from the fact that they were waiting for her to reply before coming in, Cassie knew that it wasn't Connie or Benny. 'Yes,' she sighed, and the door opened.

'Have you got a minute?' It was what's-her-name, the thin-faced girl.

'Sure,' Cassie replied, putting down the form. 'What can I do for you?'

The thin-faced girl folded herself neatly into the spare chair, like a Japanese master of origami. 'We need to discuss your future,' she said.

For a moment, Cassie felt like she'd missed a step on the escalator. 'Excuse me?'

'We should really have gone into it fully at your assessment interview,' the thin-faced girl went on. 'But that wasn't possible, because the situation hadn't really developed properly at that time. Now, however, matters have come to a head, so it would be as well to make some definite plans. If it's convenient, of course,' she added.

Cassie looked at her for a moment, then said, 'What on earth are you talking about?'

The thin-faced girl smiled. 'I see,' she said. 'My apologies – I overestimated you. I'd assumed that by now you'd have worked out for yourself the identity of the new owner of the firm.'

'Can't say as I have,' Cassie growled. 'So maybe you should just come right out with it and tell me.'

'Of course,' the thin-faced girl said. 'It's me.'

Push off, Benny had advised him, and Colin had been brought up to defer to his elders and betters. He pushed.

Finding his way out of the maze of corridors, staircases and landings was an intriguing mental challenge, for which he wasn't in the mood. He'd just about given up hope of ever seeing the sun again when he found someone to ask.

'Excuse me,' Colin said, 'I'm lost. I'm trying to get to the front office.'

The stranger, a thin-faced girl with mousy hair tucked behind her ears, pointed down the corridor he'd just emerged from. 'Down there and follow your nose,' she said. 'You can't miss it.'

'Oh,' Colin said. 'I was just there, and it didn't—'

'It does now.'

Deferring to his youngers and inferiors hadn't been part of his upbringing, so presumably he'd learned to do that all by himself. 'Thanks,' he said, and went back down the corridor.

A moment or so later, he pushed through a fire door and found himself in reception. The first thing he saw was the back of her head. Then she turned round.

'Oh,' said Fam. 'It's you.'

Nice to be reassured about something. 'Yes,' Colin said; then he remembered something that had slipped his mind during the search. 'Have you decided yet?'

'About what?'

'About coming to Vanuatu with me.'

Fam seemed to hesitate; and Colin also remembered that he'd asked her that yesterday afternoon, promising to return and hear her decision in about twenty minutes. 'You still want me to?' she said.

'More than anything.'

She frowned. 'I don't know,' she said.

Colin took a deep breath. 'Maybe we should talk about it.'

'Maybe.' The phone on Fam's desk rang, but she didn't seem to have heard it.

'But not here,' Colin added quickly. 'Come on. We can get a cup of tea or something.'

He wasn't quite sure why he'd said that; partly because he had bad memories about tea-drinking in this part of London, partly because it sounded so middle-aged. Nevertheless; she looked at him for a moment, then said, 'All right.'

'Good.'

'I'd better ring Christine and tell her I'm just popping out for a minute.'

'No.' Colin took a step closer. 'Don't do that. Just come with me.'

'All right.'

They didn't say much to each other as they walked down St Mary Axe. She asked him where he'd got to the previous evening; he replied that it was a long story and he didn't want to talk about it; she said, 'Oh all right, then,' or something to that effect. They turned a corner, and there was a tea shop.

It wasn't the sort of place you'd expect to see in the City of London. It was nestled in a tiny space between the feet of two soaring glass towers, like a hedgehog between the hooves of a giraffe. It had a bow-fronted window with chintz curtains, and the little tables each had a white lace tablecloth and a vase of wild primroses. On second thoughts, it was a work of genius, the perfect catnip to attract hassled City types. In spite of that, it was empty.

The menu came in a red plastic leatherette folder with faded gold lettering on the front cover. 'What would you like?' Colin asked, rather formally, as they sat down. 'The home-made sponge sounds good.'

'Just tea, thanks,' Fam said, perching gingerly on the edge of her chair. 'What about you?'

For some reason he couldn't fathom, he really fancied a hot chocolate with whipped cream and a macaroon. 'Just tea for me as well,' he said. A waitress decloaked off their port bow and took the order; neither of them looked at her, and she went away.

'Right, then,' Colin said, inappropriately brisk. 'Vanuatu. What about it?'

Fam looked at him; it felt like straight through him. 'I'm not sure,' she said.

Not what he'd wanted to hear. 'Yes' would've been very nice, 'No' he could've lived with, but 'Not sure' just meant it was all going to keep going on and on, and he wasn't sure he could stand that.

'Look,' he said, 'if you don't like the idea of Vanuatu, there's all sorts of other places that'd do just as well. Anchorage. Tahiti. Ulan Bator. Sutton-bloody-Coldfield. Anywhere, so long as it's a long way from here and we're together.'

Fam was still looking at him. 'Actually,' she said, 'it's not the destination.'

'Oh.'

Pause. The faceless waitress brought two cups of tea and a sugar bowl; then an interspacial void opened and swallowed her up as though she'd never existed. 'So what is it you're unsure about?'

'Whether I love you or not.'

At least it was a straight answer; no mucking about decrypting tortuous verbal defences. 'You're not sure,' Colin repeated.

Fam nodded. 'At least,' she said, 'I know how I feel, and I do love you—' She stopped, as though she'd just noticed that some part of her clothing had come undone. Then she sort of shrugged; cat out of bag, too late to go back on it now. 'I do love you,' she repeated. 'What I'm not sure about is whether you love me.'

That, as far as Colin was concerned, was the daftest thing he'd ever heard. 'Of course I bloody love you,' he snapped. 'I wouldn't be asking you to run away with me if I didn't.'

She shook her head. 'You think you do,' she replied. 'But it's only five minutes ago you were having a thing with that Cassie woman.'

Oh, for crying out— 'A *thing*?'

'I'm not stupid, you know,' Fam said angrily. 'I heard you together, in the office that time. And yesterday; you came to see her. You said you'd be coming right back to hear what I'd decided, and then, when the office closed, you were still in there with her. What did you do, Colin? Go back to her place?'

'No.'

'All right, so where were you, then?' She was scowling at him.

'I had your Dad on the phone this morning, one minute past nine, soon as the switchboard came on. He said you'd been out all night, hadn't come home, wanted to know where you were. Where were you?'

Colin hesitated. 'It's a bit awkward,' he said.

'Right.'

'No, *not* like that. I was stuck in there all night. They locked the door and I couldn't get out till the doors opened.'

That look again. 'You weren't in reception when we opened up this morning.'

Colin felt twitchy, from his feet upwards. 'I found an office to crash out in and went to sleep. I didn't wake up till after nine.'

Fam sighed. 'I don't believe you,' she said. 'You know what I think? I think you went home with her. But it didn't work, or something went wrong; she's ditched you, so you're trying me again. The rebound, isn't that what it's called? Well, that's not good enough for me, Colin.'

'But—'

Her face had gone cold and hard as stone. 'All right,' she said. 'You promise me faithfully that you don't love that Cassie Clay woman and I'll believe you. Just say it: "I promise." Well, go on.'

Colin opened his mouth, but nothing happened. It wasn't that he couldn't tell a lie; he'd been telling them all his life, though according to most people he didn't tell them very well. It wasn't even that he couldn't lie to her, because he knew he could, if he had to. But . . . maybe it was some side effect of the love potion, or possibly even hanging out with Oscar and the lads; or maybe he simply couldn't tell her a lie about *that*. 'All right,' he said, 'I do love her. A bit,' he added quickly, 'but really, it's not like that at all, it's this stupid fucking love potion that someone made me drink, and—'

Fam had stood up. 'Goodbye, Colin,' she said, and started to walk out of the tea shop.

The solution hit him like a bus. All he had to do was jump up, grab her by the arm, frogmarch her back to 70 St Mary Axe, find the Connie woman or that short man, and make them explain to her that the love philtre really did exist and that someone was playing silly buggers with his life and his happiness. He pressed his feet to the ground, ready to stand up.

Yeow!

That's the bad thing about pins and needles: no matter how much you want to stand up, you can't. Simply not possible. No blood supply to the feet, therefore no motor control. The most you can hope to achieve is toppling over and crashing to the ground in a heap. Colin tried that, but apparently it was a really acute case, and he couldn't move at all. Instead, he watched the back of Fam's head all the way from his table to the door.

And then she'd gone.

She'd left.

There's probably a mathematical formula to calculate the exact point at which it's no longer possible to set things right, when it's definitively too late. It's only ever a matter of seconds either way – if I can get to my feet and hobble to the door before I can count to five, I've got a fair chance of catching her before she's swallowed up in the crowd of pedestrians; three, four, *five* and that's that, my life has changed, irreversibly, for ever.

Colin sank back into his chair. Well, no need to hurry now, I can take my time. Got all the time in the world, now that I've lost my one true love, everything that made the world worth putting up with. Might as well wait until my feet are completely better before finding a shop that sells rope and hanging myself.

The waitress came and gave him the bill. Inexplicably, she was almost cheerful now; was it possible that she hadn't figured out what was happening here? Could anybody be that unperceptive and still remember to breathe? He grunted and picked up the scrap of paper. He looked at it, trying to remember what the hell it referred to. Tea. Tea, for crying out loud; what possible good was tea to anybody at a time like this?

Colin knew that he was supposed to pull himself together or something, but he doubted that the bits of him still had enough tensile strength to withstand the procedure. So he looked at the bill instead: two teas, £1.20 each. Total, £13.75, service not included.

He dropped the bill back onto the plate it had arrived on, loathsome and unambiguous as the head of John the Baptist. The only possible explanation for its being there was that the world simply didn't give a damn. Nobody cared; they probably hadn't even noticed. No worldwide appeals for help, no emergency relief operations or days of national mourning, no rock concerts in Hyde Park in aid of the victims. Instead, there was just him, with a broken heart and a demand for thirteen pounds seventy-five pence.

Colin frowned.

Two teas at £1.20. Total £1.75.

Not that it mattered remotely; but £1.20 times two doesn't come to £1.75, not even in leap year with Gordon Brown doing the arithmetic. It was absolutely irrelevant to anything at all, but the bastards were trying to overcharge him. No, scrub that, they were charging him too little. A consolation prize, maybe, or perhaps today they were running their Broken Hearts special offer; between 11 a.m. and 2.30 p.m., a twenty per cent discount for anybody whose one true love walks out on them during the course of the meal.

Because maths wasn't his strongest suit, Colin ran through the figures one more time. Fine. Either the laws of mathematics had broken down entirely, or else he was sixty-five pence ahead of the game. Meanwhile—

Shock, probably, freezing relays in his mental database. A lovers' quarrel in a tea shop, over a ludicrous misunderstanding; she departs in tears; he fails to follow because his foot's gone to sleep. Either the scriptwriters on Tragedy have no shame about recycling old ideas, or all this had happened before.

Funkhausen's Loop.

But that's . . . His foot was better now, much better, and Colin jumped up as though he'd sat on an electric fence. He scrabbled in his wallet, yanked out a five-pound note, and scampered to the door.

CHAPTER EIGHTEEN

Surprise, surprise; there was nobody on reception at 70 St Mary Axe when Colin burst in through the door a few minutes after leaving the tea shop. He stopped in front of the desk and looked round for a bell to ring.

'Can I help you?'

He looked up and saw the thin-faced girl he'd met earlier in the corridors. If she recognised him, she gave no sign of it.

'I need to see Connie . . .' He frowned; couldn't remember her other name. 'Connie,' he repeated. 'Followed by something complicated beginning with an S. It's urgent.'

She looked at him as though he was swimming in a Petri dish. 'If you'll just take a seat, Mr Hollingshead, I'll tell her that you're here.'

Impressed and bewildered, Colin sat down and hid from her look behind an elderly copy of *Homes & Gardens* until she'd gone away. He'd just turned the page after skipping a tedious-looking article about hollyhocks when an advert in the Classified section caught his eye: *Confused? Bewildered? Disappointed in love and wondering what the hell's going on? You must be Colin Hollingshead.*

Colin frowned, and looked at the date on the front cover. March 1976, at which time he hadn't been born; in which case, the advert must've been referring to his father. He turned back, and read—

No, you fool; not him, you. Talking of which, Benny says your horrible father is in the building right now. Visit Connie Schwartz-Alberich NOW in her comfortable, well-appointed second-floor office (just refer to the easy-to-follow sketch map below for directions) and within minutes everything will be crystal clear. But hurry – offer ends in ten minutes.

Fine, Colin thought. The sketch map – he wouldn't have known it was a map unless the advert had said so, it looked a bit like a wiring diagram, with a hint of a map of the London Underground as it might have looked if drawn by M. C. Escher – was crammed in at the bottom of the page. A cross at one end was labelled *You Are Here*; an arrow roughly in the middle pointed to *Connie's Room*. Holding the magazine, he stood up and wandered over to the fire door. Nobody about. Well, why not?

'What the hell kept you?' Connie demanded when he finally walked into her office.

'Your stupid map,' Colin answered. 'In the end I had to ask somebody. Short, beefy bloke with a beard like a doormat.'

'What? Oh, that'll have been Cas Suslowicz – he's all right. Come in, sit down, before anybody sees you.'

Colin sat down. 'That was you, right? The advert?'

'Obviously,' Connie said.

'That's all right, then. And I don't want to know how you did that, because—'

'Very sensible. You're learning, I can see that. Tea?'

Colin shuddered slightly. 'No, thanks,' he said, 'I just had some. What was all that about everything being crystal clear?'

Connie smiled faintly. 'I was exaggerating,' she said. 'A bit, anyway. It was an advert, after all, you're supposed to exaggerate slightly. So, what did you want to see me about?'

'Hang on,' Colin said. 'Why all the secrecy, anyway? Why couldn't you just come down to reception and collect me, instead of—?'

'Discretion,' Connie said. 'The fewer people who know you're here, the better. Assuming my theory's correct, but we'll come on to that in a moment. What can I do for you?'

Colin sighed. 'It's like this,' he said.

It's basic elementary psychology that men like women to be sympathetic listeners. They like to see the compassionate frown, hear the little murmurs of vicarious distress as they talk about how they've suffered. You poor thing, they want to be told, how awful for you. If, instead, they get broad grins, chuckles and merry laughter, they're inclined to get upset, and sulk.

'I don't see what's so funny about that,' Colin said, after he'd finished the sad story of how he'd lost the only girl, give or take, he'd ever loved.

'Sorry,' Connie said, smiling broadly. 'I'm not laughing at you; it's just that you've proved my theory, and I think I know what's been going on.'

'Oh,' Colin said. That was good news, of course, but he'd still have preferred a little decorum. 'Well, are you going to tell me, or not?'

It was the contract (Connie explained). That should've put me on the right track straight away, if my brains weren't totally addled by age and vicious living. It's a paradox, you see; the sort of thing we used to get set in exams at magic school. I used to hate that stuff, actually, because I always thought, that's so improbable, I'm never going to come across something like that in practice. Shows how wrong you can be.

Yes, all right, I'm getting there. Shut up and listen, and I'll tell you a story.

Once upon a time there's a boy, and he meets a girl. They like each other, and they fall in love. Usually, falling in love is a bit like those quizzes you get on phone-in shows: answer three simple questions and you win a digital radio. Well, the questions are dead simple and you know the right answers, so you phone up and leave your message on their answering machine, and that's the last you ever hear about it. Because the answers are so simple, loads of people ring in, and they just choose one at random to get the prize. Same with love. It's not exactly rocket science, falling in love. Any bloody fool can do it, but only something like one per cent of one per cent qualifies as true love and wins the prize.

But let's assume that this boy and this girl are that one per cent of one per cent. Fine. Now, as I think we explained to you before, true love is an integral part of the operational matrix of reality as we know it; makes the world go round, and so on. In consequence, if something comes along and bungs a spanner in the works, things go badly wrong. Reality starts getting bent out of shape. Imagine it as the proverbial stone chucked in a pond. The closer you are to where the stone landed, the closer together the ripples are, but they spread out and keep on going. The difference between the stone analogy and buggered-up true love is what happens when the ripples stop spreading out and start coming back in. Now that's scary, especially if you're in the middle.

Anyway. Something goes wrong. It could be something really silly and trivial – like, for example, an attack of pins and needles in a tea shop. But the effect is that true love gets star-crossed, and the universe is suddenly minutes away from crashing. The powers that be have to act. Luckily, they can take a broader view than the rest of us, since they can be a bit more creative with stuff like time and space. They can jump forward a generation, reincarnate the star-crossed lovers, pair them off and there you are – problem solved.

This is what should have happened in this case, but it didn't. Instead, the reincarnations went the wrong way. Instead of going forward in time, they went back.

No, I'm not talking drivel; listen. As a result of the screw-up, history got rewritten. People in the past who'd led perfectly ordinary, placid lives and married nice quiet girls, and sensible, steady young men with prospects all suddenly found themselves caught up in heartbreak, grand passion and melodrama, resulting in yet more star-crossedness and further potentially disastrous chaos. Put it another way: instead of there being just one set of crossed stars in the early twenty-first century, there's now a whole galaxy of the bloody things stretching back as far as the fifteenth century, maybe even further, threatening to unzip the fabric of the Einsteinian universe and reduce the whole concept of linear time to sawdust and iron filings.

With me so far? Splendid.

The obvious question is: what the hell is going on? *Why* can't the star-crossed lovers in the twenty-first century reincarnate in the future and allow the whole pig's ear to resolve itself peacefully in a civilised manner?

Well, now that I know the answer, it's howlingly obvious. If one of the lovers isn't available for reincarnation – because his soul's dropped out of the system, so to speak; disintegrated, or gone somewhere and can't come back – the whole process grinds to a halt and starts backing up, like a blocked toilet. Hence, you see, the relevance of the contract.

Think about it for a second. Suppose the boy in our scenario is you. You're destined to meet the girl of your dreams and fall in love; and it's OK, you live a blameless life, no real danger of you doing anything really bad and getting eternally damned and going to Hell; so, in the natural course of events, no danger of you dropping out of the loop. You're a safe candidate for true love, because in the unlikely event of a screw-up, the authorities can reincarnate you and get a second bite at the cherry. But – and here, I guess, is where I have to apologise on behalf of my entire profession – suppose some interfering tit comes along and replaces the natural course of events with a supernatural one; for the sake of argument, a contract where you sell your soul to the Devil. In that case—

'You?' Cassie repeated.

'Of course.' The thin-faced girl smiled thinly. 'I bought the firm when it got into financial difficulties, and I've been running it ever since.'

'Oh,' Cassie said. 'Well, that's—'

'Purely and simply,' the thin-faced girl went on, 'so that I could control you. You're rather important, you see; or, at least, we assumed you were, although it appears we may well have been mistaken. However, that's neither here nor there. Now, I'd like to introduce you to someone. His name,' she added with a frown, 'is Oscar.'

'Oscar.'

'Yes.'

'Like in Wilde, or Hammerstein?'

'Sort of.' The thin-faced girl pursed her lips. 'You may prefer to shut your eyes at this point. Oscar does take a bit of getting used to, although I should point out that you've been in contact with him, professionally speaking, for some time.'

'Professionally—' Cassie's mind leapt, impala-like, to the conclusion indicated. 'Oh,' she said.

'Quite. Like I said, he takes a bit of getting used to, but isn't it a basic tenet of enlightened twenty-first-century liberal democracy that you really shouldn't judge by appearances? Ah,' she added, as a crack appeared in the office wall. 'Talk of the—'

Through the crack, a claw squeezed, like toothpaste from a tube. The claw was followed by an arm, the arm by a torso and (broadly speaking) a head.

'Humour,' it said. 'Good morning, Ms Clay. A pleasure to put a face to the voice, after so long.'

The pleasure wasn't mutual. Cassie managed not to scream, but only because she'd always been so contemptuous of old-fashioned sci-fi heroines who howled the place down after one glimpse of an out-of-work actor in a canvas monster suit. Instead, she let her jaw flop, and tried to wriggle backwards through her chair.

'Excellent,' the thin-faced girl said, as Oscar's remaining components squeezed through the crack. 'The gang's all here. Now, I should point out that although in theory Oscar and I are on opposite sides in the perpetual war between Good and Evil, in practice our interests in this matter coincide pretty well exactly. Cosmic chaos and disorder are a pain in the bum regardless of which branch of the Service you happen to belong to. So—'

'Hold on,' Cassie interrupted; because even the flood of panic and horror sloshing through her brain at the sight of the new arrival wasn't enough to drown out the implications of that. 'So if you two are opposite sides of the same coin and he's the Devil—'

The thin-faced girl frowned. 'Oops,' she said sourly. 'That's actually restricted information, so please keep it to yourself. And no, that doesn't constitute an admission of identity on my part. Entirely off the record: yes, all my sisters and me can do an entirely adequate paso doble on the head of your average industry-standard pin. That, however, doesn't entitle you to take liberties with your duty of confidentiality, as set out in paragraph 6 (b) of your written terms of employment. Do I make myself clear?'

Cassie nodded. Although the concept of an angel being an employer, or vice versa, was so bizarre as to be incomprehensible, it would at least explain a great deal about how the universe worked.

'Oscar,' said the thin-faced girl, 'has an offer to put to you. I don't suppose it's going to influence your decision one way or the other, but you might as well know that if you accept it, you'll be doing me, and the organisation I represent, a big favour. Won't do *you* any good, mind, but— Sorry, I'm not helping, am I? Oscar, say something, before I cause a diplomatic incident.'

'With pleasure,' Oscar replied. 'Ms Clay.' It cleared its throat. 'You are of course aware that Mr Hollingshead junior is bound by a contract with my associates. You know the terms of that contract.'

Cassie nodded.

'Furthermore,' Oscar went on, 'due to circumstances which I concede were entirely beyond your control, you are presently in love with Mr Hollingshead. Am I correct?'

'Mm.'

'In that case—' Was there a tiny glint of sympathy in its small, perfectly round red eyes? 'In that case,' Oscar went on, 'I am authorised to make the following offer. If you want to save the soul of the man you love, this can be done. All you have to do is agree to take his place. That is, as and when the forfeiture clause of the contract comes into effect, you rather than he will become the guest of my associates. Do you understand?'

A bit like a dream, really. Cassie knew that her head had just bobbed up and down, a gesture signifying assent, but she wasn't aware of having had anything to do with it.

'So,' Oscar said quietly. 'Which is it to be? Yes or no?'

It wasn't unknown for Benny Shumway to grumble occasionally about his work at JWW, but he would always have been the first to admit that any job where you regularly get to bash people over the head can't be all bad. True, he wasn't entirely sure that the people he generally bashed were the people who truly needed bashing; the ratio of comparatively harmless vampires, were-wolves, zombies and rogue orcs to lawyers, local government inspectors and Members of Parliament was, in his view, not all it could have been. On this occasion, however, he was entirely sat-isfied. If ever a fellow human being cried out for a sharp tap on the skull with a bit of sawn-off scaffolding pipe, it was Colin Hollingshead senior.

Benny put the pipe down, picked up something else off the floor, considered his handiwork and smiled. Just the right amount of wristwork and follow-through, like Brian Lara driving through the covers off the back foot. Fine; now, however, he faced the usual problem. Please Dispose Of Body Tidily.

Mr Hollingshead was no featherweight, and Benny had his back to think of; so he grabbed him carefully by the ankles and dragged him out through the door, across the landing and – here Benny couldn't help grinning mischievously – into the lava-tory next to the stationery cupboard. Hollingshead senior would be safe in there – no, rephrase that. He'd be no bother to any-body in there.

True, Benny reflected as he closed the door behind him, all

manner of strange things had been known to happen to people in the second-floor lavatory, especially to those reckless enough to try and use it for its intended purpose. On the other hand, nobody had actually died or gone insane in there for ages; not for at least six years, unless you counted the poor fool who'd come to mend the shredder.

That done, Benny trotted back to his office, closed the door, put something away in the top drawer of his desk and sat down. Not bad, he thought, a certain amount of progress has been made. Now, the question was—

His door flew open, and he saw Mr Tanner standing in the doorway.

'You busy?' Mr Tanner asked.

'Yes.'

'Tough. Come with me.' Mr Tanner frowned and added, 'Bring an axe.'

Using axes was almost on a par with bashing heads as far as Benny was concerned, but there was a time and a place for everything. 'Can't it wait?' he asked. 'Only I've—'

'No.' It wasn't often that Mr Tanner raised his voice or displayed any emotion more energetic than extreme contempt. 'It can't bloody wait. Have you got an axe, or haven't you?'

Benny shrugged. 'Fine,' he said. He stood up, crossed to his filing cabinet, opened the drawer marked 'A' and took out a long, straight-handled American-pattern broad-axe. 'Are we being formal, or will this do?'

'That'll be fine,' Mr Tanner replied impatiently. 'Now come on.'

Benny followed him onto the landing, up a flight of stairs, down a corridor and through two sets of fire doors to Humphrey Wells's old office. 'Oh,' Benny said. 'Them.'

Mr Tanner nodded. 'That's right,' he said. 'The fucking auditors.'

Benny hesitated. 'All due respect,' he said, 'and I know what a pain they can be sometimes, but don't you think that killing them—?'

Mr Tanner clicked his tongue, and the sound was like a stock-man's whip cracking. 'I don't want you to kill them,' he said. 'I want you to smash in the door.'

Smashing doors wasn't quite up there with bashing heads, but it was better than doing the quarterly VAT returns or the petty-cash reconciliations. Even so, Benny asked, 'Why?'

'Because I've been knocking and shouting and God knows what for the last half-hour and they're not answering,' Mr Tanner said angrily. 'They rang down to reception for last Thursday's *Investors' Chronicle*, seventeen pairs of ladies' tights, a pipe wrench and a marmoset. I'm going to find out what's going on in there if it bloody kills me.'

Benny nodded. 'Fair enough,' he said, and swung the axe.

There's a measure of science to busting open a door with an axe. Rather than hewing wildly at the panels, the sensible man goes for the area around the lock, the idea being to cut it out as neatly as circumstances allow. It took Benny seventeen carefully placed chops, but there was a lot more to JWW doors than mere planks, dowels and glue. When the last blow had gone home and the last splinter had flown wide, Benny leaned his axe against the wall, reached out and gave the door a gentle prod with his fingertip. It swung open.

'There you are,' he said. 'Piece of cake.'

Mr Tanner took a step forward, then paused. 'After you,' he said.

Benny frowned. 'Why?' he said. 'You're not scared, are you?'

'Of course I'm bloody scared. Go on, you're the pest con-troller. Get in there.'

Benny could see the logic in that; but logic will only get you so far. When, after all, was the last time you saw a Regius professor of philosophy driving a Maserati? 'I think you ought to go in first,' he said. 'After all, you're the ex-partner, not me. It's bad enough having to go to the Bank every day, and—'

'Please,' Mr Tanner said.

'Ah.' Benny grinned. 'Since you put it like that.' He picked up the axe and slowly put his head round the door.

'Jesus,' he said.

'Well?'

'You'd better see for yourself.'

The room was in a mess. The floor was carpeted with bits of paper, file covers, scraps of shredded cloth and pizza crusts. Empty bottles and styrofoam fast-food boxes covered the desk and the bookshelves. On the wall facing the door someone had drawn a large, poorly executed picture of a peacock, apparently using a fingertip dipped in curry sauce. The cashier's-room calculator, which Benny had been looking for for days, had been cracked in two and thoroughly gutted, and the keypad numbers had been stuck to the arms of a chair with Blu-Tack in the shape of a smiley face. The phones had been ripped out of the wall, their casings cracked open like crab shells and stuffed with olive stones and pilau rice. The tights were still in their cardboard boxes, the pipe wrench lay beside the battered remains of the filing cabinet, and there was no visible trace of the marmoset. Or, for that matter, the auditors. There was also a very, very unusual smell.

'Hang on,' Benny said slowly. 'So if there's no window, and the door was locked from the inside—'

Mr Tanner, who'd been staring like a lunatic, pulled himself together, with a shudder. 'Don't worry about it,' he said. 'I mean that,' he added grimly. 'Just wipe the whole thing from your mind and pretend it never happened. Understood?'

Benny thought about that for three seconds. 'It's a bit odd, though. I mean, four accountants from Moss Berwick don't just vanish into thin air like—'

'Understood?'

'Yes.'

'Fine.' Mr Tanner held the wreck of the door open for Benny, then pulled it shut. 'I'll get Cas Suslowicz and Peter Melznic to drop by later,' he said. 'I seem to remember Peter telling me once about a spell he knows where you can seal off a room completely for ever, so nobody can ever find it again.' He frowned. 'He knows all sorts of cool stuff, that bloke,' he said. 'Pity he's such a plonker.'

Benny followed Mr Tanner through the fire doors, along the corridor and down the stairs until he was back outside his office again. There Mr Tanner paused, as if he was struggling with something.

'Thanks,' he said.

'My pleasure,' Benny replied.

'And if you could see your way about not mentioning this to—'

'No problem.'

Mr Tanner sighed. 'You know,' he said, 'you spend your whole adult life in this business and you think you've seen it all, and then—' He shrugged, and lit a cigar. 'I've got a good mind to retire come the new year,' he said. 'You know, relax, put my feet up, spend less time with the family. You ever thought about retiring?'

'Only at night,' Benny replied, 'after eating too much strong cheese. Was there anything else?' Mr Tanner shook his head. 'Mind how you go,' he said, and walked away.

'In that case,' Connie said, 'you can see for yourself what's likely to happen. You're the true lover, right? Something goes wrong, you don't get together with the girl. You die. You go to Hell. The little men with pitchforks do whatever it is that they do with the souls of the damned, and you can't be reincarnated; therefore the screw-up can't be corrected, the backed-up-toilet effect comes into play, and it's only a matter of time before the immutable laws of spatio-temporal physics are just so many manifesto promises. In other words,' Connie added, 'a right mess. Bad,' she added, 'but not so bad that attempts to set it right by well-meaning officials can't make it worse. Which,' she added with a sigh, 'is what I assume has been happening.'

Colin looked at her blankly. 'Ah,' he said.

'That's right. I'm thinking,' Connie went on, 'about the business of you and young Cassie getting dosed with the love philtre.'

'Ah,' Colin said again. 'That.'

Connie nodded. 'That. Stands to reason, someone did it on

purpose. Went to a certain degree of trouble: getting hold of the philtre, arranging things so you and she'd be together in one place at a specified time. Even,' she added, with a grim under-tone in her voice, 'a bit of A-level-standard shape-shifting, to make it seem as if it was me who gave that ditz on reception the order to take up the tray of spiked tea and bickies. Why do all that unless the guilty party believed it'd somehow help matters?'

'Why indeed?' Colin muttered.

'So.' Connie shifted a little in her chair. 'The logical assump-tion is that whoever the mystery tea-spiker was, he or she reckoned that if our Cassie fell in love with you, that'd be it, end of problem. But—' Connie shook her head and looked away for a moment. 'Well,' she said, 'it obviously hasn't worked, has it? Because although you seem to have knocked back a large enough dose of that muck to poison an elephant, you aren't actually in love with Cassie one little bit, are you?'

Colin shook his head. 'No.'

'Which is pretty remarkable in itself,' Connie observed. 'That stuff's been on the market for nigh on two hundred years: one hundred per cent success rate, until now. It seems to me,' Connie added with a thoughtful frown, 'that someone who can just shrug off something that powerful could only do so if he was already under the influence of something even stronger. Like,' she said with a slight shudder, 'genuine true love. Implications,' she added, pulling herself together. 'One: young Cassie isn't your destined soulmate. Two: someone else is. Well?' she demanded briskly. 'Yes or no?'

'Yes,' Colin replied, beetroot-faced and glowing like a nuclear meltdown. 'I told you about her just now, remember? Fam—'

'Oh yes.' Connie nodded. 'That chubby girl on reception. Well,' she said brightly, 'there you have it. The question I'd like the answer to, though, is why our phantom tea-adulterator thought the girl you needed pairing off with was young Cassie. Any ideas?'

'No.'

Connie sighed. 'Me neither. And until we know that, I put it to you that we remain conclusively screwed. There's got to be a reason,' she said angrily. 'And between you, me and the filing cabinet, I'm prepared to bet that it's also the reason why the stupid bastards who're running this outfit nowadays have given me the sack. And that,' she growled, 'is very much my business, even if the rest of it isn't.'

Colin waited for four seconds just to be sure she'd finished, then said: 'All right, so what do you think we should do about it?'

'Ah.' Connie clicked her tongue. 'There you have me, I'm afraid. There's an old saying in this business, of course: when all else fails, ask somebody. The question is, though: who do we ask? Answer,' she went on before Colin could say anything, 'the clown who put that stuff in your tea. Trouble is, we don't know who it was. Although—'

Colin leaned forward, but Connie wasn't looking at him any more. Instead, she was staring very hard at a spot on the wall about three inches above his head. Colin looked round, but there was nothing to see except the painted-over scar where a picture-hook had once been.

'What?' he demanded.

'Just occurred to me,' Connie said. 'Young Cassie used to be with Mortimers, right?'

'If you say so.'

'You don't know what that means. Right. Mortimers are the best in the business; much better firm than us, more prestigious, better chances of getting ahead, and young Cassie's pretty ambitious. But she quits Mortimers and comes here instead. I remember asking her why, and she told me it was because they offered her a ludicrously large sum of money; real offer-you-can't-refuse sort of deal. Now, Cassie's all right, but she's nothing very special. Why would anybody do that unless they needed her here for some other reason?'

'Me,' Colin mumbled.

'Exactly. Furthermore,' Connie went on, 'not so long ago, when JWW was bought out by the new people, I don't mind telling you that we were in a right old state. I remember thinking when I heard the news. Only a complete idiot would spend good money buying us. I simply couldn't see a reason. But there is one thing JWW has which no other firm in the trade can offer. You lot.'

'Excuse me?'

'You. The Hollingshead family; you've been clients of the firm for generations. So, the hypothesis runs, our new mystery proprietors bought JWW simply in order to get access to you. You and Cassie. To get the two of you together in one place. In which case,' Connie said, jumping to her feet, 'I know exactly who we need to ask in order to get the answer to my question. Come on.'

Colin wanted to say something – quite a few things – but he didn't get the chance. Connie had a firm grip on his ear, and was pulling him out of his chair towards the door.

'Well?' the thin-faced girl said.

It was a bit like trying to walk through an upended trampoline: the harder Cassie pushed toward an answer, the harder it seemed to push back. It was an impossible choice; because there was no way she'd ever make such a stupid, disastrous, idiotic gesture, not even if it was real love, instead of some horrible manipulative trick that'd come out of a bottle. It didn't help that she'd never quite managed to believe in Hell, even though she'd spoken to it so many times on the phone; to give away your soul for all eternity to something you were convinced couldn't possibly exist struck her as being pretty close to the ultimate humiliation. On the other hand—

Cassie was trying to make some sense of what she'd just heard. Since she didn't believe in it, she had no sense of what Hell could actually be. If she could draw, she could have sketched out a huge bonfire, vats of something resembling yellow porridge (what *is* brimstone, exactly?) and a crew of anatomically improbable Butlin's redcoats with pitchforks cackling wildly and prodding people in the bum. But drawing a picture wouldn't have made it any more real to her, because she knew, right down at the molecular level, that it couldn't possibly be like that. For one thing, once you'd got used to it (and she could only think of it in terms of a rather too hot bath; it's scalding when you climb in, but after a while it fades into pleasantly warm, and then it's cold and time to get out), it wouldn't be horrible and terrifying and agonising, it'd just be very boring and silly. A bit like a bad day at the office, really. Maybe that was Hell, and Bosch and Bruegel had painted in all the bird-headed fiends simply because offices hadn't been invented yet.

Or – try this one for size – maybe Hell was being made to do supremely stupid, humiliating things against your will just because someone had stuck love philtre in your tea. Perhaps it was being made to be in love with someone you'd only met a few times and didn't really like very much. Maybe Hell was Connie losing her job and Colin being stuck in the family business with his horrible father and Cas Suslowicz and Dennis Tanner having to sit behind their desks watching some ignorant clown of an angel running their firm into the ground because she simply wasn't interested in it. All those things were real enough; that's why they call it real life. But real life is tolerable because, however implausible it may seem, there's always a wispy, unrealistic flicker of hope to be clung on to – lottery win or tall, dark, handsome stranger or your immediate superior in the chain of command getting eaten by bears – and so long as there's that little hole in the roof through which you can see the stars, being stuck in the cellar isn't so bad. But suppose you *knew*, guaranteed for certain, that this was all there'd ever be: the job, home, your unsatisfactory family and disappointing friends, without even retirement to look forward to; without even death.

Benny Shumway didn't talk about it as a rule, but he'd told Cassie about it once; about death, what it was like to go to the Bank every day and see it. One thing he'd said had always stuck in her mind: it's nothing, for ever. She'd thought about that a lot, trying to figure out what he'd meant by it, and the explanation she'd come up with was scarier than anything that Stephen King and Dean Koontz could've concocted, even after a gallon of strong black coffee and a tureenful of bad magic mushrooms. Nothing, as in nothing ever happens here. For ever, as in the sun goes cold, the planet freezes into lifeless rock, collides with an asteroid, smashes into gravel and dissipates into the empty vacuum of space, and *you're still there*, as though nothing had happened; because, of course, as far as you were concerned, nothing had. So: if hell is worse than death, it's got to be pure distilled essence of nothing for ever—

'Well?' the thin-faced girl said.

On the other hand, there was love: fake, false, not real, as unreal as the brimstone porridge and the pitchforks. Cassie knew very well what it said on the label: JWW patent oxy-hydrogen love philtre, guaranteed to last for ever, till the seas run dry and the sun goes cold; for ever, this lie, this total absence of feeling. This nothing.

Colin had asked her, isn't there anything you can do? And that was just when he'd wanted to save his father from the consequences of his own lunatic stupidity. Is there anything you can do to stop it, put it right, make it go away? Such a question wouldn't have bothered Cassie if the answer had been no, because there's possible and there's impossible, and she didn't believe in miracles. She was even prepared to accept that it wasn't her fault; because yes, she hadn't read the draft contract through properly or she'd have figured out that it was Colin, not his Dad, who was in the frame; but no, because even though she'd been careless and unprofessional, she hadn't started it or suggested it or come up with the idea in the first place. Guilt couldn't make her do this supremely stupid thing, any more than love could. But he'd asked her, isn't there anything she could do, and apparently she'd been wrong when she'd replied no, nothing.

Cassie frowned. Suddenly she realised that she didn't approve of nothing, on principle. There was, after all, something she could do. It was a bloody stupid reason for doing a bloody stupid thing, but she'd go for something over nothing every time.

'Ms Clay? Yes or no?'

Cassie sighed. Maybe it was like children's parties when she was a kid; it won't be so bad once you're there.

She reached across the table, took hold of the sheaf of paper that the thin-faced girl had put down, and unclipped her pen. 'All right,' she said.

CHAPTER NINETEEN

Slightly breathless after sprinting up two flights of stairs, Connie knocked on the door and opened it, dragging Colin in behind her. Then she stopped.

'Oh,' she said, 'sorry. I was looking for—'

The thin-faced girl lifted her head and smiled. 'I know,' she said. 'You were looking for me.'

Connie wilted slightly, the way you do when you've been proved right but wish you hadn't been. 'You know what?' she said. 'I had this funny feeling that it was you, but I assumed it was just me being dozy. Hooray for intuition. So, you're the new boss, then.'

'Yes.'

'You're the one who had me sacked.'

'Yes.'

'Why?'

'Because you've been making a nuisance of yourself.'

'Ah.' Connie nodded happily. 'In that case, I forgive you. If it'd been because you thought I wasn't any good at my job, I'd have—'

'You might as well sit down,' the thin-faced girl said. Connie frowned, upset at being interrupted before she could work up a good head of righteous indignation, then did as she was told.

'I—' The thin-faced girl hesitated. 'Obviously, you've been giving the current situation a lot of thought, and I would appreciate any insights you may have to offer.'

'Coo.' Connie grinned. 'You know, that almost makes up for it. Oh, by the way,' she added. 'Who's your friend?'

The thin-faced girl smiled. 'He knows.'

He? Connie remembered about Colin, and turned round, to find him trying vainly to walk backwards through the corner of the room with his eyes shut. 'Hey, you,' she said. 'Introductions, please.'

But Colin only shook his head; apparently he was having trouble with his language skills as well as with his motor functions. Instead, the odd-looking specimen sitting next to the thin girl stood up and bowed very slightly.

'My name is Oscar,' it said.

'Charmed. I'm Connie Schwartz-Alberich. Sorry if I'm butting in on a private meeting.'

'Not at all,' the thing called Oscar said. 'As it happens, we have just concluded our business with Ms Clay, and I'm needed back at Mortlake.' It did something with its face that was presumably meant to be a smile. 'Mr Hollingshead,' it said, and Colin shuddered from head to foot. 'I must confess, I'm surprised to see you here, but in fact your presence is rather timely. I fancy that you're about to hear some good news. Farewell for ever.'

Then Oscar dipped its head, waggled its fingers in a tiny wave, and vanished, leaving behind a small yellow cloud that quickly dissipated into a bad memory and a worse smell.

'Indeed,' the thin-faced girl said, as though nothing noteworthy had happened. 'Good news, Mr Hollingshead. You're off the hook.'

'Am I?' Colin muttered. 'Oh, great. What hook?'

'The contract, of course,' the thin-faced girl said. 'It no longer applies to you, or to your father, for that matter. As far as Oscar and his associates are concerned, you're free.'

It took a moment for that to sink in; and once it had, Colin was surprised by how little he felt. Relief, yes; but not the kind and strength he'd have anticipated. It was more you-don't-have-to-go-to-tea-with-your-Aunt-Olive than saved-from-everlasting-torment. An irritation sidestepped, nothing more.

'Great,' he said. 'Why?'

'Because someone else has agreed to take your place,' the thin-faced girl said. 'Don't ask for further information, it might spoil it for you.'

Colin shook his head. 'Who was it?'

'Me.'

And that, as Connie was the first to recognise, was actually the most remarkable thing: that Colin, dosed to the eyeballs with JWW philtre, had been in the same room as Cassie for several minutes and had barely registered that she was there until she said that one word.

'You?'

Cassie nodded. 'Well,' she said, 'it's only fair. I got you into this mess.'

'No, you didn't,' Colin snapped. 'It was my stupid Dad, so it's *not* fair. You were just doing your job.'

'It's still my fault,' Cassie said, not looking at him. 'And even if it isn't, you shouldn't have to suffer. You aren't anything to do with us, the trade. You're a *civilian*.'

It took Colin a moment to realise that she meant that as an insult.

'Both of you.' The thin-faced girl could talk quite loudly when she wanted to. 'That's enough. The simple fact is, Ms Clay has made a binding contract, and neither of you can do anything about it. Accordingly, Mr Hollingshead —'

'I see.' Connie had been sitting perfectly still for an uncharacteristically long time. 'Yes, I get it. You need Colin off the hook so that he can reincarnate.'

'Quite,' said the thin-faced girl. 'Also, he is morally blameless, and my organisation's first priority—'

'Is to cover up its own messes, yes.' Connie's nostrils were flaring. 'The last thing I'd expect from you right now is a holier-than-thou attitude, even if you are.'

'Ah.' The thin-faced girl scowled. 'More intuition?'

'Yes,' Connie said firmly. 'Oh, it wasn't difficult. You buy up this firm, go to all this trouble, so that you can fix the True Love screw-up. Who else could you possibly be? I'm not quite sure,' she went on, 'if you're the with-a-flaming-sword kind or the perched-on-top-of-a-Christmas-tree variety, but I don't suppose it matters. And it still doesn't give you the right to sack people for trying to help their friends.'

'No, I suppose it doesn't.' The thin-faced girl shrugged. 'Very well. Now that there's not much point in trying to keep this wretched business confidential, I suppose you may as well have your job back.'

'No, thank you.'

'As you wish. You were a satisfactory employee but hardly irreplaceable; and besides, the affairs of this firm really don't concern me much any more. As you say, Mr Hollingshead here is now cleared for reincarnation; the discrepancy can be dealt with, that's all that matters. For my part, I've become heartily sick of this environment and I shall be delighted to go home again.'

'Fine,' Connie said. 'Push off.'

Pause. The thin-faced girl was clearly waiting for something to happen. Equally clearly, it wasn't. First she registered patience, then frustration, then irritation, finally panic. 'This isn't right,' she said, in a distinctly unhappy voice. 'I ought to be on my way home by now. I shouldn't still be here, or in this—'

'Outfit?'

'In this corporeal state,' the thin-faced girl amended. 'I should have resolved myself back into a higher plane of existence.'

This time, Connie laughed; not kindly, but with genuine warmth. 'Still here, though, aren't you? Which means,' she added crisply, 'that the balls-up hasn't been sorted out after all. Something's *still* wrong, and you *still* don't know what it is.'

The thin-faced girl gave her a scowl that you could've impaled kebabs on. 'So it would seem.'

'You don't know,' Connie repeated. 'But I'll bet you your wings and your ducky little golden harp that *I* do. Intuition,' she added ferociously, 'something you sneer at but don't have. Were those horrible bloody baseball caps your idea, by the way? If so—'

'Just a minute.' Cassie had come back to life again. 'Connie, do you really think you know what the problem is?'

'Yes. But I don't see why I should tell *her* anything. She's the one who made us do those stupid bloody assessments. And she changed the coffee from Gold Blend to Tesco's own brand. I can forgive most things, but sheer petty mean-mindedness—'

'Connie,' Cassie snapped. 'What's the problem?'

Connie wavered for a moment. 'Oh, all right, then,' she said. 'Look, it's really very simple. Margaret Thatcher here –' the thin-faced girl winced sharply but said nothing '– seems to have been basing her calculations on the assumption that you and young Colin are both reincarnations of the original star-crossed lovers, right?'

'Yes,' the thin-faced girl said. 'Actually, it's more than an assumption. We have delicate, precision-calibrated equipment that allows us to trace the passage of a soul through its various avatars; even in this case, where the incarnations have been running backwards instead of forwards. Our instruments clearly show that Ms Clay here is the fifteenth incarnation of the female star-crossed lover. As for Mr Hollingshead, it's perfectly obvious that he's also an avatar. Quite apart from our instrument readings, the fact that the pending forfeiture of his soul caused such an upheaval—'

'Sod your instruments,' Connie interrupted. 'All right, maybe Cassie's an incarnation, I'll give you that. But not young Colin. He's not a fifteenth-generation retread. He's the original.'

Stunned silence.

'That's not possible,' the thin-faced girl said eventually. 'We know who the originals were. Furthermore, Ms Clay here has actually met them. They came through the connecting door from the land of the dead to consult her.'

Cassie looked up sharply. 'How do you know about that?'

'Simple. I opened the door and let them through.'

'Did you, now?' Connie nodded thoughtfully. 'Thanks. That ties up another loose end. Really, you're being very helpful all of a sudden. But forget about that for a second. I was explaining it all to you, or had you forgotten?'

'Carry on,' the thin-faced girl replied.

Like I told you (Connie said), it's pretty straightforward once you stop and think about it. You see, you've been coming at it from the wrong direction. Typical, I might add, but I won't, because otherwise we'll be here all night.

The point about this mess, as I see it, is not just that we've got a case of true love, but a case of true love that got screwed up. So, what we need to do is find the cause of the screw-up. Now, what makes true love so important is that it's true love. It's boy meets girl, they fall in love, they live happily ever after; absolutely basic, no frills, no complications. Once their eyes have met across a crowded room, that's it. No force on earth can ever separate them, as long as they live.

Almost.

Because, of course, there *is* one force on earth that can bugger it all up, and that's J. W. Wells & Co's patent oxy-hydrogen love philtre. Guaranteed. The only way a true lover can be prised off his one true love and made to fancy someone else is five milli-litres of the good old stuff, taken internally.

That simplifies things, doesn't it? Of course, I haven't got access to all your search results and instrument data, so I can't be sure that out of all the poor sods who've been dragged into this mess by way of retrospective reincarnation or whatever, young Hollingshead's the only male partner who's ever had a dose of the big bad medicine. However, I'll bet you the knickers I'm wearing that it's true. Of course, Cassie's drunk the stuff as well, so it's possible that she was an original rather than a remake, but I don't think that's the case. You see, while all this garbage has been going on around him, Colin here reckons that he's found his one true love: stout girl, works on the front desk here, name of Famine Williams. And – no disrespect, Cassie dear – the same can't be said of our Cassie. In fact, she wouldn't know love if it bit her on the nose.

Now; once you've got that far, everything else just sort of drops nicely into place. Colin and his Fam are true lovers; but something goes wrong, with disastrous results. Fine. You and your bunch of idiots swing into action to sort out the problem. But the problem won't sort out, because the reincarnate-'em-and-fix-it-next-time-round option's not available to you, thanks to Daddy Hollingshead's ill-timed pact with the Devil. Result: incarnations back up into the past. One of them is Cassie here. You, with all your technological wizardry, assume that Cas and Colin are avatars, and you decide to force them to fall in love by spiking their tea with JWW philtre. A bit high-handed, maybe, but at least I can see where you were coming from. Like most people who do unbelievable amounts of harm and damage to others, you were only doing what you thought was for the best.

OK. Let's just stop and think about this. Something buggers up Colin and Fam's true love. We've already seen that, one, the chronology of this is all to cock, thanks to the contract with your mate Oscar; two, that only JWW philtre could've caused the screw-up in the first place. Got it?

Oh, come *on*. It's obvious. It's obvious what messed up Colin and Fam. It was you, dosing Colin with the philtre and making him fall for Cassie. See what you did? By trying to solve the problem, you bloody well caused it in the first place.

The two seconds after Connie stopped speaking were a very long time. Galaxies could have spawned in that time, and drifted from one side of the universe to the other.

'Oh,' said the thin-faced girl.

'I think that puts it rather neatly,' Connie said. '"Oh."' She breathed out through her nose, like an irritable horse. 'For crying out loud,' she snapped. 'I thought the whole point about you people is that you're supposed to be infallible, and omniscient, and all that stuff. You know, to err is human, which you most certainly aren't. But instead, you got it wrong. More than that, it's because you got it wrong that there was something to get wrong in the first place. No disrespect, but if you lot were running the brewery Christmas party, someone'd end up having to do a last-minute emergency dash to the off-licence.'

The thin-faced girl looked at her. 'Have you finished?' she said.

'For now.'

'Good.'

'Very well.' The thin-faced girl held out a piece of paper. 'I assume you're competent at simple arithmetic. Perhaps you'd be kind enough to add up the column of figures and divide the result by twenty-six.'

'You what?'

'If you'd be so kind.'

Connie shrugged. 'Whatever,' she said. A minute or so later, she said, 'Nine.'

Then something curious happened. The thin-faced girl smiled; not a humourless grin or a sardonic smirk, but a great big beaming smile. Practically angelic.

'Ah,' she said. 'So that's all right.'

Not only did the penny drop, it landed with enough force to bury itself to the rim in concrete. 'So maths is working again,' Connie said. 'Which means the cock-up is all sorted out.'

'I wouldn't go so far as to say that,' the thin-faced girl replied. 'Before that can happen, Mr Hollingshead needs to go down to the front office.'

'Me?' Colin sat up sharply. 'What've I got to do with—? Ah, right,' he added. 'But that won't do any good,' he said sadly. 'She dumped me, remember.'

'I think it may be possible to induce her to change her mind,' the thin-faced girl said. 'Provided you can do a simple thing like apologising without making a mess of it. Given the trouble we've all been to in order to secure you a happy ending, it'd be appreciated if you could see your way to making a special effort.'

Colin was about to object that all that trouble wouldn't have been necessary if a bunch of bastards hadn't decided to play funny games with his life, but he decided not to. More important things to do. He stood up. 'Right,' he said. 'Well, goodbye.'

'Goodbye.' The thin-faced girl dipped her head in a very tiny gesture of acknowledgement. 'Send us a postcard from Vanuatu.'

Colin thought for a moment. 'No,' he said, and left the room.

'Now, then.' The thin-faced girl had slipped straight back into brisk mode. 'Before we wrap up this meeting, are there any questions?'

Do angels have teeth? Connie wondered, and if so, what weapon and how much force would be needed to smash them in? 'Yes, actually,' she said. 'Why did you open the door in Benny's office? You nearly scared the poor lamb to death.'

'It was essential,' the thin-faced girl replied.

'So the dead couple could come and see me?' Cassie put in.

The thin-faced girl shook her head. 'That was merely a diversion,' she said, 'or at best an incidental benefit. The real reason was so that Mr Hollingshead could go through the connecting door into the Bank of the Dead, and then come back again.'

'Really?' Connie said. 'Why?'

This time, the thin-faced girl's smile was more of a sneer. 'Because he had drunk the philtre and fallen in love with Ms Clay, but that had failed to solve the problem. Therefore it was necessary to undo the philtre's effects. The philtre, you will recall, remains effective for as long as the person who drinks it lives.'

'But that—' Connie frowned. 'Oh, right. And going to the Bank counts as dying.'

'Correct, technically speaking. Of course, the Bank officials recognised that they had no jurisdiction over Mr Hollingshead and sent him back—'

'Just visiting,' Connie said, remembering something. 'The get-out-of-Death-free card. No, it's all right, it doesn't matter. Go on.'

'Thank you. I should point out,' the thin-faced girl went on, 'that this was something of a miscalculation on our part. Simply visiting the Bank does not, in fact, count as death, a fact subsequently pointed out to me in a memo from the Bank's acting assistant manager. Fortunately, he had the insight and the intelligence to recognise a star-crossed lover when he saw one, and send him back immediately. Otherwise—' She paused, and if it had been possible for angels to blush, she would have. 'It also follows,' she went on, 'that it couldn't have been Mr Hollingshead's visit to the Bank that released him from the effects of the philtre, and I can only conclude that you were correct and that it was his pre-existing true love for Ms Williams that achieved that result. Nonetheless, thanks to Mr Dao an awkward complication was avoided,' she said. 'For which we can all be heartily grateful.'

She wasn't expecting the awkward silence that followed. It was Connie, needless to say, who broke it.

'Some of us, at any rate,' she said.

'Excuse me?'

'Oh, for pity's sake,' Connie exploded. 'You think you've been ever so smart and clever, even though you misread the whole stupid business and nearly got us all killed, or unborn or whatever. But maybe you're overlooking the fact that poor Cassie here's been left up to her neck in it; unless, of course, you've got the power to override a duly executed binding contract.'

Before the thin-faced girl could reply, Cassie sighed and said, 'It's all right. I don't mind.'

Connie scowled at her. 'Cassie, dear, don't be so bloody stupid. Haven't you been listening? These *people*—'

'It's all right,' Cassie repeated firmly. 'It doesn't matter, because I don't believe in all that bullshit. Hell, I mean, and afterlives and stuff.'

The thin-faced girl pursed her lips. 'With respect—'

'Respect,' Cassie snapped. 'That's a laugh, coming from you. No, I don't believe in you, either. Oh, I'm prepared to accept that you're some kind of supernatural bureaucrat, because I know people like that exist, I spend half my life leaving messages on their voice mail. But that's all you are. I don't believe in you because that'd mean I had to believe you're somehow better than me, and quite obviously you're not; you're just bigger and stronger. So I don't believe in Hell, either. I think it's just ordinary death, or maybe not even that. In fact, do you know what I think Hell is, Miss whatever-your-stupid-name-is? I think it's being pushed around by the likes of you; in which case, I've put up with it this long, I can probably cope with it for ever and ever. Just knowing that whatever happens, I was in the right and you people were in the wrong will make it bearable. No, shut up, Connie,' she added sharply. 'I'm just about to get my own back, so don't interrupt. I'm going to teach this stupid cow a lesson she won't ever forget.'

The thin-faced girl's face had never been thinner. You could've shaved with it. 'Really?' she said. 'How do you propose doing that?'

Cassie's turn to smile; definitely angelic. 'Easy,' she said. 'I'm going to forgive you.'

The brief silence that followed was broken by a loud, vulgar noise from Connie: part whoop, part snort of laughter, part rebel yell. 'Cassie, that's brilliant. You go, girl. Oh, she's going to have so much trouble explaining that one away to her boss when she gets home.' She grinned savagely, like a wolf. 'I take it you do have assessments and performance reviews and stuff where you come from?'

'Of course,' the thin-faced girl said.

'And baseball caps? Tell me you have baseball caps.'

'Certainly. We find them a very potent symbol of the team ethic.'

'That settles it,' Connie said cheerfully. 'It's the Other Place for me when I go.'

'Ms Clay.' The thin-faced girl was doing icicle impressions. 'I realise that, through no fault of your own, you've been placed in a highly invidious position. Let me assure you that I will bring pressure to bear through every available channel to ensure that your stay in the environment in question will be as painless as possible. However—'

It was probably just as well for her that she got no further, given the mood that Connie was in. As it was, the door opened and Benny Shumway charged in. He was out of breath, and holding a plastic carrier bag.

'Connie,' he barked, ignoring everyone else in the room, 'I've just been talking to young Hollingshead. Is it true?'

Connie nodded. 'If you mean about the contract.'

'Yes. Right.' He turned away and faced Cassie. 'Here,' he said, reaching into the bag. 'Catch.'

He threw something. Much to her surprise, Cassie caught it.

'Thanks,' she said, 'but I'm not hungry. And anyway, I don't like apples.'

'Apples?' Connie said. 'Benny—'

The thin-faced girl had pushed back her chair and stood up. 'Ms Clay,' she said, 'please give me that.'

Cassie looked at her, and then at Benny, who said, 'Just eat the fucking apple, Cassie. Trust me.'

'What?' Cassie said. 'Disobey a direct order from the boss?'

'Yes.'

She smiled. 'No contest,' she said, and bit.

All the way home in the taxi, they hardly said a word; but when they reached Mortlake, they got out and walked up the street for a bit, until they reached a shop. Yesterday it had been a Dixons. The day before that, it had passed through a Robert Dyas phase before morphing into a Body Shop. But before that, in the distant, unreal time before the weirdness came, it had been the same travel agency for fifteen years; and, when Colin looked up at the words written on its window, that was what it was again.

Colin smiled. 'Let's go in,' he said.

Fam hesitated, but not for very long. 'All right,' she said. 'By the way, where the hell *is* Vanuatu, anyway?'

'No idea. But I want to go there anyway.'

'Oh.' Fam looked at him, then down at the ground. 'Do we

really have to?' she said. 'I mean, I do love you, and everything's all right, and I know you want to get away from all this horrible stuff that's happened to you, with your Dad and those nasty people and the love potion and everything, but—'

'No,' Colin said firmly. 'I want us to go to Vanuatu.'

She was still looking at him, but now she was smiling. 'All right,' she said.

Colin put his hand on the shop door and pushed gently. 'And then,' he said, 'I want us both to come back.'

'It was nice of her,' Benny said, putting his feet up on Connie's desk, 'to give us the company.'

Connie shrugged. 'It was the least she could do,' she replied with her mouth full. 'And anyway, you heard what she said: her lot didn't have any more use for it. Typical bureaucratic mentality; it's less hassle to get rid of it than to figure out how to write it up in the accounts. Not,' she added, 'that I'm complaining. It's just—'

Cassie looked at her. 'What?'

'Oh, I don't know.' Connie swallowed the last of her slice of apple. 'It's just that all these years I've dreamed of being made a partner, right? But— This is silly, but I'd have liked it to have been because someone finally recognised how bloody good I am at my job. Not because a senior admin-grade angel wants to keep the auditors from giving her a hard time. Spoils it,' she said. 'A bit,' she added. 'Not a big bit, though.'

'And there's eternal life on top of that,' Benny pointed out, neatly spitting an apple pip into the waste-paper basket. 'Which means—' He stopped, froze, dived into the basket like a dog chasing a ball and emerged holding the discarded pip carefully between forefinger and thumb. 'Anybody got a matchbox?'

'Benny, what are you—?'

He smiled. 'Not exactly your ordinary apple-seed, remember?'

'Oh.' Connie took an envelope from her desk drawer and handed it to him. 'You were saying?'

'Basically,' Benny mumbled as he licked the envelope flap, 'you're never ever going to have to retire.'

'True.' Connie allowed her face to slide into a grin. 'And I can't wait to see how *they* take the news. That's going to be fun.'

'Allow me to spoil it for you.' Benny yawned. 'Cas Suslowicz will burst into tears, say how happy he is for you and how much you deserve it, and give you a big hug that'll probably crack two ribs. Dennis Tanner will be livid, which means his mum'll love us all for ever. As for Jack Wells—' Benny frowned. 'Actually, that's harder to call. I wouldn't be surprised if he decided to retire.'

Connie shook her head violently. 'No way. Not in a million years.'

'I'm not so sure about that,' Benny said. 'Between us and the night and the music, I did hear a suggestion that he's been head-hunted.'

'Get out. Who by?'

'That's the good bit,' Benny said. 'Jackie Dao, of all people. Apparently, the Bank of the Dead has plans to expand into the insurance and pensions sector. Logical,' Benny added, 'when you think about it.'

'I guess so. But Jack Wells? Don't see it myself.'

'Well, I don't see him buying a bungalow by the sea and growing hollyhocks. Anyhow,' Benny went on, 'we'll know soon enough. Oh, while I think of it. Cassie.'

'Yes?'

'Thanks for letting us share the apple,' Benny said gravely.

'What? Oh that's all right.' She frowned. 'After all, you both went to a lot of trouble on my account. Besides,' she added, 'I wasn't sure you'd even want to.'

'Are you kidding?' Benny grinned, doglike. 'Living for ever and ever? Still being around when the sun goes nova? Wouldn't miss it for worlds. Oh, remind me, someone. I've still got Colin's Dad locked up in the lavatory on the second floor. Sooner or later I suppose I'll have to go and let him out.'

Cassie smiled. 'He'll be a bit fractious, I imagine.'

'I hope so,' Benny said. 'And anyway, he'll calm down fast enough when I explain to him that he may have lost a son, but he's gained a permanent supernatural workforce, contractually bound to serve his company during the lifetime of an immortal. Exactly what he wanted, so that's all right. I mean to say, he's an arsehole, but if there's servings of happy ending left over when all the good guys have had theirs it'd be churlish to begrudge him any just because he's a nasty little shit. That's forgiveness,' he added. 'Divine, apparently.'

'I wonder how they'll get on,' Connie said. 'Young Colin and his girlfriend, I mean.' She leaned forward and picked up the baseball cap that lay on her desk. It was still the same ill-advised mix of colours, but thanks to a basic transfiguration spell the JWW logo had been replaced by a gracefully inter-twined SSC – Schwartz-Alberich, Shumway, Clay & Co. She'd grown rather attached to it over the last fifteen minutes. 'True love,' she said, and sighed. 'I used to want that, when I was young. Mind you, I also wanted dark purple nail varnish, a beehive hairdo and a pony. The nice thing about getting old is growing out of things.'

'Don't knock true love,' Benny said seriously. 'Thought I'd found it, five – no, scratch that, six times' and 'Well, the first one dumped me after six months, the second one ate onions in bed, number three was all very well until I met number four, number four was Countess Judy, and the fifth one got rust in the sills and had to be scrapped. Silly really. Which isn't to say,' he added with a grin, 'that when the seventh one comes along—'

'True love,' Cassie said suddenly, 'is a joke. There's no such thing, and I don't care what that pointy-faced bitch said. It's all just biochemistry, anyhow. I mean, does it really matter if the chemicals are poured in your tea or brewed up inside you by your own glands? It's just chemicals making you do stupid things that you wouldn't dream of doing if it was up to you.'

Benny laughed. 'Just wait,' he said. 'I'll remind you of that one of these days.'

'Feel free,' Cassie replied. 'It's not going to happen. For which I'm very grateful. After all, I've got a business to run now.'

'*We*'ve got a business to run,' Connie said. 'And if you two're thinking it'll be a piece of cake, you couldn't be more wrong. I mean, just think how much of our core client base we've lost over the last eighteen months—'

'My God.' Benny shook his head. 'She's only been a boss for twenty minutes, and already she's starting to sound like one. That's sad.'

'Maybe.' Connie finished her coffee. 'But at least we're never going to wake up one morning and find we've been sold along with the client list and the office furniture.'

'Eternal life, though,' Cassie interrupted. 'Think about it, for just a second. Eternal life, and you can do magic. Think of the possibilities.'

'I've thought,' Connie said straight away. 'If you're not careful, you'll end up like her, what's-her-name – we never did find out what her name was, did we? Anyhow, just like her. Playing God.'

'Jackie Dao is going to be *really* miffed when I tell him,' Benny said. 'I have a feeling he's been looking forward rather a lot to the day when I go down there and don't get to come back again. Not that he's malicious or anything, but he does love a properly balanced ledger.'

'Anyway,' Connie said briskly. 'Now that we're the management, I think we ought to crack down on long, time-wasting coffee breaks. And since none of us has done much in the way of paying work these last few weeks—'

'Slave-driver,' Cassie said, as she stood up. 'If you're going to be like this for the rest of eternity—'

'Count on it.'

Cassie sighed. 'Maybe I'd have been better off in Hell.'

'Quite likely. Now shoo. Including you, Shumway,' Connie added, with a ferocious scowl. 'I'll trouble you to bear in mind that you two just elected me senior partner, so when I tell you to do something—'

When they'd gone, Connie sat for a while, looking up at the corner of the room. In a day or so, she'd move all her stuff into Jack Wells's room; it was bigger, it had a breathtaking view of the City – several cities, in fact, thanks to its inbuilt instantaneous-relocation charm – and most of all, it was where the boss lived. It was, of course, invidious, petty and very sad of her to care about stuff like that, but she did.

Work. She'd just been lecturing the others about it; maybe she ought to do a spot of it herself. For example, there were the last few loose ends of Cas Suslowicz's planning application. She nodded decisively. Nothing like sorting out reserved matters on a castle in the air for bringing you back down to earth.

She got up and found the file in the cabinet. When she turned round, she saw someone sitting in her chair.

'You again,' she said.

'Yes.'

'If you've come back to say you've changed your mind, you can forget about that, because you signed a legal transfer, and—'

'Certainly not,' the thin-faced girl said. 'But there's one last item of unfinished business. With all the drama earlier, it slipped my mind.'

'Drama,' Connie repeated. 'Fine. Actually, while you're here, you can clear up one thing for me. Was it your lot who kept trapping young Cassie in those stupid consequence mines and probability wells?'

The thin-faced girl frowned. 'Excuse me?'

'A few weeks back,' Connie said, 'before all this started. Seemed like every five minutes I was getting called out to go and unstick her. Now, the way I see it, either it was you or someone else, and if it was someone else, it's reasonable to assume that they're still out there, so—'

'Ah.' The thin-faced girl held up her hand. 'A simple misunderstanding. Yes, that was my organisation. We needed to conduct a number of tests on Ms Clay, to ascertain whether she was – as we then believed – a reincarnation of the female star-crossed lover. We used a number of devices to immobilise her while we carried out the tests; not the ones you mentioned, but close enough to be mistaken for them. We are, of course, sorry for any inconvenience we may have caused, but I can assure you that we had all the necessary clearances.'

'I bet,' Connie said. 'Right, that's sorted that out. What was it you wanted to ask me about?'

'Not "ask".' The thin-faced girl smiled. 'Discuss. Really, it's just curiosity.' She frowned. 'I suppose it's a side effect of having been a human for a while. It feels strange, actually, wanting to know something and not being able to.'

'I can imagine,' Connie said warily. 'So?'

'About you,' the thin-faced girl said briskly. 'For one thing, why did you never get married?'

'That's a very personal question,' Connie snapped.

'Is it? Oh.' The thin-faced girl shrugged. 'Why is that? I mean, why's it more personal than where you went on holiday last year? Is it because of the sexual connotations?'

Connie smiled at her. 'Yes.'

'I see. Well, even so, I'm interested. The truth is, in my line of work I don't get to meet many humans – not live ones, anyway – and while I've been down here, working on this project, I suppose I've realised how little I understand them. If you answer my question, it might give me valuable insights into the human mindset.'

Connie thought about it. 'If I tell you,' she said, 'will you go away?'

'If you want me to.'

'Fine.' Connie composed her thoughts. 'Well, I had my chances over the years, plenty of 'em. But—' She shrugged. 'Getting married means settling down, settling down means compromising, losing your focus. It probably sounds a bit sad, but for me the job, being a sorceress, always came first. Not because I'm a lean, hungry corporate dingo, but because it's always been *fun*. And having to divert a great big slice of my life and my energy to negotiating a relationship with some bloke – well, that's more like work than fun. It's just boring old trying to get along with people; you can't solve the problems with spells or charms, you've got to hammer them out the ordinary way. I guess you could say that in all the relationships I tried, the magic wasn't there. And magic's what I like best, you see.'

'I think so,' the thin-faced girl said. 'I'm finding this most helpful – thank you. Would you mind if we examine this in greater depth? After all,' she went on, 'unless I learn a bit more about people, the chances are that the next time I have to deal with them in the course of business I'll repeat the mistakes I made here. Surely you wouldn't want that, for your fellow humans' sake.'

Connie sighed. 'Put like that,' she said, 'you may have a point.'

'Excellent. As I understand it,' she went on, 'human social interaction is assisted by shared consumption of beverages. Tea,' she added, and a tray materialised on the desk: bone china, teapot, milk jug, another jug for the extra hot water, sugar bowl, and a silver strainer in a little three-legged pot. 'And in case you're worried,' she added, seeing the look on Connie's face, 'there's no need. I can quite see why you might be suspicious about drinking anything you hadn't made yourself, in the light of recent events; but, since we'll both be drinking from the same teapot—'

'Actually,' Connie said, 'it's more usual to use the cups. Joke,' she added. 'I'll be mother.'

'Excuse me?'

'Forget about it,' Connie said, pouring the tea and dropping in her usual two sugars. 'So, what else do you want to know about?'

'Your relationship with Mr Shumway,' the thin-faced girl said. 'My impression is that although there is no question of a romantic attachment, you share with him a bond of comradeship that is in many respects as powerful as love, or possibly more so.'

Connie thought about that. 'I suppose I do,' she said. 'Which is odd, because outside of work we wouldn't get on at all. I mean, his attitude to women, for one thing. Actually, his attitude to a lot of things. Everything, in fact. What I'm trying to say is, if we'd both got old and retired in the usual way, we'd promise each other on our last day that we'd keep in touch, no matter what, and then we'd never see each other again, ever. But here, in this building, I don't suppose there's anybody in the world I'm closer to, because, in spite of it all, we're basically on the same side. Does that make any sense?'

'Yes,' the thin-faced girl said, putting down her cup. 'And, of course, with a working relationship of that nature, anything in the way of romantic involvement would be ruinous.'

'Of course.'

'Particularly,' the thin-faced girl added with a faint smile, 'since under the prevailing circumstances you will be working together for the rest of your eternal lives.'

'It'd be so embarrassing—' Connie suddenly froze. 'Have you been drinking your tea?'

'Yes. Look, empty cup.' The thin-faced girl showed her. 'Nothing to worry about.'

'Ah,' Connie said, as her eyes closed and she started to slide towards the floor, 'that's all right then.'

'Connie?' Benny's voice, in the darkness behind her eyelids, far away. 'Connie love, are you all right?'

Ah, she thought. So I was right after all. Honestly, though; if you can't trust an angel—

(But she didn't, of course. A lifetime in the business had taught her that, apart from the few good people who work alongside you, nobody is to be trusted, ever, because sooner or later they'll let you down, sure as God made little green apples. And, when you came to think of it, hadn't that been the dirtiest trick of them all?)

Connie opened her eyes. 'Fine,' she said. 'Well, don't just stand there like a very small pyramid. Help me up off the floor.'

Benny reached down one of his broad, sausage-fingered hands, and she hauled herself up. 'Don't tell me,' she said. 'You got a call from What's-her-face. Meet her in my office pronto.'

Benny clicked his tongue. 'Oh,' he said.

'No, don't worry, it's all right.' Connie dusted herself off and sat back in her chair. A few deep breaths and she was fine. 'All right, you,' she said loudly. 'Come on out.'

Sure enough, the thin-faced girl materialised in front of them. She looked different: a floaty, sparkly dress instead of the dull-as-*Newsnight* charcoal-grey suit; a shimmering golden doughnut hovering over her head; wings. Apart from that, she was exactly the same.

'Please try not to think of it as punishment,' she said. 'More like justice. After all, you interfered in the workings of my department. In the event, no harm came of it—'

'Harm!' Benny exploded. 'You stupid bloody elf, she sorted out the mess you'd made.'

'Nevertheless,' the thin-faced girl went on, 'such meddling must be discouraged at all costs, and an appropriate reaction was called for. Ms Schwartz-Alberich, you were very helpful just now. In fact, I understand you very well. Wouldn't you agree?'

'The philtre,' Benny said quietly. Connie nodded.

'You may have been wondering,' the thin-faced girl went on, 'why I saw fit to give this firm to the three of you. Quite simple. I want you and Mr Shumway here to be working side by side, every day, for ever. In the light of what I'd assumed, which you so kindly confirmed for me—'

'Oh, quite.' Connie smiled at her. 'Listen, dear. Next time you're dancing on a pin, if you could somehow manage to slip, so the pin goes right up your—'

'Not punishment,' the thin-faced girl said serenely. 'Certainly not revenge. Simple justice. Well, now that I've cleared up the last loose end—' She hesitated, frowned, and yawned. 'I should be getting back. After all, I have plenty of work to be getting on with. A career woman, you see, just like you.'

'Just like me. I was hoping you'd say that.' Connie leaned back a bit further in her chair. She'd never realised before just how very comfortable it was. 'But here's a bit of advice, from a pathetic little mortal. When people tell you things, listen.'

The thin-faced girl arched her eyebrows. 'Meaning?'

'I told you,' Connie said pleasantly, 'that the JWW love philtre doesn't work if you dilute it with a liquid containing more than a trace of unfermented sugar. Which is why,' she went on, 'I got into the habit thirty-seven years ago of taking two sugars in my tea. Wonderful things, habits,' she added. 'You do them without thinking.'

The thin-faced girl looked at her, and then at the sugar bowl on the tray. 'Oh,' she said.

'Oh,' Connie repeated. 'I think that just about says it all. Pleasant dreams.'

'Pleasant—?' The thin-faced girl yawned again, her eyes widened to fried-egg size, and then closed.

'Another first,' Connie said. 'Never seen anybody fast asleep in mid-air before.' She stood up. 'Dozy cow assumed that just because she's an angel, it wouldn't work on her. Serves her right. I think we'd better leave now, before she wakes up.'

'In a minute.' Benny was grinning so wide that Connie was worried in case the top of his head fell off. 'Before we go— Sod it,' he added. 'There's never a stick of chalk when you need one.'

'Top drawer of the desk.'

'Thanks.'

With the chalk, Benny drew a pentagram directly underneath where the thin-faced girl was hovering. He muttered something long-winded and funny-sounding under his breath, then clicked his fingers. 'That ought to do it,' he said. 'Conjuring demons was never really my line, but it's hardly rocket science, is it?' He looked up at the thin-faced girl and shrugged. 'Well,' he said, 'she was Management. And she made us do those annoying assessments. I asked for that Oscar by name, by the way.'

Connie giggled. 'Do you think he's her type?'

Benny nodded. 'A match made in Heaven,' he said. 'Humour,' he added. He extended his elbow in a gentlemanly fashion; Connie took it. 'Come on,' he said. 'Let's get out of here and go and make some money.'